Identity

N.S. Igwe

True Essence Press

Content Warning

This novel explores themes of power, control, obsession, and emotional com-plexity, including PTSD, coercion, emotional manipulation, abduction, and sexually explicit content.
Reader discretion is advised.
Identity is a psychological suspense novel with romantic elements, blending intensity, passion, and high emotional stakes. At its core, it is a story of resilience, identity, and survival.

DEDICATION

To my Mother: It is because of your love and sacrifices that I am here today. " Pitit tig se tig".

To my Husband: Your ambition inspires mine. Your support fuels my dreams.

To my Family: Your love and belief in me encouraged me to see myself the way you see me.

To my Friends: You are my support, my community. Thank you for reading drafts, being my sounding board, never doubting me, and reassuring me when I doubted myself.

I love you all dearly.

Chapter 1

Malinda

Clay Sawyer liked expensive things—fast cars, fine whiskey, and women who were hard to catch but easy to keep. He had a reputation for always getting what he wanted. And yet, here I was, in his Aston Martin, gliding through downtown Baltimore's club district, thinking I was smarter than this. Careful. Discreet. But tonight, none of that mattered—because Clay wanted me, and I had let myself be caught.

The Aston Martin cruised through the neon-lit streets, a sleek predator cutting through the night. It screamed wealth, exclusivity—something untouchable. Eyes followed as we passed, phones lifted, cameras flashed—desperate to catch a glimpse of the A-lister they assumed was inside. But the tinted windows only deepened the mystery. If they knew Clay Sawyer, they'd know he didn't just bask in the spotlight—he commanded it.

I knew exactly what this was—Clay showing off, going overboard in his never-ending campaign to impress me. He pulled up in front of my apartment, idling the engine like he had all the time in the world. I mentally rolled my eyes.

He turned to me, his cool grey eyes taking in every curve of my body before meeting mine.

"Did you enjoy yourself tonight, Malinda?"

His voice was deep and calm, almost sensual—so different from the powerful boom he used during board meetings. I wasn't entirely sure why I had agreed to this date. I don't do dates unless I'm charming a mark. It's not my thing. Maybe I agreed just to get him off my back, or maybe—just maybe—I felt like I deserved to be wined and dined now and then. That thought unsettled me. Deserving? Since when did I believe in things like that? Dates led to emotions, attachments, and expectations—none of which I had time for.

"Yes, Clay. I did enjoy myself."

"I'm glad. I can honestly confess that I've never pursued a woman so hard and for so long just for a date. I was starting to feel like a stalker."

Stalker was an understatement. He'd asked me out every single week for nearly a year, sending flowers, cards, and emails. Anything you could think of, he had tried it. I was surprised he hadn't just shown up at my house. Clayton Sawyer wasn't used to rejection. The former party boy turned CEO, son of SparTech's current president Brian Sawyer, and grandson of the company's infamous founder William R. Sawyer, was one of the country's most desired bachelors. I just wasn't interested. He was my boss, and after this one date, there wouldn't be another.

He took my hand and gently rubbed his thumb across my palm. I knew what was coming—he was going to want a kiss. His voice lowered, turning husky.

"It's still early. Are you sure you want to go home?"

"It's 12:30, Clay. I have work in the morning."

He grinned, chuckling. "It is getting late. I guess I just don't want this night to end. How about I walk you up to your door?"

I wanted to decline, but it would've been pointless. I'd been declining him all night—correction, all year—and it hadn't deterred him one bit. Once Clay Sawyer made a decision, he followed through.

He got out of the car and came around to open my door.

Lust filled his eyes as he watched me tug down the hem of my form-fitting dress. I had nothing fancy in my closet, so I had to make do. I wasn't used to upscale lounges. Hell, I'd never even been on a real date before.

"Did I tell you that you look... amazing tonight, Malinda?"

"Yes, Clay. You mentioned it once or twice."

He extended his arm, and I reluctantly took it. His gaze never left me as we entered my building. I felt his eyes stripping me bare as we waited for the elevator. I knew he thought he was going to get lucky tonight, but that couldn't be further from the truth.

The elevator doors slid open, and as we stepped inside, the tension thickened. The air between us was charged, the space feeling smaller than it was. Clay leaned against the mirrored wall, watching me through the reflection, his lips slightly parted. I ignored the weight of his stare, keeping my gaze locked on the blinking floor numbers, silently willing them to move faster.

"Malinda." His voice was lower now, a quiet, intimate whisper.

I turned slightly. "Yes?"

He studied me, his expression unreadable. "You don't let anyone in, do you?"

My heartbeat quickened, but I kept my face impassive. "What makes you say that?"

He gave a small smirk, pushing off the wall just as the elevator dinged. "Just an observation."

Finally, at my front door, he grabbed my arm gently, pulling me into a hug. And then, just as I expected, he kissed me. His lips were firm, lingering too long. I pulled away just as his hands started to wander.

"Sorry if that was too forward, Malinda," he murmured. "But I've wanted to kiss those plump lips from the first moment I met you. Can I come in for a few minutes?"

I turned up my charm, giving him a sly grin before seductively biting my lip and playing with his lapel. I looked away briefly, as if in deep thought, and sighed.

"We both know that's not a wise decision, Clay."

His breathing quickened, his pupils dilating with lust in a matter of seconds. He leaned in closer, his voice a husky whisper.

"Are you sure?"

I stopped him with a finger to his lips, then gently tapped his nose, smirking.

"Yes, Mr. Boss Man... I'm positive."

He exhaled sharply, chuckling as he nodded. "Yeah, I guess you're right. Have a good night, Ms. Burns. See you bright and early."

Before I could react, he stole another quick kiss and strode toward the elevator.

I quickly stepped inside my apartment and locked the door behind me. Kicking off my heels, I tossed my purse toward the couch. I hated all this fancy stuff. Thankfully, I rarely had to do it.

Grabbing an organic fruit smoothie from the fridge, I walked over to my living room window—just in time to see Clay get into his car and drive off.

He could've been a good lover if I had allowed it. But Clay was too nosy, too entitled. I couldn't risk him asking questions, snooping around, showing up unannounced. I had worked at SparTech for seven years, and no one had ever known where I lived... until tonight. That realization made my stomach tighten. I would have to monitor him carefully to ensure this didn't become a habit. The last thing I needed was for him to get too comfortable.

I sighed and went into my bedroom, changed into sweatpants and a sports bra, then made my way into my office. The moment I stepped inside, the low hum of the machines filled my ears—a familiar and oddly comforting sound. The glow of multiple monitors bathed the room in an eerie blue-white light, casting shifting shadows across the walls as screens flickered with streams of data.

Rows of sleek, high-end equipment lined the desk—a custom-built PC tower with a transparent side panel revealing softly pulsing LED lights, external hard drives stacked like books, and a tangle of neatly organized cables running along the back. A secondary desk housed two additional laptops, each dedicated to different aspects of my work— one was my company-issued laptop for internal audits and legitimate financial records, the other was my custom built, encrypted laptop used for deep-dive investigations, managing my offshore accounts, and storing files on all my marks.

Against the far wall, metal filing cabinets stood locked, each drawer meticulously labeled. Recently, there was a new addition to my office—a large bulletin board covered in financial statements, various names and dates, articles, receipts, employee records, and a grainy still from a surveillance video.

I settled into my chair, the leather cool against my back, and pulled up my security system. The multiple camera feeds flickered to life on one of the larger screens, showing every angle of my hallway, the emergency stairwell, and the elevator. Satisfied that all was in order, I turned my attention to the monitors before me. The soft clicking of my keyboard filled the space as I pulled up the Instagram page of my current mark—Amy Chord.

Notorious party girl. Cocaine addict. Heiress to the Chord estate. Well-known in the Atlanta club scene.

Amy knew me as Megan Ardin, an upper-middle-class fashion enthusiast—rich enough to get her attention but not so rich that she'd ask too many questions about my pedigree. Our friendship had been cultivated over months, my presence in her life carefully curated. I knew her insecurities, her weaknesses, and most importantly, her access points.

I watched her latest story and sent heart eyes, commenting:

> **megardin_87:** Is that a new custom Birkin?! Fashionable as ever, girl!

She replied to the DM immediately, much to my expectation.

> **Amy.chord:** Thanks, Meg! Got it from one of the Crown Princes. Another for the collection!

> **megardin_87:** Slay!

> **Amy.chord:** How was Miami?!

> **Amy.chord:** I heard The Whale was insane last month.

> **megardin_87:** Ugh, Miami was a disaster. Too much tequila, not enough sleep. Tell me all about Dubai. A crown prince??

> **Amy.chord:** Girl, you have NO idea. Call me.

I smirked. Hook, line, and sinker.

Shutting down my computer, I walked over to my desk, where my briefcase sat open. My fingers hesitated before reaching inside for the manila folder. My stomach tightened. I knew what was in it—but did I really want to read the new details?

Why did they have a file on him anyway?

I sighed, tossing the folder onto the desk. A photo slipped out.

My breath caught.

A picture of my father

George Anthony Burns. The man who shaped me. My first teacher. My protector—until he wasn't.

He taught me everything I knew. How to read a mark, how to disappear, how to survive.

He was a master con artist.

And now, so was I

CHAPTER 2

MALINDA

The hum of my phone vibrating against the nightstand stirred me from restless sleep. My eyes flickered open, adjusting to the darkness of my bedroom. The clock read 3:12 AM. I reached for my phone, already knowing who it would be.

Amy Chord.

Groggily, I swiped the screen and pressed the phone to my ear, forcing my voice to remain light and engaged.

"Amy, babe." I purred, feigning exhaustion from a jet-set life I didn't actually have. "Why are we awake at this ungodly hour?"

A giggle on the other end. Amy was high. Again.

"Meg, you won't believe it!" she gushed, her words slurring slightly. "I just got off a yacht with Hassan and his friends. They flew in a Michelin-starred chef from Paris. The food was divine—but you know what's even better?"

I perked up, gripping the phone tighter. "Do tell."

"He gave me his Centurion card for the night! Can you believe it? A Black Card! Limitless, babe. Limitless."

Jackpot.

Feigning shock, I gasped. "No way! Amy, that's insane. What did you buy?"

Another giggle. "A few watches... Chanel, Cartier... nothing too crazy."

Nothing too crazy in her world meant at least fifty grand in luxury goods. But I wasn't here for the material details. I needed to know if she still had access.

"God, I wish I was with you!" I sighed dramatically. "Are you still in Dubai?"

"Yeah, but I'm flying back to Atlanta in a few days. Ugh, you *have* to come visit. We'll throw the party of the year!"

I hesitated, pretending to consider it. "You might have just convinced me. Maybe I'll fly down."

"Yay! And, Meg, you'll love Hassan's friends. They're so generous. You know what I mean?" She laughed, and I knew exactly what she meant.

I played along, letting the conversation flow effortlessly before ending the call with promises of plans.

I had gotten what I needed—confirmation that she still had access to Hassan's card, that she was reckless enough to use it freely, and he was stupid enough to let her. And lastly, that she trusted Megan Ardin implicitly.

With a sigh, I placed my phone on the nightstand. The persona of Megan Ardin was demanding, requiring constant attention to detail, but it had been worth it. Amy was an easy mark—wealthy, careless, and desperate for validation. Soon, all the time I had invested in this con would pay off.

But first, I needed to refocus. The file on my desk had been haunting me for days. I had barely made a dent in it, but tonight, I had no excuse.

I slid out of bed and walked back into my office, flipping open the manila folder. The first page was a list of financial records, but I barely skimmed them. My fingers trembled slightly as I turned to the next page.

A grainy surveillance photo of George Anthony Burns.

My father.

My pulse quickened. He looked older, rougher—but it was him. The same sharp eyes. The same arrogant tilt of his chin.

The problem? This photo was dated one year after he was supposed to be dead.

I swallowed hard, flipping through the rest of the file. Notes on offshore accounts. Correspondences. And then—an internal memo to the president of SparTech.

A reference to a SparTech hit.

My breath caught.

Why the hell was my father's name attached to this? Had he been involved with SparTech in ways I never knew? Or worse—had someone made him disappear?

I had spent my whole life avoiding the pain of losing him. But now, it seemed I had been running full speed into the web of his deceit.

No. Maybe the date on the photo was wrong. Maybe I was missing something.

Because if George Burns was alive—if he had conned SparTech and vanished—then I needed to find him. Not for closure. Not for family. For the truth.

Chapter 3

Malinda

SparTech Industries was a massive building that dominated Baltimore's financial district, its glass facade reflecting the pale morning light. A crisp spring breeze carried the scent of fresh coffee and the faint tang of exhaust from the busy streets.

I stepped out of the cab and joined the steady flow of early morning workers, the rhythmic sounds of footsteps and distant car horns filling the air. I had brought my coffee today, so I bypassed the long line at the café and headed straight for the elevators.

I reached for my badge, but it wasn't clipped to my hip as usual. Damn. I fumbled with my coffee, briefcase, and newspaper, digging through my purse to find it. Just as my mug started to slip, a hand shot out and caught it effortlessly.

The warmth of his fingers brushed mine for a fleeting second, steady and sure. The rich aroma of my coffee swirled in the air, mixing with the faint trace of his cologne—cedar and... spice?

I straightened, the sudden proximity making my skin prickle with awareness.

"Be careful, sweetheart. Don't hurt yourself."

I looked up to see Amir, grinning as he handed my coffee back.

I sighed. "Thanks, Amir."

"You're welcome, sugar." He swiped his ID and fell in step beside me. "So, when are we going on that date, Malinda? Cirque du Soleil is in town. We could catch a show this weekend."

I suppressed an internal groan. "This weekend isn't good for me. Sorry."

His smile didn't falter, but I could tell he was disappointed. Still, he didn't press. That was what made Amir different from the others. The elevator doors opened on the 22nd floor, and I made a quick escape.

I greeted my assistant, Shirley, as she handed me my messages. "Mr. Sawyer wants to see you in his office immediately following the nine o'clock staff meeting."

I stilled. My heart sank. What did Clay want now?

I kept my expression neutral, nodding as I took my seat and scanned through my messages. I pushed away the unease creeping in. I'd gone on the damn date. It was over. He'd gotten what he wanted, and now he'd move on. Right?

I sat through our quarterly staff meeting, taking notes and avoiding Clay's gaze like it was my full-time job. I knew he was watching me. I could feel it—the weight of his unrelenting stare burning into the side of my face. My pen moved automatically across the page, but my mind was elsewhere, hyper-aware of his presence.

When the meeting ended, I returned to my desk, pretending to be deeply absorbed in my work. But at 10:30, Shirley paged me again.

"Ms. Burns, Mr. Sawyer called again. He wants to see you immediately."

No more avoiding it.

I exhaled slowly, grabbed my notepad, and headed upstairs to the 30th floor.

I stepped into his office, noticing that the privacy blinds were drawn. Keeping my posture composed, I walked toward him.

Clay was perched on the edge of his massive mahogany desk, focused and in control. He tossed a lime-green stress ball between his hands, the motion smooth, rhythmic. It wasn't nervous energy—it was measured, precise. Like even his idle movements had intention.

His office was modern yet classic—glass, steel, and dark wood—minimalistic but commanding. Floor-to-ceiling windows overlooked the city.

Even the air carried his presence—expensive cologne, leather, a faint charge of intensity. This wasn't just his workspace. It was his battleground. And right now, I was standing in it.

He motioned for me to sit, finishing a call before turning his full attention to me. His gray eyes lingered as he smiled.

"Good morning, Ms. Burns. How are you?"

"I'm well, Mr. Sawyer. Thanks for asking."

"You look lovely this morning." His gaze traveled over me, slow and deliberate.

I resisted the urge to fidget. I wasn't wearing anything special—a button-down, pencil skirt, and my everyday Louboutins.

Maybe it was my hair. I stumbled upon a YouTube channel dedicated to natural hair and decided to try out a few styles. My high bun might have been a bit much, but it turned out lovely—a nice change from my usual neat French braid. Maybe that was what caught his attention.

"Thank you, sir."

Before I had time to process, he was standing, reaching for my hand and pulling me up without a word. My breath hitched as my body tensed, my muscles instinctively locking up. His grip was firm but not forceful, yet the suddenness of it sent a shiver down my spine. My fingers twitched at my sides, uncertain whether to push him away or steady myself.

The air between us thickened, charged with something unspoken and dangerous.

I stiffened as he positioned me between his legs, his hands resting on my waist.

"Mr. Saw—"

"Cut the formalities, Malinda." His voice was low, intimate. "Last night was the best date I've ever had. You're different from any woman I've met, and I can't stop thinking about you."

I swallowed hard. His intensity was overwhelming. His grip felt... possessive almost.

"Clay, let me go. We're at work."

"I know it's unprofessional, boo, but I want more time with you. Meet me for a long lunch today."

I nearly laughed. Boo? Clay Sawyer did not say things like that. This side of him was new, and it was fascinating.

I searched for the right words. "Clay, you're my boss. We can't do this."

He smirked. "I am the boss. That means we can."

I sighed and stepped back. "I need to get back to work, Mr. Sawyer."

I turned, but he caught my wrist, spinning me back into him. His lips crashed against mine before I could protest. One arm wrapped around my waist, the other cupping the back of my neck.

I tensed, my mind racing, strategizing. Biting my boss would certainly get me fired, and this was the best cover I'd ever had. I could control the moment if I gave in.

So, I played along.

I let my hands slide up his chest, around his neck, deepening the kiss. His grip tightened as he groaned against my mouth.

That was my cue.

I bit his lip—just hard enough to startle him—then pulled away.

He exhaled sharply, his eyes dark with desire. "Damn, Malinda... Kissing me like that only makes me want you more."

I smoothed my skirt and stepped away. "I need to get back to work."

His fingers brushed my chin. "Of course. Just one more."

This kiss was different. Soft. Lingering. No dominance, no urgency. Just... sweet.

I hated that it made my stomach flip.

I stumbled over my words. "Um... I—I should go."

His grin was slow, knowing. "Alright, boo. The car will be ready at 1:00."

Before I could argue, his assistant's voice crackled over the intercom. "Mr. Sawyer, your eleven o'clock conference call is on line three."

The moment snapped. His expression shifted back to business mode as he turned away.

I took my chance to escape, willing my pulse to slow.

I was late.

Not by much, but enough to prove to myself that this lunch didn't matter.

After freshening up, I made my way downstairs around 1:15. Clay was already inside the car, on a call. When I slid in, he took my hand and kissed it absentmindedly. I stared at him. Romantic now? He was full of surprises.

The drive was quiet, aside from his conversation. I listened discreetly—you never know what useful information you might pick up by simply keeping your ear open.

Twenty minutes later, we pulled up to Sotto Sopra.

"I hope you like Italian, boo." He smirked, pressing a quick kiss to my lips.

I barely had time to react before the host greeted him. "Good afternoon, Mr. Sawyer. Will you be dining in a private room today?"

"Yes, Phil. The usual accommodations."

Clay took my hand, guiding me through the softly lit restaurant. The warm scent of roasted garlic and fresh herbs filled the air, mingling with the low hum of conversation and the gentle clinking of glasses. The walls were adorned with rich, abstract paintings that added a touch of modern elegance to the cozy atmosphere.

We followed Phil to the back, where the lighting was even dimmer somehow, offering an intimate escape from the bustling main floor. It was a beautiful place.

"Walter will be your waiter today, and if it's no inconvenience to you, he's training a new waiter," Phil informed us.

"That's fine." Clay said smoothly.

He pulled out my chair before taking his seat across from me, studying me with an intensity that made my skin prickle.

"You're tense." he noted. "Relax, Malinda. It's just a meal."

"Then why does it feel like something else?" I countered, unfolding my napkin.

His lips twitched. "Because everything with you is electric." He leaned forward, eyes darkening. "You feel it too."

Walter bowed slightly as he greeted us. "Good afternoon, Mr. Sawyer. Ma'am. Shall we start with a wine?"

"Whatever you recommend, Walter. And how's the wife doing?"

"She's doing well, sir. Recovering nicely after the knee replacement surgery. That specialist you recommended is a miracle worker."

Clay nodded, his voice softening just a touch. "Glad to hear it. I had a gift sent over—just something to make her smile. Let me know if she needs anything else."

Walter looked genuinely touched. "Yes, we received it. That was incredibly kind of you, sir. Thank you. She loved the flowers and the spa basket. Said you've got better taste than I do."

Clay smirked. "She's not wrong. Call my office—Marsha will give you the name of a great physical therapist I know, when she's ready to start recovery."

"Yes. Of course. Thank you, sir. I'll be back shortly with your wine. In the meantime, Lucas will be taking your order."

He gestured toward a young man who looked barely old enough to drink. Lucas walked over, feigning confidence, his notepad trembling just slightly in his hands.

Clay leaned back in his seat, casual but composed, giving Lucas the kind of patient attention that only made the kid more nervous.

"Good afternoon, sir. What will we be having today?" His voice shook.

Clay didn't miss a beat. "We'll start with the prosciutto flatbread and some sautéed calamari. For the main course, my stunning companion and I will both have the duck."

He grinned at me, casual and charming, and I felt a sharp twitch in my pelvis. Ugh. I hated that my body reacted before my brain could shut it down.

"I—I'm sorry. Dinner isn't available until five, sir."

Clay's expression didn't change, but the look he gave Lucas could've frozen molten lava. Steel-gray eyes narrowed just slightly. The air between them tightened. The poor kid looked like he was about to faint.

Walter reappeared like magic, clearly sensing the shift in atmosphere, and waved Lucas off with a tight smile.

"My apologies, Mr. Sawyer. He's unaware."

Walter poured our wine, calm and practiced, then took Clay's order again like the last few seconds hadn't happened.

Unaware of what, exactly?

That Clay had his own menu? A standing arrangement? A script? Did he text his orders ahead of time and expect the staff to play along?

Of course he did. Men like Clay always had special privileges—they didn't just play the game, they rewrote the rules.

That whole exchange with Walter? It was smooth. Polished. Measured generosity wrapped in warmth. Probably just another piece of the Clay Sawyer brand.

And yet...

There was something about the way his voice softened when he asked about Walter's wife. Something in the way he looked genuinely pleased that the gift had been well-received. Maybe it was part of the performance. Or maybe he really did care.

I hated that I couldn't tell the difference.

I hadn't even looked at the menu. Not that it would've mattered—Clay had already decided for me before I could get a word in. The arrogance was annoying. The confidence? Infuriating. And yet, I couldn't stop watching him.

Everything he did was intentional. The calculated charm, the tailored suit, the way he folded his napkin with precise fingers like he wasn't trying to impress me—but absolutely was.

I was supposed to be immune to men like him. I'd made a life out of studying them, outsmarting them, staying three moves ahead. But somehow, I had let myself end up here, across from Clay Sawyer, in a restaurant too expensive for my tax bracket, trying not to feel the heat crawling up the back of my neck.

I crossed my legs under the table, squeezing my thighs together as if I could trap the heat building there and make it disappear. My body was betraying me, but I forced my mind to steady, my focus sharper—stomping down any hint of attraction that dared to creep in. I needed to remember who I was. What this was.

Just lunch. Just strategy. Nothing more.

Chapter 4

Malinda

Lunch was delightful. Clay was a great conversationalist, knowledgeable on so many different topics. We discussed everything from pop culture to major world news. Before either of us realized, it was 3:30. My phone buzzed, alerting me of my next meeting at 4:15.

Clay took my hand and kissed it tenderly. "I know, babe. We should be heading back. I'm just having such a good time with you."

"This was lovely. Thank you for treating me to lunch."

He sighed, got up from the table, and took my hand. We headed out of the restaurant and back to the car. The ride back to the office was quick, the city passing in a blur. As we pulled into the garage, I waited for Clay to get out, but instead, he rolled up the partition and turned to me. His eyes, dark with lust, locked onto mine.

"We have a few minutes to spare, boo. Let me taste you."

A sharp twitch shot through my pelvis. My body betrayed me. I kept telling myself it was only because I hadn't had any in over two years. Clay leaned in, kissing me gently, then with growing intensity. His hands explored and groped me with a controlled yet passionate hunger. Then his fingers slid between my thighs, shifting my thong aside. When his fingers pushed into me with shocking precision, a moan tore from my throat.

"Wet already, boo? Is that all for me?" His voice was a raspy whisper against my skin.

I barely had time to react before his mouth found my nipple, his fingers working me into a fevered, desperate mess. I tried to focus, to regain control, but I was slipping, spiraling in all the sensations. He watched me, eyes locked on mine as the pleasure built. When he curved his fingers, I shattered. He grinned, withdrawing his fingers and licking them.

"You taste so sweet." He muttered, "Fuck the meeting."

His kiss was deep, almost uncontrollable, and what little logic I had left vanished. Before I could think, I was straddling him, his zipper down, his hardness pressing against me. He kissed my neck, rough hands tugging my skirt up as he guided my hips forward. With a thrust, he was inside me. I tensed as a yelp escaped me.

"Malinda. Fuck, baby. You're so fucking wet."

The sensation overwhelmed me. Clay filled me so deeply that I needed a moment to adjust. He sensed it, maneuvering me down on my back, pulling out just slightly.

"Better?"

I nodded. He started slow, gentle, then thrust deep until I took all of him. He pinched my nipple, bit my neck, and drove me to an explosive orgasm. But he didn't stop, didn't let up. His eyes bore into mine.

"Fuck, Malinda. You're so gorgeous. Come for me one more time, boo."

His voice, his touch, his intensity—it was all too much. He rubbed my clit, triggering another release, and this time, he followed, moaning against my lips as his body tensed.

Clay collapsed against me, catching his breath, but he recovered quickly. He pulled out, kissed me again, and smirked. "I hope you enjoyed that, boo. Next time, I'll take more time adoring that body of yours."

I was in a daze. How much time had passed? It felt like an hour, but when I checked my phone, only twenty minutes had gone by. I felt disoriented. How was Clay so calm? He was grinning at me like he'd won a prize.

"Speechless?" He kissed my forehead. "We have about seven minutes, boo. I have a call I need to get on."

He was back to business, but there was still tenderness in his voice.

"Do you want privacy to fix your hair?"

I shook my head, quickly pulling out my compact mirror. Adjusting my clothing, fixing my hair, touching up my makeup—I needed to look composed. I took a deep breath. "I'm ready."

He cupped my chin and kissed me—sweetly, innocently. But the moment the car door opened and a cool breeze hit me, reality crashed in. What the hell did I just allow to happen?

I had been intimate with Clay. This could ruin everything. I should have stopped him. My mind was a tangled mess.

We stepped into the elevator. Clay was already back in no-nonsense mode, phone in hand, typing out an email. I stole a glance at him. He looked up, caught my eye, and winked.

The elevator doors slid open to my floor, and I stepped out quickly, eager to put as much distance as possible between me and what had just happened.

"Wait."

I froze. My heart slammed against my ribs as I turned back to him. He was still inside the elevator, his posture relaxed, one hand keeping the doors open while he glanced at his phone.

"Come up to my office, Malinda," he said, his tone smooth, unreadable. "I have something to discuss with you."

I hesitated, my pulse still too high, my body still too aware of what we'd just done.

"It'll only take a moment," he added, glancing at his phone again, already half-distracted.

I should say no. Walk away. Pretend like this never happened.

Instead, I nodded.

Fuck.

The ride up to his office was silent. My mind wasn't. I was spiraling, the weight of my recklessness pressing down on me. What the hell had I just done?

Had I lost my damn mind? This wasn't me. I didn't do things like this—wild, impulsive, messy.

And Clay... Clay was still composed. Still effortlessly in control, standing beside me with his phone in hand, skimming emails like he hadn't just had me falling apart under him less than twenty minutes ago.

The moment we stepped into his office, he shut the door, flicked a switch to close the privacy blinds, then turned to me. Before I could react, he pulled me into a hug, wrapping me in his warmth.

I tensed.

What the hell was this?

"I have a quick call," he said, letting go just as fast, already walking toward his desk, his focus shifting. "Should only take about twenty minutes." He tapped out something on his phone, barely sparing me a glance. "There's a shower in my bathroom if you want to freshen up. Then we'll talk."

"I—I can't..."

I needed to get out of here. I needed to get back to my floor, my desk, my sanity.

I opened my mouth to say as much, to push back—but Clay was already seated at his desk, fingers gliding across his keyboard, completely unshaken.

Like this was normal.

And maybe, for him, it was.

His former party-boy lifestyle had to be full of moments like this—wild, reckless, meaningless sex in the middle of the day before slipping right back into work without missing a beat.

I, however, wasn't built like that. My pulse was still erratic, my body still thrumming with aftershocks, my mind still trying to process how I had let myself lose control so easily.

"Right... your meeting," he said, his voice absentminded as he scrolled through emails, still not looking at me. "I'm sure they can manage without you. Correct?"

It wasn't a question. It was a statement.

And that irked me.

My meetings mattered too. I had responsibilities. My time wasn't his to dictate. Why was I the one expected to bend?

I bristled, jaw tightening, but Clay didn't notice. Or maybe he did and simply didn't care. Either way, there was no room for discussion.

"Yeah. Sure," I mumbled, hating how it felt like an agreement when it wasn't.

I grabbed my phone, my movements stiff, and typed out a quick email excusing myself from the meeting I should have been at.

Fuck.

I went into the bathroom as Clay sat at his desk. Staring at myself in the mirror, I felt sick with disappointment.

I couldn't believe I let this happen. Raw at that. The look in his eyes—he was smitten. Now everything was ruined. I had to quit.

Clay would want more, and that would lead him to dig into my life. A high-profile guy like him? I couldn't afford that attention.

I had to figure this out.

Quickly, I undressed and washed up. By the time I stepped out, Clay was on the couch, phone in hand again.

"Call go well?" I asked.

He looked up and smiled. "Come sit, Malinda. Let's chat."

As I walked over, he gestured for me to sit beside him, but I hesitated before lowering myself onto the couch. He took my hand, his thumb grazing my palm in a way that sent a shiver through me. His touch was warm, but there was something measured about it now—controlled.

"How are you feeling?" he asked, his voice softer than I expected.

I didn't answer right away—too busy noticing how he reached for my hand as if we were lovers. Like nothing had changed. Like this was some kind of tender aftercare moment.

"I'm fine. What do you want to discuss?" I kept my tone clipped and measured—like I hadn't just let him wreck me in the back of a car. Like I hadn't come undone for a man I swore had no power over me.

He exhaled, rubbing the back of his neck. "Earlier... I just want you to know that was impulsive. Under normal circumstances, I'd never have made a move on you like that, not in the backseat of a car. But lunch went so well, and last night was..." He trailed off, shaking his head with a self-deprecating chuckle. "I lost myself, Malinda. I just want to make sure you're okay about it all."

I forced a small smile, trying to project indifference. "As long as things don't get weird. You're still my boss, and I value my career. I worked hard to get here—"

"Malinda." His voice was gentle but firm, interrupting me before I could spiral further. "I'd never abuse my position. Whatever this turns out to be, I'll follow your lead."

I studied him, searching for cracks in his sincerity, but there were none. Clay was confident and powerful, the kind of man who made decisions and expected the world to follow. And yet, in this moment, he was handing me the reins.

"Okay," I said finally, though the knot in my stomach remained. He seemed sincere but I knew better than this. Once feelings get involved and egos get bruised, things turn ugly, logic goes out the window.

His smirk was slow, wicked. "And about earlier... I didn't plan it, so using protection was the last thing on my mind."

My lips twitched despite myself. "Worried you knocked me up?"

His expression shifted, something darker flickering in his gaze. "Hoping."

A strange, hot sensation swept through me, both thrilling and terrifying. I scoffed to mask it. "You're out of luck. I have my birth control implant."

His eyes narrowed slightly. "What?"

I took his hand and guided it to my bicep. "Feel it?"

His fingertips brushed over the tiny rod beneath my skin, his expression unreadable. "Technology." he murmured.

I winked flirtatiously, but before I could pull away, his grip tightened.

"So," he murmured, his voice dropping an octave. "Does that mean you're down for another round?"

His voice was thick with desire, and teasing, but with a promise behind it. His gaze flicked over me, dark and knowing, before he leaned in. "I've had fantasies of bending you over my desk, watching that perfect ass bounce as I fuck you until you come so hard you cry."

A sharp pulse of need clenched deep in my core. How did he do this to me? How did he make my body react so effortlessly?

I was frozen, trapped in the image he painted so vividly in my mind.

Before I could gather myself, Clay's lips were at mine again, his kiss searing and insistent.

I pulled back abruptly, pressing a hand to his chest. "Clay, wait, I—I can't. I have meetings."

His fingers traced up my thigh, slow, deliberate. "But you want to. Fuck those meetings. They can be rescheduled." His lips brushed my jaw, his breath warm against my skin. "You're so pretty when you come. That perfect O your plump lips make when you break apart? It's addictive."

His mouth crashed against mine, stealing my breath, my thoughts, my control. My mind went blank as his hands roamed, claiming and coaxing. And then—

We were at his desk. I gasped as he spun me around, pressing me over his desk, roughly bunching my skirt up around my waist.

I barely had time to register the shift before I felt him stroke himself behind me, teasing. Anticipation tightened every nerve in my body. I expected the sudden push of him inside me, but instead—

"Clay..."

"Shh, baby."

His hands parted my thighs, spreading me open, and then—his tongue.

"Oh—fuck!"

A sharp moan ripped from me as he licked me slowly, savoring, teasing. He groaned against me, the vibrations sending electric pleasure through my limbs.

"Soon." he murmured against my skin, the words dripping with promise. He sucked at my throbbing clit, dragging his tongue over me in long, torturous strokes. I bit my lip hard, but it was useless—Clay was relentless.

"Let me hear you love this, babe." He said between licks, his voice thick with satisfaction. "This room is soundproof."

He devoured me, his grip firm, his mouth insatiable. My legs trembled as he pushed me toward the edge, licking, sucking, fucking me with his tongue until I was shaking apart in his hands.

Then, I felt his lips on the back of my thigh, kissing, biting, leaving his mark.

The unmistakable tear of a condom wrapper filled the air, and then—

A stretch. A slow, deep push.

I gripped the desk, gasping as he filled me inch by inch, his thickness a perfect fit. He held still for a moment, letting me feel every part of him. Then, his hips rolled, finding that rhythm—deep, slow, deliberate.

My fingers clawed at the wood as he played out his fantasy, his thrusts measured but devastating. He knew exactly what he was doing, exactly where to hit, exactly how to drag me toward that consuming, mind-numbing pleasure.

"Make a fucking mess on me, Malinda." His voice was strained, desperate. "Oh fuck—come on me, baby."

I was losing it. Completely unraveling.

"Fuck. Clay!"

He groaned, a deep, guttural sound, and then—he snapped.

His pace turned brutal, his strokes impossibly deep, tearing pleasure from me until I was nearly sobbing from the intensity. My orgasm tore through me, sudden and all-consuming, like a live wire snapping loose. A sharp cry ripped from my throat as my body seized, every muscle tightening, pleasure cresting so intensely I could barely hold myself up. My grip on the desk slipped, my legs trembling beneath me, helpless against the waves crashing over me, pulling me under.

Clay felt it the moment I shattered. His pace slowed, dragging out every pulse, every clench, every tremor that wracked my body. He was savoring this, prolonging my pleasure, forcing me to feel every last second of my undoing. I gasped as his hands tightened on my hips, steadying me, holding me right where he wanted me.

He groaned, low and deep, but didn't let himself go. Instead, he withdrew slowly, his touch gentle as he guided me upright, pressing his chest against my back. His lips brushed my ear, his breath ragged but controlled.

"Not finished with you yet, boo," he murmured, voice thick with restraint. "Turn around."

He turned me in his arms, tilting my chin up to meet his gaze.

"You're so fucking beautiful." He murmured. His thumb traced my jaw as he stared at me like he was memorizing my face. "How are you this beautiful?"

I had no answer. I could barely breathe.

He kissed me again, slow, deep, like he was trying to pull me back under.

Then, in one swift move, he hooked his arms beneath my thighs, lifting me onto the edge of his desk. His eyes burned into mine as he pushed inside me again, sinking into my still-quivering heat. My head fell back, pleasure overwhelming me all over again.

"You love me inside you, boo." He rasped. "Why'd you deny us this for so long?"

His slow thrusts were maddening, torturous, his eyes locked onto mine, refusing to let me escape the intimacy of it. I cupped his face, lost in the way his gaze bore into me.

Too much. Too deep.

He groaned softly. "You feel so fucking good."

I clenched around him, testing him, and he faltered, his breath hitching.

"Shit, Malinda—I'm barely holding on as it is."

I smirked and did it again. His eyes snapped shut, his jaw tightening as a deep, helpless groan ripped from his throat.

"You're gonna make me bust, baby."

I bit his lip, moaning against his mouth.

"Good."

That was all it took.

He cursed, his thrusts turning wild, and erratic before his body froze, and he came with a deep, shuddering moan.

Clay collapsed into his chair, pulling me into his lap, his grip firm. I was still trembling, my body was spent, but the moment he buried his face in my neck, pressing slow, lingering kisses to my skin, unease prickled down my spine.

I hated this part. The aftermath. The warmth of another person wrapped around me, the weight of strong arms keeping me close. Sex, I could handle. Affection? That was harder.

His lips brushed my temple, then my cheek, his breath still uneven. "That was insane, boo." He murmured, his voice low, sated. His hold tightened like he had no intention of letting me go.

I forced myself to stay still, to relax into him. To pretend that I was comfortable. But the longer we sat like that, tangled together, the more my skin itched. This wasn't me.

And then his phone rang.

I stiffened.

Reality... Fuck.

Clay let out a low sigh, fingers flexing against my waist, but didn't reach for his phone. He didn't want to move. Didn't want to let me go.

I did.

I needed to.

I sat up, shifting against him. "You should get that," I said, my voice hoarse. "We've been MIA for hours.

He shrugged. "I don't care."

I smirked, slipping off his lap. "Yes, you do."

His jaw ticked, his reluctance obvious, but after a beat, he reached for his phone. I exhaled, relief flooding my chest.

He caught my wrist. "Please stay, babe."

I shook my head, smoothing my skirt. "Get back to work, Mr. Boss Man."

He chuckled, watching me as I walked to the bathroom.

The moment I shut the door, the weight of it all came crashing down.

What the fuck am I doing?

I pressed my hands to the sink, staring at my reflection. The flush in my cheeks, the dazed look in my eyes—it was all because of him.

Clay was dangerous. Too consuming. Too addictive.

I needed to get out of here. I needed to clear my head.

I grabbed my phone and emailed Shirley.

Hey Shirley, can you cancel my meetings for the rest of the day? I think I'm coming down with something. Reschedule them for next Tuesday and hold all my calls as well.

Her response was almost immediate. *Yes, Ms. Burns.*

I quickly washed up and stepped back into Clay's office. He was on a call, his expression focused, but the moment he saw me, his eyes softened. I waved, signaling that I was leaving. He motioned for me to wait, but I shook my head and slipped out, ignoring the way his brows furrowed in response.

By the time I hit the street, my heart was pounding. My body still buzzed from him—his touch, his voice, the way he looked at me like he owned me. My mind, however, was screaming for distance.

What am I doing? How do I fix this? I need to get out of here. I need to clear my head.

Then I thought of Amy. My mark. My escape. She hadn't texted in a few hours—maybe she was busy, or maybe she was already high. Either way, she was exactly the distraction I needed. I pulled out my burner phone.

> **Megan:** Heyyy hoee. Where have you been today??

Her response was almost instant.

> **Amy:** Girlllll. I wish you were here. I'm so hungover right now. What are you up to?

> **Megan:** Well, I saw on your Instagram that you were in Cannes?

> **Megan:** I thought you were coming back state-side?

> **Amy:** Yup! Last minute change. Hassan wanted to go to his friend's yacht event this weekend.

Amy: It's wild out here already. You should come!

Megan: You know what? I will.

Amy: What?? Yes omg! Send me your flight details, and I'll have Franco get you at the airport.

Megan: Awesome. Thanks.

Amy: Of course! Can't wait to see you. Bisou!

I exhaled, feeling a sliver of relief. A getaway. Space. A reset. Then my phone pinged.

Clay: Sorry, I was stuck on that call…

Clay: I tried to reach you at your desk, but I heard you left for the day. I hope you're feeling okay.

Clay: I'll call you later.

I stared at the message.

I'm fucked.

Clay is into me. Deeply. And there's no easy way to turn him down that won't leave him hurt, angry, or worse—obsessed.

The only way out of this is to quit. To disappear. Start over somewhere else.

But I can't do that overnight. I've been at SparTech too long. My life is rooted here. I launder my money through this. Uprooting everything would take planning and precision.

I never should've gone on that stupid date with him.

I'll take this trip, get some space, get my head back on right. I'll play the long game as long as I can.

I'm Malinda Burns. I can handle Clayton Sawyer.

Treat him like a mark. Do what I need to do.
And don't get attached.

The Mediterranean air was thick with salt and the quiet hum of excess, the kind of wealth that made even the filthiest of rich feel like outsiders. I stepped off the private jet and into a chauffeured Rolls-Royce, where Amy's driver, Franco, greeted me with a charming smile and dark sunglasses that barely hid the exhaustion in his eyes. The drive to the villa was lined with palm trees, high-end boutiques, and million-dollar yachts moored along the marina—an endless display of everything money could buy.

By the time we arrived at the sprawling estate overlooking the Riviera, the sun was setting, casting golden hues over the infinity pool. Amy met me at the door, barefoot despite the sequined mini dress clinging to her frame, a champagne flute dangling between manicured fingers. Everything about her dripped with designer labels and the casual indifference of the ultra-rich.

"You made it, bitch!" she squealed, pulling me into a tight hug. "God, you look hot. We're hitting a yacht party in an hour. Get dressed."

I didn't argue. I needed the distraction, the noise, the champagne, and the artificiality of it all. I slipped into a slinky emerald-green gown that hugged my curves and stepped into a world where indulgence was survival, where excess drowned out reality.

The yacht was obscene—gaudy and dripping in wealth, a floating palace of ice sculptures, Dom Pérignon fountains, and a guest list that included European royalty, A-list actors, and men whose pockets were lined with oil money. The music pulsed, a deep bass thrumming through my chest, numbing me to the nagging thoughts I had come here to escape.

I danced, I drank, I laughed. I let the flirtations of foreign billionaires wash over me without letting them stick. Amy was in her element, clinking glasses with a sheikh's son while I watched the crowd, calculating angles like I always did. But something felt different. Hollow.

Later, in a private cabana, Amy sprawled across a chaise lounge, her skin glowing from liquor and luxury. She swiped through her phone lazily, pouting. "Ugh, I need another Hermès bag. Should I get this one?" She turned the screen toward me, showcasing a $35,000 crocodile-skin Birkin.

"Sure. Why not?" I said, feeling the weight of my indifference.

Amy groaned, tossing her phone onto the cushion beside her. "My AmEx is maxed out. Stupid Daddy cut me off again."

I smirked. "Give me a minute."

It was second nature by now, the muscle memory of the con. I drifted toward the bar, phone in hand, my movements smooth, unremarkable.

I scanned the room taking my time. Then I saw him. My mark was exactly what I was looking for—older, wealthy, and full of himself. Mid-fifties, thick gold watch, and dressed in a tailored Tom Ford suit. His platinum card flashed carelessly as he waved down the bartender, his other hand resting too familiarly on the bare shoulder of a woman half his age. She leaned away, smiling politely, but he didn't notice. He was too busy plying a group of beautiful women with drinks, boasting about his offshore ventures, and his connections in high places.

I waited.

His attention flickered when a new distraction entered the room—a striking brunette, legs for days, sauntering past in a silk slip dress. His gaze latched onto her like a heat-seeking missile, the women at his table momentarily forgotten. That was all I needed.

I hovered nearby, casually opening my burner phone. A preloaded phishing link, disguised as a routine hotel survey, popped up on his screen. A careless swipe and I was in. The moment he opened it, his screen mirrored mine. His saved card details lay exposed, vulnerable.

One swipe and I had his card information. A few more taps, and the funds funneled through a shell company, bounced through offshore accounts, and disappeared into the ether.

Less than five minutes. Half a million dollars rerouted. Enough for Amy's bag, an entire season's wardrobe, and more.

The transaction cleared. I waited for the familiar rush, the thrill of a perfect con.

Nothing. No spark. No satisfaction. Just emptiness.

Back at the villa, I sat by the pool long after the party had ended, my feet skimming the water, the stars stretching endlessly above me. The world was quiet, but my mind was anything but.

I had more money than I could ever need. A stable job. A life I had built for myself. And yet, I kept dipping back into the game, like an addict chasing a high that no longer hit.

Amy wasn't a mark. She never should have been. She had her issues, and her vices, but in the end, she was just searching for something real. And I had made her collateral damage.

I had to end this. Walk away. Ghost her. She didn't deserve this.

After tonight, she'd never hear from me again.

If I was done—if I meant it this time—then what the hell was I still chasing?

I exhaled, rubbing my temples, the answer settling like a weight in my chest. George.

Because no matter how much I tried to move forward, his ghost always pulled me back.

But if I was truly leaving this life, where did that leave me? Could I really walk away from the underworld—the fences, the fixers, the whispers in the dark—and still find answers?

No. Of course not.

He was a lifelong conman, and to find him meant stepping back into the world I had spent years mastering. Maybe I didn't have to run scams anymore, but deception? That was still my greatest tool.

My father had always said: *Once a con, always a con.*

But did I have to be? Could it be different for me?

I wasn't sure. But I was about to find out.

I thought about my father and the lessons he had drilled into me. *Survival. Manipulation. Control.*

But I had survived. And I have more control now than I ever did as a con artist.

Maybe it was exhaustion. Maybe it was something deeper. But by the time I left the villa, I knew—this was it. No more cons. No more old habits.

I was done.

At least, that's what I told myself.

By the time I landed back in Baltimore, I had a plan. A real one. A way to handle Clay. No cons—just calculated deception. A way to take back control of my life on my terms.

CHAPTER 5

MALINDA

I came back to the States refreshed, motivated, and re-focused. I hadn't spoken to Clay since that day in his office. I told him I'd be unreachable for a few days, but that didn't stop the texts from coming.

My plan was simple: keep things casual with Clay, set firm boundaries, and keep digging into my father's past until I had enough information. Then I'd disappear without a trace.

I'd always wanted to live in California. I could make it work—if Clay behaved.

I hated relying on others to pull off a plan. But this time, I didn't have a choice.

I was back at work early Tuesday morning for several reasons. I had too much to catch up on after the chaos with Clay disrupted my schedule. Thursday had been a disaster, and Friday through Monday was a complete loss as I fled the country to clear my head. Getting in early also gave me the privacy I needed to continue my investigation into why my dad's name was associated with these specific accounts.

The quiet hum of my office was a welcome solace. I worked diligently for two hours, my fingers flying over my keyboard, my mind deep in files and numbers, searching for patterns, anomalies—anything that could give me a lead. As my colleagues trickled in and the energy of the office shifted with conversations and laughter, I knew I had to wrap up.

Balancing work and my investigation was becoming harder. Every time I tried to focus on a task, my mind drifted back to those accounts. I needed answers. I needed clarity. But Clay... Clay was becoming a problem. His presence, his intensity, the way he pulled me in without even trying—it was all a distraction I couldn't afford. I had to compartmentalize, had to shove the emotions, the temptation, the chaos of him into a box so I could function. I told myself I was in control, but deep down, I knew I was slipping.

I skipped the weekly all-hands meeting to avoid another distraction. At 10:30, Shirley buzzed me.

"Ms. Burns?"

"Yes, Shirley?"

"Mr. Sawyer is requesting to see you in his office immediately."

I rolled my eyes. "Please take a message and let him know that I have a full schedule today."

"Will do."

I spent the next thirty minutes reviewing my presentation slides. My phone pinged.

Clay: Seriously, Malinda?

Clay: I want to see you.

I sighed and ignored his message. At eleven, I led my first meeting, then retreated to my office for a protein shake and prep before my second meeting at one.

My second presentation started smoothly—until about five minutes in when Clay walked in and took a seat. My heart jumped into my throat. He looked agitated, his gaze burning into me as if daring me to acknowledge him. I forced myself to remain calm, pressing forward while ignoring the confused glances from my colleagues. The weight of his presence was suffocating. I felt his gaze strip me bare, reliving our last encounter. My skin prickled with heat.

By the time the meeting wrapped up at two, I was drained, but Clay lingered. He feigned small talk with a few people, but it was obvious he was waiting for me. I took my time packing up, hoping he would get bored and leave. No such luck.

"Great presentation, Malinda," he said smoothly as I finally turned to face him.

"Thank you."

I couldn't meet his eyes. Not with the way he was looking at me. The air between us was charged, thick with something unspoken, something undeniable.

"Is there a reason you skipped the all-hands meeting this morning?" His voice was deceptively casual.

"I apologize, Mr. Sawyer. I lost track of time catching up on work."

He nodded; his expression unreadable. "Sure. I can understand that. Please be sure to read the minutes. There's a lot of important information regarding upcoming Q3 projects."

"Will do." I attempted to walk past him, but he moved swiftly, blocking my path. My breath hitched. He was too close. Too consuming. The tension thickened, an invisible thread pulling us together. My body betrayed me, responding to the warmth radiating from his frame, to the scent of his cologne—dark, intoxicating.

"Why did you refuse to see me earlier?"

His voice had dropped, the commanding edge sending a shiver through me.

"I had to prepare for my meetings." He nodded again then stepped closer to me. He lowered his voice and my whole body lit up.

"Baby...why have you been avoiding me? Hmm?" I was breathless. The rumble of his baritone caused my pelvis to twitch.

"Mr. Sawyer-..."

He sucked his teeth in irritation. "Cut that shit out, babe. It's just us in here. Talk to me."

I exhaled sharply, trying to steady myself. I knew this game. I played this game. And yet, with him, it was different. Clay wasn't a mark. He wasn't someone I could manipulate and move past. He was something else entirely—something I wasn't prepared for.

"Clay... I'm fine."

His eyes studied me, searching for the truth beneath my words. "Doesn't seem like it."

"Well, I am."

He smirked as if he knew I was full of shit. "Fine. Then meet me for dinner later."

"I can't, Clay. I'm staying late to finish up some things."

His grin deepened, playful yet laced with something possessive. "Even better. I'm always here late. We can just leave from here."

"Clay—"

"Come up to my office at 6:45, then we'll head out." His voice left no room for argument. "Don't make me come looking for you again, boo."

Irritation crept up my neck. There he goes again—dictating my time

He turned and walked out, leaving me standing there, pulse-pounding.

I was in trouble. The kind I wanted to escape. The kind that threatened to drown me.

I inhaled sharply, running a trembling hand through my hair. I had to stay focused. I had to remind myself why I was here. Clay was a complication I couldn't afford, but he was also an unavoidable force. If I wasn't careful, he'd pull me under. And this time, I wasn't sure I'd make it back up for air.

CHAPTER 6

CLAY

Malinda is hard to figure out. I can admit last week was intense. I just wanted her so damn bad I made a poor decision. Taking her down in the backseat is high school shit. I shouldn't have treated her that way. And then playing out my fantasy with her in my office was crossing a line. I'd been dreaming of her for years, but I know this is all fresh for her. Still...leaving the country and ghosting me was a larger reaction than I had expected.

I'm trying to make it up to her, but seeing her in action during her presentation only fueled the flame in me that burns for her. She's so assertive, direct, and intelligent. The way she formulates and communicates her thoughts makes me melt. Ugh, she's one hell of a woman. I had a spring in my step as I made my way down the hall to my meeting with the board.

I walked in, and my business mask slid firmly into place.

"Jerry, brief me on the Sylvan acquisition. Where do we stand?"

"It's nearly finalized, Clay."

"That's what I like to hear. Walk me through the numbers."

"We started at 95 million. They countered with 150 and a 2% equity stake. We responded with 110, and they came back with 120 plus the 2%. We accepted. This gives us full control of their domestic operations along with their Beijing and Berlin locations. Just need your final sign-off."

"Good work. Draw up the final paperwork and get it to me. I'll give Logan Sylvan a call to congratulate him on a deal well done. He's walking away with 120 million, and we're securing international expansion. It's a win."

"Absolutely."

I clapped my hands together. "Once the ink is dry, we'll celebrate properly. Dinner's on me."

The board members chuckled and nodded in approval.

After the meeting, I strode back to my office, still riding the high of a well-played deal. My phone buzzed, and my mood soured immediately. A text from Brooke. I deleted it without reading it. Blocking her outright would only stir up unnecessary drama. Instead, I turned my focus to dinner plans.

Beacon had been courting me for months to check out their new flagship restaurant and lounge. A quick search revealed its concept—Southern comfort meets Asian fusion. That could work. I paged Marsha.

"Yes, Mr. Sawyer?"

"Get me a two-person reservation at Beacon for 7:30."

"Right away."

Fifteen minutes later, she emailed me the confirmation. I exhaled, satisfied. Tonight needed to go well. Malinda had to see how much I wanted her—not just in the obvious way, but all of her.

At 6:45, she knocked on my office door, punctual as always. I knew she was being a smart-ass about it, and that only made it sexier. I grinned as I called out, "Come in."

The moment she stepped inside, memories of last week crashed over me. Her expression shifted slightly as her gaze flickered to my desk. I knew she was thinking about it too.

"Hey, Malinda. Grab a seat."

She glanced at the chair I gestured to, then sauntered to the window instead. "I'm fine standing."

"Alright. I should be ready in a few minutes. Would you like to freshen up before dinner?" I bit my cheek to suppress my smirk.

She turned, amusement dancing in her eyes.

I sighed "Babe, let's not make this awkward, okay? We both know what happened here last week."

"You're the one making it awkward," she shot back, smirking.

She laughed, shaking her head. "Yes, I'd like to retouch my makeup. Thanks."

She disappeared into my private bathroom. I exhaled. I needed to pull myself together. One deep breath later, I called my driver.

Beacon was a masterpiece of ambiance. Stepping inside felt like entering a modern-day speakeasy—dim lighting, jewel-toned velvet seating, and a polished elegance that screamed exclusivity.

The moment we walked in, the owner greeted us personally. I turned on the charm, shaking hands and making easy conversation. Business talk flowed effortlessly, and before I knew it, he was nodding in admiration, promising special accommodations anytime I visited.

I felt Malinda watching me. When I turned to her, she smirked, but there was something else in her expression—something warmer, something like awe.

"Wow. Look at you go," she mused.

"What do you mean?"

She tilted her head, studying me. "Watching you in action is... impressive. I get why you close so many deals, Prince Charming."

Her voice held genuine admiration, and I had to work to keep my cool and not blush. The heat in her gaze sent blood rushing in an entirely different direction, which, for once, I was grateful for. I smirked.

"I'm a man of many talents, boo."

I winked, and she bit her lip before quickly looking down at her menu, hiding her smile.

"What looks good to you?" she asked.

I wanted to tell her she did. That she was the only thing I wanted to devour tonight. Instead, I reined myself in. I needed to ease up, to stop overwhelming her with my intensity.

"It all looks appetizing," I said smoothly.

"It does. Plantain fritters, smoked rib dumplings, southern soul egg rolls... ooh, Korean fried chicken & waffles with sweet chili glaze?" She glanced up, eyes dancing with excitement. "This is going to be hard to choose."

"Then we won't choose," I said. "Let's get a sampler of everything."

She laughed. "That's excessive."

"And yet, here we are." I flagged the waiter and ordered a spread, adding a bottle of wine for good measure.

The meal was a journey. We built combinations, fed each other bites, and debated the best flavor pairings. Conversations flowed, easy and unforced, weaving between work, music, and the latest headlines. She challenged me, made me laugh, and made me forget everything outside of that moment. Before I knew it, three hours had passed, and we were two bottles of wine deep.

When dessert arrived, I leaned back, watching her, taking her in. The candlelight softened her sharp edges, her skin glowing under its flicker. She looked radiant, almost surreal.

"You ready to go, babe?" I asked softly.

She dabbed her lips with a napkin, considering. "I must admit... this was an enjoyable outing."

Something in my chest tightened at the way she said it. I reached for her hand, bringing it to my lips, kissing her knuckle slowly.

"I'm glad you had a good time," I murmured. "But the night's still young. Come over for a nightcap."

CHAPTER 7

MALINDA

He led me into his penthouse from the car elevator, and my breath hitched. The sheer scale of opulence was staggering—20-foot ceilings, floor-to-ceiling windows that offered an uninterrupted panorama of the city, and marble finishes so pristine they gleamed under the warm glow of custom lighting. The living space was immaculate yet inviting, designed for both indulgence and intimidation. The space was curated, not just designed, every detail meticulously chosen to exude power and precision. A baby grand piano sat adjacent to an oversized sectional, its black lacquered surface reflecting the skyline's twinkling lights. Everything about this place exuded power, wealth, and control—it felt both intimidating and strangely intimate just like its owner.

I wandered toward the window, unable to tear my eyes away from the breathtaking view. Baltimore stretched beneath me in a glittering sprawl, the harbor illuminated like a necklace of diamonds. I'd always thought my apartment had an impressive view, but this? This was another level.

I didn't hear Clay approach, but I felt the warmth of his body before his arm slipped around my waist. He pressed a slow, lingering kiss to my neck, sending a shiver down my spine. In his other hand, he held a glass of wine, which he extended toward me.

"What's on your mind, babe?" His voice was low, intimate.

I took the glass, exhaling softly. "Nothing..."

He studied me for a moment before taking my hand. "Come."

I followed him to the couch, sinking into the butter-soft leather as he turned to face me. His gaze was probing, assessing, stripping away layers I didn't even know I had.

"Look," he said, voice measured. "I know what happened between us might have been too much, too soon. I get that. I'm usually a lot more chill than that."

I couldn't help the grin that spread across my lips. He chuckled, shaking his head.

"What's so funny?" he asked.

"You? Chill?" I arched a brow.

His mouth twitched in amusement. "Yes, me. But with you..." He exhaled, running a hand through his hair. "I lost control. And that doesn't happen to me. Ever. But you? You are so wonderfully different. It's hard to find someone real, especially when you come from a family like mine. Everyone who interacts with me wants something."

I tilted my head slightly, watching him. "That sounds... exhausting."

A humorless laugh left his lips. "You have no idea. My entire life, I've been used. For my name. My money. My connections. Women pretend to care, but it always comes down to what I can offer. My family expects me to be a perfect CEO, to carry the legacy without question. My father had a stroke, and suddenly, my life wasn't mine anymore. I had to step up, no choice. Meanwhile, my brother, Titan, gets to live however he wants. No responsibilities. No expectations. Just... freedom."

There was something almost bitter in his tone. Envy. I hadn't expected that. "Titan?" I echoed.

He nodded. "My younger brother. He lives here, same building, fifteenth floor. When he's not here, he's in Montecito for the winter. No obligations—just working out, partying, and investing in startups for fun. His mornings are spent at the gym, then the rest of the day? Whatever the hell he feels like. And me? I have to be the heir, the leader, the one who cleans up every mess." He exhaled heavily, swirling the wine in his glass. "I know I sound like an entitled asshole complaining about privilege, but I never had a choice in this. I was born into it, raised for it."

I listened quietly, absorbing his words. Beneath the arrogance, beneath the relentless pursuit, there was something else. The weight of a crown he never asked for.

"I get it," I murmured. "More than you think."

His gaze sharpened like he wanted to pry deeper, but I wasn't about to give him more than that.

"Clay, if I'm honest, you're right. It's been a lot. Too much, too fast. I'll admit—I'm a little freaked out."

He nodded slowly, absorbing my words. Then, gently, he reached out and brushed his fingers against my cheek. "This is more than just physical for me," he murmured. "So tell me—what do you need to be willing to consider something deeper?"

Panic flared in my chest. Fuck. He wanted more than just a hookup. I needed to recalibrate—find a way to slow this down, to keep him at arm's length without tipping my hand.

"I need us to take things slow," I said carefully.

His eyes held mine for a beat before he nodded. "Okay. Slow... Let's start with getting to know each other better."

A quiet dread settled over me. I couldn't let him know too much. I had to stay on guard.

"Okay," I said cautiously. "What do you want to know?"

His lips quirked. "What do you like to do when you're not being a badass at work?"

I smiled despite myself. "The usual, I guess."

"Like what?"

"Hiking, reading, painting."

His brows lifted. "You paint?"

"Mhmm."

A slow grin spread across his face. "I'd love to see some of your work."

I sipped my wine. "Maybe one day... What about you?"

He shrugged. "I'm always working."

"Being a CEO is demanding."

"Extremely. But when I do step away, I love boating. Being out on the water, disconnected from the world, no calls, no meetings—it's the only time I feel free. Oh, and music. Jazz, R&B, especially the kind I can play on the piano."

I studied him as he stared off into the distance, lost in thought. The way he spoke about the water, about music, about escape—it was almost wistful. The urge to reach out and touch him was sudden and visceral, but I forced myself to resist.

"That sounds beautiful, Clay."

He glanced at me then, eyes soft. He took a sip of his wine, then asked, "What about your friends? Do you hang out with them often?"

I shrugged. "I don't really have friends. I mean, I have acquaintances, but actual friends? Not so much."

His expression didn't change, but something flickered in his eyes. "I get it. Same with me. We're alike in more ways than one."

Our eyes locked, and then he leaned in and kissed me. His lips were warm, coaxing, and before I could think twice, I was kissing him back. A kiss didn't mean anything. I tried to convince myself. The taste of red wine and something uniquely Clay lingered on my tongue as he deepened the kiss. His hand cupped the side of my neck, thumb stroking my skin as if memorizing the shape of me. Then his hands began to explore, his fingers skimming my waist, trailing up my ribs. His touch was firm and deliberate, and my pulse spiked. A kiss didn't mean anything I repeated desperately in my mind. But then he was cupping my breast, teasing the peak through my blouse, and suddenly my mind went blank.

How did he do this to me?

I needed to stop this. I had to keep my head straight. But before I could fully form a coherent thought, my blouse was unbuttoned, and his lips were trailing down my chest.

"Clay..." I managed.

He lifted his head, brushing his lips over mine. "What's wrong?"

"We shouldn't..."

His mouth found my neck, his thumb sweeping over my hardened nipple. Heat coiled low in my stomach.

"Why not?" he whispered, his voice like velvet and sin.

"We have work tomorrow."

He smirked. "And what does that have to do with tonight?"

His hand slid down my body, gripping my thigh.

"It's late," I tried, though my argument was weak.

He kissed me deeply before pulling back just enough to murmur, "Are you saying you don't want me to make you come?"

I was speechless.

He kissed me again, and then his forehead rested against mine, breath warm against my lips.

"Stay," he murmured. A simple word, but laced with so much weight. "Last time was just a taste," he said, voice dark and promising. "Tonight, I guarantee it'll be better."

I should've left.

Instead, I whispered, "Okay."

Logic screamed at me to walk away, to regain control. But my body had already decided. The next thing I knew, I was in Clay's bedroom, his fingers peeling away my clothes with aching slowness. The mattress was luxurious, the sheets softer than anything I'd ever felt against my skin. And then there was Clay, standing at the foot of the bed, undressing, his eyes raking over me with pure, unfiltered desire.

"Malinda..." His voice was hushed, reverent. "You're fucking gorgeous. I wish I could take a picture to remember this moment forever."

Chapter 8

CLAY

She lay there in my bed. Malinda. The woman I've spent three years craving—aching for. I stared down at her, trying to soak it all in, to memorize every breathtaking detail. Her long, coily hair fanned out like a halo around her, as if she were something divine, something too perfect for this world. Her smooth chestnut skin gleamed against the cream sheets, a striking contrast that made my chest tighten with awe. My Goddess.

I traced the curves of her body with my eyes, lingering on the way her full, perky breasts rose and fell with every breath. Her dusky nipples stood erect, waiting for me, calling to me. I clenched my fists to keep myself from grabbing her too soon. I needed to savor this. The other day hadn't been enough—it had only deepened my need for her and made my desire spiral further into something unstoppable. She had ensnared me, and I welcomed it.

I stood before her, bare, and her eyes widened as she drank me in. Was that desire flickering there? That dark, hooded gaze, the way her lips parted slightly—God, I hoped so. The thought that she wanted me, craved me the way I craved her, sent a thrill straight to my core.

I leaned over her, pressing my lips to hers, swallowing the soft moan that escaped her. My body responded instantly, my cock twitching at the sound.

Fuck, she was so sexy. But I couldn't rush this. No, I needed to take my time, to painstakingly worship her body until she had no choice but to fall apart for me. I wanted to ruin her for any other man, to brand myself into her soul the way she had unknowingly done to me.

My hands glided over her, reverent, savoring every inch of silk-smooth skin. She whimpered at my touch, a sweet, delicate sound that made my eyes flutter shut in pleasure. Her fingers wove into my hair, gripping, tugging, pulling me deeper into the kiss, and I groaned against her mouth. She was letting go. Finally. Right now, I wasn't her boss. I wasn't a CEO. I was just a man, desperate and hungry for the woman before me.

Breaking the kiss, I kneeled at the foot of the bed taking her right foot in my hands, lifting it with care. I placed a slow, heated kiss on her heel, breathing her in, letting the warmth of her skin seep into me. Everything about her was so damn soft. I ran my tongue up the arch of her foot, savoring the way her breath hitched, the way her fingers tightened in my sheets. When I took her toe into my mouth and sucked, a sharp, breathy moan escaped her lips. My cock twitched at the sound.

I glanced up at her, drinking in the sight before me. Her hooded eyes, and her perfectly plump, pillow-soft lips parted just enough for more delicious moans and whimpers to slip through. She was stunning, utterly fucking mesmerizing. I wanted to memorize this moment and brand it into my brain for the rest of my life.

I forced myself to focus, to stay on task. I placed a searing kiss behind her knee, letting my lips linger, letting my breath fan over her heated skin. My hands roamed up her thighs, spreading her open, teasing her. Her scent filled my senses, intoxicating and warm, an invitation I had to fight not to take just yet. My patience was fraying, but the slow burn—the slow, torturous build-up—would be worth it.

I left a love bite dangerously close to where she needed me most, and she inhaled sharply, her body shivering in response. That sound, that reaction, fueled something primal in me. I kissed the same path down her left leg, worshiping her, marking her, making sure she knew she belonged to me.

Her delicate folds glistened, her arousal dripping, waiting. My voice was hoarse when I finally spoke.

"Do you want this?"

She bit her lip and nodded, her breath shaky.

That was all I needed.

I spread her open and dragged my tongue from her honeyed entrance up to the sensitive bud at the apex, groaning at the first taste of her. My mind blanked. There was no space for thought, no space for anything but this—her taste, her heat, her soft, desperate gasps. I dove in, my lips and tongue worshiping her with slow, deliberate strokes. I licked and sucked her folds like she was my last meal, savoring every drop of her.

Her fingers tangled in my hair, yanking me closer, holding me right where she needed me. I let her guide me, let her grind against my mouth, let her use me the way I wanted to use her. I slipped two fingers inside her, curling them just right, rubbing against that spot that made her legs tremble.

A choked moan tore from her throat as her back arched off the bed. I pressed my other hand against her pelvis, holding her down, pinning her to the bed so she had no choice but to take every ounce of pleasure I gave her. She shattered beneath me.

"Oh God, Clay!"

Her body convulsed, her climax wracking through her like a storm, her walls pulsing around my fingers. I groaned against her, pressing more kisses to her heat, to her trembling thighs, trailing my way up her body as she tried to catch her breath.

Her body trembled with aftershocks, and I let her come down slowly, licking, soothing, never rushing. Her nipples hardened beneath my tongue as I lavished attention on them, teasing and playing as she sighed in pleasure.

Then, suddenly, she moved. With a burst of energy, she pushed me onto my back, surprising me. Her hands were on my chest, her body straddling me, and fuck, the sight of her above me stole what little breath I had left.

She kissed me, tasting herself on my lips, and the possessive part of me growled in satisfaction. Then, she trailed down my body, her lips searing over my neck, my chest, and my abs. My muscles tensed in anticipation.

"Oh, Malinda. You're so fucking hot."

She kissed my V-cut, and my body jerked in response. Then, her hands wrapped around my cock, stroking me, teasing me, pulling a ragged groan from my throat. I clenched my jaw, trying not to lose control too soon, but when she took me into her mouth, my restraint unraveled.

I tried to think about something else—anything else—to keep from cumming embarrassingly fast. A frustrating business call, a board meeting, something mundane. But her technique dragged me back into the present, making it impossible to focus on anything but her tongue, her lips, the way she sucked and stroked me like she wanted to own me.

I hissed, gripping her head. "Slow down, baby... fuck."

She did, smirking up at me. Extremely pleased with herself for having me at her mercy. I tried to catch my breath. Then, she did something—some magic with her tongue, a twisting, sucking motion that spartan kicked me off the edge, crashing me deep into the drowning waters of my orgasm. Heat shot through my entire body, from the tips of my fingers to my toes, converging in one explosive release. I was launched off this plane of existence as my body tensed up. I felt my face redden and my jaw locked up with how intensely I came down her throat.

She swallowed every drop, licking me clean, teasing me until I was a shuddering mess beneath her. Then, she crawled back up, curling beside me. I wrapped my arms around her, pulling her close, and nuzzling into her neck.

I could have sworn I felt her body tense up.

I thought I felt it the other day, too, when I held her after we finished.

But I pushed it out of my mind.

Because right now, I needed to gather myself.

Because I was nowhere near done with her yet.

CHAPTER 9

MALINDA

Clay was cuddling me. I was all tensed up. But I powered through it. He would let go soon enough. It never ended well when I told men not to cuddle me. They always either got offended or launched into an interrogation, trying to understand why that type of affection made my skin crawl.

But Clay was different. He didn't prod. He didn't ask for explanations I wouldn't give. Instead, he traced slow, lazy circles on my back, his breathing warm against my neck. His touch was almost reverent. Worshipful.

And it terrified me.

I felt his lips press against my shoulder, then trail along my jaw. His fingers skimmed down my spine, sending a tremor through my body.

"I want you so fucking bad, Malinda."

His voice was deep, thick with need. His body, all hard planes, and heat, pressed against me, the evidence of his arousal insistent against my belly. I bit my lip, trying to suppress the shudder that rolled through me.

I shouldn't want this again. But I did. I ached for it.

He rolled me onto my back, settling between my legs. I barely had time to catch my breath before his mouth was on mine again—hungry, consuming, unraveling me piece by piece. My fingers tangled in his hair, pulling him closer, needing more.

Clay reached over, and grabbed a condom from the nightstand, tearing it open with his teeth. His eyes never left mine. There was something possessive in them, something that made my stomach tighten and my breath hitch.

"I can't get enough of you, baby. You're like my drug."

I watched as he rolled it on, my body already anticipating what was coming. He nudged my thighs apart, positioning himself at my entrance. The first push was slow, and deliberate, stretching me inch by inch, giving my body time to adjust to his girth. My nails dug into his shoulders as pleasure and pressure coiled deep in my belly.

Clay groaned, his forehead dropping to mine. "Fuck, Malinda..."

He started to move, slow at first, teasing, savoring the way I clenched around him. Then, as I arched beneath him, he picked up the pace, finding that rhythm, that perfect angle that had my toes curling and my breath coming in desperate gasps.

The noises coming from us both were feral. He pushed me to the edge over and over, never letting me tip over completely. His lips found my throat, my collarbone, the curve of my breast, his hands mapping every inch of me, memorizing me. He was taking his time. Worshiping me. Like he wanted to leave his mark on my soul, not just my body.

And it was working.

"Look at me," he whispered. "Let me see you."

I forced my eyes open, meeting his gaze. His pupils were blown, his expression raw, unguarded. It stole my breath away.

Clay reached between us, his fingers finding that sensitive bundle of nerves, pressing, circling, coaxing me higher. My body tightened, every nerve alight with pleasure.

"Come for me, baby."

With one final thrust, I shattered, pleasure washing over me in waves so intense I could barely breathe. Clay followed a heartbeat later, burying himself deep, groaning my name as he lost himself inside me.

He collapsed beside me, both of us breathless, spent. My whole body trembled with the aftershocks. I barely registered the sound of him disposing of the condom before he was back, pulling me into his arms, wrapping me in warmth.

I should pull away. I should leave now, while I still had some control. But I didn't move. I couldn't.

His lips pressed against my forehead. "You're so pure and sweet. Beautiful and innocent, Malinda. Like a Dove. My Dove."

His words made my stomach twist. I forced a smile, but Clay just held me tighter, spooning me, his chest warm against my back, breathing me in like he couldn't get enough.

I lay still until his breathing evened out, slow and steady. He was asleep. I checked the clock on his bedside. Almost one in the morning. I stared at the ceiling, wide awake. My mind raced, battling the heat still lingering in my body, the warning bells screaming in my head.

This isn't what I planned. I can't keep doing this with him.

At 2:45, I slipped out of his grasp, moving silently as I gathered my clothes. I called an Uber and left his apartment without a second glance.

By the time I got home, it was nearly 3:30. I stepped into the shower, letting the water scald my skin, trying to wash away the weight of his touch, his words.

I laid out my clothes for work, climbed into bed, and stared at the ceiling, sleep refusing to come.

In a few hours, I'd have to face Clay again.

So, I had to find a way to end this before it consumed me whole.

CHAPTER 10

CLAY

I woke up to my bedside alarm ringing around 5:30. I sleepily turned it off and turned to cuddle Malinda, but her side of the bed was empty. My arm met cold sheets. I sat up, my chest tightening as I glanced around the dimly lit bedroom.

"Malinda?" I called, knowing full well she wouldn't answer.

Silence. My jaw clenched. She fucking left.

Frustration burned through me as I scrubbed a hand down my face. Why would she just leave in the middle of the night like that? Running away from me. Again.

She's such a fucking enigma. One minute she's right there with me, her body soft and willing, taking everything I give her, and the next, she's slipping away like I'm just another mistake she regrets.

I exhaled sharply and swung my legs over the side of the bed, rubbing the tension from the back of my neck.

I got dressed for my morning workout, throwing on a fitted compression shirt and gym shorts before heading downstairs. I stopped by the grocery mart on the 10th floor for a power bar and ran into my brother inside.

"You're late this morning," Titan quipped, grabbing a protein shake from the fridge.

I grunted in response and shoved my headphones in. Not in the mood.

Malinda was the only thing lately that made me genuinely smile, and yet, she refused to let me have her fully. She let me in physically but pulled away the second that things felt real.

Last night had been mind-blowing. I've had good sex before–, great sex even. But with Malinda, it was—otherworldly. But I bet money she's gonna ghost me today. Again.

I pushed myself harder than usual during my workout, increasing the weights and pushing myself to failure in every set. Sweat dripped down my forehead, but it wasn't enough. Nothing was enough to shake this frustration out of my system.

"Damn, Clay," Titan said after I finished my last set. "You're in beast mode today. What's your deal?"

"Let it go, Titan. I obviously don't wanna talk about it."

"Whatever, bro." He rolled his eyes. "Are you going to the gala this weekend?"

I scoffed. "Do I ever have a choice?"

Titan grinned. "You do, but we both know you'll show up anyway. Our dear parents would hunt you down otherwise."

"So not much of a fucking choice then huh?" I spat back bitterly. I hopped on the treadmill and did a 5-mile run.

I got back up to my apartment at 6:45. My mood still sour. I felt her presence before I even saw her at my kitchen island sipping coffee like she owned the place. Dread filled me as I turned the corner. My mother.

What the fuck. I groaned internally.

I exhaled hard, pinching the bridge of my nose. "Mom. Please. I asked you to ask my permission before coming over. And only use my key in an emergency."

She smiled as if she didn't hear me. That fake smile she uses when she's agitated. The one that never reached her eyes and left her looking deranged. "What a way to greet your dear mother, Clayton."

I rolled my eyes. "Good morning, Mother. How can I help you?"

She waved a manicured hand toward the living room. "I see you had company last night." Her sharp gaze landed on the two wine glasses on the coffee table, eyes narrowing critically.

I didn't take the bait. Instead, I turned to the fridge, grabbed a bottle of water, and twisted the cap off.

She tsked and pulled a tabloid out of her purse, sliding it across the counter toward me like it was evidence in a trial. I glanced down and felt my stomach tighten.

There, on the cover, was a picture of me leaving the lounge last week. Malinda's face was mostly obscured by her hair, but that didn't matter. The headline screamed: "Eligible Bachelor Clayton Sawyer With New Mystery Woman."

"How do you think Brooke feels seeing this?" My mother demanded, her voice like cold steel. "And she told me you haven't been taking her calls."

I snorted but held my tongue.

"Well whatever it is you think you're getting into with them, I just hope these young women have no hopes of anything serious with you. Since you're already engaged to Brooke.

I felt my rage bubbling up to the surface, sharpening my tongue.

"If she wants to get married so badly, then Titan can have her."

"Clayton Dominic Sawyer!" She gasped, scandalized. "Brooke is not a toy to be passed around. She is your soon-to-be wife. Respect her. We have a dynasty to protect, and I will not have you ruining it all with your reckless actions."

I laughed humorlessly. "Reckless? You mean living my life? Doing what I want instead of what you and Dad dictate? Titan is out partying every night, yet you never say a damn word to him."

She leaned in, eyes sharp. "You're so selfish and immature. Titan is the younger brother. He has the luxury of freedom. You do not. You are the head of this family's legacy, and we will not have our name dragged through the mud because of your childish whims."

I clenched my fists, feeling the heat rise in my chest. It's been years since I let her words get to me. But this time it hurt. *I'm* selfish? Everything I do is in the best interest of this fucking family. I counted to 10 in my head so that I didn't explode on her.

"I. Am. Not. Engaged to her," I bit out. "Dad made that 'deal' when I was barely thirteen. That has nothing to do with me. I didn't consent."

She exhaled, exasperated. "You don't have to. It's your duty. And whether you like it or not, you will fall in line."

I glared at my mom. My jaw clenched with rage. I'm sick of this damn family and their "dynasty".

I tried to regulate but my words came out clipped. I forced a slow breath through my nose. "I have to get ready for work. See yourself out."

I walked away from her. I hate being the 1st born son. My brother gets all the fun without any of the responsibilities. I on the other hand was sacked with the CEO title at 30 after my dad got sick, on top of the burden of continuing our legacy and strengthening our dynasty.

I hopped in the shower and then got dressed. On the ride to Maribella, my father's fine dining restaurant, for breakfast, I couldn't resist the urge to text Malinda.

Good morning, Dove. You didn't have to sneak away in the night. I wasn't holding you hostage.

I closed her thread before I could overthink it and switched to answering emails.

My car pulled up to the restaurant and I was greeted at the door by the host. Even though they don't officially open until lunch and dinner service my father would have his meetings daily on the rooftop weather permitting. Ever since his stroke left him unable to take the stress of running a Fortune 500-level company, he's leaned into his foodie side and built up his fine dining restaurant.

"Good morning, Mr. Sawyer. Your father is on the sky deck this morning."

"Thanks, Sasha. Bring me a double espresso. Extra strong."

I made my way up and found my father sitting at his usual table, reading the *Financial Times*.

"Good morning, Pop."

He grunted. "Tell me you've closed the Sylvan deal, and then it'll be a good morning."

"Then my original statement stands."

He smirked, folding the paper. "Atta boy. You're my son through and through. Are all the details worked out?"

"Got the confirmation email this morning."

"Good. Let's eat."

We talked about stocks and the economy, but then he blindsided me.

He cleared his throat, shifting in his seat like he didn't even want to say it. "Clayton... your mother has been pestering me about this, and I'm inclined to agree with her."

I sighed. "Pops, please, not you too."

"You're thirty-four. You're not getting any younger. It's time you and Brooke settled down and had a few kids. The Sawyer name must live on."

I gritted my teeth. "I don't love Brooke. I'm not marrying her."

He let out a dry chuckle. "Who said anything about love?" He held my gaze. " I thought you would have understood by now. It's business, son." He shook his head in disbelief. As if *I* was the one with the messed up logic. He looked toward the trees taking a moment to think. He turned back to me and studied my face. I'm sure processing the look of misery in my eyes. "Look, let's compromise. You can be with whoever you want...but on the side. A mistress. Like the long-legged honey-brown skin model. The one the tabloids have you pictured with. You can keep her around. But Brooke will be your wife. That is the reality. No discussion."

Our breakfast arrived, but my appetite was gone. I stared at the plate, my father's words circling in my head.

I pushed the plate aside and checked my phone. No response from Malinda.

Today was going to be a long fucking day.

CHAPTER II

MALINDA

I arrived at the office early again, Clay's text from this morning lingering in my mind. Guilt twisted in my stomach, but I couldn't fathom waking up next to him in the morning. The thought unsettled me in a way I couldn't quite place. I quickly typed out a response.

> *Wanted to get ready for work at home.*

I hit send just as I rounded the corner—and walked straight into Amir.

"Whoa there, Speed Racer." His hands caught my arms before I could stumble.

"Sorry, Amir."

He grinned. "No need to apologize. Seems like the only times we talk is when we're literally bumping into each other."

I forced a smile. "Yeah, always in a rush." I stepped to the side, but he mirrored me, blocking my path.

"Hey... I know you never show up, but I still wanted to invite you to my annual summer kickoff in June. Same place in Federal Hill."

"Oh... um, I'll check my calendar."

"Mmhmm." His grin was skeptical.

"Also, correction—I *did* go to that Super Bowl thing you threw."

"Five years ago. One time in, what, eight, nine years?" He shook his head with a laugh.

I shrugged. "Told you—parties aren't my thing. It's the effort that counts."

"Well, I hope to see you there. I'm a grill master, so you *know* the food's gonna be great."

I smiled and walked past him, shaking my head. That man would never give up.

I made it through the entire workday without a single text from Clay. The most productive I'd been all week. Hours flew by as I pored over files, caught up on reports, and even found time to track an account tied to my father's tenure at SparTech. The familiar rush hit me like a drug—chasing anomalies, connecting the dots, uncovering secrets buried in numbers. It was a high nothing else could match. That's how I fell in love with Accounting to begin with. Numbers aren't complicated.

I stopped by Shirley's desk on my way out and my heart nearly stopped. A gossip magazine lay open, featuring a *gigantic* photo of Clay and me leaving the lounge last week. My hair shielded most of my face, but not enough. I grabbed the magazine and stuffed it into my purse, my pulse hammering as I beelined for the elevator.

This. This was exactly what I was afraid of.

I couldn't deal with him. He was too high-profile. Too reckless. I stormed straight to the 30th floor, knocked once, and pushed his office door open. He was pacing by the window, his hands shoved into his pockets. The second he saw me, his face softened into a smile.

"Hey, Dove. How was your day?"

I flung the magazine onto his desk. "What the *fuck* is this, Clay?"

His jaw tightened. He exhaled slowly, then picked up the magazine, barely glancing at it before tossing it onto a nearby table.

"I hate when you curse, Malinda. Please refrain from doing so in front of me."

I blinked. This version of Clay was new.

"I don't give a fu—"

"*Seriously.* Don't test me." His tone was lethal, clipped. The air in the room shifted, thick with something I couldn't quite name.

I folded my arms. Raised a brow. Waiting.

He dragged a hand through his hair, exhaling sharply. "I already knew about this. Paparazzi were outside the club. It happens."

"What are you going to do about it?"

"Nothing." He leaned against his desk. "Your face was mostly covered. No one knows it's you. They've already moved on."

I scoffed. "It'll take *no* effort to figure it out. How many Black women do you take out, Clay? How many even work for you?"

His gaze darkened. "I've been photographed with women of all races all over the world." His tone was measured, but defensive. "And even if someone *does* realize it's you—why does it matter? Is it so horrible being seen with me?"

I clenched my jaw. "Don't be naive. If people find out, my career is over. I'll never be taken seriously in corporate spaces again. My *privacy* is gone. *Your* life is too high-profile for me."

I turned to leave, but he was on me in seconds, gripping my wrist.

"Baby, wait." His voice was raw, urgent. "What are you saying?"

I swallowed. "I can't do this with you."

His grip tightened, then softened. He lifted my hand to his lips, brushing a kiss over my knuckles. "I know it's been a lot. I'm sorry. I'm just so used to it, I don't even think about it anymore. But I know you're not. You said you wanted to take it slow—so let's do that. *Please.* Don't end this before we even know what it could be."

I hesitated. "What does 'slow' mean to you?"

He exhaled. "What do *you* need?"

I took a breath. This was my chance to set boundaries. Make this bearable—until I disappeared.

"Work is off-limits," I said firmly. "No daily lunches, no sneaking into my meetings, no calling me up here unless it's work-related."

His brows furrowed. "But, Dove—"

"*Off-limits, Clay.*"

A muscle in his jaw ticked. "Fine. What else?"

I folded my arms. "Dates are weekends only."

He sighed. "So I never get to see you?"

"You do. But I need my beauty sleep, and I need to focus at work."

His lips twitched. "You're gorgeous, so I guess there's no arguing that." Then, after a beat—"Counteroffer: one night a week, dinner at my place. No going out, no pressure. Just food, wine, maybe a movie."

I eyed him warily.

His cheeks pinked. "*Just* dinner, Dove. Anything else... only if we both want it. I promise I won't push."

I studied him for a beat before sighing. "Fine."

His lips curved. "Great." He kissed me, slow and teasing. "On the weekends, we can find other things to do."

"Like?"

He smiled, eyes gleaming. "All kinds of things. Boating, hiking—since I know you like that. Museums, shows, parties, vineyards. The world is our oyster." He grinned like a schoolboy, completely pleased with himself.

"Sounds fun. But what stops more pictures from getting out, Clay?"

His fingers brushed my jaw, the touch light but possessive. "I'll have security. My guy Rick—you've seen him before. He'll make sure no one gets a shot of us. And if something *does* slip through the cracks, I'll shut it down before it spreads." His lips twitched. "Right now, the internet thinks the woman in that photo is some Ethiopian supermodel in town for a Gucci shoot."

I exhaled, studying him. This could be a fun summer. So why not? Besides, I'd never actually been in a *real* relationship. Everyone I'd been with, even briefly, had been a mark. The thought caught me off guard, and I quickly reframed.

Clay was *not* my boyfriend.

This was *not* a relationship.

I nodded. He grinned. "Perfect. We've set the ground rules, and taking it slow starts *now.* Though, full disclosure—I can't guarantee I won't flirt with you in public. That's asking too much."

I rolled my eyes. He grinned and kissed me again.

He took my hand in his, thumb grazing over my knuckles. "You done for the day?"

"Yeah, I was just heading out."

"Want a drink before you go? I wanna hear about your day."

I hesitated, then shrugged. "Sure."

He got up, moving toward his bar cart. "Wine?"

"Yes. White, preferably."

He turned, smirking slyly.

I narrowed my eyes. Heat flooding my face. "Oh, *please,* Clay. You *know* what I mean."

He chuckled and poured my wine, then fixed himself a scotch.

"How was your day, Dove? Hope things went smoothly."

I sipped my drink and nodded. "Yeah, things went well. I got a lot done. Another internal audit is coming up, so there's just a ton of paperwork and delegating."

"I see."

"And I have to present to the board and stakeholders in three weeks, so everything has to be *perfect.*"

His gaze softened. "I'm sure it will be." He lifted my hand, pressing a slow kiss to my knuckles. His eyes lingered on mine, something deep and unreadable in them.

I quickly changed the subject. "What about you? How was your day?"

His expression flickered, a shadow crossing his face. "It was... okay. Closed the deal with Sylvan Corp. Meetings were good."

"That's great news. Congratulations." I studied him. "But you seem off. What's wrong?"

He took a sip of his scotch, gaze distant. "Nothing... just the usual family stuff."

I hesitated, then reached out, my fingers brushing over his forearm. "Well... whatever it is, I hope it works out for the better."

He turned his head, eyes locking onto mine. Then, without a word, he leaned in and kissed me. The taste of scotch lingered on his lips, warm and intoxicating.

"Thank you, Dove."

We lingered there, talking for a little while longer, finishing off our drinks.

Finally, Clay set down his glass. "Would you like a ride home?"

I exhaled. "I'd appreciate that. Thank you."

And just like that, I let myself sink a little deeper.

Chapter 12

Clay

I got dressed in my tux and sat on my bed, trying to hype myself up. These society events are all the same—a bunch of rich, boring people stuffed in a ballroom, peacocking and trying to one-up each other while outbidding one another to win the title of the most generous donor for whichever charity is being fundraised that night. I'm sick of it. I've been attending these things with my parents since I was a kid. After taking over as CEO, it's now mandatory for me to make an appearance.

I wish so deeply in my soul that Malinda was my date tonight. I can picture her now—dolled up in couture, her hand tucked in the crook of my arm, stealing my attention with just a glance. If she were here, the night wouldn't feel so unbearable.

The car arrived, and Titan was already in the lobby by the time I went down. We dapped up, and he let out a low whistle as he caught our reflection in the mirror.

"The Sawyer boys looking spiffy tonight," he said, adjusting his cuffs before snapping a few mirror selfies.

I rolled my eyes and straightened my bowtie. "Let's just get this over with."

Once we arrived at the banquet, we posed for the paparazzi, flashing polite, effortless smiles before heading inside. Titan went off to locate our parents while I slid my businessman mask into place, schmoozing and charming donors for a large chunk of the night. It was all routine—tight handshakes, forced laughter, fake interest in conversations I had no desire to be a part of.

After what felt like an eternity, I made my way to the bar for a drink. Just as the bartender placed the glass in front of me, I felt a delicate yet firm hand slip around my arm.

"Hey, darling."

I stiffened. I knew who it was before I even turned around.

"Hi, Brooke."

"I've been calling you, babe." Her tone was light, but there was an underlying edge to it.

I turned to face her. Brooke was conventionally attractive—flawless dirty blonde hair styled in an elegant knot, impeccably done makeup, straight white teeth, and a perfectly even spray tan that barely concealed how artificial it all was. Everything about her was manufactured, and curated. She and her circle would swear under oath that her nose had always been that perfectly proportionate and her cheekbones naturally that high. But I remembered her original face.

"I've been preoccupied," I replied flatly. "As you may have heard, SparTech is going international. It's a very involved process."

"I have heard. Congratulations are in order." She smiled, tilting her head slightly. "How will we celebrate?"

"Brooke..." I sighed, already exhausted by this conversation.

"Don't be difficult, darling. You deserve some fun." She leaned in, her perfume so strong it was suffocating. "Preferably with your fiancée and not some hooker at a club. I know boys will have their fun, but next time, try leaving out the back to avoid the scandal of a front-page exposé."

My blood ran cold. My grip on my glass tightened. Did she just insult my Dove? I took a slow, measured breath, forcing down the impulse to snap.

"Am I engaged?" I turned to her fully, my expression unreadable. "Because I don't recall buying a ring or getting on a knee."

She blinked at me, stunned into silence for a beat before recovering.

"I don't get why you constantly try to hurt me, Clayton. I don't complain when you have your whores—"

"Watch. Your. Mouth." My voice was low, tight with barely restrained fury.

Her expression faltered for a split second, but she quickly masked it with a haughty look. She huffed, grabbing a champagne flute from a passing waiter.

"You know what? You're stressed, so I'll just leave you to your thoughts." She released my arm. "Have you seen Rose?"

Before I could answer, she was already striding away, off to find my mother.

I didn't mean to be harsh, but we truly didn't get along. We never had. When I was fifteen, my father sat me down for 'the talk'—not just about women, but about Brooke. What it actually meant to be "promised" to each other. It was more than just going to the same private schools and summer vacations at our estate. I was meant to court and eventually marry her.

I gave it a try. I truly did. We went on dates. Sure, I wasn't polished or charming yet, but she made it impossible to find her likable. We drifted apart, and dated other people in college, but when we tried again in our early twenties, she was even worse—brattier, more entitled, and completely devoid of any real personality.

Now here we were again. Ever since I became CEO, my parents have been pushing me toward marriage with her, whispering promises to her about our future. But my heart was already spoken for. I had found my match, and they couldn't force me to give her up. Not for anything in this world.

Chapter 13

Clay

I knocked on her door, takeout in one hand, the other braced against the doorframe to steady myself. The world tilted slightly, but I barely noticed. My chest was too tight, my mind too full. The gala had drained me. The same faces, the same conversations, the same exhausting expectations. And Brooke...

I clenched my jaw. I didn't want to think about her. I didn't want to think about any of it. I just wanted Malinda.

I knocked again, louder this time. The sound of locks clicking sent relief washing over me.

The door cracked open, and Malinda stood there in an oversized T-shirt, her curls piled high on her head. Her face was bare, tired, and still the most beautiful thing I'd ever seen.

She sighed. "Clay."

"Dove," I murmured, the word slurring slightly.

Her eyes flickered over me, taking in my loosened bowtie, and my slightly unsteady stance. "You're drunk."

"Tipsy," I corrected, offering the bag of takeout as a peace offering. "And I brought food."

She didn't take it. Her fingers tapped against the doorframe instead. "Go home, Clay."

I huffed, stepping past her into the apartment before she could stop me. "I don't wanna go home."

"Clay—"

I turned to her, pleading. "Just let me stay."

She crossed her arms. "Why?"

I licked my lips, searching for the right words, but everything felt too raw. Too much.

"Because I need you." My voice came out hoarse. "Because I don't wanna be alone. And because I missed you, Dove. So fucking much."

Her expression softened, but she stayed planted in place. "That's not my problem."

I let out a humorless laugh, raking a hand through my hair. "Yeah, I know. But you're still the only thing that makes me feel okay."

She exhaled sharply, glancing at the takeout bag. "What did you bring?"

My lips twitched. She was giving in, just a little. "Your favorite." I lifted the bag, shaking it slightly. "Peking duck, those dumplings you liked from Beacon and their plantain fritters."

Her gaze lingered on me for a moment before she snatched the bag from my hand with a small huff. "You're impossible."

"And you're irresistible," I murmured, watching as she walked into the kitchen.

She shot me a glare over her shoulder but didn't kick me out.

I shrugged off my tuxedo jacket and slumped onto her couch, rubbing my face. The exhaustion hit me all at once.

She placed a container of dumplings on the coffee table, then hesitated before sitting on the opposite end of the couch. "What happened tonight?"

I leaned back, letting my head rest against the cushions. "Same shit. Same people. Brooke was there."

Her expression didn't change, but I caught the flicker in her eyes.

"Brooke?"

Shit. My tongue was too loose. Malinda didn't know about her and I didn't want to elaborate.

"Family friend..." That wasn't a lie— technically.

"So what's the issue?" She grabbed a dumpling with the chopsticks and bit into it.

"She just reminded me why I hate her." I turned my head toward Malinda, studying her. "I don't want to talk about her. I don't want to talk about the Gala. I don't want to focus on anyone but you."

She scoffed, popping the rest of the dumpling into her mouth. "I don't need your drunk confessions, Clay."

"I mean it." My voice was rough, my body weighed down with emotion. "You're the only thing that feels real."

She went quiet, focusing on her food, but I saw the way her shoulders tensed.

I sat up, leaning toward her. "Come here."

"No."

I reached for her hand. "Dove, please."

She let out a frustrated breath. "You're just drunk and lonely right now."

"Yeah," I admitted, squeezing her fingers. "And I want to be drunk and lonely with you."

She stared at me for a long moment before sighing and setting her food down. Then, with an exaggerated eye roll, she scooted closer. "Just for a little while."

That was all the invitation I needed. I pulled her into my arms, settling her against my chest. My whole body exhaled. She was warm, soft, everything I craved.

She didn't relax right away, but after a few minutes, her body melted against mine, her fingers curling slightly against my shirt.

I pressed my lips against her forehead, closing my eyes. "Just let me hold you, baby."

She didn't answer, but she didn't pull away either. And for now, that was enough.

I stirred awake at the sound of movement. The soft rustle of fabric. The faint clink of something—keys? A water bottle? My head throbbed dully, but it wasn't unbearable. What pulled me out of sleep fully wasn't the headache, though. It was her.

I cracked one eye open.

Malinda stood near the dresser, tying the laces of her hiking boots, her curls piled high again, her skin fresh and dewy from her morning routine. Sunlight filtered through the window, casting a warm glow over her, making her look almost... ethereal.

I swallowed. I've always thought she was beautiful, but there was something about seeing her like this, in her own space, getting ready for something that had nothing to do with me, that made my chest ache.

"You're up," she noted without turning around.

I groaned, dragging a hand down my face. "Unfortunately."

She smirked, tossing a small bottle my way. "Electrolytes. You'll need them."

I barely caught it before it smacked me in the chest. "Jesus, Dove." I rubbed the point of impact. I cracked the bottle open, downing half in one go, then wiped my mouth with the back of my hand. "Where are you going?"

"Hiking." She stood, rolling her shoulders, testing the weight of the small pack on her back. "I go every Saturday."

I grunted, rubbing my temple. "And you were just gonna leave me here?"

"No," she said simply, grabbing her water bottle. "Thought you were going home."

Malinda was such a direct communicator that it sometimes threw me off.

I exhaled, stretching my sore limbs. "I'll just come with you." I really didn't want to be back home.

She turned, raising a brow. "You?"

"Yeah." I rolled my neck, wincing slightly. "Fresh air, exercise. Might sweat out this hangover."

She eyed me skeptically. "You're in a tux, Clay."

"I'll text Rick." I reached for my phone, already typing a message to my driver. "Ask him to bring me some stuff from home."

Malinda sighed, arms crossed. "Last night really was impulsive huh?"

I nodded almost instantly regretting it as my head throbbed harder. I winced gently rubbing my temples.

She snorted.

"You really think you can survive a hike today?"

"Yup." I dropped my phone onto the nightstand. "Gotta make sure you don't get eaten by a bear or something."

She scoffed. "There are no bears where we're going."

"I don't know that." I stood, stretching. "But what I do know is I'd rather be with you than sitting in the back of a town car regretting every life choice I've ever made."

She rolled her eyes. "Fine. But don't slow me down."

I smirked, sitting up in bed. "Wouldn't dream of it."

I wiped the sweat from my brow, exhaling through my nose as we made our way up a narrow dirt path. I'm not out of shape—I work out every day for christ sake —but this was different. The terrain was uneven, and the incline steep at times. Malinda, on the other hand, moved effortlessly, like she belonged here.

She was in her element.

She barely glanced at her feet, knowing exactly where to step, her breathing steady and controlled. Her eyes scanned the trees, occasionally pointing something out—a red-tailed hawk soaring above us, a small patch of wildflowers, a barely visible deer trail cutting through the underbrush.

I wasn't used to seeing her like this. In the office, she was sharp and calculating. With me, she was guarded and evasive. But here... here she was at peace.

"You do this every Saturday?" I asked, adjusting the strap of the borrowed backpack Rick had delivered.

"Every Saturday," she confirmed.

I huffed, stepping over a large root. "And you never get tired of it?"

"Nope." She shot me a smirk over her shoulder. "Unlike you."

"I'm fine," I lied.

She snorted. "You're dying."

"I am not dying," I grumbled.

She laughed, the sound light and easy, and for a moment, I forgot about my aching calves. I just watched her, the way the morning light played in her eyes, the way she moved like she was a part of the landscape.

She caught me staring, her brows furrowing. "What?"

I shook my head, smirking. "Nothing. Just wondering how I managed to get you to let me come along."

She shrugged. "You didn't."

"Then why am I here?"

She was quiet for a beat, then sighed, gaze flickering to the treetops. "Maybe I didn't feel like being alone today."

My heart fluttered.

I wanted to press, to ask her why, but I knew better by now. Instead, I just nodded, matching her pace.

For the first time in a long time, I wasn't trying to win her over. I wasn't trying to seduce her or convince her of something.

I was just here with her.

And it felt like the best damn thing in the world.

The door shut softly behind us. The scent of warm spices and grilled vegetables from the wraps we picked up on the way home lingered between us, but neither of us moved toward the kitchen.

Malinda dropped her pack by the door, rolling her shoulders. I tossed my borrowed gear onto the couch, running a hand through my damp hair. We were both tired, and sore, but there was something else beneath the fatigue—a slow-burning heat, an unspoken pull.

I watched her as she toed off her boots, flexing her fingers, and stretching the muscles in her legs. The way her body moved, the way her skin glowed from exertion, had me aching with something deeper than hunger.

Malinda exhaled, finally glancing up.

That was all it took.

I was on her in seconds, my mouth claiming hers, hands anchoring at her hips. She gasped, but there was no hesitation, no resistance. She met me just as fiercely, sinking into me like she'd been waiting for this.

My fingers slipped beneath the hem of her shirt, dragging over her heated skin. She shivered, pressing closer. "Clay—"

I groaned at the way she said my name, low and wanting, but this time, there was no rush. No frantic tearing at clothes, no reckless desperation. This was something else.

Something deeper.

My hands slid down, gripping the backs of her thighs, lifting her easily. Her legs wrapped around me, and I carried her to the bathroom, never breaking our kiss.

Steam filled the space as the shower roared to life, fogging up the glass, and surrounding us in warmth. I peeled her clothes from her body, slow and deliberate, drinking in every inch of her.

She stood before me, bare and beautiful, her chest rising and falling with quiet anticipation. My fingers traced the curve of her waist, the dip of her spine.

"You're incredible," I murmured, my voice rough.

She didn't respond—not with words. Instead, she hooked a finger at the waist of my shorts and boxers. I smirked and pulled my shirt up over my head, making quick work of the rest of my clothes. She pulled me into the spray, tilting her head back as the hot water cascaded over us. I followed her lead, my lips trailing along the column of her throat, over the damp skin of her shoulder, my hands mapping her body like she was something sacred.

She sighed against me, her fingers threading into my hair, guiding my mouth back to hers. The kiss was unhurried, and deep, tongues sliding, bodies melting into one another.

When I lifted her again, pressing her back against the cool tile, she exhaled sharply, her nails digging into my arms.

I forced eye contact as I slowly pushed into her. I needed to see her affected by me. Her eyes fluttered, and a soft moan escaped her lips. That's exactly what I needed to see. I buried my face in the crook of her neck, peppering kisses along her collarbone as I moved inside her with slow, deliberate strokes. I got lost in how good she felt—hot and tight like a glove. My forehead rested against hers as I periodically stole her moans with a kiss, my breath mixing with hers.

No words were spoken, but everything was felt—the weight of it, the intensity, the way our bodies fit like they were made for this.

Malinda's lips parted, her head falling back, eyes fluttering shut. "Clay—" she was close.

"Shh, I got you," I whispered, kissing the side of her face, her jaw, the edge of her mouth. My grip tightened at her hips, steadying her as I buried myself deeper, harder. I needed to be deeper. Her hips began to roll, matching my intensity as she clung to me, her body trembling, her breaths turning to soft, choked gasps.

It was different this time. Not a game, not a power struggle.

I didn't rush, didn't push—just held her, moved with her until her soft moans turned into something more. Something begging, needing, desperate. Until she shattered against me, her nails digging into my back, my name breaking from her lips.

I followed moments later, burying myself in her warmth, her name pouring from my lips as I lost myself in the way she felt, in the way she *let* me have her like this.

And for the first time, I didn't feel like she was pulling away.

For the first time, she was right there with me.

And it was everything.

The smell of warm spices and roasted vegetables filled Malinda's apartment as we sat cross-legged on the couch, the remnants of our wraps spread out on the coffee table between us. The TV was off. Our phones were mostly ignored—except for when mine buzzed with work notifications that I couldn't seem to resist.

"You ever just not answer an email the second it comes in?" Malinda asked, watching as I typed out a response with the kind of intensity usually reserved for boardroom negotiations.

I didn't even glance up. "No."

She smirked. "Wow. And here I thought you were paying attention during the very recent management meeting about how to avoid burnout. Didn't you lead that discussion?"

I finally looked up, leveling her with a deadpan stare. "I was paying attention."

"Uh-huh." She stretched out lazily, popping the last bite of her wrap into her mouth. "Could've fooled me."

My brows twitched, and before she could react, I lunged, grabbing her around the waist and pulling her into my lap.

"Clay—! No, don't you dare—"

But it was too late. My fingers pressed against her sides, and she shrieked, twisting in my grip as I tickled her mercilessly.

"Say you were wrong," I teased, my voice low against her ear.

"I wasn't—" She gasped, squirming, laughter spilling out uncontrollably. "You literally—Clay!"

I grinned, tightening my hold as she thrashed. "Admit it, Dove. You just like getting under my skin."

"Maybe." She gasped between laughs, trying to pry my hands off her waist. "Or maybe you're just that easy to mess with."

I chuckled, loosening my grip but not letting her go entirely. She was breathless, flushed, and still half-laughing when I tilted my head, brushing my lips against hers.

The shift was subtle—one moment playful, the next something softer, deeper.

She stilled against me as my mouth pressed more firmly to hers, slow and unrushed. There was nothing urgent about the way I kissed her now. It wasn't desperate or claiming—it was exploring, savoring.

She sighed into me, her fingers finding the back of my neck, pulling me closer. I hummed in approval, my hands moving to cradle her face, my thumb stroking along her jaw.

Sweet moments like this were new to me. I'd never really had this with anyone else. Malinda brought comfort and peace to my life which was unexpected.

I could get used to this.

As the night stretched on, we found ourselves in the kitchen, moving around each other in an easy rhythm.

The kitchen was a mess.

Not a disaster, but certainly not the pristine, efficient workspace I was used to seeing in restaurants or my penthouse. And that was mostly because of Malinda.

She stood at the stove, staring at the pan of half-sautéed vegetables with a frown, arms crossed over her chest like she was trying to will them into submission.

Leaning against the counter, I bit back a smirk as I popped a piece of sliced bell pepper into my mouth. "You do know you have to stir those, right?"

She shot me a look. "I know that."

"Do you?"

"Yes, Clay." She grabbed the wooden spoon and gave the pan a few aggressive, choppy stirs. "See? Stirring."

I sighed dramatically. "Alright, move over, Dove."

Malinda raised a brow. "Oh? So you know how to cook?"

"I'm decent," I admitted, taking the spoon from her. "I mean, I never had to learn. Had chefs my whole life. But I wanted to."

She crossed her arms, watching me now. "Why?"

I hesitated, glancing down at the pan, watching the steam curl up in soft tendrils. It was a simple meal. A stir-fry, nothing extravagant. But the act of making it—making something for her—felt significant in a way I didn't want to examine too closely.

Instead, I shrugged. "Figured it's something I should know. Might come in handy."

"You know," she said, standing entirely too close as she studied what I was doing, "I am capable of cooking."

I arched a brow. "Are you?" My words were laced with disbelief, a smirk tugging at the corner of my lips.

"Yes." She grinned. "I know how to delegate." She handed me a small bowl. "Time for the garlic."

I snorted. "That's not cooking. That's bossing people around."

She smiled fully now as I met her eyes. "Exactly."

I chuckled, rolling my eyes.

Malinda hummed, a soft melody beside me as I stirred the contents of the wok. "Alright, chef. Show me what you got," she quipped.

Turns out, I was decent.

I wasn't perfect—I overestimated how fast the onions would cook and nearly burned the garlic—but compared to Malinda, I was practically a pro.

"You're so smug right now," she accused as I expertly flipped the chicken in the pan, brow furrowed in focus.

"Who, me?" I glanced at her with mock innocence.

"Yes, you."

"Maybe a little," I admitted, grinning. "I think you're just mad I'm better at this."

She scoffed. "You are not better. You just have a slight advantage."

I gave her a look. "Dove, you almost put the rice in without washing it first."

"It's pre-washed!"

"It wasn't."

She huffed, but there was no real annoyance in it. Just playful defiance.

Still, we fumbled through it together and made it work—between stolen bites of food, me guiding her through the steps, light teasing, and her occasionally challenging my logic just to be difficult. We made it work. The meal came together. And when we finally sat down to eat, something settled between us—something quiet, something normal.

No interruptions. No phones. No outside world. Just us.

And me—I dreaded the end of this.

By Monday, it would be back to boardrooms, back to endless calls, back to the weight of my family's expectations.

But tonight, I wasn't the CEO of SparTech.

I wasn't the son of Brian Sawyer.

I wasn't anything except hers.

The next morning, I woke up first.

It was rare for me to be up so early—I was usually sleeping off late nights and stress-heavy weeks on Sundays. But something pulled me from sleep, and the moment I opened my eyes, I knew what it was.

Malinda.

She lay on her side, still deep in slumber, her face relaxed, lips slightly parted. Her satin bonnet was slightly askew, allowing some dark brown tendrils to hang free. The golden morning light streamed through the blinds of her balcony door, casting her in a warm, almost ethereal glow.

If I were a religious man, I'd swear this was what looking into the face of an angel felt like.

It staggered me.

The softness of her. The quiet. The way she existed so fully in her own world, separate from everything else. Untouchable.

I lay there for a long moment, simply taking her in.

Eventually, I exhaled, slowly slipping out of bed, careful not to disturb her. I grabbed my boxers from the floor, tugging them on as I shuffled barefoot into the kitchen.

Coffee. We needed coffee.

I moved on autopilot, filling the machine with water, measuring out the grounds, and setting it to brew. The rich aroma soon filled the air, grounding me.

While I waited, I reached for the cabinet, grabbing two mugs. That's when I looked around.

Malinda's apartment was... nice.

Modern, with sleek finishes and elegant yet understated décor. It wasn't showy, but it was expensive—high-rise living in Baltimore wasn't cheap.

Must have cost her a decent chunk to live here.

The thought was fleeting, but another followed, uninvited.

Maybe her parents help her out.

She never talked about them. Not once.

I shook the thought away, taking slow steps toward the floor-to-ceiling windows, coffee still brewing in the background.

That's when something caught my eye.

A manila envelope, half-hidden under the couch.

Curiosity got the best of me.

I crouched down, fingers brushing over the corner of the envelope, pulling it free. My thumb slid under the flap, about to open it—

"What the fuck are you doing?"

Her voice, sharp and tight, sliced through the air.

I jerked up, turning to see her standing in the bedroom doorway, wrapped in the sheets, hair fully out of her bonnet and wild from sleep, eyes sharp with suspicion. My stomach dropped. Shame hit fast.

"Shit," I muttered. "I wasn't—" I exhaled, setting the envelope down. "I wasn't thinking. I'm sorry."

Her shoulders remained tense, her dark eyes watching me carefully, walls snapping back into place.

I hated it.

Hated that I made her feel like she had to be on guard.

After a long, weighted pause, she walked over, grabbed the envelope, and tucked it into a drawer without another word.

I raked a hand through my hair, feeling like an asshole. "Seriously, Malinda. I wasn't trying to—"

"I know," she said, voice clipped, distant. "Just... don't do that again."

A beat of silence. Then—

"The coffee's ready."

And just like that, the tension cracked. Not fully, but enough.

We grabbed our mugs and went back to bed, spending most of the day in comfortable quiet, watching TV and movies, barely talking. By dinner, things had mostly returned to normal. We ordered takeout and shared a bottle of wine. And then another.

And then—

She rode me.

Hard. Unapologetic. Reckless.

I had never been taken like this before.

Malinda moved over me with devastating precision, hips rolling in a way that made my head spin. She dug her nails into my chest, dragging them down, leaving scorching trails that would mark me for days.

"Fuck, Dove," I groaned, hands gripping her hips, hanging on.

She ignored my attempts at slowing her down. Kept working me, pushing me higher, harder.

She played with my nipples, dragged her nails over my abs, and controlled me in ways no one else ever had. No one ever dared.

My toes curled.

I was unraveling beneath her, utterly at her mercy. Hers.

When she shattered around me, tight and trembling, I broke.

My climax hit so hard that I saw stars.

By the time it was over, by the time my body stopped trembling, and my heart slowed from its wild, desperate hammering, she collapsed onto me.

I barely had the strength to wrap my arms around her.

I had never—never—felt this spent.

And for the first time in months, I drifted into the deepest, most restful sleep of my life.

The next morning, the sun barely up, I kissed her awake.

"Good morning, baby."

She mumbled incoherently, making me chuckle. I kissed her again, trailing my lips over her bare shoulder.

"I'm gonna head home, hit the gym, and get ready for work."

She cracked one eye open. "What time is it?"

"5:13."

"Too early."

"I know, my darling. Go back to sleep." I kissed her forehead before slipping out.

At the gym, Titan spotted me and smirked. "Surprised you're here, bro. Thought you ran off to some other country."

"Why?" I questioned as I put my things down near the weights.

"One minute you're at the gala, the next you disappear without a trace. No calls, no texts."

I shrugged, a sudden image of Malinda's laughter flashing in my mind. I smiled involuntarily.

Titan's eyes narrowed. "Whoa. You're smiling. Nah, who were you with? That mystery girl?"

I rolled my eyes but couldn't wipe the grin off my face. "Mind your business, Titan." I did a lighter workout today and went up to shower and get ready for work. My apartment felt empty. After 3 nights with Malinda, I'm feeling her absence.

On the drive to Maribela, I texted Malinda:

CHAPTER 14

MALINDA

Monday morning came too fast.

I sat at my desk, eyes skimming a financial report, but my mind was far away. The weekend felt like a fever dream—something surreal and dangerous. I exhaled sharply, shifting in my seat, trying to shake the remnants of Clay's presence from my skin.

It wasn't just that he had been in my space. It was that he had entered it so easily, slipping past my guard, past my carefully laid boundaries.

He had shown up at my door unannounced, and that had pissed me off. I had been in the middle of something important when the knock came. Chasing a lead, reconnecting with an old fence I hadn't spoken to in years, trying to unearth anything that might prove what I had begun to suspect: my father hadn't died. He had disappeared. And I needed to know why.

I remembered checking the cameras and seeing Clay standing there, wobbly, unsteady, nothing like CEO Clayton Sawyer. Still, he had been entitled as hell, showing up like he had every right to be there. Like this was normal.

For a moment, I had considered ignoring him, letting him knock himself out and go home. But Clay was persistent. Insistent. And I didn't need him waking up my neighbors. I had quickly shut down my system, locked the server room with a key, and cracked the door open just enough to let him know this was not okay and that he needed to go home. But he had slipped past me anyway, like he belonged there.

That moment had sent a wave of panic through me. I had barely managed to sweep up files, tuck envelopes into drawers, and—most crucially—kick a very important file under the couch. The one he had nearly found on Sunday. If he had seen the blown-up, grainy security image of my father? There would have been no way to explain it away.

And yet... I had let him stay. Let him distract me. Let him touch me. And by Saturday night, as I stood beside him in the kitchen, watching him fumble with a knife, all of my frustration had turned into something softer, something unfamiliar and dangerous.

I had gotten lost in him.

It had started that morning, on the hike.

I had let him talk me into bringing him along, even though my nature time was sacred. A moment where I could escape and just be in the quiet, smell the fresh air, clear my mind. Hearing him huff and puff behind me had been entertaining. Seeing the perfectly polished Clay struggle with hiking did something to me.

I had laughed more than I should have and teased him when he stumbled over a tree root. But at the end of it all, as he stood at the top of the viewpoint, staring at the vastness before him with awe and appreciation, I had felt close to him. Connected. He had appreciated the beauty, and that had meant a lot to me.

By the time we stood in my kitchen that night, I had been staring at the peppers and onions sautéing, feeling somber, lost in my thoughts. I should have known how to cook. My heritage was rich, my bloodline a blend of Bolivian, Afro-Colombian, and Haitian roots—food should have been second nature to me. But my parents had never stayed anywhere long enough for my mother to teach me. My father had been too preoccupied with the next con, then with SparTech. I had learned to survive, but cooking had never been part of that.

Clay had pulled me out of that train of thought, making a joke about stirring the peppers, and I had bantered with him despite myself. I had let myself enjoy it. Let my guard down. And that was dangerous.

Sunday had been a stark reminder of why I couldn't afford to do that.

I had secrets. He could never find out. This was not real. He was not my boyfriend. I needed to remember that. I needed to treat him like a mark—get in, play the game, don't get attached, and ghost. The weekend had messed with my head and made me forget the rules. But I couldn't afford to slip. Not with him

And yet, when I had straddled him Sunday night, watching him break into pieces beneath me, I had liked it. Too much. I had gotten off on seeing him unravel, on taking control of him in a way I never had before. It terrified me—how much I had enjoyed it; how much I had wanted to break past every one of his masks until there was nothing left but my name on his lips.

I shifted in my seat, trying to push it all out of my mind.

A sharp buzz from my intercom snapped me back to reality. "Ms. Burns, you have a call on line three."

My pulse steadied. Right. Back to work.

I reached for the phone, clearing my throat before pressing the button. "Malinda Burns."

It was a quick call. Just answering a question for one of my team members. But as I wrapped up, a buzzing came from my purse. My cell phone was next to me on the desk, so it could only be my burner. My pulse quickened.

I grabbed my bag, dug to the bottom, and pulled out the phone, swiping the screen to answer.

The line crackled slightly, and then a voice I hadn't heard in years snaked through the receiver.

"Hey, Butter. How you doin', baby?"

I went still. Ghost.

My former fence. The one I'd been chatting with when Clay showed up Friday night.

"You disappeared in the chat, so I wanted to check on my favorite girl, just to keep up the convo."

I rolled my eyes. He was a slimeball—oily, slick-tongued, and only loyal to the highest bidder. But then again, most of us who operated in the underbelly of crime and scams were. He didn't care about me—he cared about the payday. I had offered him five grand for a lead.

"Still need that info, sweet thing?"

I stiffened. The hairs on my nape prickled. I glanced at my office door, making sure it was shut before lowering my voice. "What do you know?"

A low chuckle snaked through the receiver. "More than you do."

I exhaled sharply. That was always his game—always just enough bait to keep me on the hook. I hated him for it.

"Meet me. Same place as last time. I only take crypto now," he added lazily, like this was just another transaction.

My pulse kicked up. *That place.* The shady bar tucked in the mountains of Virginia, the one with the busted neon sign, where dirty money exchanged hands under the table and nobody asked questions. The Pines. Secluded, not far off the Appalachian Trail, and barely accessible by car. I was young and dumb back then, trekking up that winding road like I had nothing to lose, knowing each time might be my last.

I exhaled through my nose, already calculating the risks. "That was ten years ago, Ghost. I'm not the same idiot you met back then."

"No, you're not. But you still want answers."

I gritted my teeth. He had me. And he knew it.

"What do you have?" I asked, my voice tight.

"A lead."

My stomach flipped.

"On George?"

A beat of silence. Then, "Meet me and find out."

Silence stretched between us, thick and suffocating.

"Fine. Text me the details."

The line went dead.

I leaned back in my chair, staring at the ceiling.

My weekend with Clay was officially over.

I stood in my living room Saturday afternoon, double-checking my pack. Flashlight. Protein bars. Hygiene items in case I can't get back home until tomorrow. My self-defense kit—pepper spray, a compact stun gun, my knife.

My fingers wrapped around the worn leather grip, tracing the familiar ridges. It had been a gift from my father on my thirteenth birthday. *Every girl should know how to protect herself,* he'd told me, pressing it into my hands with a rare flicker of fatherly concern.

I had never had to use it. *Almost* once, years ago, when a mark got too handsy. But never seriously. Never in a way that would make me feel the weight of it afterward.

I prayed I wouldn't have to tonight.

Ghost was annoying as hell for choosing such a late time to meet. It was intentional—I knew that. He wanted me off balance, uneasy. But I adapted. I had my defenses. My mind was in the right place. I'd be fine.

My phone buzzed.

> **Clay:** *Miss you. I wanna see you so bad.*

I exhaled sharply, setting the knife down and typing back.

> **Malinda:** *Wish I could, but I have that hiking club outing today.*

The dots appeared. Disappeared. Reappeared.

> **Clay:** *Damn. You should've told me sooner, Dove.*

> **Clay:** I would've moved some things around to go with you.

I smirked, shaking my head.

Malinda: You can come to the next one. It's a group of pros this time.

Malinda: Real hikers.

Malinda: No room for amateurs who almost passed out halfway up the trail.

A beat.

Clay: Almost?

Clay: Be serious babe. I was hungover and still crushed it.

I rolled my eyes. Here we go.

Malinda: Mmhmm. Sure.

Malinda: Pretty sure I had to bribe you with trail mix just to keep you moving.

Malinda: Wouldn't want you falling behind and embarrassing yourself in front of these guys.

Clay: Falling behind?

Clay: Me? Cute.

Clay: You fed me lies and peanuts, and I still dominated. Imagine what I could've done sober.

Malinda: So you keep saying.

Clay: Let me come next time.

Clay: I'll bring snacks and stamina.

Malinda: The same stamina you had passed out on my couch after the last hike?

Clay: That was after the other workout—holding your fine ass up on that shower wall, dicking you down till you cried my name.

Malinda: You tryna say I'm heavy?

Clay: Not at all baby. I love a good cardio/strength training combo.

I huffed out a laugh, shaking my head.

Clay: But if you wanted to see me struggle, you could've just asked, baby.

Clay: I'd have taken you on a real hike—bare skin against the sheets, long night, plenty of cardio.

Malinda: Sounds exhausting.

Clay: Sounds like the best kind of workout.

Clay: You should've invited me.

Malinda: Next time.

I laughed, shaking my head.

It was effortless, lying to him. I didn't feel guilty. He asked too many questions.

Six hours later, I stepped off the Greyhound bus and shouldered my bag, the straps digging into my hoodie. The air was thick with the scent of pine and damp earth, the forest stretching wide and endless before me. The trailhead loomed ahead, nothing but a sliver of dirt cutting through towering trees.

I hesitated. Just for a second.

Then I adjusted my ballcap lower over my eyes, tightened the straps of my bag, and started walking.

The climb was steep, the dirt path winding uphill with cruel indifference. My boots dug into the uneven ground, every step sinking slightly into the softened soil. The baggy cargo pants I'd worn for disguise—not function—clung to my legs with sweat, slowing me down. My hoodie, loose-fitting and oversized, was stifling in the humid air. My hair was braided down, tucked neatly beneath my hat, every strand concealed.

It was all intentional.

When I was younger, I hadn't thought much about how I dressed in places like this. I assumed strength was in confidence, in letting people see me—letting them want me—using my looks to my advantage without strategy. I had been reckless. Drawn the wrong attention. Had too many close calls that should have been warnings, but instead became lessons.

Now, I understand the value of blending in. Of removing distractions. Of shifting perception in my favor.

Still, despite the weight of my gear and the burn in my legs, the beauty of the trail was undeniable. Sunlight filtered through a shifting canopy, golden beams dancing across the path. Above me, the sky had vanished beneath a living tapestry of leaves, rustling softly in the wind. The world smelled untouched, crisp, ancient. Birds called to one another in the distance, hidden somewhere in the branches.

A fleeting thought crossed my mind—how the hell did a bar stay in business if only thru-hikers and those in the know could reach it?

Then the answer hit me. Crime. Duh.

I shook my head, forcing the thought away. I needed to stop wondering about things that weren't my business. Wondering led to asking questions, and asking questions got people killed.

By the time The Pines came into view, the sky had started to darken.

The place looked like it had been standing since Prohibition and had barely survived it. A wooden shack with a sagging roof, warped windows, and a busted neon sign hanging crookedly above the door, buzzing dimly. Dust coated the glass. The wooden porch groaned under the weight of its decay, the edges eaten away by time and neglect.

And yet, it was still very much in business.

Another thought formed—maybe they keep it looking this way on purpose. A deterrent. A signal.

Then I mentally kicked myself. Stop wondering.

I wiped the sweat from my brow, took a slow breath, and stepped inside.

The air inside was thick—stale beer, cigarette smoke, and something damp and metallic that clung to the back of my throat.

I stepped in far enough to let the door swing shut behind me, scanning the room without lingering. The place was small, but not cramped—just enough space for hushed conversations to carry from the nearby booths, for whispered deals to exchange hands in the dim lighting.

I immediately clocked the back exit.

The bartender—a woman, surprisingly—stood behind the bar, wiping down a glass with slow, practiced motions. She looked to be in her thirties, solidly built, with sharp eyes that missed nothing.

A handful of men sat at the bar, hunched over drinks, murmuring in low voices. One of them caught my attention—a broad, heavyset guy with a jagged scar slashing diagonally across his face. A warning carved into his skin.

Be wary of him.

I kept moving.

A deal was going down in one of the booths—a man sliding an envelope across the table, another nodding as he palmed it, tucking it into his jacket like it never existed.

I walked with purpose, my steps even, my shoulders squared. Not too fast. Not too slow. Just another body in the room.

Still, I felt them watching.

Eyes trailing over me, taking note.

This place wasn't meant for women. Certainly not a woman alone.

The floor stuck to the soles of my boots as I crossed toward the back.

And there he was.

Ghost.

Slouched in the farthest booth, twirling a toothpick between his fingers, a greasy smirk tugging at his lips. I slid into the seat across from him, my back hitting the cracked vinyl as Ghost grinned, flashing a missing canine.

That's new.

"Well, well, look what the cat dragged in," he drawled, stretching out like he owned the place. "Didn't think I'd ever see you back in a dump like this, Butter."

I ignored the nickname. "Do you have what I asked for?"

Ghost let out a long, exaggerated sigh, lounging back like he had all the time in the world. "Not even a how you been, Ghost? Miss me? Nothing?" He tsked. "You're no fucking fun, you know that?"

I didn't react. Just watched him.

He smirked, rolling the toothpick between his fingers. "Damn shame you're dressed like a dude, though. Was hopin' for a little trip down memory lane, see if that body still looks as good as I remember.

My lip curled. "Your creepy-ass leer didn't get me to fuck you back then, and it sure as hell won't now. Keep wasting my time, and I'll carve a new memory into you."

Ghost barked out a laugh, shaking his head. "Damn, still got that sharp tongue, huh? Same ol' Butter."

I waited; expression blank.

He sighed, dropping the act. "Fine. You wanna play it like that, we'll play it like that." He tapped the table. "Why you lookin' for George Burns?"

My jaw tightened. "Last I checked, curiosity got people killed. I pay for answers, not your nosy ass."

Ghost spread his hands in mock innocence. "I'm helping you, remember?"

"You're not helping me," I said flatly. "You're selling me scraps—same as you always did when I was green."

His smirk turned lazy. "Sugar, I was your guide in this life. You learned from me."

I let out a sharp laugh. "No, you robbed me blind. Gave me half of what I was owed—if that—and the last time? You took me for everything. I should make you pay for that."

Ghost just shrugged, casual as ever, dismissing the truth like it didn't matter. His grin stretched wider, something sinister curling beneath it. "If you don't know how to play the game," he said, voice slick, "the game plays you, sugar."

I leaned forward; my voice low. "Lucky for me, I learned."

He lifted his phone, shaking it lightly. "You got my payment?"

I pulled out mine, finger hovering over the transaction screen. "You got the drive?"

He slid a flash drive across the table with a flourish. "Right here."

I didn't touch it. Not yet.

"How do I know this isn't bullshit?"

He leaned back, smirking. "You don't."

We locked eyes. The air between us tightened.

But my pulse stayed even. My fingers didn't shake. I'd been here before. I knew this game.

Without looking away, I pressed send.

Ghost checked his phone, nodded once, and then tapped the flash drive. "Pleasure doin' business, Butter."

I picked it up and slid it into my pocket. Cold. Small. Potentially useless.

I stood without another word, turned, and walked out the same way I came.

The night air hit me—sharp, cool, laced with pine and danger. I didn't let myself relax. Not yet. Not until I was far, far away from here.

Chapter 15

Malinda

It had been two weeks since I'd stepped back into the underworld for answers—two weeks since I let Ghost con me out of five grand for a flash drive full of nothing. The frustration lingered, but summer had arrived, bringing with it a strange sense of ease I didn't know what to do with. SparTech's summer hours meant that Fridays were mine, a luxury I *should* have used to push my search forward. But after weeks of chasing leads that only led to dead ends, I needed to step back.

I wasn't sure why I had felt such urgency in the first place—my father had been gone for years. If he was alive, he wasn't in any hurry to make contact. So why was I running myself in circles? Acting like time was slipping away? Instead of driving myself mad, I had allowed something else to take up space in my life—Clay.

Our Wednesday dinners at his house after work had become something I *looked forward* to. I hated that.

To my surprise, he had respected my professional boundaries. He stayed in his lane at work, only breaking our unspoken rules once—texting me a simple *Good luck* before my board presentation. The pride in his eyes afterward had unnerved me.

And yet, every Thursday evening, I still found myself in his office at the end of the workday. It had become routine now—slipping into his private bathroom, where a bag of my clothes always waited, changing out of the armor of Malinda Burns, internal auditor, and stepping into something softer. Then, we would go to the docks, spending the weekend—weather permitting—on his yacht.

At first, I told myself it was an escape. Something casual. A break from the world. I would read on the deck while he took meetings inside. Sometimes, I would work on reports while he made calls. Other times, we would sit together, watching the sun sink into the water, drinking expensive wine, and swapping stories.

I had learned so much about him—his childhood, his family, his friendships, and the reckless, indulgent mess of his party-boy past. Details I could weaponize if I wanted to.

But I didn't. That was the problem.

Clay Sawyer was multi-layered. Cocky, obsessive, emotional. A little paranoid. The product of two people who had no business raising a child. He was entitled in ways that made me bristle, but lonely in a way that made me ache. I *recognized* the loneliness. I knew the shape of it, the way it twisted inside, how it hollowed you out.

I wasn't supposed to care. That wasn't part of the plan. I tried to treat him like a mark—something to manage, not feel. But the more time I spent with him, the harder it was to keep myself at a distance.

When I let myself relax—when I let my mind drift—I thought about the little things. The way he watched me when he thought I wasn't paying attention. The way he gripped the back of my neck like he needed to feel my pulse under his fingertips. The way his breath hitched every time I said his name in the dark.

When I looked at him, I saw the potential for destruction. Not just for him—for *me.*

I needed to get my head back on straight. I *would.*

Just not right now.

For now, I would let him hold me. Let myself be consumed by him. Let the warmth of summer and the lull of the waves convince me, for just a little while longer, that this was safe.

CHAPTER 16

MALINDA

The tension had been simmering all afternoon.

I knew going to Amir's cookout with Clay there was a mistake. Not because I didn't want him there, but because I knew *him*. He had been trying—really *trying*—to play it cool, to act like I was just any other employee in a social setting. But Clay was possessive by nature. And patience was not his strong suit.

I felt his eyes on me the entire time. Not just watching—*tracking*. Measuring every interaction, every laugh, every touch that wasn't his. He stayed on the other side of the yard, drink in hand, making conversation with a few executives from work, but I wasn't fooled. The tension in his shoulders, the way his jaw ticked, how he checked his phone every few minutes—I knew exactly what he was doing.

He was waiting for me to slip up.

I had tried to keep a respectable distance, making sure not to linger too long in his space, but it didn't matter. Clay found reasons to touch me. A hand grazed my lower back as he passed, fingertips brushing my wrist when he handed me a drink. When I glanced at my phone, I found a series of messages that made my stomach flip:

> **Clay:** *You're ignoring me.*

> **Clay:** *That dress should be illegal.*

> **Clay:** *Come find me.*

> **Clay:** *Now.*

I swallowed hard, typing out a quick response.

> **Malinda:** *Behave.*

His reply came almost instantly.

> **Clay:** *Make me.*

The scent of grilled meat and smoky barbecue sauce hung thick in the humid summer air, mingling with the sound of old-school R&B pouring from the speakers Amir had set up on the deck. The cookout was in full swing, with guests laughing, drinks flowing, and the sun casting a golden glow over the yard. Yet here I am hovering near the refreshment table, swirling the ice in my drink, trying to ignore the weight of Clay's gaze on me from across the lawn and not trigger his weird possessiveness over me. I'm losing control of this thing with him, and I don't like it.

"You look tense," Amir's voice broke through my thoughts, warm and teasing. "You good?"

I turned to find him leaning against the edge of the table, plate in hand, easygoing as ever. He was dressed in a simple Hawaiian tee and khaki shorts, but somehow, he still managed to look like the most put-together person here.

"I'm fine," I said, forcing a small smile. "Why wouldn't I be?"

Amir raised a brow, unconvinced. "I don't know, boo—you just look like you're either plotting something or trying *not* to commit a crime. Either way, I figured I should check in."

I rolled my eyes, but the corner of my mouth lifted. "I'm not plotting *anything*. Just enjoying the party."

His gaze flicked over me, assessing. "Uh-huh. You sure that drink isn't just for show?"

I took a sip to prove my point, arching a brow as I swallowed. "Happy?"

"For now," he said with a grin. "So, what's the verdict? Food up to your standards?"

"You mean the food *you* made?" I tilted my head. "Cocky much?"

He smirked, feigning offense. "Excuse me, but I slaved over that grill."

"Slaved?" I echoed. "You handed out a few instructions and then stood around looking important."

Amir gasped dramatically. "Wow. Just lying straight to my face."

I let out a small laugh. "Fine. The food is great. Happy?"

"Very." He nudged my cup with his knuckles. "And the playlist? Don't think I didn't see you nodding along a few minutes ago."

I exhaled, shaking my head. "Okay, okay—you win. You've got good taste."

He grinned, clearly satisfied. "Damn right. Glad you're enjoying yourself." Then, lowering his voice slightly, he added, "Can't say the same for the boss over there though."

My stomach tightened. "What?"

Amir nodded subtly across the yard. "Clay. He's been shooting daggers at me all afternoon. You'd think I insulted his entire bloodline. I mean sure I turned in the performance evals for my department a little late but killing me is an unjust punishment for the crime don't ya think?"

I chuckled and forced an easy shrug, swirling my drink. "He's probably just stressed about the merger. He's been up everyone's ass about it. Going international in 2 separate countries at the same time is ambitious."

"Mm." Amir hummed, unconvinced. "I guess." He took a casual sip of his drink, studying me. "It's just funny, though."

I kept my expression neutral. "What is?"

" I think he may be into you. The way he's been looking at you," Amir mused. "Like he wants to eat you alive, but also like he's mad about it."

My fingers tensed around my cup, but I made a show of rolling my eyes. "Now who's lying straight to *my* face?"

Amir chuckled, shaking his head. "Hey, I call it like I see it. But truthfully, who wouldn't be looking at you like that? Your dress is...very flattering. I could tell he was holding back to be respectful but his eyes leered.

I blushed trying to suppress my smirk.

"Thanks."

He shot me a playful wink. "But let's get to the real question—when are you finally gonna say yes and let me take you out?"

I let out a breathy laugh, shaking my head. "Amir."

"What?" He grinned, all charm and mischief. "I ask every year. Gotta keep the tradition alive."

"And every year, I say no. Technically it's been twice this year."

"Hey, Cirque du Soleil being in town is a special occasion in my books."

I snorted. "Whatever you say."

He tsked, undeterred. "One day, you're gonna surprise me."

I smirked. "Don't hold your breath."

"Noted," he said with a mock-serious nod. Then, with a slow wink, he added, "Next time."

And with that, he strolled off, leaving me standing there, sipping my drink, being very much aware that Clay was *still* watching.

When I glanced back across the yard, Clay was staring at me, his expression dark, and unreadable. But I *felt* his anger from where I stood. It curled in the air between us like a storm cloud. And at that moment, I knew—It was time to go.

I made my excuses, grabbed my things, and left. But I wasn't free of him. Not even close.

The moment I stepped into my apartment, my phone rang. I hesitated before answering. "Clay—"

"Open the door."

My pulse jumped. "Are you serious?"

"I'm outside, Malinda. Open the fucking door."

I took a steadying breath before unlocking it. The second I did, Clay pushed inside, slamming it shut behind him. He rounded on me.

"Clay, what the hell is wrong with you?"

"You're gonna stand there and act like I imagined that?" His voice was low, tight with barely restrained anger.

I sighed, already exhausted. "Clay—"

"Don't," he snapped, running a hand through his hair. "Don't sit there and tell me Amir is just *like that with everyone.* I have *eyes,* Malinda."

I folded my arms, keeping my tone even. "And what did your *eyes* see, exactly? Someone making conversation? Joking around?"

Clay laughed, but there was no humor in it. "*Joking?*" He took a step closer. "I saw the way he looked at you. I saw the way you *smiled* at him. And you think I'm just supposed to pretend that doesn't mean anything?"

I clenched my jaw, forcing myself to stay calm. "Amir is flirtatious with *everyone,* Clay. That's just his personality. It doesn't mean anything. You're reading into something that isn't there."

His eyes darkened. "Don't fucking gaslight me."

My breath caught, surprised at the sharpness in his tone.

"You think I don't *know* attraction when I see it?" he demanded. "*Both* of you—laughing, whispering— him leaning in like he had every right to be close to you." He exhaled harshly, pacing. "So tell me, Malinda. Is it just *him* that flirts with everyone, or do you flirt back?"

I stiffened. "*Excuse me?*"

"Do you have *any* idea how fucking hard it is to pretend like you're just another employee when you're standing there looking like *that*—letting him get that close to you?" His voice was low and seething.

"I wasn't *letting* him do anything. Amir is just my *colleague.*"

Clay scoffed, running his tongue over his teeth and stepping closer. "That's cute. Does he know that?"

I clenched my jaw. "This is exactly why I didn't want you there."

He stilled. "What the hell does that mean?"

"It means you don't *do* casual. You don't know how to be normal about things." I exhaled sharply, rubbing my temples.

Clay turned; his expression unreadable. "Are you hooking up with him?"

The question hit me like a slap. My stomach twisted. "What the *fuck* did you just ask me?"

His jaw flexed. "You heard me. Are you fucking him? He more your type? Better in bed?"

Anger flared hot in my chest. "Are you seriously implying that because Amir and I are Black, I must be fucking him?"

"You said it. Not me." He held my gaze unflinching. But I could sense that he knew he crossed a line. He exhaled angrily, running his fingers through his hair but backing down.

"Get out." My voice was sharp, ice-cold.

I saw a shadow of panic cross his face.

"Wait—"

"Get the *fuck* out, Clay." My hands were shaking. "I put up with a lot from you, but I will *not* let you disrespect me. What next!? You gonna ask me what our favorite fried chicken shop is? Or admire how "articulate" I fucking am?!"

Clay took a step back, his face crumpling. "Shit. No, baby, that's not what I—" He stopped himself, exhaling shakily. He dragged his hands down his face, then through his hair again, suddenly looking wrecked. "*Fuck.*"

I swallowed hard, my heart hammering as I watched him.

"You have no idea what this is like for me," he muttered, shaking his head. "Keeping this secret. Pretending like I don't *need* you the way I do." He looked at me then, and something in his eyes made my breath hitch. "I just want to *claim* you, Malinda." His voice cracked. "I wanted to put my arm around you at that fucking cookout and let everyone know you *belong* to me."

I swallowed; my throat tight. "You don't own me, Clay."

"I *know* that." he said quickly, taking another step toward me. "I just—" His breath shuddered. "*Please*. I didn't mean it like that. I swear, Malinda. Just—don't shut me out." His hands trembled at his sides. "I want you so fucking bad it's driving me insane."

Clay, we agreed to *this*—being just between *us*...

"I know... I just want you too much. I can't fucking stand watching other men think they have a chance with you"

"You're acting possessive."

A muscle ticked in his jaw. "Is that what you think this is?"

"How else can you explain getting this upset over a conversation at a cookout?"

He sighed after a moment of silence. He searched my eyes desperately.

"Baby... half the time you act like you don't want me." I stilled. "You think I don't see how hard you fight our attraction? You're so desperate to keep me at a distance, to make me *temporary*."

He stepped closer to me. "You can lie to yourself all you want, Dove," he murmured, fingers brushing my wrist. "But don't lie to me."

My chest ached, my anger warring with the sheer desperation in his voice. He had crossed a line. But seeing him like this, breaking in front of me, tugged at something deep inside me.

And *that* was the real problem. Because no matter how much I fought it, Clay Sawyer had already dug himself under my skin.

CHAPTER 17

CLAY

The rest of the summer went by in a blur. I still can't believe I acted like such an ass to Malinda during that fight. Things between us have been better since then, but I can feel the shift—her guard is back up. She's careful now, more measured in her words and reactions, and I hate it. I miss the way she let herself melt into me without hesitation. Our sex life is still mind-blowing, but I know better than to think that means everything is fine. Still, we've found a balance—quality time spent talking, going to concerts, discussing the company, and me running international expansion strategies by her over late-night dinners.

Today was one of those days where we just couldn't keep our hands off each other. Maybe it was the storm outside. Thunder rolled through the city like a war drum, shaking the very walls of my penthouse. The rain pelted against the windows in heavy sheets, the sound rhythmic and unrelenting, a force as uncontrollable as the pull between us. The room would light up in a violent flash, only to be swallowed by darkness again before the deep, guttural crack of thunder vibrated through the air. It was primal, electric, like the world outside had decided to mirror what was happening between us. We lost count of how many times we gave in to our need for each other, the heat between us rivaling the storm itself.

I was lying on my side, catching my breath, while Malinda massaged my calf. I'd been ambitious, trying out a new position, and our climax had been insane—but now I was paying for it with the worst charley horse of my life. I clenched my jaw, trying to breathe through the pain, but Malinda was all giggles, entirely unsympathetic.

"Damn, Clay. Does this mean you're getting old?" she teased, her fingers kneading into my calf muscle.

I exhaled a rough laugh, shaking my head. "As long as I keep sending you into orbit with these orgasms, I think I'll be just fine."

She hummed, clearly pleased, and I seized the opportunity to pull her down into my arms, pressing her body against mine. Our legs tangled, the warmth of her skin against me sending a lazy, satisfied ache through my body. I sighed, inhaling the faint traces of vanilla and whatever sinful thing her skin naturally smelled like. Outside, another crack of thunder split through the sky, its echo rolling over the city like a warning.

Tonight had been different. The most fun we'd had in a while. The tension between us had started to erode, and for the first time in weeks, I felt like I had her again, like she wasn't actively holding a part of herself back from me.

I'd planned it that way. I made sure Kent, my private chef, took the night off so I could cook for her myself. It reminded me of the first weekend I spent with her. She had…limitations in the kitchen, so I handled most of the cooking. But I wanted it to be sexy, intimate, something to pull us back to that space we'd once occupied so effortlessly. I turned off all the lights, lit candles, and we played out a little fantasy—her, my naughty sous chef, and me, her stern and mysterious executive chef.

She emerged from the bedroom in only an apron, a thong, and the new YSL heels I'd bought her. I damn near dropped the pan in my hand. I tried to focus on the meal, I did. But then she bent over just slightly, showcasing that perfect ass of hers, and I almost burned the steak and knocked over a candle all in the same breath. She burst into laughter, the sound like honey, dripping thick and sweet, making me fall harder for her in ways I never thought I would.

"You feeling better?" Her voice pulled me from the memory, her fingers still tracing over my leg absentmindedly.

I stared at her, studying the way the candlelight flickered against her features, casting soft shadows across her cheekbones. A slow smile spread across my lips as I nodded.

"Dove?"

"Hm?" She reached for her phone on the nightstand, and I caught her wrist before she could grab it.

"I want to take you on a trip."

She froze. "A trip?"

"Yeah. Next week."

She narrowed her eyes, already skeptical. "Clay, we're in the thick of Q3."

I smirked, planting a soft kiss against her forehead. "I'm aware, and I don't think the company will go under if we take a few days off."

"Why the spontaneity?"

I sighed, the thing I'd been dreading finally surfacing. I ran a hand through my hair before pressing another kiss to her temple, stalling. "September is around the corner. The merger with Sylvan Corp is going to be taking up a ton of my time. I'll be back and forth between Beijing, Berlin, and Baltimore for the next six to nine months to ensure a smooth transition."

Her expression shifted, something unreadable flashing across her face. "Oh..."

"Yeah. I mean, of course, Jerry and Emmett are going to be based there for at least a year, but I'm particular. I like to be hands-on to make sure things are done correctly."

"I see."

I hated the way she said it. Like she was already preparing herself to detach. Like she was quietly taking stock of the time we had left.

"Yeah, so since the amount of time we can spend together is going to be limited, I want to make the most of it."

She was quiet. Too quiet. And I didn't like it.

I tilted her chin up, forcing her to meet my gaze. "Come on, babe. Please don't think about things too deeply. Let's just have a good time. I want to take you to Spain."

Her brows lifted slightly. "Spain?"

"Yeah. I have a villa in Mallorca. Just a quick trip. Four days."

I searched her face for any hint of excitement, any sign that she was on the verge of saying yes. I didn't just want to take her away—I needed to. The way things had been lately, the walls she'd rebuilt between us... I needed to remind her of what we had. Needed her to look at me like she used to, like I was the only thing that made sense in her world.

Outside, another flash of lightning illuminated the room, the boom of thunder shaking the glass of the balcony doors. I watched the shadows dance across her face, the way her lips parted slightly, like she was weighing something unspoken. I had her, I just had to be careful not to let her slip through my fingers.

She was still mine—I just had to make sure she never forgot it.

CHAPTER 18

MALINDA

We flew private. Clay's wealth was a sort of muted elegance versus the ostentatious displays put on by some of the marks I've conned over the years. It's difficult to conceptualize just how wealthy Clay Sawyer is. Even knowing his family's legacy, and seeing the casual opulence woven into his life, it never quite settled in my mind.

The minute we landed, he shut off his phone.

"Clay... what if someone needs to reach you?"

He wrapped his arms around me, pulling me close as the warm Spanish sun bathed us in golden light. He placed a gentle kiss on my head, his breath tickling my hair.

"Everyone I need to talk to is right here."

I rolled my eyes but couldn't suppress the warmth curling in my chest. "That's reckless. What if the company burns down?"

He smirked. "Then I guess we'll have to stay in Spain forever."

I wanted to remind myself that this was temporary. That I had an end date now, and soon, I'd have to leave. I needed to start planning my exit. But every time I tried to focus on that reality, Clay would do something—smile at me a certain way, pull me into a spontaneous kiss, make me laugh—and it would all slip away. For now, I let myself pretend. Just for the weekend.

His villa was breathtaking. Nestled along the coast, it was all stone and glass, blending seamlessly with the landscape. Terracotta roofs, whitewashed walls, and balconies opened to endless views of the Mediterranean. The scent of saltwater and jasmine drifted through the air, carried by the coastal breeze. A private infinity pool shimmered under the sun, and the sound of waves crashing in the distance gave everything an almost dreamlike quality.

"Clay," I breathed, turning in slow circles to take it all in. "This is breath-taking."

He watched me with quiet amusement, hands in his pockets. "Glad you like it."

"Does it sit empty when you're not visiting?" I asked, running my hand along the smooth marble railing of the terrace.

He stepped behind me, his arms encircling my waist. "Nah. Luxury short-term rental."

I nodded, impressed. "Smart idea."

He grinned. "I have those every once in a while."

I shot him a knowing look. "Only every once in a while? I feel like you have a thousand business schemes up your sleeve."

Clay grinned, tilting his head as if considering. Then, he leaned in, his lips grazing my ear as he murmured, "Mmm, maybe a thousand and one. But right now, my only scheme is keeping you all to myself."

We spent four blissful days together. Shopping in cobblestone streets lined with boutiques. Attending a yacht event where champagne flowed like water. Long afternoons spent tangled in sheets, our bodies moving in a rhythm as old as time. Floating in the pool, letting the Spanish sun warm our skin, stealing lazy kisses between sips of sangria.

It was like being in another world. A different reality where I wasn't who I was, and there was a real chance for us to be happy together.

And that thought—that dangerous, foolish thought—was the most un-settling of all.

I wasn't supposed to be happy with Clay. I wasn't supposed to be swept away by the way he laughed, by the carefree way he carried himself here, light and unburdened. I wasn't supposed to ache at the idea of this ending. But I did. And every time I tried to bring myself back to reality, his hand would find mine, his lips would brush against my skin, and the walls I kept trying to rebuild would crumble.

Clay was different here. Lighter. Laughing almost constantly, teasing me, playing pranks like a mischievous schoolboy. He was a man unburdened, a man I rarely saw in the polished, composed CEO who dictated boardrooms with an iron grip. He had a streak of boyishness in him—a playful charm that made it easy to forget the weight of his name, his title, his responsibilities.

He was so romantic.

We took the tram in Sóller to the sea, where we had lunch overlooking the water. The restaurant was a charming little place, nestled against the cliffs, with tables shaded by lemon trees. The scent of grilled seafood and freshly baked bread filled the air. Clay ordered for both of us, his Spanish smooth and confident, and I found myself watching him, enthralled.

"You know, you're kind of showing off," I said as he spoke effortlessly to the waiter.

He shot me a playful look. "Am I? Or are you just impressed?"

I rolled my eyes, but I was.

At one point, as we walked along the winding coastal path, he suddenly veered off, stepping onto a small patch of wildflowers growing along the edge of the road. He crouched down, plucked a few, and turned back to me with a playful smile.

"For you," he said, holding out the small bouquet.

I stared at him, caught between amusement and something much softer, something dangerously close to affection.

"You picked me flowers?" I teased, raising an eyebrow.

He shrugged, grinning. "Don't tell anyone. It might ruin my reputation."

I laughed despite myself, taking the flowers from his hand. The petals were delicate, almost translucent in the sunlight.

"Your secret's safe with me," I murmured, twirling one between my fingers.

The yacht event was lavish, but not in the gaudy way I expected. The people there, Clay's friends from around the world, were just as wealthy as him—easily billionaires, heirs, or tech moguls—but they were warm, engaging, and genuinely interested in conversation.

I found myself talking to a French art dealer who spoke passionately about his latest gallery opening, a Brazilian philanthropist funding clean water initiatives, and an Italian fashion designer whose brand I'd admired for years. They were polished, accomplished, and entirely different from the arrogant, shallow elites I was used to conning.

"Malinda, you're quite the mystery," the art dealer, Jacques, mused over his champagne. "Clay never brings anyone to these events."

Clay leaned back with an easy grin and simply said, "She's special."

My stomach twisted at that because I knew he meant it. He thought I was something special while I was plotting to leave him. I had never dealt with a man like him. These last few months had been a dream. But I had always known it wouldn't last. The merger presented a natural end, an easy way out.

And yet, as the night continued, as we laughed and drank under the star-drenched sky, I let myself lean into the illusion.

Later, we dined at an exclusive restaurant, seated at a long table overlooking the city lights. The conversation flowed effortlessly, and for once, I wasn't on guard. I laughed at inside jokes, debated art and business, and let myself be part of the moment.

Clay reached for my hand under the table, lacing our fingers together. I should've pulled away. Instead, I held on just a little tighter.

But soon, this would end. And I had to remember that.

CHAPTER 19

MALINDA

We leave in the morning. I can't believe how fast the weekend slipped through my fingers, real life looming just beyond the horizon. Today had been slow, and indulgent. Clay spent hours sprawled out under the sun, deepening his tan, while I stayed cool under a beach umbrella, absorbed in my book.

"I've planned a dinner for us tonight," he said casually, breaking the silence.

I didn't look up. "Oh?"

"It's our last night in Spain... for now." His voice dipped lower, edged with something unspoken. "I want to do something special. Romantic."

I flicked my gaze up at him, catching the smirk on his face.

"What?"

He held my stare for a beat, then licked his lips, the smirk fading slightly. "What I've planned... I need you to trust me."

That made me pause. Trust him? In what way? I don't trust people. He didn't need to know that, though. I kept my tone light.

"I don't eat squid, Clay," I deadpanned. "I don't care how fancy they try to make it sound—calamari is still just a slimy sea blob."

He chuckled, deep and amused. "No, nothing like that, baby." His voice took on a velvety edge. "It's a surprise. A journey, so to speak. I just need you to trust that I won't do anything outlandish."

I hesitated, rolling the thought around in my mind. I wasn't sure what unsettled me more—the request itself or the way he said it, like he was inviting me into something I'd never experienced before.

Finally, I nodded. "Okay. I trust you."

He hummed his approval, a slow, pleased sound that sent a strange thrill down my spine. I forced my focus back to my book, but the words blurred together.

I had no idea what Clay had planned. But the way he looked at me just now?

I wasn't sure I was ready.

The sun hung low in the sky, casting a golden glow over the villa as we returned from the beach. My skin was still warm from the Spanish sun, grains of fine sand clinging to my legs as I kicked off my sandals in the foyer. I stretched, sighing contentedly, before turning to find Clay watching me with that familiar intensity—equal parts reverence and hunger.

"Go upstairs," he murmured, his voice smooth, assured. "I have something waiting for you."

I arched an eyebrow, but he only smirked and walked past me, speaking in hushed tones to the staff as they bustled around, preparing for the evening ahead. I lingered for a moment, observing the way his jaw tensed, the way he ran a hand through his sun-bleached hair, making sure every detail was perfect.

Curiosity piqued, I ascended the grand staircase and found the bedroom bathed in warm afternoon light. The scent of lavender and jojoba greeted me, mingling with the salty ocean breeze wafting through the open balcony doors. A low, melodic hum of soft instrumental music played from the sound system.

Then I saw her.

A woman in all white, standing by the massage table that had been set up in the center of the room. The masseuse smiled warmly, gesturing for me to come closer.

"Señor Sawyer has arranged a special treatment for you," she said, her accent lilting, inviting.

I hesitated, but the thought of sinking into warm oils and skilled hands was too tempting to resist. I undressed and laid face down on the table, sighing as the masseuse draped a steaming hot towel across my back, the heat seeping deep into my muscles.

My tension unraveled with each stroke, each deliberate press of strong, experienced hands kneading away the remnants of my resistance. Warm fragrant oil cascaded over my skin, slick and decadent, gliding along the slopes of my shoulders, and down the curve of my spine. By the time she was done, I felt boneless, my limbs heavy with pleasure, my mind hazy with relaxation.

I sat up slowly, stretching my arms above my head. That's when I noticed the bed.

A rust-colored silk dress was draped elegantly across the sheets, accompanied by a delicate lace lingerie set in the same hue. A pair of strappy heels sat neatly beside a box of glittering jewels, and at the center of it all, a handwritten note on thick, expensive paper.

I picked it up, recognizing Clay's bold, slanted handwriting.

> *My Dove,*
> *Tonight, let me worship you.*
> *Come to me at sunset, draped in silk and precious jewels,*
> *Embark with me on this journey where wine, music, and my hands will be your only indulgence.*
> *Forget the world—just for tonight. Let me make you feel adored.*
> *Yours always,*
> *Clay*

Heat pooled in my stomach at his words, but I pushed it down, reminding myself—this was just for fun. Just an indulgence. Nothing more.

And yet, as I slipped the silk dress over my freshly oiled skin, fastening the delicate chain of diamonds around my throat, I couldn't deny the anticipation thrumming through my veins.

By the time I stepped onto the terrace, the sun had begun its descent, painting the sky in breathtaking strokes of amber, blush, and violet.

The terrace had been transformed.

Flowers in rich shades of orange, deep reds, soft pinks, and crisp whites overflowed from golden vases, their fragrance intoxicating. The air was laced with the deep, sultry strum of a Spanish guitar playing softly in the background. A small, intimate table for two was set, candlelight flickering against crystal glassware, the promise of a lavish evening lingering in the air.

Then I saw him.

Clay stood at the edge of the terrace, his back to me, staring out over the cliffs where the ocean stretched endlessly beyond the horizon. He was dressed simply—linen slacks, an open-collared white linen shirt, his tanned skin glowing against the crisp fabric.

At the sound of my heels clicking against the tile, he turned.

His eyes found mine, and in that moment, I swore the world around us stilled.

He looked at me as though I had descended from the heavens themselves, as though I were the most exquisite thing he had ever laid eyes on. His pupils darkened slightly, his lips parted as he exhaled, his gaze roaming over me like a reverent touch.

I reached for the champagne flute he offered, but he didn't let go immediately, holding it steady between us as his fingers grazed mine.

"You take my breath away, Dove." His voice was low, rough with something unspoken. He leaned in, brushing a lingering kiss against my cheek, his scent enveloping me—clean linen, expensive cologne, a hint of the sea.

My pulse fluttered as I met his gaze, the weight of his devotion pressing against me like a tangible thing.

And then, we sat.

Chapter 20

Malinda

The night unfolded like a dream, each course a decadent step toward surrender. The villa's balcony, bathed in candlelight, became a private sanctuary overlooking the endless expanse of the Mediterranean. Spanish guitar hummed softly in the background, blending with the rhythmic crashing of waves below. The air was rich with the scent of jasmine and sea salt, a heady mixture that seemed to thicken with each passing moment.

I had agreed before I could stop myself. *Trust me,* he had said. And for some reason, I did.

The seven-course meal was an intricate seduction, each dish meticulously prepared with aphrodisiacs—truffle-infused oysters, saffron-laced risotto, a filet drizzled with dark chocolate balsamic reduction. The chef had explained each dish before retreating into the night, leaving us alone under the sky, nothing but flickering candlelight between us.

Every sip of wine, every decadent bite heightened my awareness, making my skin more sensitive, and my body more attuned to Clay's presence. It started with innocent touches—his fingers grazing mine as he refilled my glass, his knee pressing lightly against mine beneath the table. But there was nothing innocent about the way his gaze burned into me as I licked a smear of honey from my lips.

By the time dessert arrived—chili-infused dark chocolate paired with a vintage port—I felt the shift. The mild hallucinogens in our meal seeped into my bloodstream like liquid heat, amplifying every sensation. The brush of Clay's thumb against my wrist sent shivers racing down my spine. The air itself felt electric.

My breath hitched when he leaned in, his lips a whisper away from my ear. "Do you feel it, Dove?"

I nodded, my pulse fluttering. Everything was *more.* More intense. More consuming. More dangerous.

His fingers traced the delicate line of my collarbone, barely touching my skin, but I felt it everywhere. A slow burn spread through me, pooling low in my belly, making my thighs press together in search of relief. He smirked, sensing it. *Enjoying* it.

"Come here," he murmured, his voice thick with desire.

I rose, letting him pull me into his lap. The moment my body met his, I felt the hardness beneath his slacks, and my breath stuttered. His hands roamed over me, slow and reverent, exploring the silk of my dress, and the curves beneath. The wine glass in my hand trembled as I tried to take another sip, but Clay caught my wrist, guiding it to his lips instead. He drank from it, eyes locked on mine, then set it aside before kissing me deeply.

The moment our lips met; I was lost. His tongue slid against mine, teasing, taking, and I moaned into his mouth. Every nerve in my body was alight, responding to him as if he was the only thing that existed in the world. I didn't even realize he had lifted me until I felt the cool stone of the balcony railing against my back.

My dress slipped from my shoulders, pooling at my waist, and the night air kissed my exposed skin. Clay's mouth followed, tracing heated patterns down my neck, and across my chest. The scrape of his teeth against my nipple sent a jolt of white-hot pleasure straight to my core, and I gasped, my fingers threading through his hair to hold him there.

"Clay—"

"I know," he growled, his voice strained. "I feel it too."

His hands gripped my thighs, spreading me wider as he settled between them. The ocean breeze ghosted over my fevered skin, heightening every sensation, and making me tremble. When he finally pushed inside me, it was too much and not enough all at once. A strangled moan ripped from my throat as I clung to him, my nails digging into his back.

The world blurred. The sounds of the ocean, the flicker of candlelight, the scent of him—leather, spice, raw masculinity—all of it consumed me. Clay's movements were deliberate, and controlled at first, but the drugs, the desire, the sheer need between us unraveled that control quickly.

He turned me around, bending me over the balcony ledge, and the next thrust nearly shattered me. The position left me vulnerable, completely open to him, and he took full advantage, fucking me deep and slow before picking up the pace. The impact sent shocks of pleasure through my body, my walls gripping him tight as he pounded into me from behind.

"Oh my—fuck," I sobbed, my fingers curling against the cool stone.

Clay groaned, a guttural sound ripped from his chest as he held my hips, dragging me back onto him with each thrust. "You take me so well, Dove. So fucking tight."

The sensations were too much—his grip on me, the way he filled me perfectly, the sheer intensity of it all. My body clenched around him as my orgasm built, cresting like the waves below us. When it finally hit, it was devastating. I came with a cry, my legs trembling, my body convulsing around him. Clay wasn't far behind, his rhythm stuttering as he spilled into me with a deep, shuddering groan.

For a long moment, neither of us moved, our bodies locked together, our breath mingling in the night air. Slowly, he pulled me back against his chest, his lips finding my shoulder in a tender kiss. The waves crashed below, the scent of salt and sex lingering in the air. His arms wrapped around me, grounding me. I still felt as if I were floating, but at least in all of this, I could grip onto him as my anchor.

Night had fallen by the time we moved inside, the moon casting silver beams through the sheer curtains of the open balcony doors, bathing the bed in ethereal light. A warm breeze wafted through the room, carrying the ocean scents, mingling with the lingering spices of our decadent dinner. The air itself felt thick with anticipation, charged with the promise of what was to come.

On the bed, an array of silk ties, a blindfold, nipple clamps, strawberries, manuka honey, body dust, and a sleek riding crop awaited. My breath hitched at the sight, arousal coiling low in my belly. The aphrodisiacs still hummed through my veins, making my skin more sensitive, my body more pliant, and my desire more raw.

Clay stood behind me, his fingers ghosting along my arms, his breath hot against the shell of my ear. "Do you still trust me?"

A beat passed, my pulse hammering in my throat as I nodded.

"Good girl."

A shudder ran through me at the dark satisfaction in his tone. He slipped the blindfold over my eyes, the loss of sight sharpening every other sensation. I heard the rustling of fabric, the quiet creak of the bed as he moved, the steady control in his breath as he positioned me just how he wanted.

Silk ties encased my wrists, binding them securely to the headboard, leaving me open, vulnerable, utterly at his mercy.

He started light, peppering featherlight kisses on my face and neck. I suddenly felt him pressing something sweet against my lips. Honey? I licked at it—a strawberry coated in honey.

"Bite it," he commanded, his voice laced with desire.

I obeyed; my lips coated in sticky sweetness. Clay licked away some of the honey left on my lips, his breath warm against my mouth.

"Beautiful," he whispered breathlessly.

The mattress dipped as he climbed onto the bed, and I felt the soft tickle of the riding crop as he traced it along my skin—down the curve of my throat, over my collarbone, teasing over the swell of my breasts before sliding lower, along the sensitive plane of my stomach.

"You're so fucking perfect like this," Clay murmured, his voice thick with hunger. "Completely mine."

The crop flicked lightly against my thigh, making me gasp. He did it again, just a whisper of a touch, teasing rather than punishing. The contrast of silk bindings and the subtle sting of leather sent sparks shooting straight to my core.

Then came the pinch of the nipple clamps. A sharp intake of breath escaped my lips as my back arched involuntarily. Clay hummed his approval.

"That's it, Dove. Let me hear you. Let me feel you."

A slick heat pooled between my thighs as he trailed kisses down my body, his mouth following the path the riding crop had mapped. His tongue flicked over one sensitized nipple, then the other, sending a jolt of pleasure-pain through me. His hands roamed lower, fingers dipping between my folds, spreading me open, testing just how soaked I was for him.

"Fuck, you're dripping," he rasped, rubbing slow, torturous circles over my clit. "So needy. You love this, don't you? Being at my mercy."

A whimper escaped my throat, my body twisting beneath him, seeking more.

He chuckled, dark and low. "Oh, I'm going to ruin you tonight."

And then his mouth was on me, his tongue lapping at my core, alternating between slow, languid strokes and quick flicks that left me trembling. The blindfold heightened every sensation—the wet heat of his mouth, the firm grip of his hands keeping me in place, the vibrations of his groan against me as he tasted me.

Then came the soft hum of a toy. The moment the vibrator pressed against my clit, I jerked against the restraints, a strangled moan breaking free.

"Clay—oh God—"

"That's it, sweetheart," he coaxed, licking into me as he pressed the toy more firmly against me. "Come for me. I want to hear you fall apart."

He worked me expertly, keeping me teetering at the edge, pushing me closer and closer until I shattered with a cry, my entire body trembling against the silk bonds. He didn't stop. He kept his mouth on me, drinking me in, wringing every last ounce of pleasure from me as I writhed beneath him.

When I thought I couldn't take anymore, Clay ripped the blindfold off.

"Look at me. I need to see you."

My heavy-lidded eyes met his, dark with need, with something deeper, something unspoken. There was no pretense, no game. Just us, stripped bare, vulnerable.

He untied my wrists as he positioned himself between my legs, pushing into me slowly, and deliberately. A guttural moan ripped from his throat as he filled me. He set a deep, unhurried pace, rocking into me, letting me feel every inch, every pulse, every ounce of his restraint slipping away.

"You feel so fucking good," he groaned against my mouth, pressing fevered kisses along my jaw, my neck. "You were made for me."

Tears brimmed in my eyes as pleasure overwhelmed me, as something terrifying and beautiful cracked open inside me. He pressed his forehead to mine, his strokes deep, reverent. Our bodies moved in perfect harmony, in sync in a way neither of us dared put into words.

Because the moment we did, it would be real.

When the final wave crashed over us, when our bodies finally unraveled together, Clay held me as though letting go would destroy him.

After, we soaked in a warm bubble bath, wrapped in silence. The water lapped gently around us, the faint scent of lavender and sea salt filling the air. Clay stroked my hair, pressing butterfly kisses along my temple, my cheek, and the curve of my shoulder. The world had slowed, but inside, something restless stirred.

For the first time in a long time, my heart broke thinking about the future. About leaving. About what was coming next.

For tonight, though, I let myself belong to him.

CHAPTER 21

CLAY

The next morning, we sat on the balcony, bathed in golden sunlight, the scent of strong coffee and sea air mingling between us. The Mediterranean stretched endlessly before us, its sapphire waves lapping against the shore below. The warmth of last night lingered between us, but real life loomed on the horizon.

"This has been a wonderful trip, Clay. Thank you for taking me."

Her voice was soft, almost wistful.

"This is the most fun I've ever had on any vacation, Dove. Thank you for agreeing to come. I'm just sad that it's ending."

I took her hand, tracing my thumb along her knuckles before pressing a lingering kiss to them. Her skin was warm against my lips, familiar, intoxicating.

"After the merger is settled, we can go to the Alps for a little while. You'd like Gstaad." I glanced at her. "Do you ski?"

She shook her head. "I don't."

"I can teach you," I said smoothly. "Or we can do something else. Switzerland is magical in the winter."

Something flickered across her face, so quickly I almost missed it—a shadow, a slight stiffening in her posture, like she was bracing herself. But outwardly, she remained composed, her expression betraying nothing as she turned her gaze to the horizon.

"That sounds lovely."

I brought her hand to my lips again, exhaling slowly. My nerves were wrecked all of a sudden, my stomach tight with something I rarely felt—uncertainty.

"Malinda?"

She turned to me, her deep brown eyes locking onto mine.

"Hmm?"

I swallowed, my pulse hammering. "These last few months with you have been... indescribable." My voice was rougher than I intended. "You've helped me tap back into a joy I haven't felt in decades." A beat of silence. Then, my heart in my throat, I asked, "Will you be my girlfriend? Officially?"

For the first time since I met her, Malinda looked genuinely caught off guard. Her lips parted slightly, eyes widening with something raw and unreadable. She froze as if thousands of thoughts were rushing through her mind at once, overwhelming her. Slowly, almost cautiously, she pulled her hand from mine and sat up straighter.

"Clay..."

The way she said my name, like she was preparing to break something, made my stomach drop. My shoulders slumped, the weight of her hesitation pressing down on me like a vise.

"I need to think about it..." she finally said, her voice measured, careful.

I stared at her, uncomprehending. A sharp pang of disbelief lanced through me. *Think about what?* All this time, all we'd shared—what did she think this was leading to?

"Think about what?" My voice was level, but barely. The agony bled through despite my best efforts to keep it in check. "Hasn't our time together here solidified that we're right for each other?"

She exhaled, her fingers twisting in her lap.

"Clay... you're high profile. Extremely busy. Very social. And you're about to leave for nine months." She paused, searching for words, before exhaling again. "Committing to you means committing to your lifestyle. And it's..."

"Overwhelming," I finished for her, my chest tightening.

She gave a small, regretful nod. "Yeah... I just need some time to consider it all."

Silence settled between us. I forced myself to absorb her words, to process them instead of reacting on instinct.

Slowly, I reached for her hand again, bringing it to my lips. This time, I let the kiss linger, as if I could will her hesitation away. Finally, I found my voice, though it came out quieter than I expected.

"Okay." My throat tightened. "I understand."

But I didn't. Not really. And as we sat there, the sun warming my skin, the taste of rejection thick on my tongue, I realized something unsettling.

No wasn't an answer I knew how to accept.

The flight back to Baltimore was silent, the cabin thick with the unspoken. Malinda sat beside me, curled up in her seat with her eyes closed, but I knew she wasn't asleep. She was thinking—processing—calculating. And it killed me that I had no clue what conclusion she was coming to.

I barely touched my drink. I was too busy replaying our breakfast over and over, dissecting her every word, every glance away, every hesitation. Her rejection—if I could even call it that—was still raw.

I just need some time to consider it all

I wanted to push. I wanted to make her see that she didn't need to think. That we fit. That she was already mine, even if she refused to say the words.

She had met my friends. No one meets my friends. And they loved her. She fit right into my world, acing a test that neither of us knew she was taking. The texts of approval from my circle rolled in after we left. Everyone can see that we're good together. What more was there to consider? But I knew her well enough to know pressure would make her retreat further. So, I let it go. For now.

By the time the jet touched down, real life was waiting for me like a wrecking ball. The moment I turned my phone on, it vibrated so aggressively in my palm that I had to clench my fist to stop myself from throwing it across the cabin.

Missed calls from my father. From my executives. From Brooke. My voicemail notifications stacked like bricks, each one a fresh headache waiting to be opened.

I exhaled sharply and glanced at Malinda. She was stretching, rolling the tension from her neck, looking unfairly beautiful even in exhaustion. She caught me watching, and for a second, something flickered in her eyes—something softer. It almost made me forget the avalanche waiting for me outside this jet.

"I'll see you later?" I asked, knowing she needed space but hoping anyway.

She gave me a small smile, but it didn't reach her eyes. "We'll talk soon, Clay."

Soon. A vague, meaningless word. But it was all I had.

By the time I stepped into my apartment, the loneliness was suffocating. Three days. Three days with her in my arms, her laughter filling my space, her scent lingering on my skin. And now, nothing.

I didn't have time to dwell on it. My father's call came before I even had a chance to pour a drink.

"Three days, Clay. Three fucking days you went silent in the middle of the most critical business move we've made in years!" Brian Sawyer's voice was sharp, cutting, filled with the kind of disappointment I had long since grown immune to.

I pinched the bridge of my nose. "I needed a break."

"A break? Do you think I had the luxury of breaks when I was building this empire? When I was negotiating million-dollar deals while keeping this company afloat?" he barked. "You vanish, leaving your executives scrambling, the Berlin team confused, and Beijing questioning if you're serious about this merger!"

I exhaled slowly. "Everything is under control."

"That's the kind of naive thinking that gets a company eaten alive," he spat. "Do you know who's been calling? The investors. The board. The press wants a statement on why the CEO of SparTech disappeared while the biggest deal of the year is happening. And do you know who had to clean up your mess? Me!"

I clenched my jaw, my patience wearing dangerously thin. "I'll handle it."

"You better. And Clay—" his voice dipped into something quieter, more menacing "—whatever this distraction is, cut it out. We don't have time for your little indulgences."

My grip on the phone tightened. "I'll handle it," I repeated before hanging up.

I barely had a moment to process before another call came in—this time from the Berlin team, then another from Beijing. Each conversation chipped away at the peace I had stolen over the weekend. Each one a reminder of the life I lived. The obligations. The expectations. The constant need to be present, available, and on top of everything at all times.

By the time I got off the final call, it was well past midnight, and I was exhausted, but not in the way sleep could fix. My apartment was too quiet. Too empty. I ran a hand through my hair, exhaling sharply as my thoughts drifted back to Malinda.

How could today have gone so horribly wrong? I had woken up with her in my arms, feeling whole in a way I never have. I had been so sure that this was it—that she was it. And now, I was right back where I started. Alone. Miserable. And she still wasn't mine.

The next few weeks passed in a blur of meetings, calls, and damage control. My Summer Fridays disappeared under the weight of back-to-back crises. The Beijing merger required more of my attention than expected, and my executives were restless, demanding my full focus.

Wednesday nights with Malinda, once something I anticipated all week, turned into rushed dinners where I had one hand on my phone, jug-gling last-minute Zoom meetings and urgent calls. I saw her walls rebuilding—brick by brick, stronger and taller than before. And this time, I wasn't sure if I had the energy to tear them down.

She was slipping away, and I was too fucking busy to stop it.

The worst part? She never complained. She didn't sulk or demand my attention. She just adjusted, withdrawing, detaching. I saw it in the way she stopped reaching for me, in the way she took longer to respond to my messages, in the way her eyes cooled whenever I had to step away mid-conversation.

It was like watching sand slip through my fingers, and no matter how tightly I clenched my fist, I couldn't hold on.

I wasn't going to let this stand. Malinda was hesitant, but I knew she felt what I did. She just needed to see that this could work. That I could make it work.

I'd give her space, but not too much. She needed to know I wasn't letting her go. Because Malinda Burns was my future. And I'd do whatever it took to make her realize it, too.

CHAPTER 22

MALINDA

He was cuddling me on the couch, his body warm and solid against mine, his fingers tracing slow, absentminded circles on my arm. The low hum of the TV played in the background, but neither of us was paying attention. We had barely spoken in the last twenty minutes, yet the silence between us felt like it was crackling with unspoken words.

"Malinda..." Clay's voice was soft, hesitant. "I leave for Beijing tomorrow. I'll be gone for four weeks, Dove. It would be nice to know where we stand."

I sighed, staring at the flickering light from the TV. I had been expecting this. He had been holding onto me tighter these last few weeks, trying to tether me to him before I slipped away completely.

"Clay..." I started, but he didn't let me finish. He turned my face to his and kissed me—desperate, searching, as if he could pull the answer he wanted from my lips alone.

"Please don't say no, baby," he murmured against my mouth, his breath warm, his lips coaxing. "We're so good together." He kissed me again, deeper this time, stealing my response before I could give it.

I knew that Clay and I would never be together, and I knew I would miss him. I had already started to pull away, putting distance between us in preparation for what had to come next. But right now, feeling the heat of his body, the way he held me like I was something precious, I wanted to give us this one last time.

I shifted in his lap, straddling him, taking control of the kiss. His groan vibrated through me as I slid my hands under his shirt, feeling the hard planes of his stomach. I pulled the fabric over his head, tossing it aside as I ran my nails lightly down his chest. His muscles tensed under my touch, and a sharp inhale escaped him when I leaned in to suck his earlobe, trailing kisses down his neck. He shuddered as I bit down, leaving a mark on his skin. I heard him mutter under his breath; his voice raw.

"Mark me, baby. I'm yours."

For a moment, the words caught me off guard. He believed it. He still believed that I could be his. My fingers hesitated on his skin, but then he shifted beneath me, his arousal pressing against my heat, and all my thoughts scattered. Clay undid the buttons of my dress, peeling it open with impatient hands. His mouth found my breast, taking my nipple between his lips, sucking and teasing as I moaned into his ear. My fingers tangled in his hair, tugging as I rocked against him. He yanked my dress up further, moving my thong aside with a rough impatience that sent a thrill through me. He freed himself from his sweats, his length hot and heavy against my thigh.

He gripped my waist, his fingers digging in as he guided me down onto him in one rough, aching thrust. I cried out, the sudden fullness a delicious mix of pleasure and pain. He groaned, his head falling back against the couch, his jaw tight as he fought for control.

"Fuck, Malinda..."

I rode him mercilessly, needing to chase the feeling, needing to memorize the way he felt inside me, the way he looked—his eyes dark with need, his lips parted as he whispered my name like a prayer. He squeezed my hips, guiding my movements, his grip tightening as he let out a low, strangled moan.

"You drive me fucking insane," he ground out, his hands roaming my body, possessive and desperate. He spanked me, his palm landing with a sharp sting that only made me grind down harder. The sounds we made were primal, raw. My nails dragged over his shoulders, leaving red trails in their wake, and

I leaned down to kiss him, to taste him, to commit every inch of him to memory.

Then his hand wrapped around my throat, applying just the right amount of pressure to send me over the edge. My hips bucked wildly; my moan muffled against his lips as I shattered around him.

Clay slowed, giving me a moment to catch my breath, his lips brushing against my jaw. He eased us down onto the floor, laying me back against the plush shag rug. My dress was discarded completely now, leaving me bare beneath him. He gazed down at me, his expression adoring as his fingers traced my skin.

He ran his hands up my thighs, pausing to squeeze, to explore, to take his time memorizing my body. His fingers played with my nipples, making me arch beneath him, my breath catching as he slid his hand between my legs and teased my clit.

"Damn, baby... how will I survive a month without you?" he murmured, his lips brushing against my temple as he slowly rocked into me.

I matched his rhythm, wrapping my legs around his waist to pull him deeper, and he groaned into my ear, his breath hot against my skin.

"You are everything to me, baby," he whispered, his voice hoarse with emotion. "Everything."

His movements turned desperate, his pace increasing as he buried his face in the crook of my neck. His body tensed, his breath shuddering against my skin as he spilled into me with a final, guttural moan. We lay there for a while, tangled together on the floor, our bodies slick with sweat, our breathing gradually slowing. He played with my curls absentmindedly, his fingers twining in the strands like he was grounding himself in me. Then, after a moment, he moved my hair aside and pressed a soft kiss to the nape of my neck.

"Dove... you know how much I want you," he murmured, his lips brushing against my skin. "But I don't want you to feel pressured, so... hold off on answering me, okay? Take some more time to think, and when I get back from Beijing, we'll talk."

I nodded, but I was grateful he couldn't see my face. Because unbeknownst to him, this was goodbye.

Part 2

"Emotions make you reckless. Attachments make you weak. The greatest con isn't the one you run—it's the one your heart runs on you. Love is the most dangerous game."

CHAPTER 23

MALINDA

I wiped the sweat off my forehead and threw my keys on the kitchen counter. I hated working out, but my building had such an amazing facility, and I paid a fee every month anyway, so I might as well stay in shape. My muscles ached pleasantly as I walked over to the fridge, grabbing the salad I'd prepped earlier today along with my special avocado cream dressing.

As I took a bite, I wandered across the cool oak floors of my living room and into my server room. The screens glowed softly as I powered them on, bringing up the surveillance monitors. I installed micro cameras in the hallways, elevators, and stairwells when I first moved in five years ago. You can never be too cautious, especially with the life I live. I set my salad down, feeling a familiar sense of comfort watching the empty hallways and stairwells. My fortress. My safe place.

Or at least, it used to be.

I glanced at the clock. 9:00 p.m. The day had slipped away from me again. Since quitting SparTech three months ago, my routine had become almost obsessive—long hours of research, picking apart old records, trying to connect the threads of whatever my father had done to SparTech that made them keep a file on him. He conned them, clearly. That man couldn't hold a legit job if he tried. But what did he take? Money? Information? And why was SparTech still paying a PI all these years later?

I sighed and leaned back in my chair, rubbing my temples. If I'd just played Clay a little longer, I could still have access to their internal network. Now, everything took twice as long. Hacking into their systems was a different beast than simply logging in under the guise of my job.

I wasn't some expert—I had above-average skills compared to a regular person, sure. Years of hobby coding, online forums, and the kind of software tricks that helped with my degree and with scamming. But in the world of real hackers? I barely scratched the surface.

I should've asked for help. There were people out there who could do this in half the time. But I couldn't risk that. This was personal. Too many buried secrets, too much at stake. I knew enough to get by, but not enough to make this easy. It was slow, methodical work, and I hated every second of it.

My plan to move to L.A. was taking longer than expected. I'd packed a little, but never seriously. Clay had been too much of a distraction. And despite everything, leaving SparTech—leaving my team—was harder than I thought. I'd spent eight years there. It was my home. And now? Now I was adrift.

Shaking off the melancholy, I walked to the kitchen and grabbed my fruit smoothie. As I sipped, I let my eyes drift to the floor-to-ceiling windows. The Baltimore skyline twinkled back at me, beautiful and distant, like a world I no longer belonged to. I took a deep breath, forcing myself to focus. First thing in the morning, I'd call a realtor. I needed to move on.

Then I heard it.

The soft, unmistakable jiggle of my front door handle.

I froze, my fingers tightening around my glass. The sound sliced through the quiet, subtle but deliberate. My skin prickled. I strained my ears. Maybe I imagined it. Maybe—

There it was again.

My pulse spiked as I darted back to my office, my hands flying over the keyboard to pull up my hallway feed. Two men stood at my door. Rough-looking. Dressed in dark clothing. One crouched, working the lock with careful precision.

Not a random break-in.

A cold weight settled in my stomach. I didn't live in a neighborhood where things like this happened—not on the 23rd floor of a luxury high-rise, not with the security in place. These men weren't here by accident.

They were here for me.

Adrenaline shot through my veins. I sprinted to my bedroom, locking the door and shoving my heavy oak dresser in front of it. The carpet muffled the sound, but I knew I had seconds, maybe less. I had an escape plan—I'd gone over it a thousand times in my head. I just never thought I'd have to use it.

How did they find me? I'd been so careful.

Clay.

A sick feeling twisted in my gut. Did he do this? Was this payback for ghosting him? No, that was too extreme—even for him. But if he found out about my father...

I shoved the thought away and bolted into my closet, digging into the back until my fingers closed around my pre-packed messenger bag. I emptied my safe, grabbing the cash, flash drives, and, most importantly, the file on my father. That's what they were here for. They had to be.

A loud crash echoed through the apartment. My door.

I swallowed a curse. No time.

Yanking on jeans over my workout shorts, I laced up my sneakers with shaking hands. Footsteps pounded outside. They were inside.

I slipped onto the balcony, rain immediately pelting my skin. Cold and relentless, it soaked through my clothes in seconds. My breath came fast and shallow. The city stretched out beneath me, dazzling and indifferent.

This was insane.

I swung a leg over the edge, gripping the rain-slick railing as the wind howled past. My bag weighed me down, throwing me off balance. The metal was freezing against my palm, slick and treacherous. I exhaled sharply, repositioned my grip, and jumped.

The impact knocked the air from my lungs. My knee slammed into the metal railing of the balcony below, sending a jolt of pain through my leg. My bag caught on the ledge, nearly yanking me over. I bit down on a scream, muscles straining as I wrenched it free and collapsed against the wet floor, chest heaving.

A muffled voice carried down from my apartment. They were still up there. They hadn't seen me.

Move. I urged myself

I forced my shaking legs to cooperate, slipping inside the darkened apartment through the balcony door. The old woman who lived here was a creature of routine—she'd be fast asleep. I crept to the front door, cracked it open, and scanned the hallway. Empty.

I slipped into the stairwell and ran. Twenty flights down. My lungs burned, and my knee throbbed, but I didn't stop. I couldn't.

By the time I reached the lobby, I forced myself to slow. I pulled up my hood, walked calmly through the entrance, and stepped into the rain.

I walked for what felt like hours, the downpour relentless, soaking me to the bone. My limbs were heavy, my knee screaming in protest, but I pressed on. As I neared a CVS, I glanced up—and froze.

Two figures in black stepped inside ahead of me.

My stomach dropped. Were they following me? My pulse pounded as I hesitated, then forced myself to keep moving. I couldn't afford paranoia. Not now.

I ducked inside, the fluorescent lights harsh against my eyes, The CVS was pretty empty except for a customer in the greeting card aisle. I ducked into the bathroom and locked the door. I slumped onto the floor with my head in my hands, trying to calm myself. I had to come up with a plan. I couldn't stay in one place for too long. What if I was being followed? I needed to figure it all out. I opened my messenger bag and counted my cash. I didn't have any of my debit or credit cards with me. All I had was 200 dollars in cash. I couldn't go anywhere significant with that. I needed somewhere to stay until the morning so I could figure out what I would do. I grabbed my phone and to my horror, the screen was black and wasn't responding. I desperately searched for an outlet to figure out if it was water-damaged or just dead, but there weren't any in the bathroom. I took a few deep breaths. I need a plan. Now was not the time to freak out.

Whose number or address do I know where I can quickly get to? I wracked my brain for a few minutes.

Amir.

The thought hit me suddenly. He lived nearby. Federal Hill. He had always been kind to me, always made a point to check in, to invite me to his gatherings even when I turned him down. He was funny, warm, and perceptive in a way that made it easy to be around him without feeling suffocated. I felt a surge of adrenaline. I had a plan, a loose one but a plan, nonetheless.

I had no right to show up at his door like this, but I had nowhere else to go. Hopefully, he hasn't moved in the 3 months since I left SparTech Industries.

I pulled off my hoodie and tried to wring it out and dry it as much as I could. I forced myself back into the rain, shivering violently. Every step was agony, my body spent, but I kept moving until I reached his Brownstone. Knocking felt impossible with how badly I shook, but I banged on his door, desperate.

The lock turned, and the door cracked open.

Amir stood there, shirtless, eyes heavy with confusion, before they widened.

"Malinda?" His voice was rough with sleep. "What the hell—"

I shivered violently, dripping onto his doorstep. "Can I come in?"

CHAPTER 24

MALINDA

"M alinda, are you okay? It's past midnight. Damn, girl, you're shivering."

He let me in and led me through the house into the kitchen.

Suddenly, I felt weak. The adrenaline rush I'd been functioning on for the past few hours was wearing off, and all I remembered was trying to grab the counter on the way down before everything went black.

I woke up a short while later, disoriented and forgetting where I was. The dim glow of a lamp cast long shadows across the room, unfamiliar yet strangely comforting. Instinct took over, and I jerked upright, my breath coming in short bursts as I scanned my surroundings.

"Whoa, easy," Amir's voice broke through my haze, low and steady.

I turned to see him walking back into the living room with a bottle of water in one hand and a towel in the other. He had changed into a beater, his expression calm but watchful.

"Good, you're up. I was gonna wait a few more minutes before I took you to the ER," he said, crouching in front of me. "Sit down, Malinda. Here, drink this."

He handed me the water, his fingers brushing against mine, warm and grounding.

"I don't know what's going on, but I take it you'll be spending the night. So here." He passed me a t-shirt and pajama bottoms. "Go change out of those damp clothes before you catch hypothermia or pneumonia or something. Get warm, and then come fill me in."

I hesitated for a moment but took the clothes, using the opportunity to gather my thoughts. When I returned, towel-drying my damp hair, Amir was sitting on the couch, waiting patiently. The air between us was thick with unspoken questions.

"Thanks, Amir."

He brightened up. "And she speaks!" He smirked. "I was starting to think you'd gone mute."

I managed a weak grin. "Sorry if I freaked you out. I know you weren't expecting me to drop by this late."

"No need to apologize, mama. Any visit from you is graciously welcomed." His tone was light, but his eyes searched mine carefully. "I haven't seen you since you left SparTech a few months back."

"How's the company doing?"

"Eh, different day, same shit. Everyone is stressed about the merger transitioning smoothly, and Clay has been on a warpath for the last six weeks." He leaned back, stretching his legs out. "But you are looking at the new Director of Marketing."

"You got promoted? That's great news." I tried to focus on his words, but my eyes kept darting around the room, my nerves still on edge.

"Thanks..." Amir studied me carefully. "Tell me what's going on, Malinda. You seem super heightened right now like you're being chased."

I stiffened, and his expression darkened with concern.

"Are you? Is someone hurting you? Are you in danger?" His voice dropped, more serious now. "Do you know who? Or why? Did you call the cops?" He reached for his phone, but I grabbed his arm, shaking my head.

"I—I'm fine, Amir. I just need a place to stay for a few hours, and then I'll be out of your hair."

"Hey..." He placed his hands on my shoulders, his grip firm yet gentle. "You're safe here, okay? Stay as long as you need."

I swallowed hard, unable to meet his gaze. He sounded so sincere. Truthfully, I might have to take him up on that offer. I suspected it was Clay's guys who broke in tonight, but it could have been anyone. Over the years, I've screwed over a lot of high-profile and dangerous people. Any one of them could be after me.

A wave of exhaustion hit, and I barely stifled a yawn.

"Thanks for all this, Amir."

"Of course." He hesitated. "How did you get here?"

"I—I walked."

" In this weather!? " He exhaled sharply, rubbing the back of his neck. "No wonder you look exhausted. Let's get you rested. It's almost two. We'll talk more in the morning."

He led me upstairs to a guest bedroom, talking lightly as he grabbed extra blankets. I barely registered his words. The moment my body recognized safety, it allowed all the panic I had suppressed to surge through me, crashing over me in waves. My breaths came too fast, too shallow, and I hadn't even realized I was hyperventilating until I heard him say my name.

"Malinda?" His voice softened. "Hey, look at me."

I couldn't answer. His voice sounded so far away, muffled, like I was underwater. I was shaking uncontrollably.

We locked eyes, and I saw something in him melt. He whispered, "Come here, boo..." and pulled me into a hug.

It felt surprisingly good. I usually hated being touched, but this was... different. His chest rose and fell rhythmically, his heartbeat strong and steady against my cheek. I focused on it, matching my breathing to his until the panic ebbed away. His hands ran slow, soothing circles down my back, grounding me.

For a moment, I let myself melt into him. His warmth, his strength—it made me feel, if only briefly, like I wasn't completely alone. His hand cupped the back of my head, his thumb stroking absentmindedly against my damp hair. It was intimate and reassuring.

His voice was husky when he finally spoke. "You want me to stay with you tonight?"

That was when it hit me. How close we were. How easily I had let him in. The realization snapped me back into myself. The comfort I had found in his arms moments ago now felt dangerous. Vulnerability was a liability. My guard shot up, sky-high.

I exhaled shakily and gently pushed myself away. "Thank you, Amir. I'm fine. I guess I just needed a hug."

The wanting in his eyes flickered before he slipped back into his usual flirtatious self. He grinned. "No problem, mama. I'm hug central."

He reached out and touched my cheek lightly. "Sleep well, boo. I'm down the hall if you need me."

I managed a small smile, but as soon as he left, I turned and locked the guest room door. It wasn't personal. It was survival. Trusting no one kept me alive.

I climbed into bed, my body finally giving out. I would figure everything out later. Right now, I just needed sleep.

CHAPTER 25

MALINDA

I woke up to the warm smell of pancakes drifting in from the kitchen. It shocked my senses, dragging me out of the haze of sleep with an unexpected wave of nostalgia. The last person who ever made me pancakes was George. My chest tightened at the thought.

I blinked against the soft morning light and took in my surroundings. Unfamiliar walls. A guest room. The events of last night slammed back into me all at once. Damn it. It really happened. I was hoping that it was all just a bad dream. At least I got out with the files.

Clay had to be behind this. No one else knew where I lived. I'd never run jobs in Maryland, never given anyone a reason to come looking for me here. The files held the answers—I just needed to get somewhere safe to go through them.

I stretched, trying to shake the lingering stiffness from my body, and glanced around for my messenger bag. It wasn't in sight.

Panic surged. My heart kicked up. Where the hell was it?

I shoved back the covers and bolted from the room; my bare feet silent against the hardwood as I made my way downstairs. The scent of sizzling bacon mixed with sweet maple and cinnamon filled the air, but I barely registered it. My eyes darted around the open space until they landed on my bag hanging on a hook by the door. Relief hit so hard that my knees almost buckled.

I took a slow breath, centering myself before my attention snapped to the sight before me.

Amir was in the kitchen, blasting old-school hip-hop, rapping along with Black Sheep while frying bacon. Shirtless. He moved with effortless ease, completely at home in his space, his body swaying slightly to the beat. He shook his tooshie with absolutely no shame, attempting a few dance steps so terrible I almost laughed.

I lingered at the edge of the kitchen, hesitant, watching. The energy in the room was warm. Uncomplicated. Something I wasn't used to.

"Your mama never taught you that hot bacon grease burns?" I called over the music.

He jumped slightly before turning, flashing his signature megawatt grin. "I live on the wild side, baby."

He strolled over to the speaker, turning the volume down, and I caught myself tracking the way he moved—fluid, confident like nothing ever rattled him. He always carried himself with ease. I'd never noticed before. Maybe because we only interacted in passing at work, where everything was buttoned up and polished. Or maybe because I never let myself pay attention.

His eyes flicked over me, amusement sparking. "You checking me out?"

I rolled my eyes, refusing to give him the satisfaction. "In your dreams."

He laughed, grabbing his t-shirt and tugging it over his head. "Alright, alright. I'll spare you the temptation."

I ignored him, my gaze shifting to my bag. I needed to get to it without making it obvious that I was desperate to snatch it up. Casually, I walked over and grabbed it, clutching it tight against me.

Amir, either oblivious or just letting me have my moment, turned back to the stove. "I hope you're hungry, Malinda. We got bacon, a garden omelet, pancakes with my special peach-glazed syrup, and sausage. If that doesn't tickle your fancy, I can whip up some cheddar grits or waffles. There's fresh-cut fruit chilling in the fridge. And for drinks, freshly squeezed orange juice, grapefruit juice, a wide variety of teas, and my signature blend of coffee."

I blinked. "Do you run a bed and breakfast on the side?"

He smirked. "Just a little sutin' for you."

I hesitated. Eating meant staying. Sitting. Letting my guard down, even a little. But he was already plating the food, setting it on the counter with an expectant look.

I sighed, relenting. "Fine. But only because I don't trust you not to burn the house down."

"Damn, no faith in me at all," he teased, sliding a plate in front of me.

Breakfast was... comfortable. He kept the conversation light, filling the silence with easy chatter about anything and everything except what happened last night. It was like he knew I wasn't ready to talk. I appreciated it more than I let on.

I kept my bag on my lap the entire time, my grip never loosening. The moment the plates were cleared, I made my move.

"I'm gonna go freshen up," I said, standing and gripping my bag tighter.

Amir nodded easily, his attention already shifting to cleaning up. "Take your time."

I slipped back upstairs, shutting the guestroom door behind me and finally letting out the breath I'd been holding. I sat on the edge of the bed, pried open my bag, and pulled out my laptop. The second I pressed the power button, nothing happened.

I tried again. And again.

My stomach twisted into a tight knot. No. No, no, no.

I turned it over, inspecting every inch until I saw it—a faint shimmer of dried water damage near the vent.

My breath hitched. My fingers trembled.

My laptop wasn't just a laptop. It was my lifeline. My offshore accounts. My research into my dad. Years of careful record-keeping on old marks. Everything. My encrypted USBs are useless without the decryption program that only my laptop has.

And now, when I needed it most, it was useless.

I squeezed my eyes shut, willing the sting of frustration away. Stay calm. Think.

I needed to fix it. I needed parts. That meant I needed time.

I inhaled sharply, pushing down the sheer panic clawing at my throat, and forced myself to my feet. I made my way downstairs, slower this time, every step heavier than the last. Amir was in the living room now, lounging on the couch, one arm draped casually over the backrest, phone in hand, scrolling and texting.

He glanced up when he saw me, his expression open and easy. "You good?"

I hesitated. I hated this. Hated asking. "Would it be cool if I stayed a bit longer? Just until the parts I need arrive?"

His answer was immediate. No hesitation. No conditions. "Malinda, you can stay as long as you need."

Relief warred with frustration inside me. I wasn't used to this. Wasn't used to needing help. Wasn't used to someone offering it so freely.

I exhaled, nodding. "Thanks."

CHAPTER 26

MALINDA

Days turned into a week, then two, then three, and now a month of living in Amir's home, wearing his clothes, using his toiletries, and slipping into a routine that was both comforting and unfamiliar. He never pried, never asked for more than I was willing to give, but his presence was a constant warmth I hadn't realized I'd come to depend on. He cooked for me without question and encouraged me to join him for dinner, to watch TV, and even to play video games, though I declined that more often than not. And yet, when he left for work in the morning, I felt his absence in ways I couldn't quite explain.

The trauma of my escape haunted my dreams. I woke up drenched in sweat, heart pounding, gasping for air as images of the fall that almost was, replayed over and over in my mind. The way the wind had roared in my ears. The way the rain had slicked the balcony ledge, nearly pulling me over. I could still feel the burn of my muscles straining to pull myself into safety. And then there was the constant paranoia—the fear of being found. Of being cornered. I couldn't even make a mental plan to leave the house without hyperventilating. Every time I was alone in the house at night, the panic crept in, seizing my body in an iron grip. Sometimes I sat curled up in Amir's guest bed, clutching my knees, forcing myself to breathe, reminding myself I was safe here.

But I hated this feeling. This weakness. I hated that I had to rely on anyone, even someone as easygoing and kind as Amir.

And to make matters worse, my investigation had stalled. The part I needed to fix my laptop was still on backorder from Japan. Every time I checked, the estimated arrival date had been pushed back again. Without my laptop, I couldn't access my offshore accounts. I had no money, no resources, no way to move forward. I was stuck, and the frustration gnawed at me daily.

It was two weeks into my stay with Amir, Thanksgiving morning when I realized how much he had begun to see me. I had spent the past few years ignoring holidays, pretending they didn't exist. They were just another day. But when I came downstairs that morning, Amir had turned the kitchen into something out of a cozy, nostalgic dream.

"Surprise!" He grinned, setting down a plate. "Figured you probably weren't heading home for the holiday, so... Happy Thanksgiving."

A full Thanksgiving brunch spread was laid out on the table—fluffy biscuits, spiced apple cider, sweet potato waffles, pumpkin pancakes, glazed ham cheddar egg bites, stuffing balls, scrambled eggs with caramelized onions, turkey bacon, cranberry compote, and harvest fruit salad.

I stared at the food, at the effort, at him, and something deep inside me twisted painfully.

No one had ever considered me like that before. No one had ever thought about what I might need, what might make me feel seen. I felt a lump in my throat but swallowed it down, giving him an easy smile.

"You didn't have to do this." My voice was tight, foreign to my ears.

"I wanted to." He shrugged. "Besides, I'll be with my family later. But I figured you might want to celebrate too." He had said like it was no big deal. But it was.

Celebrate? I hadn't celebrated anything in years. And yet, sitting across from him, eating a meal that he had made just for me, I felt that lump in my throat fighting its way back. I swallowed it down with hot apple cider and let myself pretend, just for a moment, that this was normal. That I was normal.

That Amir wasn't making me feel things I had no business feeling.

We were sitting in the living room watching a movie he had chosen for movie night. Some comedy. This had become our routine. Amir made dinner of course. He's an amazing cook and extremely thoughtful. It's been nice being somewhere safe. He reached over to the coffee table and topped off our glasses of wine, emptying the bottle.

"Amir, this shrimp Scampi is to die for. You missed your calling. You should be a chef."

He rubbed the back of his neck, grinning like someone who wasn't used to being complimented.

"Think so?"

"Yes definitely. You're wasting your talents in corporate marketing."

He exhaled a soft laugh, shaking his head.

"Thanks, Malinda. That means a lot. If I'm honest. I've actually been toying around with the idea of opening up a restaurant or starting a catering business for a few years now."

"You should absolutely make that idea a reality."

He turned toward me, his gaze lingering. My heart skipped a beat. "Would you be my business partner?"

I sipped my wine, hoping that it would help me cool off a bit.

"Sure I would. Just don't let me cook any of the food." He laughed.

"Fine... I'll come up with the menu and you... can be my taste tester."

Something in the way he said "taste tester" made something in my stomach tighten. I quickly turned back to the TV. "Deal."

We continued watching the movie and I continued to sip on my 3rd glass of wine for the night.

Amir kept up with his hilarious commentary as he usually did. But tonight felt different. I was more giggly.

The wine was making me woozy, wrapping around my senses like a slow, creeping fog. My body felt warm and heavy. Lulled into a state of ease I hadn't let myself feel in a long time. Without thinking, I rested my head against Amir's shoulder, the weight of it bridging the space between us.

I felt the way he stiffened slightly, just for a second, before relaxing again, his breath catching in his throat. The soft thud of his heartbeat against my cheek, steady and strong, was strangely soothing. Amir and I didn't get close like this. We had an understanding—an unspoken boundary we hadn't crossed in all the weeks I'd been here. But over time, he had become...comfort. A quiet, steady presence in the storm that was my life.

I told myself it was just the wine, just the haze of a lazy evening, but I was too aware of him—of his scent, the heat of his body, the way his fingers twitched slightly like he wanted to reach for me but wouldn't dare.

My gaze flickered to his hands. Hands that had only ever offered me kindness. Hands that cooked for me, that gave me space, that never asked for anything in return.

And then his fingers brushed against my cheek. Light. Tentative.

I froze.

I should have pulled away. I should have made a joke, pushed him off, done anything to stop this moment from shifting into something I wasn't prepared for.

But I didn't.

Instead, I tilted my chin up slightly, meeting his gaze. Amir's dark brown eyes searched mine, and there was something so open about the way he looked at me—so unguarded, so patient.

He leaned in.

A slow, quiet movement.

Like he had been waiting for this moment for years.

I didn't move away.

Didn't stop him.

Before I could process it, our lips met.

It was slow at first, hesitant as if he was giving me the space to change my mind. His lips were warm, soft, and firm all at once, moving against mine with an aching desire. His fingers slid into my hair, tilting my head back, and deepening the kiss. My stomach dipped, a slow, curling heat working its way through me as my body instinctively reacted to him.

His hands were steady, patient, exploring like he was memorizing every inch of me. My fingers found his bearded chin, tracing the sharp edge of his jaw, the warmth of his skin grounding me in the moment. I lost track of time as the kiss deepened, the heat between us building and surging until I found myself shifting into his lap.

His breath hitched as I straddled him, his hands splaying across my back, his grip firm, steady. My palms pressed against his chest, feeling the solid muscle beneath my fingertips. A deep groan rumbled from his throat as I pressed closer, and that sound—God, that sound—sent a rush of heat straight between my legs.

His hands slipped under my shirt, teasing the bare skin of my lower back. My head spun, and suddenly, my shirt was off, my bare skin against his.

I felt him.

Hard, thick, pressing against my heat through the thin fabric of his basketball shorts.

His hands dragged up my sides, fingers brushing just under my bra, teasing. He tugged at the straps, his lips trailing down my jaw to my neck, and I felt myself unraveling beneath his touch. A moan slipped out before I could stop it.

And that's when everything snapped back into focus.

It was too much. It felt too good. Too genuine. Too real.

His hands on my body, his lips against my skin, his voice murmuring in my ear.

A rush of panic hit me like ice water.

I yanked back violently, breathless, my heart pounding so hard I thought it might crack my ribs.

Amir blinked, disoriented, lips slightly parted, his pupils dark and blown wide. His hands hovered at my waist, still holding me, but looser now.

"Your lips are so soft..." he murmured, his thumb brushing over my bottom lip.

His voice was deep, thick with arousal.

He leaned in for another kiss and I fucking panicked.

"Amir...no."

I scrambled off his lap like I'd been burned, chest heaving, arms wrapping around myself to cover my exposed skin.

His brows furrowed, confusion flashing across his face. "Baby...are you alright? I—I'm sorry." His voice was laced with concern, with something softer, something hesitant.

I couldn't look at him. I shook my head, trying to find words, but everything in me was a tangled mess of emotions. "No. It's not you. I just... I—" My voice cracked. "I think I drank too much. I need to go to bed."

I turned quickly, grabbing my shirt off the couch, trying to cover myself, to retreat before I made things worse.

I barely made it a few steps before his hand caught my wrist—not hard, just a light touch, like he was trying to get me to look at him. "Malinda..." His voice was softer now, pleading. "Talk to me."

I swallowed hard. I couldn't.

Because if I did, I'd have to admit that I was making the same mistake all over again. That I was letting someone in when I knew better. That I was letting myself be comforted, held, wanted.

And I couldn't afford that.

Not again.

Not ever.

I pulled away. "I just can't, Amir. I'm sorry."

I turned and walked out, my vision blurring, my heart pounding so loud in my ears that I barely heard him sigh behind me.

I reached my room, locked the door, and collapsed onto the bed, knees pulled to my chest, trying to force my mind to go blank.

This should never have happened.

I had to leave.

I had to get out before I made another mistake.

A soft knock came at my door.

"Baby...open the door. Let's talk. Please. We should discuss what just happened."

I stayed silent, pressing my forehead against my knees.

"Malinda... I'm sorry. I... I don't want you to feel uncomfortable, okay? It was just a kiss."

He waited a few more moments, but I never answered. Eventually, I heard his quiet sigh, the sound of him retreating to his room.

I waited.

An hour passed. Then another.

When I was sure he was asleep, I opened my door and crept toward the stairs, keeping my movements light.

But as I turned the corner, I saw him.

His bedroom door was open, and he was awake, sitting on the edge of his bed, staring right at me.

He didn't look angry. Just...hurt.

"Malinda...please." His voice was soft, aching.

Something in me twisted, but I ignored it.

I ignored the way my chest felt tight.

I just shook my head, looking away.

"I can't, Amir."

He exhaled sharply but nodded, like he understood, even if it hurt. "Okay."

I turned back toward my room, shutting the door behind me.

Chapter 27

AMIR

I threw myself onto my bed, exhaling sharply as I ran a hand down my face. My mind was racing. The weight of Malinda's reaction sat heavy in my chest, gnawing at me. I grabbed my phone and texted the one person who could give me some real advice.

Dorian had been my best friend since preschool, the brother I never had. He was the kind of person who saw through my bullshit instantly—The one person who always gave it to me straight, whether I wanted to hear it or not.

Amir: *Man, I need advice.*

A few seconds later, the typing bubble appeared.

Dorian: *What's up bro?*

Amir: *Remember that girl I've been crushing on for the last few years?*

Dorian: *The one from your job?*

Dorian: *Thick thighs?*

I chuckled despite myself. Dorian had a memory like a steel trap.

Amir: *Yeah, her.*

Dorian: *What about her?*

Amir: *She's been staying with me for the past month.*

The typing bubble disappeared. Then reappeared. Then disappeared again.

Dorian: *…what??? Are you hooking up with her?*

Amir: *No.*

Dorian: *Huh?*

Amir: *Something happened with her apartment. She needed a place to crash.*

Dorian: *So, you've been living with your dream girl for a month and you ain't hit?*

I sighed, rubbing my temple.

Amir: *It's not like that, man.*

Dorian: *I'm lost AF, bro. Help me understand.*

Dorian: *You've been in the trenches for this girl for YEARS, and she's in your house, up in your personal space, using your shower, and you're telling me nothing's happened?*

Amir: *Not until tonight.*

A pause.

Dorian: *...oh shit. What happened?*

Amir: *We kissed. And it was...*

I hesitated before typing. No words could truly describe what I felt. That kiss had undone me.

Amir: *Out of this world, man. Like, I've never felt something like that before.*

Dorian: *Okayyy. So, what's the issue? Ask her out.*

Amir: *I can't. She freaked out. Like, full-on panic mode. Locked herself in the guest room.*

Another long pause.

Dorian: *Damn. Over a kiss? You ain't whip your dick out or something, right?*

Amir: *Bruh, NO.*

Amir: *It wasn't even like that. It was just a kiss.*

Amir: *But I could feel it, man. She felt it too.*

Amir: *And then she ran from it.*

Dorian: *That's a huge reaction...*

Dorian: *You sure she even likes you like that?*

I hesitated before responding. That's what messed me up the most—I *knew* she wanted me. The way she kissed me back, the way she moaned against my mouth, the way her body moved against mine—it was real. It had to be.

Amir: *She wants me. I know she does.*

Amir: *But she's scared of it. Scared of me. Scared of... something.*

Dorian: *Orrr she just don't want you like that and you're reading too deep into it.*

Amir: *Nah, bro. It's not that simple.*

Amir: *Malinda's not like other women. She's got walls up like Fort Knox.*

Amir: *I think I'm the first person who's ever gotten this close to her.*

Dorian: *That's the thing though—some walls aren't meant to come down.*

Dorian: *She's been curving you for years, Amir.*

Dorian: *YEARS. And suddenly she's in your space? That don't seem like a red flag to you?*

Amir: *She needed help. What was I supposed to do? Leave her out in the cold?*

Dorian: *That's not what I'm saying.*

Dorian: *I know you, bro.*

Dorian: *You get attached. You fall hard. But this ain't no fairy tale.*

Dorian: *If she ain't ready, she ain't ready.*

Amir: *I don't have a choice, man. I'm already in too deep.*

Dorian: *So what, you gonna wait around hoping one day she finally decides she wants you?*

Dorian: *Meanwhile, you curving women left and right who actually WANT to be with you?*

Amir: *Dorian… it's Malinda. It's different.*

Dorian: *Man, Lorraine is literally begging to be with you. And you ain't giving her the time of day.*

Dorian: *But this chick—who barely acknowledges she likes you—is the one you're willing to suffer over?*

I clenched my jaw. I knew Dorian was right, in theory. Lorraine had been good to me—cool, fun, no drama. She made it clear she wanted more, and I made it just as clear that I didn't. But *Malinda*? I couldn't even think straight when it came to her.

Dorian: *You been chasing this girl for five years, Amir.*

Dorian: *Five years, man. And she's still running.*

Dorian: *At what point do you stop and let her go?*

I didn't have an answer to that.

I stared at the screen, my jaw tight. I knew Dorian was coming from a place of love. Of logic. But logic didn't mean shit when my heart was screaming Malinda's name.

I sighed heavily and tossed my phone onto the nightstand, Dorian's words still rattling around in my head. *Why not invest all them feelings into someone who actually wants you?*

I scrubbed a hand down my face, sinking deeper into the mattress. I had really fucked up tonight.

For weeks, I had done everything right. I hadn't pushed, hadn't pried, hadn't even let myself think too hard about why Malinda was really here. Because it didn't matter. She was here. And I'd be lying if I said I hadn't loved every second of it.

Coming home to someone—to *her*—was something I didn't even realize I had craved so badly. The easy companionship, the shared meals, the quiet moments of her curled up on my couch, stealing my blankets, side-eyeing my TV choices, even the way she'd act like she wasn't listening when I played music—only to hum along under her breath minutes later.

It had all felt so damn good.

And I had to go and ruin it.

I groaned, pinching the bridge of my nose. I hadn't even planned on making a move. But when she rested her head on my shoulder, when she looked at me with those dark, unreadable eyes, something inside me snapped.

I had wanted her for *years*—years—and for the first time, she wasn't holding me at a distance. She was close, soft, and warm, looking at me in a way that made it impossible to think straight.

But I *should* have.

I should have reminded myself why she was here in the first place. She didn't need me complicating things. She just needed a safe, reliable place to stay. And instead of being that for her, I let my feelings get in the way.

Now she was behind a locked door, probably regretting ever coming here.

I stared up at the ceiling, my jaw clenching. The idea of her leaving—of walking back into this house without her in it—hit me harder than I wanted to admit. Because no matter how much I tried to reason with myself, the truth was simple.

I *didn't* want her to go.

Even if she never felt for me what I felt for her. Even if she only saw me as a place to crash, a temporary reprieve before she moved on to whatever was next.

It didn't matter.

I just wanted her here.

And now, I had made her uncomfortable.

I exhaled sharply, rolling onto my side, and staring at the door. I wanted to knock again, to apologize, to fix it. But I knew Malinda. She wasn't the type to let people in—not easily. And after tonight, that wall I had been carefully chipping away at was probably back up—thicker and higher than before.

And I had no one to blame but my damn self.

CHAPTER 28

MALINDA

I felt even worse now, but I had to sort my feelings out before I could talk to him. I keep getting myself into these scenarios with men. First with Clay and now with Amir. What the hell is wrong with me? The only way to get my head on straight is to leave.

I packed my messenger bag and quietly left Amir's house around three in the morning.

The night air was sharp, biting through my hoodie as I stepped outside.

My breath fogged in front of me, and for a split second, I hesitated at the bottom of the steps. My pulse pounded in my ears, and I shoved my hands into my pockets as I walked to the Uber, every shadow along the street feeling sharper, more menacing.

The city felt too open, too quiet, after spending weeks tucked away in Amir's safe little world.

I slid into the back seat of the Uber, settling in and pulling my hood tighter around my face. A strange, hollow sensation settled in my chest as I watched Amir's house disappear in the side mirror. I refused to acknowledge it. I was just tired. That's all. I watched the empty familiar streets roll past in the window's reflection. A blur of neon lights. The world quiet, still asleep. I exhaled, feeling the tension in my shoulders ease—only slightly.

When my building finally came into view, my pulse slowed. Towering and pristine against the night sky, glowing under the bright city lights. My sanctuary. My home. The one place that had always been mine, untouched by my past. For the first time in a month, I felt a sense of relief wash over me.

As the car pulled up to the entrance, the glow of the bright lobby spilled onto the sidewalk, a warm contrast to the coldness creeping into my bones. I stepped out of the car, my sneakers barely making a sound against the polished marble floors as I entered the building.

The sleek white marble lobby was illuminated by soft, ambient lighting, the high ceilings making the space feel vast and open. The faint scent of fresh-cut flowers lingered in the air, clean and crisp. I silently made my way through as I adjusted my bag on my shoulder.

The concierge at the front desk barely glanced up, offering a polite nod as I walked by. That was one of the things I loved about this place—no unnecessary questions, no small talk. Just anonymity.

I reached into my pocket, pulled out my key fob, and scanned it at the private elevator. The soft beep was the only sound in the stillness. The elevator doors slid open, and I stepped inside, pressing the button for the 23rd floor, my reflection staring back at me from the mirrored walls. I barely recognized myself. Dark circles under my eyes, my jaw clenched too tight, and my shoulders hunched as if I were still bracing for an impact that had already come.

As the elevator rose and the doors opened to my floor, I let out a slow breath. Home.

I walked down the hallway to my door. Just the sight of the busted knob caused my stomach to churn. I hesitated but ultimately stepped inside.

And my heart shattered.

My sanctuary—ransacked.

The air left my lungs in a violent exhale.

Papers were strewn across the floor like discarded confetti. My cozy, modern furniture was overturned, glass shards littering my oak floors, catching the dim glow from the city lights outside. I glanced over to the kitchen—once pristine, once mine—was wrecked. Cabinets were thrown open, and their contents shattered across the counters.

I staggered forward, the nausea rising fast. My hand shot out to grip the edge of the wall, grounding myself.

My breath hitched as my gaze landed on the coffee table—split down the middle like someone had stomped on it. My legs barely held me up as I unsteadily stumbled my way down the hallway toward my bedroom, glass crunching under my shoes. The door to my server room was barely on the hinges. They busted through with brute force. My security monitor was damaged, with lines and distorted images on the screen. My safe, tucked behind a false panel in the closet, had been wrenched open.

A tremor ran through me, cold and violent. They had been looking for something.

A flicker of movement in the corner of my eye made me jolt—but it was only my reflection in the shattered remains of the hall mirror. One of the only things that I kept from my childhood home, now utterly destroyed.

I swallowed thickly; my throat raw.

This place had been my oasis. The only thing in my life I had full control over. And now—now it was nothing but wreckage. A violation.

Clay caused me to lose the only place I felt safe in years.

My ears rang as the walls felt like they were closing in.

I turned on my heel, propelling myself forward, forcing myself to see my bedroom. My hands trembled as I gripped the doorknob, hesitating. Please... please. I silently prayed.

I pushed it open. The dresser I had barricaded the door with was tipped forward, partially blocking the path to my bed and bathroom. But other than that, it was relatively untouched.

My bed was still made, blankets undisturbed, the nightstand drawers half open. My closet was ajar, clothes shoved to one side, but nothing had been taken. It was all pretty much exactly how I left it.

A bitter laugh caught in my throat. How generous of them to spare this space.

The tension in my chest eased up slightly.

I felt a small sense of... relief? But not safety.

My exhaustion overtook me as I made a choice.

My sanctuary was gone. My escape was gone.

And the only thing left was a cold, gnawing sense of inevitability.

I didn't belong here anymore.

But I had nowhere else to go. For now, this would have to do.

I locked the door, dropped my bag onto the chair, and collapsed onto my bed. I didn't even bother changing clothes. Sleep took me under almost immediately.

Chapter 29

MALINDA

When I woke up, the sun was high and bright in the sky, streaming through the balcony blinds and blinding me. For a fleeting second, I forgot everything. Just a second. Then it all rushed back. My body ached; my mind scrambled to keep up.

I stretched and checked my phone. Noon. I had slept for hours. I ran a hand over my face and forced myself up. If I let myself linger in bed, I might never leave it. I needed to move, and plan.

I turned on the shower, letting the bathroom fill with steam. Then, I walked into my closet and pulled out an outfit for the day. As I ran my fingers over the fabric, a wave of purpose settled over me. This was what I needed—to focus, to act, to move forward. I couldn't afford to let Clay, Amir, or my confusion cloud my judgment. I had wasted a month being comfortable and distracted. No more.

Today, I was finding Sergei. I can't believe it took me so long to make this major connection.

It all came together during my first week at Amir's house. Late one evening, he was stuck at work, and I was in the guest bedroom reflecting on my life. My mind drifted back to something I had buried for years. A name. A business card.

Sergei.

I had seen it before. Felt the rough, yellowed edges of the card when I was just a teenager. A week before my father disappeared, he had pulled it from his wallet and handed it to me. "Keep this," he had said, his voice serious in a way that sent a shiver down my spine. "If you ever need anything—anything at all—Sergei can help."

I never understood what he meant. And after my father was gone, the trauma buried that memory deep. Until now.

I came across the name again, years later, in a different context. During a long con, I overheard a mark whisper about a man who could find anyone, anywhere. "A ghost-finder," they called him. "A man who knows how to find the unfindable."

At the time, I thought nothing of it. Just another whisper among criminals. But at that moment with my mind finally idle, trying to figure out my next steps, it clicked.

Sergei. The same name.

I knelt in the closet and pushed through my things, searching until I found the old memory box I had stashed away in the back of my closet years ago. I opened the lid pulling out old pictures, report cards, a friendship bracelet...and there it was—the ratty, faded card my father had given me.

Now, staring at it again in the present, my pulse quickened. If Sergei could find anyone, then he could find my father. Or at least tell me what happened to him.

I closed my fingers around the card, determination settling in my chest. I had wasted too much time. It was time to track him down.

I rushed into the bathroom and stepped into the scalding water, letting it wash away the grime and exhaustion. I hadn't realized how much I missed my arsenal of hair care products until now. The familiar scent of hibiscus and honey soothed me as I worked the conditioner through my curls. I turned on the steam function, closed my eyes, and took deep, measured breaths.

Forty minutes later, I stepped out, refreshed but still on edge. I lathered my skin in my favorite lotion and then topped it with scented oil, taking my time to massage it all in, sealing in the moisture. It was something I'd always done—not just for vanity, but to ground myself. The ritual made me feel like me.

After my wash-and-go air-dried, I defined my curls with my diffuser. I did a light makeup look. Then, I got dressed: dark-wash ripped jeans, an auburn bodysuit, my oversized army fatigue trench, and my favorite cognac combat boots. The weight of the outfit, the way it fit, the way I looked in the mirror—it gave me a small dose of control.

My phone had been on silent all night, but now, I turned it over and saw the inevitable. Dozens of missed calls and messages from Amir. I clenched my jaw. I refused to read them. Not now. Not when I needed to stay focused.

Once I had all the info I needed, I would run off to L.A. I was giving myself one week. One week to find Sergei, to figure out what my father had hidden, and to disappear.

I ordered a rideshare, typing in the address that was scribbled under the name. I slung my messenger bag over my shoulder, stepped out of my bedroom, and exhaled. Seeing the destruction in the daylight was worse somehow. The stark reality of it all sat heavy in my chest.

I walked into the kitchen, opened the fridge, and grabbed a Naked juice. My fingers checked the expiration date by habit before I unscrewed the cap and downed half of it. I leaned against the counter, surveying the wreckage one last time. The cost to repair, to replace—to fix—would be outrageous. And yet, standing here, it already felt beyond saving.

Focus, Malinda.

At 4 p.m., I slipped into an Uber. The car ride was silent as I stared out the window, gripping my bag tightly. The ride to Virginia would take 45 minutes. And then, my real work would begin.

As soon as the car rolled to a stop, I hesitated.

This couldn't be right.

I checked the address again. It matched. But instead of some secretive safe house or a discreet meeting location, I was staring at an unassuming office building.

Not the kind of place you find a ghost.

I leaned forward and met the driver's gaze in the rearview mirror. "Hey. Can you wait here for me? I won't be long."

The driver nodded, barely interested, and I stepped out, feeling the cold Virginia air bite at my cheeks.

Inside, the lobby was nearly silent, the kind of unsettling quiet that came with abandonment. The security desk was unmanned, and dust clung to the edges of the marble floors. The monitors behind the desk flickered with grainy surveillance footage, the only sign of life.

I glanced at the directory, but there was no mention of Sergei.

Figures.

I turned toward the elevators, already recalculating my next move when a voice cut through the quiet.

"Excuse me! Miss, can I help you?"

I inhaled sharply, schooling my expression into one of polite curiosity before turning around.

An older man in an ill-fitting security uniform was watching me, his posture shifting as soon as I met his eyes. The minute my smile appeared; his suspicion softened.

Bingo.

"Yes, sir," I said, stepping toward him with careful confidence. "I'm looking for a man named Sergei. Would you happen to know on which floor his offices are located?"

His eyes scanned me slowly, lingering just a bit too long. His skepticism wavered under my pleasant tone.

"That name sounds familiar." He motioned for me to follow him to the security desk, where he sat and cracked his knuckles before tapping a series of keys.

I leaned against the desk just enough to give the illusion of ease, a delicate balance between casual and interested. His fingers stilled for a moment, and I caught the glance he made at my chest before clearing his throat and refocusing.

I fought the urge to roll my eyes. Some things were just too easy.

"Yup," he grunted. "Sergei, private consultant. Moved outta here five years ago, sweet peach."

Sweet peach? I nearly gagged but forced a demure blush instead, lowering my lashes. "Oh... well, that's disappointing."

His eyes flicked to my lips, and I saw it—the hesitation, the tiny crack in his resolve.

I leaned in just slightly, lowering my voice. "You wouldn't happen to have any forwarding information, would you?"

He frowned. "Only have a personal address, and I can't give that out. Sorry."

I let my shoulders sag, just enough to look vulnerable, my expression a mix of frustration and desperation. Wide, sad eyes. The same look I used to give my father when I wanted something.

"Oh... it's just that I really need to speak to him. It's important. A—An awful situation, really. I don't know where else to turn."

I glanced at his name tag and added a small, hopeful smile. "Marcus?"

His throat bobbed as he swallowed, and I saw the moment his better judgment wavered.

"I—" He licked his lips, his eyes raking over me. "I guess it is public knowledge anyway..."

He scribbled something onto a piece of paper, his hand moving fast like he was worried he'd change his mind. As he slid it toward me, I reached for it, but he caught my hand.

Too rough. Too eager.

His fingers curled around mine as he grinned. "What are you doing later today, sweet peach? I'd love to have someone as beautiful and sexy as you on my arm at the lounge tonight."

I resisted the urge to yank my hand away, keeping my expression effortlessly sweet instead.

"Aw, that's real sweet, Marcus." I slowly pulled my fingers from his grip. "But I'm not from around here. Just passing through."

His expression darkened momentarily before he quickly scrawled his number on the corner of the paper. "Text me. Next time you're in town, let's get together."

I let out a soft laugh, tucking the address and his number into my bag as I flashed my megawatt smile. "We'll see."

I winked at him for good measure before strolling out the door, slipping back into the cold.

I didn't breathe until I was inside the car, the door safely shut.

"Where to now?" the driver asked.

I unfolded the paper in my lap, staring at the address.

CHAPTER 30

MALINDA

I asked the driver to take me home. I don't just show up places without a plan—I do my research first. And right now, I needed to regroup, figure out my next move, and determine how to approach Sergei.

By the time we reached my apartment building, the sky had darkened into a deep navy. The thing I hate most about winter is how early night falls. It was barely 6 PM, but the city felt abandoned, the cold air sharp against my skin. I pulled my trench coat tighter around me, shifting my messenger bag closer to my side as I stepped out of the car. The street was quiet. Too quiet.

Something in my gut twisted.

As I approached the alley leading to the back entrance of my building, I noticed a sleek black Jaguar parked near the door. Tinted windows. Engine off. No one inside—or at least, no one I could see. My footsteps slowed.

Every nerve in my body screamed at me to turn around.

I kept my movements calm and casual, pivoting on my heel and walking toward the front of the building instead. I wasn't going to chance it. Not after everything that had happened.

Then, just as I was about to make it to the street, the car doors clicked open.

Two large men stepped out.

I stopped mid-step, my breath catching.

The taller one of the two grinned, his teeth stark white. "Ms. Burns. Come with us."

His voice was smooth, too smooth, like he was enjoying this.

I turned back toward the door—only to realize I had nowhere to go.

Fuck.

These had to be Clay's people. No one else knew where I lived. No one else would be waiting for me like this.

I swallowed down the rising panic and tightened my grip on the strap of my messenger bag. I wasn't going down without a fight.

The taller one took a slow, deliberate step forward.

I exhaled through my nose, my mind racing. Two against one. They were bigger than me, stronger, but I was faster. I could use my size to my advantage. I wasn't defenseless. I just needed to wait for my moment.

The two men advanced at the same time.

I struck first.

I swung at the smaller of the two, my fist connecting with his mouth in a sharp, brutal impact. His head snapped back, and he let out a strangled curse, covering his bleeding lip.

Then, his face twisted with rage.

"You fucking bitch."

Before I could react, his hand came down hard across my face, the force snapping my head to the side. My vision blurred, pain stinging down my jaw.

Then, another blow.

Fist this time.

Pain exploded across my cheekbone as my head snapped back. I stumbled, momentarily dazed.

The bigger one didn't hesitate. His arms wrapped around me like a steel vice, locking me in place. I reacted on instinct—I bared my teeth and sank them into his forearm. Hard.

He yelped but didn't let go. Instead, he growled and squeezed tighter, his arm pressing against my ribs, forcing the air from my lungs.

"Fucking bitch bit me," he snarled.

The smaller one was still touching his mouth, blood seeping through his fingers. He spat onto the ground; eyes filled with pure hatred. "Let's take this bitch to the boss before someone sees us—or I wring her fucking neck."

My stomach dropped.

Boss?

Clay?

I screamed, or at least I tried to. The large one clamped a rough hand over my mouth, muffling the sound. I kicked wildly, my boots connecting with the smaller man's shoulder, then his face. He stumbled back with a grunt before recovering, his hands shooting forward to grab my legs and pin them together.

"No more games, sweetheart."

They started hauling me toward the car.

Panic set in, hot and suffocating.

No. No, no, no.

I thrashed as hard as I could, kicking, twisting, trying anything to break free. My pulse pounded in my ears. The cold metal of the trunk loomed closer, and I fought harder. I couldn't let them get me in that car. I knew what happened to people who got thrown into trunks.

My nails clawed at the taller one's wrist, my muffled screams growing frantic. My vision blurred with desperation.

And then—

A brutal shove. A sharp impact against the metal frame of the car.

Pain exploded at the back of my skull, white-hot and searing.

The world tilted.

Then everything went dark.

I groggily came to, my head throbbing as I realized I was trapped in the trunk of a moving vehicle. My wrists were double zip-tied so tight that it was cutting my flesh. They must have done it when I was knocked out. It was pitch black, the air thick with the scent of oil and rubber, my body aching from being curled up in the confined space. I couldn't see anything and was starting to become dizzy from all the turns we were making. Panic clawed at my chest, but I forced myself to breathe through it. I need to think.

What will happen to me? What will Clay do to me? Is this the end for me? I have no one who will miss me...other than Amir maybe. But I've already ruined that. I disappeared in the middle of the night when all he was trying to do was show me he cared about me. What the hell is wrong with me? Why is this the life I chose? This is not the life my mom or dad wanted for me.

As the car rumbled beneath me, my mind drifted back to a time I had long buried—a time before I had learned to fend for myself. The week before my father disappeared had been strange. He had been more present than usual, asking me odd questions about what I wanted in life, or if I ever thought about settling down somewhere. At the time, I had been a restless teenager, more concerned with drama with friends than any far-off future.

But now, with the distance of years, I see the cracks I had ignored. The way his eyes lingered on me when he thought I wasn't looking. The way he hesitated before speaking, as if weighing his words carefully. The night before he vanished, he had hugged me tight—tighter than he ever had before. And then, the next day, he was gone.

I had waited for him. At first, I told myself he'd be back in a few hours. Then a day. Then a week. When the weeks turned into months, the betrayal hardened into something else—anger. He had left me to clean up the mess of his life, to survive on my own with nothing but the skills he had taught me. Skills that had both saved and damned me.

And now, I'm here. Stuffed in a trunk, in danger because of a man who hadn't even cared enough to say goodbye.

Tears burned in my eyes, but I blinked them away. I had survived before. I will survive this too.

The car seemed to be slowing. I tensed, preparing myself. I'm not that abandoned little girl anymore. And if they think they can break me, they are dead wrong.

My thoughts were interrupted when the car came to an abrupt halt. I rolled forward, slamming my face into the hatch of the trunk, pain blooming across my forehead and nose. My stomach churned as the air was knocked out of my lungs, disoriented from the impact.

I barely had time to gather my senses before I heard car doors slamming, followed by the thud of heavy boots. The sound of keys rattling sent fresh panic shooting through me.

Then—light. The trunk popped open, and harsh fluorescent light flooded my vision, momentarily blinding me. Rough hands grabbed me, yanking me out with no regard for the way my limbs twisted awkwardly, banging various parts of my head and body on the car, my head whipping back from the force of their grip.

I tried to get a clear look at where I was. A warehouse. Vast and mostly empty, except for scattered crates, rusted machinery, and the scent of dust and motor oil hanging thick in the air. My wrists ached from the too-tight zip ties, my face throbbing with the certainty that my nose was bleeding.

I was carried up a narrow metal staircase, my body jostling with every unsteady step, and then I was dumped onto a chair in a small, dimly lit office space. The bigger goon roughly forced me into place, gripping my arm hard enough to bruise.

I kept my expression blank, refusing to let them see the pain radiating through me. I wouldn't give them the satisfaction.

My mind was racing. What will happen next? Are they going to shoot me? I waited in terror for what felt like forever.

Then I heard it—a car pulling into the warehouse, the tires screeching to a sharp stop. A car door flung open. Fast, precise footsteps ascended the stairs, growing louder, and heavier.

He walked in.

Clay's presence swallowed the room whole. The moment he entered, his sharp gaze immediately locked onto me a cocky smirk on his face. But the moment he took in my bruised face, the cut on my lip, the blood leaking from my nose, —something inside him snapped. His smirk vanished. His entire body stiffened, jaw tightened, his nostrils flaring, his breathing coming sharp and fast, and then—

A storm erupted.

Before I could process it, Clay turned on the bigger goon—the one who had yanked me out of the trunk like I was garbage. The man barely had time to react before Clay's fist slammed into his jaw with a sickening crack. The goon stumbled back, groaning, blood spurting from his lip.

"What the *fuck* did you idiots do to her?" Clay's voice was lethal, a serrated blade cutting through the air sending a wave of panic washing over me.

I had *never* seen him like this before. He was always so controlled, so calculated. But this? This was unrestrained fury.

The larger goon barely had time to catch his breath before Clay struck him again—this time, his fist connecting brutally with the guy's chin sending him crashing to the floor. A chair toppled over in the process, clattering loudly as the man let out a strangled grunt of pain.

The smaller goon cleared his throat, his voice nervous. "Boss, she put up a fight."

Clay turned so fast that the man flinched. And before he could even react Clay had him by the collar, shoving him so hard against the wall that the metal shelves behind him rattled.

"She's *five-foot-three*," Clay growled, his voice low, shaking with quiet rage. "I told you to keep her unharmed." His grip tightened, knuckles white against the fabric of the goon's jacket. "Do you not understand simple instructions?"

The larger goon coughed, wiping his busted lip with the back of his hand. "She fought back hard" he wheezed.

"Yeah. She bit him and kicked me in the face." Added the one he was holding by the collar, his voice trembling. Clay's expression darkened.

His knee drove into his stomach, a sharp, devastating hit that made the man double over with a strangled grunt. "And you're telling me you couldn't handle that without putting your fucking hands on her?" His voice was eerily calm now, but that only made it more dangerous.

I swallowed hard, watching the fury radiate off him watching Clay *unravel*.

My body ached, my head still swimming from the impact of being thrown around, but none of that mattered right now.

He wasn't just angry. He was enraged—unpredictable. Not at all the man I thought I understood. I thought I knew him. Thought I had peeled back enough layers to understand who he was beneath all the cocky charm, the expensive suits, and the calculated power plays.

But this? This was something else.

This was a man on a warpath willing to destroy anyone who hurt me. But why?

A quiet, dangerous realization settled into my bones.

Clay Sawyer is dangerous. He's not just furious. He's *possessive*. He doesn't like it when things slip out of his control. Like I had. This was a message.

Clay let go, watching as the man staggered, clutching his ribs.

He turned his back toward the two men, rolling his shoulders like he was shaking off the residual need for violence.

"You disobeyed me." His voice was smooth now, back to its usual composed state, but the underlying menace hadn't faded. If anything, it had sharpened. "Both of you—get the fuck out of my face." He adjusted his cuffs as if the whole thing had been a mild inconvenience.

"We'll continue this discussion later," he added darkly, his gaze cutting into them. "Send Rick in here."

The two goons didn't hesitate. They scrambled out of the room, not even daring to look back.

He tugged a handkerchief out of his pocket, wiping his hand against it like the very act of touching them was beneath him.

Silence stretched between me and Clay.

The adrenaline in my veins hadn't settled yet. My hands were still trembling, my body still aching from the fight, but my mind was clear.

Clay turned to me. His breathing was still uneven, his chest rising and falling sharply, his jaw clenched so tight I thought it might snap. His hands were still curled into fists.

He hadn't calmed down yet.

He studied me, his gaze raking over my injuries again.

I stayed silent, watching as he exhaled sharply and dragged a hand down his face.

Then, finally, his gaze softened.

His expression morphed into something soft and remorseful. I stared defiantly at him. He reached for me, and I flinched. He looked pained at my reaction.

"Dove..." His voice was low, almost desperate like he was still trying to steady himself. It wasn't the usual endearment, soft with possessive admiration. This was something else—raw, conflicted. Like he was trying to reconcile the woman in front of him with the one he had built in his mind.

"You're shaking. They hurt you. That's not how this was supposed to go."

He lifted my chin, forcing me to meet his gaze. I steeled myself, and with the courage I had left I spat bitterly "Go to hell, Clay."

His lips pressed into a thin line, and for a moment, I saw the warring emotions flicker across his face. Anger. Betrayal. Possession. And something deeper—something that scared him just as much as it did me.

He exhaled sharply, rubbing a hand over his mouth. To my surprise, he knelt in front of me reaching for my bound wrists.

With a tender touch, he began loosening the restraints. The moment I was free, I crossed my arms holding myself tightly, biting back a wince. It was a self-soothing technique I used to use at night after my dad left and my panic attacks would dominate me. Clay reached out like he wanted to touch me, to confirm I was real, but I jerked away.

His jaw tensed. "Your lip is bleeding". He caressed my face.

"Thanks to you," I shot back.

Regret flickered in his expression, but it was gone as quickly as it came, masked beneath something harder. "You left me no choice, Malinda."

I scoffed. "There's always a choice."

He stared at me, eyes dark and unreadable. Then, so softly I almost didn't hear it, he said, "Not with you."

I forced myself to steady my voice, to summon whatever courage I had left. "Why am I here? What do you want, Clay?"

A knock at the door pulled his attention away. He glanced at me for a beat—like he was debating something—before stepping out into the hall. As soon as he was gone, I scanned the room, my pulse pounding. No weapons, no real cover. Just an old desk, a few chairs, and one exit. Rushing for the door would be reckless. I had to be smart. I had to figure out what Clay wanted before I made my move.

The sound of his footsteps returning made me tense, but when he stepped back into the room, he wasn't holding a weapon and wasn't wearing that cold, calculating mask. Instead, in his hands was a small first aid kit.

Clay kneeled back down to my level, his expression unreadable, a mask of cool detachment as he examined my face. He reached out, dabbing at my lip with gauze, soaking up the blood with clinical precision. Then he wiped it down with alcohol.

The sting forced me to inhale sharply.

"I know, Dove. I'm almost done, darling." His voice was a low murmur, intimate, as though we were anywhere but here—me bruised and bloodied, him my captor. He moved to a cut on my cheek, tending to it with the same gentle care, his fingertips grazing my skin. A lover's touch, but with an underlying tremor I couldn't quite name.

After a few moments, he finished, tilting my chin slightly as he studied his handiwork. "Hopefully, you won't bruise too much. I don't want your beautiful skin to scar." His eyes finally met mine, and for a fleeting second, there was something raw in them. Something that made my pulse stutter.

"What do you want from me, Clay? Why did you send your goons after me?"

"You're a hard woman to catch."

"Then stop chasing."

His eyes sparked with amusement, and he tried—and failed—to suppress the smirk forming on his lips. "You're still just as witty as ever. One of the many reasons I still want you so badly."

Then he kissed me. Desperately. Hungrily. A man drowning and grasping for the only thing keeping him afloat.

I didn't return it.

He exhaled sharply and kissed my forehead instead, lingering there as if trying to imprint something on me. "I just couldn't help myself, Malinda. Your lips... I've never been able to resist them."

And then, just like that, he pulled away, straightened his tie, adjusted his cuffs, and cleared his throat. The transformation was immediate. The lover vanished, replaced by the CEO—composed, unreadable, detached.

Another knock at the door. The door opened and a familiar face walked in. Rick. I had spent months around him, having him be my chauffeur and bodyguard when Clay and I went out. Any hopes that he could be my savior vanished as he avoided eye contact and handed a briefcase to Clay.

Clay turned and accepted the briefcase and a bottle of water from Rick. Returning to the desk, he placed the briefcase down and handed me the bottle.

I stared at it.

"Drink the water, babe. It's not poisoned." He cracked the seal and took a sip himself. "See? It's safe."

I hesitated, then took a sip.

"What do you want from me, Clay?" My voice was firmer now, demanding. "Your people broke into my house, trashed it, and now kidnapped me. I'm assuming on your orders. You're going to all this trouble for what?"

"As I said earlier, Dove, I was disobeyed. I told them to find you and bring you to me, not to assault you." His voice was even, calculated. "I'd never order such a thing."

"And my apartment?"

He gave me a deadpan stare, his expression shifting, hardening into something colder. "Why did you quit your job at SparTech, Malinda?"

The question caught me off guard.

"I already had my exit interview with HR, Clay."

A ghost of a smirk flickered across his lips, but there was nothing amused about it. "If you know what's good for you, Malinda... you'll stop being a smart-ass."

My mouth went dry. His voice was calm, almost soft, but laced with something dangerous underneath. A warning.

"I—I left because I wanted to explore my career options."

He scoffed, shaking his head. "That's the story you're sticking with?" His eyes bore into mine, searching, demanding something real. "So, you're saying it had nothing to do with us?"

I forced a frown. "Us?" I played dumb. "What do you mean?"

His jaw clenched, and for a moment, I saw the cracks forming in his control. The man who had been cold and ruthless just minutes ago, pummeling those goons, was struggling to maintain the same level of detachment with me.

"You disappeared while I was in Beijing," he said, his tone clipped but too raw for comfort. "You didn't just quit your job—you left me. Without a word. No call, no explanation. Just gone." He exhaled sharply, pacing now, like standing still made this harder to swallow. "Our sex life was amazing. Our conversations were top-tier. Our dates? Enjoyable. Spain..." His voice faltered for a split second, something unspoken lingering in the air. "Then I ask you to be my girlfriend, and a week after I leave, you vanish."

I looked away, my stomach twisting.

"No," I said, voice barely above a whisper. "It had nothing to do with that."

Lies.

I felt his gaze lingering on me, sharp and heavy, like he could hear all the things I wasn't saying. And maybe he could. Because Clay wasn't stupid. And I wasn't as indifferent as I pretended to be.

"Bullshit."

His voice was so sharp, so certain, that it made my head snap back toward him.

"I don't believe you."

I swallowed hard. "That's not my problem."

His nostrils flared, his tongue running over his bottom lip, the way it did when he was trying to control himself. "So let me get this straight," he said slowly, his tone deceptively even. "You enjoyed my company, you enjoyed the sex, you enjoyed my fucking time, but you just—what? Got bored? Decided you didn't want it anymore?"

I didn't answer.

His jaw tightened. "I deserve the truth."

I met his eyes then, forcing myself to stay still, forcing the walls inside me to go higher, thicker. The more he pushed, the colder I became.

"I already told you."

He took a step forward, invading my space, his gaze relentless. "You ran, Malinda. Not just from the job. You ran from me."

I stayed quiet.

"Say it."

Nothing.

"Fucking say it."

I let out a breath, my face impassive, my body still. "Fine. I ran."

Clay's entire body tensed, like I had punched him square in the chest. He blinked once, twice, like he wasn't sure he had heard me right.

A long, heavy silence stretched between us.

Then, quietly, almost brokenly, he asked, "Why?"

I thought about telling him. I thought about breaking my silence, about explaining, about letting him see even a fraction of what was going on in my head.

But what would be the point?

I had already gone too far. The damage was done.

So instead, I did what I always did when things got too close.

I shrugged.

Clay stared at me for a long time, his expression unreadable. Then, with a slow, bitter chuckle, he took a step back.

"Got it."

His voice was hollow now, and something inside of me ached at the sound of it. But I forced myself to hold his gaze, to keep my posture relaxed, to act like none of this meant anything.

Even as a sick, sinking feeling settled deep in my stomach.

He stared at me for a long beat, then turned, opening his briefcase. He pulled out a file and placed it on the desk.

"Explain something to me. Why is it that if anyone pulls up your employee information, it lists a fake address, and a fake birthday? Even your social security number is a tax ID linked to a shell corporation in Delaware, with offshore accounts in the Bahamas."

My pulse pounded.

"I like my privacy."

He smirked, shaking his head. "That's not even the best part. I took it upon myself to review the last files you accessed before quitting. And what do you know? All of them are tied to a former employee. George Matthew Burns." He leaned in slightly, eyes dark with something unreadable. "Ring any bells?"

I swallowed hard. My cover was blown. But maybe I could salvage this.

"I worked for you for nearly eight years, Clay. I don't remember every file I looked at. My job as an internal auditor was to—"

He kicked a chair out of his way and was in my face before I could blink.

"How fucking stupid do you think I am?!" His voice cracked like a whip. "I can't believe I never connected the dots. Your father damn near ruined our company! He stole three hundred and fifteen million dollars from SparTech twenty years ago! And I've been here—" his voice wavered, something breaking through. "—lusting after his daughter. My father would have a fucking heart attack if he knew what was happening. Grandpop must be rolling in his grave".

I stayed quiet. The less I talk the better. I've never seen Clay so...unhinged.

He backed away, running a hand through his hair. His mask slipped. For the first time, I saw it—the hurt, the betrayal.

"After everything we've talked about. I opened up to you. I was fucking vulnerable with you. And you knew who I was this whole time. Was that your plan all along? To seduce me and rob me blind like your thieving father?!"

"No!" I snapped, my voice shaking. "I had no clue about my dad's history with SparTech! I stumbled across those files—"

"Bullshit!" He rounded on me, his fury barely contained. "You live a lavish life, Malinda. I saw your place. I know what we paid you. It doesn't add up."

"I'm an accountant. I have great money management skills."

He scoffed. "You know what I think? I think your father cut you a piece of the pie. At first, I thought you were skimming from our revenue accounts but nope. Everything checks out. So, it must be the former."

"My father is dead, Clay." My heart was racing. Clay doesn't need to ever know how I built my wealth.

"Do you think I believe that shit?!"

"It's the truth. Why do you even care about it? It was way before your time."

"He ruined our lives!" For a flash of a second Clay's mask slipped again and I saw hurt overtake his features. He pulled himself together speaking in a calmer tone. "The company is still recovering from that blow. You don't seem to understand the severity of what your dad did to my family."

"He's dead Clay. Why are you tormenting me? I had nothing to do with it."

"I don't give a fuck about whether he's dead or alive Malinda. If I could recover even a third of what he stole from us, then I'd be satisfied."

"I still don't understand what that has to do with me."

"Don't play stupid with me Malinda. I did my research. I know everything about you. You're my obsession. Your father left you an inheritance and a storage locker full of crap which was all released to you on your 18th birthday."

"He left me his life savings, it was only 20k. I used it for college. I swear. That's all I know."

"You knew who I fucking was. What was your angle there huh? Why even apply at my company?"

"Clayton..." He paused. I have never used his full name. "All I knew as a child was that when we moved to Baltimore, my dad got a job at a company named SparTech. Then he died. Last year as I was completing an audit, I saw his name pop up. I had no idea he was connected with you."

"You're a fucking liar."

"You pursued me! For years. What kind of shitty criminal would I be if I ignored my supposed target?"

He paced back and forth in silence for what felt like an eternity, running a hand through his hair, jaw tight, eyes dark with something unreadable. He exhaled, dragging a hand down his face.

When he finally stopped, his gaze locked onto mine, sharp and unyielding.

"Fine, Malinda," he said, voice eerily calm. "Since you claim you don't know, then you're going to find out." He stepped closer, invading my space, his presence suffocating. "I want you to continue your investigation. Find my fucking money." His eyes flickered with something dangerous, something final. "If you try to run, I will find you. If you lie to me..." He tilted his head slightly, considering his words, then smiled—cold, detached. "Just don't lie to me, Dove. For your sake."

He let that linger, the weight of his warning pressing down on me like a vice. Then, as if nothing had happened, he straightened his cuffs, smoothing out the tension from his suit, the perfect picture of control once more. "I'll be in touch," he said, voice crisp, businesslike. As if he hadn't just ripped my world apart. And just like that, I was his prisoner. His obsession.

Clay strolled to the door and pulled it open with a measured calm as if he hadn't just threatened to unravel my entire life. The two goons stepped inside, their presence a suffocating force in the already stifling room. The bigger one had dried blood crusted at his temple and a split lip. The other held his side gingerly, wincing slightly as he reached for my arm. I didn't have to wonder why—they had gone off-script, and Clay forced me to witness the consequences of disobeying him.

Their grip was iron-clad as they yanked me forward, forcing me to follow Clay and Rick out of the warehouse and into the night. My legs felt unsteady, my body sore from the rough handling, but I bit down on my fear and forced myself to keep up. We went outside and behind the warehouse. The air was thick with the scent of damp asphalt and gasoline as they led me to the waiting black Escalade. My breath came in short, panicked bursts. This felt like a dream—no, a nightmare—one I couldn't wake up from.

Clay slid into the front seat with the same air of control he always carried, adjusting his cuffs as if this were nothing more than a business transaction. Rick drove in silence, his knuckles white against the steering wheel. The goons flanked me in the back, their bruises and cuts making them even more menacing in the dim streetlights that flickered past.

The drive felt endless, a period where my pulse never settled, where every second felt like it could end with something worse than what had already happened. But then—familiarity. A sharp left turn. My street.

The SUV slowed, then stopped.

Without warning, rough hands shoved me forward. My feet caught on the curb, and I hit the wet pavement hard, my palms scraping against the unforgiving concrete. Pain shot through my knees, but I barely registered it over the thundering of my heart. I turned just in time to see the taillights disappear into the night; the sound of the engine swallowed by the rain.

Everything hurt. My ribs, my face, my pride.

I tried to push myself up, rain soaking into my clothes, making every movement heavier, and slower.   But then—

"Malinda?"

A voice cut through the darkness, warm and familiar.

I jerked my head up, my breath catching in my throat.

Amir.

He was jogging toward me, panic and concern etched into his face, his steps quickening the moment he saw me. The relief that crashed over me was instant, overwhelming.

I wasn't alone.

Chapter 31

Malinda

"**M**alinda, what the hell is going on? Who were those people who just threw you out of the car?"

I barely had time to process before Amir's arms wrapped around me, his warmth cutting through the icy rain. I clung to him, my body trembling from more than just the cold.

"I was so fucking worried about you," he murmured into my hair, his grip tightening like he was afraid to let go.

He pulled back, his gaze raking over my face. The moment his eyes landed on the bruises, the worry in them darkened into something more dangerous.

"Look at your face! What happened to you?"

A sudden awareness crashed over me. We were standing in the rain, voices too loud, too exposed.

"I'll tell you once we get inside."

I stepped back, breaking the hold between us, and made my way toward my building. Amir stayed close, his presence grounding me as we slipped through the lobby, doing our best to stay inconspicuous. When we reached the elevator, I swiped my key fob and pressed the button for the 23rd floor.

"This is where you live, boo?"

I nodded without meeting his gaze. Letting people into my world, into my space, was what got me into this mess in the first place. My stomach twisted, overwhelmed by too many emotions at once.

When the elevator doors slid open, I led the way down the hall, unlocking my door with shaky hands.

Amir stepped inside—and stopped dead in his tracks. His eyes swept across the wreckage, the overturned furniture, the shattered glass.

"Malinda...what happened here?" His voice was low, and controlled, but I could hear the barely contained anger beneath it. "Is this the same people who hurt you? Are they the ones who did this?"

He turned toward me, reaching out, but I took a small step back. I needed space. I needed to breathe.

"Amir...I'll answer your questions, but I just need an hour to collect myself. Please."

His expression softened. "Okay, Malinda. How can I help?"

"You've done enough, Amir. Thank you. Come with me."

I led him toward my bedroom—the only untouched part of my home. The only place that still felt like mine.

His eyes widened slightly as he took it in. "Damn, you got a walk-in closet? And a balcony?" Then he spotted the bathroom. "Wait...you got a steam shower? Oh, you fancy, huh?"

His grin was so unexpected, so normal, I couldn't help the small chuckle that slipped past my lips.

"Make yourself comfortable," I said, nodding toward the bed. "I just need to shower and clear my head."

"And then we'll talk?" His voice was steady, but the way he looked at me—intense, searching—made my breath hitch.

I hesitated. How much could I really tell him? The more he knew, the more danger he'd be in.

I sighed. "Yes, Amir. Then we'll talk."

I handed him the remote and disappeared into my closet. I peeled off my jacket, tossed it into the dry-clean bin, and grabbed a towel before making my way back through the room. I caught Amir watching me—his gaze drifting, his jaw tightening—before he quickly turned his attention back to the TV.

In the bathroom, I took my time, letting the hot water work through the tension in my muscles, clearing my mind. I scrubbed my skin, using my favorite bath soaps, washing away the lingering scent of Clay and that goddamn trunk, making sure to wash my hair again with my favorite products to get the gunk out of it, and then twisted it. I treated my bruises, and my cuts, then let the steam surround me, pressing my forehead against the cool tile.

For the first time since Clay's men grabbed me, I let myself think. Really think. About what happened. About what I needed to do next.

By the time I stepped out, wrapped in a towel, I was steadier. But when I walked back into my bedroom, Amir did a double take, his eyes dragging over me before he licked his lips and looked away.

"Sorry. Just passing through."

He arched a brow, smirking. "No worries, boo. This is your space."

I hurried into my closet, changed into leggings and a tank top, and emerged to find him still lounging on my bed. I got in bed next to him.

I never liked having people in my space. With Clay, I made sure to always go to his place, apart from the one time he drunkenly invited himself over. But with Amir...it was different. Maybe because I'd been living with him for the past month. Or maybe because, for the first time in a long time, I wasn't alone.

Except last night.

That kiss. Kissing him felt too good. I liked it too much. I know I can't stay with him for too long so why emotionally invest in a person I have to leave? I can't do that again.

I shoved the thought away.

Amir turned to face me, and the air between us thickened. Tension. Heat. Something unspoken.

"So...are you ready to talk?" His voice was deep, slow. Innocent question, but the way it sounded, the way his breath ghosted over my skin, sent a warmth curling through my stomach.

I cleared my throat. "Yeah, I am. What would you like to know?"

He met my gaze, and something about the way he looked at me made me want to curl into him.

"Whatever you're comfortable telling me."

I swallowed. "I...I don't know where to start."

"Who were those people from earlier?"

I hesitated. "They work for Clay."

He frowned. "Clay? Our boss? Well...I mean, my boss."

"Yeah."

His expression darkened. "Those were some shady-looking guys, Malinda. And they hurt you. Why were you with them?"

"They took me."

His body tensed. "What do you mean?"

"I was coming back here earlier today when those guys cornered me in the alley entrance. I fought back. That's how I got these injuries."

"What did they want with you?"

I hesitated too long.

"Malinda." His voice was firmer now. "What are you involved in? Is it drugs? Gambling?"

"No," I said quickly. "It's personal. Between me and Clay."

"Personal?" His jaw clenched. "Personal enough for him to send hitmen after you?"

"Amir, I don't want you involved in this. You've already done more than enough."

He looked torn, like he wanted to push, but after a moment, he exhaled. "Okay, Malinda. What's your plan?"

I hesitated. "I have to contact a few people...that's all I can tell you."

His lips pressed together. He wasn't happy about that answer, but he let it go. Instead, he reached out, cupping my face, forcing me to look at him.

"What do you need right now? Tonight?"

I swallowed the lump in my throat. "I just need to rest."

"Okay," he said softly. "Let's grab some clothes and go home."

I stiffened. "I can't go with you, Amir. You've done enough."

His expression turned stormy. "No way. No fucking way am I leaving you here alone."

"Amir—"

"No, Malinda. These people know where you live. They got to you once. You think they won't try again? Come back home with me, I can keep you safe there."

"I-I know. But this is my space Amir. This is my home."

"And you can come back here when this is over and you're safe. But that's not the reality right now." I was silent.

I did not argue about that. I knew he was right. But the idea of being ordered around made my stubborn streak flare.

He saw the resistance in my eyes and sighed.

"Fine, boo." He peeled off his jacket and sweater, settling back against the headboard. "If you're staying, then so am I."

"What? But you have work—"

"Tomorrow's Friday. I'll call in sick. Monday, I'll work from here. Point is, I'm not leaving you."

I stared at him, overwhelmed, grateful, scared of how much I needed him.

He softened. "Did you eat today?"

I shook my head.

"Alright, I'll order takeout. Are you cool with Indian? I'm in the mood for Samosas"

I smirked and nodded.

An hour later, we sat in bed, eating and watching *The Fresh Prince of Bel-Air*, but my mind wasn't on the TV.

It was on him.

I'd never met anyone like Amir. This is the first time in my life that I've met anyone so genuine. The feelings that have been developing grew 10-fold tonight. I've never felt like this about anyone before.

And that terrified me.

He glanced in my direction and caught me staring. I quickly looked away, my heart hammering in my chest. After a beat, he paused the show.

"You okay, boo?" His voice was low, careful.

"Yeah," I said softly, but I knew he didn't believe me.

He studied me for a moment, then sighed. "You look exhausted. It's late... let's go to bed."

I nodded, not trusting my voice. He moved off the bed, gathering up the leftovers and taking them to the fridge. When he returned, he hesitated near the door, locking it before slowly making his way back to the bed. The air between us was thick, charged with everything unspoken.

Amir sat down stiffly, rubbing the back of his neck. "Uh... d-do you want me to hold you?" His voice was cautious, unsure.

My breath caught. I did. God, I did. But saying yes meant acknowledging this pull between us, the way his presence made me feel safe in a way I didn't want to need. My walls were cracking, and I was terrified of what would happen if they crumbled completely.

Still, my body moved before my mind could argue. I nodded, and the tears slipped down my face before I could stop them.

He swallowed, his throat bobbing, then shut off the light. Slowly, almost tentatively, he lifted the covers and pulled me close. He was warm, his grip strong but careful, as if he was afraid I'd push him away. I rested my head against his chest, feeling his heart pound beneath my cheek.

His hand hovered near my back before he finally settled it, stroking it in slow, soothing circles.

"Tonight was... a lot," he murmured, his lips near my hair. "I can only imagine what you've been through. But just know—when I'm around, you're safe."

A choked sob escaped me, and I clung to him tighter. I wanted to believe him. Needed to.

He didn't speak again, just held me, his fingers gently stroking my hair until, for the first time in what felt like forever, sleep finally took me.

CHAPTER 32

CLAY

I'm so fucking angry with her. I never thought that could be possible. I thought she was this perfect goddess who came into my life and made me the happiest I've been in a decade. But it must have been all part of her little game.

She knew who I was this whole time. She said that's not true, but it's been established that she's a fucking liar, so how can I trust anything that comes out of her mouth? I can't shake the idea that she's just like her father. This must be part of their long game. I told her things—sensitive things about myself, my family, the company. Shit she can use against us. She's been in my house and had access to so much information. She could take us down, tank the Sylvan deal, or sell industry secrets to our competitors. My stomach twisted just thinking about it.

I pressed my fingers against my temples, trying to ground myself, but it didn't work. The car was silent except for my breathing, heavy and uneven. My chest felt tight like it was closing in on me. I've been played before, but never like this. Never by someone who made me believe I was safe with them.

Tonight didn't go as planned. I never wanted her hurt. I just needed her found. I needed to understand how she could just vanish like that, as if I meant nothing to her. The past few months had been a fucking whirlwind. Coming home from Beijing, I had been excited—desperate—to see her, to hold her, to hear her voice, to feel her touch. Only to hear she hadn't been in the office. I figured she was just taking time off. Malinda had a habit of taking impromptu trips and she ran her department like a well-oiled machine so it was never an issue.

She never answered my calls or texts. At first, I thought she was just pissed. That she needed space. That eventually, I'd walk into the office, and she'd be there, pretending I didn't drive her crazy.

The twelve-hour time difference made it impossible to keep up with her the way I wanted. I sent flowers, and a card, then got pulled right back in, flying to Berlin for six weeks. But the whole time, something felt off. I felt her slipping away, but I refused to believe it.

I cut my trip short to get back to her, only to find out from HR that she was just... gone. She put in her official resignation weeks before. No reason. No warning. No fucking explanation. That's when the paranoia set in. I needed answers. I put the investigator we already had on the books—originally looking into George fucking Burns—on her case.

The fucking irony. How this all connected. How blind I had been. My father and grandfather had spent decades hunting George Burns, trying to track him down, desperate for answers. And now, years later, here I was—the new CEO—sending the same fucking investigator after Malinda. His daughter. The woman who had captured my soul.

And still, none of it told me where she was.

That's when I sent guys to her apartment to bring her to me.

Yeah, they trashed her place, but I didn't order that. I didn't want her hurt. Just answers. Just *her*. But she slipped away again.

It sucks having to outsource this type of stuff, but after tonight, I'm done with those guys. They're unprofessional and don't follow orders.

And then today.

Rick had texted me while I was still on the tarmac. They spotted her leaving her apartment and were waiting for her return. My adrenaline spiked instantly. I came straight here, barely able to sit still on the ride over. I was *finally* going to get the truth. But I wasn't fucking ready for it.

Finding out she is George Burns' daughter? That was the biggest shock of my life. It was like hearing a ghost come back to haunt me.

I was too young to fully understand what was happening back then, but I remember how my grandfather cursed his name. How he took George under his wing and treated him like family. He trusted that bastard. My dad trusted him. They played golf together, drank scotch, and shared secrets with him—and he fucking gutted them. My grandfather was so obsessed with finding that motherfucker that he hired the PI firm that we have on retainer till this day, to track down any scent of him. That betrayal is what sent Granddaddy to an early grave.

SparTech nearly went under. Three hundred and fifteen million dollars, stolen. Years of hard work, destroyed. The company was forced to delay going public for another seven years.

Granddad took out a high-interest loan against the company to keep it afloat and keep the scandal quiet, to keep the truth buried. A loan that's still on our books today. A bad loan with horrible interest terms, but they were desperate.

That desperation seeped into my life too. I'm stuck with Brooke because of my dad and granddad's desperation to keep SparTech standing. Because Charles Whitmore Spencer—shipping magnate, business tycoon, and one of the last true American aristocrats—didn't just invest. He bought his way into the company, securing shares, leveraging influence, and quietly keeping us afloat when we needed it most. But there was only one thing he wanted in return. Not power. Not profits. Just a marriage. A union between the Sawyers and the Spencers, binding our families together like a fucking medieval alliance. King Louis and Marie Antoinette. Henry VIII and Catherine of Aragon. And me? I was the sacrificial lamb, sent to slaughter. All because they trusted George Burns.

And now I'm the idiot falling for his daughter. *Fell* for her. Still fucking falling.

It makes me sick. I clenched my fists so hard my knuckles turned white. My jaw locked so tight it ached. Because despite all of that, despite knowing exactly who she is now, I still want her.

I still fucking want her.

I want to hate her. I want to punish her, destroy her. I want to forget her.

But all I can think about is how badly I still fucking want to see her, hold her, touch her, love on her, kiss her until she's breathless until she *feels* what I feel—this fucking madness she's left me in.

Memories of her flood my mind, and I can't stop them. Flashbacks of our time together are like an iron grip around my throat, suffocating me. The way she looked at me. The way she laughs, low and throaty when she's genuinely amused, when she lets her guard down, like music I never wanted to stop hearing. The way she melted under me. The way she challenged me, the way she pushed back. That fire in her eyes when she thought I was being impossible. And that softness in them when she thought I wasn't looking.The way she feels underneath me, around me, how she melts for me.

None of that could've been fake. It couldn't have been.

How did I not see it?

How did I not put two and two together? *Burns.* The name that's been a stain on my family for twenty years. I've heard my father spit it out like venom more times than I can count. And yet, I didn't even *question* it when it came to her. Because I was blinded. I thought back to our conversations, to how effortlessly she made me talk. The way she got me to open up about things I never tell anyone. How did I not figure it out? And that's when it hit me.

I never really *knew* her. She made damn sure of that. I don't know anything about her.

Everything she's ever told me has been surface-level or work-related. Nothing deep. No family stories, no childhood memories. I was so caught up in the way she made me feel that I didn't realize how little she revealed about herself. She let me believe I was getting closer while keeping me at arm's length the entire time.

The car came to a stop outside the warehouse. Bruce and Chuck got out without a word. I didn't move. I ran my hands down my face, my entire body tense.

The silence inside the car was suffocating. I let my head fall back against the seat, staring at the ceiling. My fingers clenched into fists, then loosened, then clenched again. My jaw ached from grinding my teeth. I exhaled sharply and turned to Rick.

"If I ever see those fuckers again—"

"I promise, Clay. You won't." Rick's voice was steady, unshaken, the same way it had been for the past six years. He knows me better than I know myself sometimes—he has to. My dad hired him back when I was in my reckless playboy era, drowning in booze, partying too hard, and cycling through women like I had something to prove. I was the perfect target to get mugged, set up, or worse. Rick was supposed to keep me out of trouble, but over the years, he became more than just my bodyguard. He became my fixer, my reality check, the one person who didn't just follow orders blindly. He never hesitated to call me out when I needed it.

But this? This was different. This wasn't smoothing things over with an NDA or cleaning up some drunken mistake. This was hiring men to hunt someone down. And I knew he had a soft spot for Malinda. He was there all spring and summer, watching as she tangled herself into my life. He saw the stolen glances, the quiet touches, the way I fucking melted for her. He tried to talk me out of this, but I was too pissed off, too consumed by my own need for answers. I nearly fired him for hesitating.

What he doesn't know is the real reason behind it all. He doesn't know about her father. He doesn't know the wreckage George Burns left in his wake, the way his betrayal still poisons my family to this day. And I won't tell him. That's our shame to bear. Our fucking mistake for trusting the wrong man, for letting a silver-tongued con artist inside our ranks.

I grunted, my fingers digging into my temples, trying to rub the tension away. My head pounded, and my whole body felt tight like I'd been holding back a scream for hours.

I turned my head slightly, leveling my gaze at him. "Find me guys with some fucking decorum." My voice came out low and controlled, but it still carried the weight of everything pressing down on me.

I rubbed a hand down my face, trying to pull myself back into reality.

Rick nodded. "Got it."

Rick watched me for a moment before speaking.

"Today seemed rough. How are you dealing, man?"

I scoffed, shaking my head. "I don't even fucking know right now. I just need a drink."

Rick nodded knowingly. "Let's go to Tassels. A lap dance will do you some good."

I didn't answer immediately. My body was telling me to move, to do something before I spiral even further. I reached for the door handle, hesitating for just a second.

I should say no. I should go home. I should figure out my next move. But I don't. I can't.

Because I know the moment I'm alone, all I'll be able to think about is *her*. Because even as I sit here, seething in anger, drowning in betrayal, I already know that no drink, no lap dance, and no amount of distraction is going to make me forget Malinda Burns.

CHAPTER 33

MALINDA

I woke up to the low murmur of Amir's voice, the sound of him rescheduling meetings on his phone while still holding me against him. His body was warm, solid, and familiar. I stretched, and he glanced down at me before setting his phone aside, his full attention shifting to me.

"Good morning, boo."

I yawned. "Good morning," I mumbled, my voice thick with sleep. "What time is it?"

"It's 11:30. You slept so peacefully I didn't want to wake you."

I blinked up at him, processing the time. "Damn. I was exhausted."

"I bet you were." His voice was soft, but there was an undertone of concern. "How do you feel?" He was giving me his undivided attention, his voice soft, his eyes warm. I shifted to sit up, immediately regretting it as an ache spread through my body. I groaned. "I'm so freaking sore. I feel like I'm sixty."

"Well, to be fair, you had an intense day yesterday."

"Yeah... true."

I pulled myself out of bed, stretching as best I could before heading to the bathroom. I splashed cold water on my face, trying to push away the weight of everything from the day before. When I returned to my bedroom, Amir was perched on the edge of my bed, watching me with quiet intensity.

"Malinda?"

"Yeah?"

"Come back home with me. Pack up as much as you need, but let's leave here."

I froze for half a second before shaking my head. "Amir—"

"Can we talk about why you left in the first place?" His voice was gentle and calm, but there was no mistaking the frustration there. His eyes searched mine. "You snuck away in the middle of the night... because we kissed?"

I froze in place. The mention of it sent a rush of heat through me. Just thinking about that kiss made my stomach tighten and my pulse race. My knees felt weak, and I hated that he had this effect on me.

I swallowed hard. "I—I can't discuss this right now."

I turned toward the door, but Amir was up in an instant, his hand catching my arm—gently, but firmly enough that I couldn't just walk away from this.

"Why not, Malinda? Was it that unenjoyable?"

I felt his breath on my neck, and shivers ran down my spine. My heart pounded. The air between us was thick, electric. I struggled to find my voice, my mind a mess of warnings and desires. I could still taste the last time he kissed me.

"It wasn't," I admitted softly. My voice was barely above a whisper. How could I tell him that it was amazing? That I wanted him more than I should? That it shook me? Just thinking about kissing him causes my stomach to do flips and makes my knees weak. That being around him makes me feel like a schoolgirl. I know he likes me, and this will just make things so much more complicated. I can't get into another situation with a guy. I saw how things turned out with Clay.

I felt his breath on my skin, and shivers ran through me.

His grip on my arm tightened just slightly. "Then why did you leave me?" His voice was low and slow, sensual, deliberate, laced with something that made it impossible to ignore, wrapping around me, and pulling me in.

I opened my mouth, but no words came. He stepped closer, his fingers tilting my chin up, so I had no choice but to meet his gaze.

"What's complicated about it?" he asked. "We felt something... and we acted on it."

Before I could stop myself, I was leaning in. Or maybe he was. Our lips met and I was lost. His lips were on mine, warm, insistent, tasting, claiming. Slow at first, tentative. But the moment I responded—when I sighed against him when I opened for him—it turned into something urgent, raw, feverish.

One second, I was pressed against the wall, my fingers threading through his hair, my arms locking around his neck, pulling him closer. His hands were firm and sure, gripping my waist, pulling me in as if he needed me, as if I was the only thing keeping him steady. The next, we were tumbling onto the bed, and I was on top of him, my thighs straddling his waist, his hands running up my waist gripping me, guiding me. His lips found my neck, the spot that made my head tilt back, the moan slipping out before I could stop it.

The moment blurred—his hands roaming, our breaths heavy, ragged. He groaned, flipping me onto my back, his weight pressing into me, his hips grinding against mine. I felt the hard length of him through his jeans, pressing exactly where I needed him most, and I gasped at the friction. His mouth was on my breast, his tongue teasing, his hands kneading, exploring. Pleasure crashed over me, and I lost myself in it, in him. A moan escaped before I could stop it. I felt the deep, desperate ache between my thighs, felt the way his body responded to mine. My legs wrapped around his waist. It was dizzying. Addictive. Dangerous.

"A-Amir..." My voice was barely a breath.

"Yes, baby," he groaned against my skin, his voice rough, wanting. His lips trailing, sucking, branding me. He kissed along my collarbone, then my throat, before sucking just below my ear, and a sharp inhale turned into a helpless moan.

I was spiraling. I couldn't think straight. His body was heat and pressure and something dangerous, something I wanted too much. My fingers dug into his shoulders. My legs tightened around him, pulling him closer.

This was dangerous.

This was too much.

"Amir... stop. Please."

I was losing myself in him.

I had to stop this.

He froze instantly. His breath was heavy against my skin, his body tense with restraint. Slowly, he pulled back, his dark eyes searching mine, filled with need, confusion, and concern.

"What's wrong, boo?"

I pushed at his chest. He rolled off me, sitting up. He was so aroused I could feel it in the way his body vibrated, in the way he ran a hand down his face as if trying to get himself under control.

I swallowed hard and sat up, wrapping my arms around myself creating more distance between us. My body protested, my skin still burning where he had touched me.

"We can't do this." I needed space. I needed air.

I pushed off the bed and stepped onto the balcony, the cold December air hitting me like a slap, shocking me back into reality. I took deep, slow breaths, sucking in lungfuls of frigid air, trying to calm my racing heart. My body was still hot from his touch, my lips swollen, aching for more. I squeezed my eyes shut.

When I turned, Amir was standing in the doorway, watching me.

"Malinda... if you don't like it—"

"I didn't say that."

He looked bewildered. Then he ran a hand over his face, exhaling sharply. "You obviously don't, Malinda."

I shut my eyes again and covered my face with my hands. "I'm not good with feelings, Amir. I never have been. I have a ton of baggage, and I don't need things in my life getting any more complicated."

"Babe—"

"I'm a hot mess, Amir. You don't want this. I promise."

He took a step closer, his voice steady, sure. "Malinda... I really like you. I have for years, and I know you know it. I haven't exactly been subtle." He let out a weak chuckle, then his face softened. "The better I get to know you, the deeper I fall."

My stomach clenched.

"That being said," he continued, "I'm not going to force anything on you. If we kiss or anything else, it doesn't have to mean that I expect some kind of emotional commitment. We're two consenting adults. I'm not adding extra meaning to what does or doesn't happen between us. No pressure. No expectations."

I opened my mouth, but he wasn't finished.

"I want you to feel safe and comfortable with me. My house isn't a prison. You don't need to escape from it... or me. And you don't ever have to feel anxious about some horny dude cornering you and pressuring you for anything ever. I promise."

I exhaled shakily. His words were everything I needed to hear, but they also made it harder to resist him.

"Can I hug you?" he asked, a teasing edge to his voice. "I promise to keep my lips to myself."

I chuckled despite myself and nodded.

He pulled me into his arms, holding me close, tight and it felt... good. Too good. It felt like something deeper than our kiss, something intimate and safe. When he finally pulled away, he smiled softly.

"Okay," he said. "So let's pack up some stuff and go home. We can grab lunch on the way, or I can make something when we get back."

I sighed. "Okay, Amir."

As we moved back inside, the tension between us still crackled. I locked and secured the balcony door. Just having the door closed caused the tension between us to rise instantly again. He kept his distance, true to his word, but I could feel his presence, the way his eyes lingered on me. The pull between us was undeniable. Why am I so drawn to him? I glanced at him and could see that he felt it too. I have no idea how much longer I can fight this. He shifted uncomfortably and cleared his throat.

I'm gonna finish answering emails while you get set. Let me know when you're ready, Malinda.

I nodded and avoided locking eyes with him. I can't trust myself in this closed space with him. I haven't ever had anyone touch me with such affection the way Amir has. With Clay, it was pure eager desire, but Amir is so different. I feel like I'm falling for him. I quickly shook the thought out of my head. I need to focus on the tasks at hand, not daydreaming about being intimate with Amir.

I went into my closet and took a few deep breaths. I grabbed my duffel bag and 2 suitcases. I packed some essential outfit pieces, loungewear, intimates, shoes, and sweaters now that the weather was getting cold. I grabbed the duffel bag, went into my bathroom, and packed all of my hair care products, skincare products, makeup, and soaps. Amir had been great with letting me use whatever I needed but I'm tired of smelling like Old Spice.

I came out of the bathroom and Amir was perched on the corner of my bed still tapping away on his phone. I put all my luggage at the door, and I cleared my throat.

He addressed me without even looking up.

"Ready?"

"Yeah", I said softly. He glanced at my suitcases and smirked.

"You need all that boo?" He got up and walked over to me.

"I most definitely do. Clothes shoes and hair/skin care. I am not surviving on just Old Spice and musk anymore."

He grinned. "I thought you liked smelling like me. Rugged pine and musk, not your thing?" His voice was playful, but his gaze was heavy, lingering. I swallowed. I needed to get out of this room. As if our thoughts were synched, he took a step back, grabbed the handle of both of my suitcases, and opened the door of the bedroom to wheel them out.

"I think we should order something and pick it up on the way home. I have some things to do for work and I won't have time to cook when we get home. Sounds good?" He asked over his shoulder.

I cleared my throat.

"Yeah, that sounds great."

As we walked down the hall, I stopped at my server room. I grabbed some external hard drives, more USB drives, and cash from my safe. Amir stepped in behind me, his eyes widening at the wall of screens, the blinking towers, the intricate security feeds.

"Whoa. Boo, are you a hacker or something?"

I ignored the question, shoving the drives into my bag. I could feel his gaze still on me, lingering with unspoken questions.

"Come on," I said, walking past him.

He followed, but I could tell—this wasn't the last time he'd ask about it.

CHAPTER 34

AMIR

Over the next three weeks, Christmas crept into the house slowly, piece by piece. It started with the garland I strung along the staircase, then the twinkling lights I convinced Malinda to help me hang around the windows. She rolled her eyes but didn't fight me, and that felt like a victory.

For me, Christmas had always meant warmth, laughter, and family filling every space. It was the smell of cinnamon and pine, the sound of my mother humming in the kitchen, the chaos of kids tearing into gifts before dawn.

It was home.

And for the first time in years, my home didn't feel so empty.

Since she couldn't go out, we scrolled through online stores together, picking out gifts for my nieces, nephews, and cousins. She sat beside me on the couch, laptop balanced on her knees, carefully reading reviews and weighing options.

I watched the way she deliberated, her fingers tapping against the trackpad, her brow furrowing in concentration. She had an eye for quality, an instinct for the perfect thing. She pretended she didn't care, but she did.

That, too, felt like a victory.

"Get them something they'll actually use," Malinda muttered, scrolling past the plastic toy set I pointed out. "You know kids don't care about half this stuff after a week."

"You act like I don't know my own family," I teased, nudging her lightly. "Besides, what's Christmas without some unnecessary junk?"

She shot me a look, unimpressed. "I bet you were that kid, weren't you?"

I grinned. "Hell yeah. But I always made sure my sister got the good stuff. Gotta make sure she knew her worth early on. Teach 'em young."

Malinda bit back a soft smile and kept scrolling.

Every night leading up to Christmas, we watched a different holiday movie. She scoffed at the cheesy ones, but I caught her smiling more than once. I didn't call her out on it.

Some things were better left unspoken.

On Christmas Eve, I made hot chocolate, topping hers with extra whipped cream. We sat on the couch, lights from the tree flickering against the walls, *The Preacher's Wife* queued up and ready to play.

"What do you mean you've never seen this movie?" I stated, astonished. "This is a 90's classic!"

"Ok, Mr. Movie critic. Close your jaw. It better be as good as you're making it out to be."

I grinned. "Oh, it is. This was a holiday staple in the Stevens' household when I was a kid."

She rolled her eyes playfully as she took the hot chocolate from me and curled up, ready to watch the movie.

For a moment, I let myself imagine this was our life—quiet, easy, the kind of normal I never realized I wanted so badly. Whatever had her so guarded before seemed to soften. The weight she'd been carrying felt lighter. She seemed less preoccupied, like her mind wasn't somewhere else for once. It was like she let herself be here, fully present. With me. Just for a little while.

On Christmas morning I woke up early to cook. It was my favorite part. The smell of cinnamon and nutmeg filled the house as I flipped thick slices of French toast, the edges crisped to golden perfection. Eggs, maple sausage, fruit, and mimosas—I went all out.

When Malinda walked into the kitchen, sleepy-eyed in one of my hoodies, something deep and unshakable settled in my chest.

She was it.

She probably didn't even realize what it did to me, seeing her like that—comfortable, at ease, wearing something of mine like she belonged here. I tightened my grip on the spatula, forcing myself to play it cool.

"Merry Christmas, boo." I grinned, plating her food.

She took the plate and yawned. "You really did all this?"

"You're acting like you don't know me."

She sat, fork in hand, watching me for a beat. "Merry Christmas, Amir."

After breakfast, I gave her a small gift—something simple, a silver bracelet with a delicate engraving on the inside. I didn't expect much of a reaction, but when she traced her finger over it, quiet, something in her eyes softened.

"Amir..." she started, and I braced myself, half-expecting her to push it away. Instead, she pulled a box from beside her and handed it to me.

I hadn't expected a gift. I didn't think she'd go that far. When I unwrapped it and saw the monogrammed professional-grade chef's apron, I let out a low whistle.

"Damn, boo." I turned it over in my hands, weighing the heavy canvas, tracing the stitching of my initials, and admiring the leather detailing around the pockets. "This is..." I swallowed hard, gulping down my emotions so I wouldn't freak her out. "This is really nice."

I pulled her into a hug, tight and warm. She stiffened at first like she always did when caught off guard by touch, but then she melted into it. I felt her hands press lightly against my back, her face burying against my shoulder.

It was small, but it was *everything.*

New Year's Eve was quieter. I had an event to attend—a networking thing, full of polite smiles and empty conversations—but the whole time, I found myself checking my watch, thinking about Malinda alone in my house.

So, I left early.

When I walked through the door just before midnight, she was curled up on the couch with a book, and a half-empty glass of wine on the table. Her brows lifted. "You're home early."

"Yeah, well," I said, pulling a bottle of champagne from the fridge. "Thought I'd rather spend New Year's with someone who doesn't bore the hell out of me."

She huffed a small laugh, shaking her head, but she let me top up her glass.

The countdown started on TV, the hum of voices filling the room. When the ball dropped, I turned to her, and before I could overthink it, she kissed me. Soft, unhurried. A kiss meant just for us, in the quiet of my home, away from the world.

I wanted more. God, I wanted more. But I kept my promise—to myself, to her. I wouldn't push. I wouldn't make this mean something more than she was ready for.

"Happy New Year," she murmured, her fingers grazing my jaw.

"Happy New Year, boo."

We kissed a few more times that night, slow and lingering. And for the first time, when we went to bed, she didn't return to the guest room. She lay beside me, our hands brushing, our breaths evening out in the dark.

"You tired?" I asked softly.

"No," she admitted. "You?"

"No."

We talked for hours—about everything and nothing. I didn't ask about her past. She didn't offer. But she was there, fully present, and that was enough.

For now, that was enough.

CHAPTER 35

MALINDA

I t was Valentine's Day. Amir made me dinner, doing his best to keep things casual, to not get caught up in the romance of it all. But the effort was wasted—we both felt it thick in the air between us, simmering beneath every glance, every brush of our hands as we moved around his kitchen.

Wine always seemed to be the culprit in my reduced judgment. He poured a vintage, rich, and velvety, and we spent hours talking—about nothing, about everything—until the night stretched into the morning. Somewhere between laughter and longing, we found ourselves moving upstairs. My body was warm from the alcohol and his presence, but clarity hit when we reached the hallway. I turned toward my room, but Amir caught my wrist, his touch light yet certain.

Desire darkened his eyes. "Stay."

Before I could protest, he pulled me to him, his lips grazing mine with a featherlight touch. It was a whisper of a kiss, hesitant yet full of promise. My heart pounded as he pressed his forehead against mine, his breath warm against my lips. His fingers traced slow circles along my wrist, sending shivers up my spine.

I tilted my head slightly, and that was all the invitation he needed. His lips found mine again, lingering this time, savoring the moment rather than rushing through it. The kiss deepened, not in hunger but in tenderness, in the slow unraveling of restraint we both had held onto for so long. His hands cupped my face, his thumbs brushing against my cheekbones as if memorizing every curve.

My breath hitched as he pulled me closer, my body molding against his. His lips moved down to my jaw, then lower, tracing the line of my neck with barely-there kisses that set my skin aflame. I sighed, my fingers curling into the fabric of his shirt. Every touch, every press of his lips spoke of devotion, of unspoken emotions that neither of us dared to put into words.

"Amir..." His name left my lips in a breathless whisper, and he stilled, lifting his gaze to mine. The tenderness in his eyes made my chest tighten. He was looking at me like I was something sacred, something to be cherished.

He took my hand and led me to his bed, easing me down onto the mattress with such care that it made my throat constrict. He hovered over me, studying my face, giving me every opportunity to change my mind. But I didn't want to. Not anymore.

Before I could protest, he pulled me to him, his lips claiming mine in a kiss that sent fire through my veins. My resistance crumbled instantly. One kiss turned into another, deeper, hungrier, until the next thing I knew, I was straddling him, my fingers dragging through his beard, savoring the feel of it against my skin as his hands gripped my waist.

Our breathing was heavy but in sync, the weight of everything unspoken pressing down on us. As my mind sobered, panic crept in. This was too real, too much. I tried to pull back, but Amir's grip on my hips tightened, grounding me.

"Baby... you can't keep leaving me like this," he murmured, tugging gently at my curls before kissing me again.

"Amir... I..."

"Nah, baby. You know how I feel about you. You know how I've always felt about you. Just give us a shot."

I sat up, my breath catching as his arousal pressed against me through the barrier of our clothes. The heat pooling between my thighs spread to him, and I felt him thicken beneath me. His hands roamed my body, worshiping every curve. Desperate for more.

"Give me a chance, boo," he whispered, kissing my neck, his lips leaving a trail of fire in their wake.

I wanted to resist, to say something to break the moment before we went too far, but my body betrayed me. I pressed against him, seeking relief from the ache he stirred in me. He groaned, gripping my hips tighter.

"You like me, right?" His voice was rough with frustration and longing. I hesitated, then nodded.

"Then what's the problem, Malinda? Why won't you let yourself have this?"

Instead of answering, I kissed him deeply, pouring every ounce of my turmoil into it. If I spoke, I'd have to tell him the truth—that I was falling for him, that I'd been here before and it didn't end well, that I was scared, that Clay was dangerous and would hurt him if he knew how much I cared.

He pulled away and I kissed his neck. He groaned.

"Don't tease me, baby. I can't take it. I wanna make love to you. I can't hide it anymore. I wanna touch the deepest part of your soul." He ran his hands up my body. I had no response. Every moment we've spent together these past 4 months, as we tiptoed around our attraction to each other, has led us to this moment. I know he's been trying to be respectful of my boundaries. Especially after what happened after our first kiss. But tonight, the lust and longing in his eyes was unmistakable.

Amir took my silence as permission and flipped me onto my back, spreading my legs with ease. The way he looked at me, like I was something precious and sacred, sent a shiver through me.

He kissed me again, deep and slow, his hands mapping the contours of my body with reverence. My pulse quickened as he brushed his fingers down my arms, and my waist, his touch igniting heat in its wake. He slipped the straps of my top down my shoulders, pressing soft kisses to my collarbone, each one more intoxicating than the last.

"You want me, baby?" His voice was hoarse, thick with need.

"Yes," I admitted in a whisper.

He kissed down my body. By the time his lips found my stomach, my breathing was ragged, and my body aching for more. He groaned,

He kissed the inside of my thigh while peeling away my shorts, his hands gripping my hips as he settled between them. The first brush of his tongue against me sent a shockwave through my system, making me arch off the bed. He groaned his satisfaction and pressed his mouth to my core. He took his time, savoring every reaction, murmuring sweet words against my skin, his hands gripping my thighs as he feasted on me, savoring every reaction.

I came too fast, overwhelmed by months of tension, finally snapping. He licked his lips, watching me with a heated gaze.

"Tell me you want me."

I pulled him over me, feeling him hard and insistent at my entrance. I bit his ear and whispered, "I want you."

His breath hitched. "What do you want me to do to you, Malinda?"

"Fuck me, Amir."

He pushed into me slowly, cursing softly at the tight heat wrapping around him. He stretched me perfectly, filling every space inside me. He stilled, giving me time to adjust, then moved—grinding, teasing, pushing me to the edge all over again.

"God, Amir..."

He kissed me, worshiped me, touched me in ways that weren't just physical. He made love to me like he was trying to brand himself into my soul. His strokes were deep, controlled, and maddeningly perfect. Every roll of his hips sent another wave of pleasure crashing over me.

He stopped suddenly, flipping me onto my stomach. I gasped as he entered me again from behind, pressing his body flush against mine, his fingers lacing with mine. He kissed the back of my neck, whispering sweet words into my ear.

"Damn, my love... I'm bouta come."

I reached back, stopping him. "Not yet."

"Please, don't stop me, boo." He kissed me, desperate, pleading.

"Let me ride you."

He pulled out and lay back, breathing hard. I straddled him, taking my time as I sank onto him again. He groaned, his hands gripping my hips, his head falling back in bliss.

I rode him slowly, savoring the way he felt inside me. When I clenched around him, his body went rigid, his breath shuddering. His hands trembled against my skin as he lost control, pulsing deep within me.

I collapsed on top of him, and he wrapped his arms around me, holding me close. For a brief moment, everything felt right. He was still inside me, his warmth cocooning me, and I could almost pretend we existed in a world where this wasn't dangerous.

But then reality crashed down.

I pulled away, the weight of what we'd done settling in my chest like a boulder. Now that we've done this, and crossed this boundary, nothing will ever be the same. We're in too deep. Amir watched me, still basking in the afterglow. He reached for me, tugging at my curls playfully.

"That was amazing, baby." He kissed my forehead. "How are you feeling?"

I sat up, slipping out of bed. "Fine."

His brows furrowed. "Where are you going?"

"Out."

"But it's five a.m." His voice was tinged with frustration. "Malinda, don't do this."

I didn't answer. I pulled on my clothes and moved toward the door.

He sat up, rubbing his face. "I hate when you act like this, Malinda."

I ignored him, forcing myself to move quickly. I showered, scrubbing away the scent of him, trying not to think about what had just happened. I should've never done this. Because now, when I leave, it'll hurt more—for both of us. And I have to leave him. I can't drag him deeper into this mess of a situation. I keep repeating the same patterns over and over with these men in my life. What is wrong with me? I kept kicking myself mentally as I dressed.

Amir wants a girlfriend. I'm not her.

By the time I was dressed, Amir was waiting at the door, arms crossed, his expression unreadable.

"Stop running from this," he said, his voice low, edged with something raw. "We both have strong feelings for each other. There's nothing wrong with that. So stop fighting it."

I swallowed hard. "Amir, I have to go."

"Go where?! It's six in the morning. We just made love, Malinda. You don't even want to talk about it. You just wanna run. Again."

I clenched my jaw. "I don't need this right now."

I pushed past him and climbed into the waiting cab, leaving behind the one man who had ever truly seen me.

CHAPTER 36

AMIR

The back door slammed shut, and I felt a sharp sting of hurt and annoyance. Did I push her too far? I don't understand Malinda at all. She broke the boundary and kissed me last month—so why is she running away now? I've been letting her take the lead on anything intimate, giving her space, never pressuring her.

Finally connecting with her in such an intimate way was everything I dreamed it would be. The image of her riding me, her body moving with mine, is something I'll never forget. But what am I supposed to do now? I never thought past a moment like this. If I had it my way, I'd ask her to be my girl and then marry her. But if Malinda freaked out over something as small as a kiss, she'd probably leave the country if I even mentioned anything about marriage.

I tried to wash up and catch some sleep. We did not sleep all night. I tossed and turned until 8:30 and then tried to power through some work. That was a joke—I couldn't focus on anything. My head was too full of her. I had a meeting with the marketing team at 10, but my mind wasn't in it. I listened with half an ear as they discussed campaign strategies for the upcoming quarter, nodding along while my thoughts kept drifting back to

Malinda. Had she eaten? Was she thinking about me? Was she regretting last night? Every time my phone buzzed, my heart jumped, but it was never her—just emails, Slack messages, or one of my casual hookups checking in. I ignored them all. None of them mattered anymore.

By noon, I gave up pretending to be productive and decided to go to the grocery store. Bad idea. The entire place was still decked out in Valentine's Day decorations—heart-shaped balloons, discounted candy, and those ridiculous stuffed bears holding "I love you" signs. It felt like a cruel joke. Just yesterday, Malinda had been in my arms, and now I was here, alone, glaring at a wall of pink and red. I grabbed a frozen pizza and a six-pack, avoiding eye contact with the happy couples roaming the aisles.

Back home, I threw the pizza in the oven and sat at the kitchen table, staring at my phone. I'd reached for it a dozen times already today, wanting to text Malinda, wanting to demand an explanation, but every time I stopped myself. She needed space. But the longer the silence stretched, the more pissed off I got.

By the time the sun started setting, my resolve cracked. I needed to talk to someone, so I texted my twin sister.

Amir: You busy?

Aria: Nope, what's up?

Amir: Your gender is confusing as hell, Ri.

Aria: Oh boy, hold on. Let me put the twins down.

I smirked despite myself. A minute later, my phone rang.

"Lady troubles?" she asked as soon as I picked up.

"Sorta."

"What did you do and who did you do it to?"

I rolled my eyes. "I didn't do anything... it's just that girl."

"Lorraine?"

"Nah... the one from work."

"Ohhh, Malinda," she said, drawing it out like she already knew this was going to be a mess. "Okay, what happened? Did she finally agree to go out with you?"

I had to choose my words carefully. I told my sister everything, but I promised Malinda I'd be discreet.

"I made her dinner last night and we hooked up."

"Okay, so what's the problem? Sounds like a great Valentine's Day."

I exhaled. "She got all weird after."

"What do you mean?"

"She ran out on me right after we—"

"Oh God, stop. Spare me the details."

I smirked despite myself. "You asked."

"I asked what you meant, not for an explicit play-by-play of you getting your freak on."

I laughed.

"Freak on?!" I could practically hear her eyes rolling.

"So, it sucked? It's cool, bro, it takes time to learn."

I groaned. "Shut up! It did not suck. I know what I'm doing."

Aria cackled. "Alright, alright. So, what's the problem? You finally had your big, romantic moment, and Malinda did what Malinda does best—ran for the hills?"

"It's not funny."

"It's a little funny. She's been curving you for like 5 years."

I exhaled sharply. " Six...But it's different this time, Aria. I know she—"

"Oh, please, Manny. Different how? Because she doesn't feed your hopeless romantic delusions? Because she won't give you the picture-perfect love story you've been chasing since high school?"

"I'm in love with her. I want her to be my girlfriend." She sighed heavily

"So, ask her. See what she does after you profess your love" she stated sarcastically.

"That's not fair."

"No, what's not fair is you continuously throwing yourself at someone who's made it painfully clear she can't—no, won't—give you what you want.

And instead of accepting that, you keep letting her string you along because you think if you love her hard enough, she'll magically change."

I was silent, jaw tight. Aria sighed.

"Look, I love you, idiot. But you do this every time. You go all in, head over heels, and then get mad when the other person doesn't match your level of intensity. That's the problem with you. Since we were kids, you always fall in love with or go after the girls who either treat you horribly, don't deserve you, or act like they don't want you. Meanwhile, you ignore the girls who are DYING to be with you. Remember Lexi?"

"Lexi had her issues, and I just wasn't into her. But that was back in high school, and that's not the point."

"It is tho. Malinda's not even pretending to be in this the way you are. She's got one foot out the door at all times. Homegirl has commitment issues."

I sighed heavily, weighing my sister's words.

"I don't know what to do next. I'm trying to give her space, but I want her to realize that I'm the perfect guy for her. It's so annoying because we spend so much time together anyway."

Aria sighed. "Have you two communicated about exclusivity?"

I rubbed my face. "Kinda."

"Okay. What's her take?"

"She said she has too much baggage and her life is a mess right now. But I don't care about all that. I just want her."

"You're literally just proving my earlier points." Aria groaned, exasperated.

"You don't know her like I do."

"You're right. But I know you. And I know that no matter how much you try to downplay it, this is killing you. So, what are you gonna do about it?"

I pinched the bridge of my nose. "I don't know."

"Yes, you do. You just don't like the answer."

I swallowed hard, holding my head in my hands. The house felt too big, too empty. "I just thought last night meant something."

Her voice softened. "I'm sure it did. To you. But you need to ask yourself—when has Malinda ever let you believe she wanted something serious?

And more importantly, how much longer are you willing to keep doing this dance with her?"

I closed my eyes. "I don't know."

Aria was quiet for a second before she said, "Are you sure it's not just lust?"

"It's love, Ri."

She sighed dramatically. "I think you should give yourself some space from her. And if you still feel the same, then talk to her about it. I mean, she told you clearly that she's not looking for commitment, but you're willing to do this situationship thing because you're hoping she changes her mind. That's on you, bro."

I groaned. "Fine, I'll try to give her some space."

"Good. Now go eat something. And stop moping because you're lovesick over a woman who doesn't want to be loved. It's pathetic."

She hung up, leaving me alone with my thoughts. My sister was annoying. And right. So damn right. Giving Malinda space? Easier said than done.

Chapter 37

Malinda

The train ride was long, but I barely noticed. My body moved on autopilot, the rhythmic rumbling beneath me and the occasional metallic screech of the tracks lulling me into a state somewhere between exhaustion and hyper-awareness.

It was still dark when I left Amir's house, slipping out past him. Leaving him standing there. I stopped myself mid-thought. I can't go there right now. I hadn't allowed myself to think about the night before. The feel of Amir's lips, the heat between us, the way I lost myself in him until panic took over. I shoved those thoughts deep down, locking them in the same place I had stored every other feeling I couldn't afford to acknowledge.

I needed to escape. This time, it wasn't just from my tangled mess of emotions toward him—it was everything. The fact that my investigation had gone stagnant. The fact that every lead I'd followed since May had led me absolutely nowhere. The fact that I had become *comfortable*, hiding away in Amir's home while the truth about my father haunted me.

I stared out the window as the scenery blurred past, gray skies stretching endlessly over barren winter trees. I should have felt something—anticipation, maybe. Hope, at the very least. But instead, all I felt was dread.

What if this is another dead end? What if I've been chasing a ghost this entire time? What if my father is alive? It had been easier to believe my father was dead than to believe that he had planned and prepared to abandon me.

I clenched my jaw and turned my gaze away from my reflection in the glass. I didn't have the luxury of doubting myself. Not now.

The train hissed to a stop, and I stepped onto the platform. Wilmington, Delaware. The air was sharp, biting through the layers of my coat and scarf as I pulled them tighter around me. I shoved my hands into my pockets and walked with purpose, but the pit in my stomach only deepened the closer I got to my destination.

The address was easy enough to find. A straight walk from the station, past a couple of rundown storefronts and a gas station with flickering neon lights. But when I finally reached the location, my stomach dropped.

It wasn't an apartment building anymore. It was a damn parking garage.

I stared at the massive concrete structure, my breath coming out in quick, uneven clouds of condensation. *No. No, no, no.*

This couldn't be right.

I double-checked the address, my hands shaking slightly as I pulled the slip of paper from my bag. *2025 Fairview Drive.* That's what was written, clear as day. But the building was gone. Completely erased, like it had never even existed.

I paced along the sidewalk, my boots crunching against patches of ice and slush. Maybe someone around here remembers. Maybe there's a lead I haven't considered yet.

I spent hours searching. Asking around, striking up conversations in corner stores, diners, and even a laundromat. I switched on my old persona—the one that was quick-witted, charming, and able to get people talking without them realizing they were giving anything away. But every person I spoke to had the same response.

"That old building? Torn down years ago." "Never heard of a Sergei." "Try city hall, maybe they have records."

By lunchtime, my fingers were numb, my patience threadbare. I stopped at a diner and sipped lukewarm coffee, scrolling through old public records, property sales, *anything* that could give me a clue as to where Sergei might have gone.

"I don't have time for this," I muttered under my breath, refreshing the search page on my phone for the tenth time. My knee bounced under the diner table, fingers tapping anxiously against my coffee cup. Every second wasted felt like another door closing.

By five o'clock, my entire body ached with exhaustion and bitter disappointment.

Nothing. I had nothing. *Another dead end.*

I trudged back toward the train station, the wind picking up, biting at my exposed skin. The adrenaline I'd been running on all day was gone, leaving only fatigue in its place. My limbs felt heavy; my thoughts sluggish.

The train station was relatively empty, save for a few other stragglers waiting for the last evening routes. A group of teenagers huddled in a corner, laughing over something on one of their phones. A man in a heavy coat sat a few rows away from me, nodding off. A woman balanced a toddler on her lap, humming softly while rocking him back and forth.

I sank into the stiff plastic seat, letting out a long breath.

The train arrived, and I boarded without thinking, dropping into an empty seat by the window. As we pulled away from the platform, I let my forehead rest against the cold glass.

The train rattled beneath me, a dull vibration in my bones. The heater was on full blast, but I still couldn't stop shivering. My fingers were stiff inside my gloves, my toes were numb in my boots. My body ached from the constant motion—hours of walking, stopping in random shops and diners, asking pointless questions to people who didn't know or didn't care to know.

This was all a mistake.

All of it. I was out all damn day trying to track down Serge. *If my dad knew that one day I might need this, then why was this guy so hard to find?* Frustration burned hot in my chest. My fingers tightened around the strap of my bag. *Why give me the damn card if it led to nowhere? Why mention Sergei at all if he was just another dead end?*

The months I had spent chasing down leads that led nowhere weighed heavy. The time I had wasted believing I could find the answers to something that had happened over a decade ago.

And what if I did? What if I eventually found Sergei and he confirmed what I had always feared?

That my father wasn't gone. That he abandoned me, choosing a con over his own kid.

I squeezed my eyes shut. The thought left a bitter taste in my mouth.

No. I couldn't afford to think like that.

I just needed to regroup. Make a new plan.

The train jerked as we neared Baltimore, and I sighed, pressing my forehead against the cold glass of the window. The city lights blurred together, streaks of yellow and red bleeding into the darkness. My reflection stared back at me—tired eyes, chapped lips, and exhaustion written all over my face.

I had nothing to show for today. No leads. No information. Just more questions and a creeping sense of hopelessness that I was running in circles.

The cold was sharper when I stepped off the train, slicing through my coat like it wasn't even there. The temperature had dropped significantly in the hours I had been gone. I tugged my coat tighter around me and called an Uber, too tired to care about the extra cost.

Stuffing my hands into my pockets, I made my way through the near-empty station and to the ride-share pick-up lane. My joints were stiff from the hours of travel, my knees locking with every step.

By the time I arrived at Amir's house, I felt like I had been run over. Every muscle in my body ached, my head was pounding, and my fingers were still numb from the cold. I trudged up the steps, unlocking the door with the key he had given me weeks ago, grabbing a package left on the stoop as I went.

The warmth of his house wrapped around me instantly, and I felt relieved to be back here.

That terrified me more than anything.

I sighed, putting the box down, peeling off my coat, and kicking off my boots, the scent of dinner lingering in the air.

CHAPTER 38

MALINDA

I shuffled down the hall toward the kitchen, my body heavy with exhaustion, but the moment I saw him, I stopped cold.

Amir was in the living room, shirtless, wearing a pair of loose gray sweats, his toned arms resting lazily on the couch. The low flicker of the television cast soft shadows over his face, his expression unreadable. But my body didn't need to read it.

The flashbacks hit like a punch to the gut. His lips on mine, the way his hands explored my body with deliberate, aching reverence. The warmth of his breath against my skin, the way I came undone in his arms. My knees nearly buckled under me, and I gripped the counter, grounding myself.

Get it together, Malinda.

I took a deep breath and glanced at the kitchen island. My stomach twisted when I saw a pizza sitting there.

Amir ordered out?

That was...unexpected. He never ordered out. And definitely not something as basic as a plain takeout pizza. This was a man who took pleasure in seasoning cast iron pans, in slow-cooking sauces to perfection, in plating a dish like it belonged in a five-star restaurant.

This wasn't just about food.

I moved to the fridge, grabbed the pitcher of his homemade iced tea, and poured myself a glass, the clinking of ice the only sound between us. The silence was unbearable.

I finally spoke. "Hey."

He didn't look at me. His eyes stayed fixed on the TV, his fingers tapping idly against his thigh.

"Hey."

His voice was cold. Emotionless. It stung more than I was prepared for.

I clenched my jaw and kept my composure, refusing to let the hurt show. "Do you mind if I grab a few slices?"

His eyes didn't waver from the screen. "All yours."

My chest tightened, anger bubbling up beneath the surface. Why did he have this effect on me? Why did his distance bother me this much?

I threw the pizza in the microwave, watching the seconds tick down, my fingers gripping the counter as I tried to push down the irrational urge to explain myself—to tell him why things had to be this way.

You can't, Malinda. You can't drag him into this.

I took my plate and settled on the couch near him. The moment I sat, I felt it—the tension. It filled the space between us, thick and charged, electric. He shifted slightly, adjusting his position, but still refused to look at me.

A few minutes passed. I couldn't take it anymore.

"Amir...about earlier..."

"Don't sweat it."

His voice was clipped, dismissive. I exhaled sharply, pressing my lips together. He was making this difficult.

"Can you please just look at me, Amir?"

His jaw flexed. His grip on the remote tightened. But finally, he turned, pinning me with a glare that sent a shiver down my spine.

"Why?" His voice was low, and controlled, but there was a sharp edge beneath it. "What is that gonna change?"

His eyes burned into mine, and for the first time since this morning, I saw it—the raw emotion swirling beneath his frustration. The hurt.

It hit me like a gut punch.

I had done this.

I had made him feel this way.

And yet, despite all the logical reasons I had for keeping my distance, I found myself leaning in. My body betrayed every ounce of self-preservation I had left.

I kissed him.

He groaned against my lips, his body tensing before melting into me. The kiss deepened, raw, desperate, familiar. The taste of wine from earlier still lingered between us, warm and intoxicating. My fingers instinctively curled into the back of his head, tugging gently, feeling the slight hitch in his breath.

But then, just as quickly as he gave in, he pulled away.

"Stop it, Malinda." His voice was rough, strained. He exhaled harshly, shaking his head.

"Amir, I did enjoy it," I whispered, my heart pounding. "I get weak in the knees just thinking about this morning. It was...amazing."

His chest rose and fell heavily as he stared at me.

"Then why did you run out of here and leave me?"

I swallowed hard. I couldn't give him the answer he wanted.

"I just had to."

His lips curled into something bitter, something that made my stomach sink.

"Here we go again," he muttered under his breath, shaking his head as he stood up abruptly. "I can't believe I'm sitting here, begging and being all emotional over you."

I opened my mouth, but nothing came out.

He exhaled sharply, running a hand over his beard before turning away. Without another word, he headed upstairs, his steps slow, deliberate.

I sat there, the weight of the evening pressing down on me, my food untouched.

Eventually, I forced myself to eat, but everything tasted bitter in my mouth.

CHAPTER 39

MALINDA

When I finally dragged myself upstairs, the house was silent except for the distant hum of the shower running in Amir's bathroom. My feet hesitated outside his bedroom door, my heart pounding harder than it should have, my body torn between fleeing and surrendering. I should just go to bed. I should let him cool off. I should give myself space to think. But my limbs had a mind of their own, moving before my logic could stop them. I stepped into the room hearing his shower playlist low and somber as my feet moved me to his bathroom door. Every logical part of me screamed to turn around, to crawl into the guest bed, to put distance between us. But my body had its own ideas.

I stepped inside, drawn to the sound of running water like a moth to a flame.

Steam rolled through the bathroom, the air thick with heat, curling around my skin like an invitation. The faint scent of his body wash—deep musk and cedar, attacked my senses, something uniquely him. Amir was in the shower, under the spray, his broad, muscular back turned to me, head tilted forward, droplets cascading over his sculpted shoulders, gliding down the deep ridges of his spine. He was beautiful, every inch of him was raw power and fluid grace.

He hadn't noticed me yet. I should have walked away, but instead, I reached for the hem of my shirt, pulled it over my head, and stripped out of the rest of my clothes, letting them fall silently to the floor. My breath was uneven, anticipation and nerves tingling inside me. This wasn't me. This wasn't the plan. But right now, I didn't care. I needed him.

I stepped into the shower. The moment the warm spray hit my skin; Amir turned. His dark eyes widened slightly, his sharp gaze locking onto mine.

His whole body tensed. Water beaded on his skin, running down the ridges of his abs, pooling at the deep V-cut of his waist.

I moved closer, placing tentative hands on his chest, my fingers trailing over the firm muscle, the smooth heat of his damp skin. I leaned up, trying to kiss him, but he caught my chin between his fingers, holding me just out of reach.

His dark eyes scanned my face, his breathing uneven, jaw tight.

"Malinda..." His voice was raw, as if he didn't trust himself to speak.

My heart pounded. "I'm sorry, Amir. I didn't mean to hurt you. I just...had to go... I wish you could understand." My voice was unsteady. I wanted him to understand, even if I couldn't fully explain.

He released my chin. Holding my gaze searching for what, I had no clue. The rest of the soap suds rinsed off his body, trailing down his thighs. His expression was unreadable, but something flickered in his gaze—an emotion I couldn't name, something deeper than frustration or desire.

I suddenly felt exposed in a way I wasn't used to. My impulse had led me here, but now, standing under the hot water, inches away from him, my vulnerability felt suffocating. I swallowed hard and turned to leave.

Before I could step out, he grabbed me—gently but firmly—pulling me back to him. He said nothing at first, just took me in—slowly, hungrily.

"You drive me crazy, you know that?" he murmured, more to himself than to me. Then, without another word, he pulled me into him, crushing his lips to mine, urgent, searching, devouring. The warmth of his skin met mine, and I melted into his embrace before I could stop myself.

His kiss was deep, and consuming, his grip strong and sure. His hands slid down my back, gripping my hips, pressing me against his hard, aching body. The heat of him, the way he fit so perfectly against me, sent my mind spinning.

Then, without breaking the kiss, he reached behind me, grabbing the shower puff and soap.

He pulled away. My breaths were shallow. My lips were swollen, my breath stolen.

I watched as he lathered up the shower puff, taking his time, his movements deliberate.

His eyes flickered up to mine, filled with something heavy, something deep, and then he started washing me.

Slow, methodical, worshipful. His movements were unhurried, and deliberate, igniting goosebumps in its wake.

He started with my hand, bringing it to his lips before scrubbing up my arm, over my shoulder, and then down to my collarbone. The gentle friction sent shivers through me. His touch was reverent, a stark contrast to the storm that had been between us only an hour ago. When he ran the puff over my breasts, my nipples pebbled under the light abrasion, my breath hitching.

His eyes darkened as he slowed down. He took his time, circling each peak with maddening slowness.

"You like that, baby?" His voice was molten, thick with lust.

I bit my lip, nodding. A wicked smirk tugged at his lips before he continued, moving lower, focused, as if he were memorizing every inch of me.

He turned me away from him, dragging the puff down my back, over the curve of my ass, then lower.

He pulled me to him, pressing my back against his chest, his erection hard against me. I trembled, feeling my body respond to him, my resolve breaking. The water beat down on us, the steam wrapping us in a cocoon.

"You're shaking," he murmured into my ear, his lips brushing my neck, his free hand trailing down my body. He reached down, lifting one of my legs and resting it on the shower bench. The moment his hand brushed my inner thigh, my pulse skyrocketed. He let the puff fall, his fingers replacing it. Soft at first, then firmer, his fingers pressed against my folds, teasing, testing.

"Show me how you like it," he murmured, his breath hot against my neck.

I shuddered. His voice was thick, laced with desire. My hands covered his, guiding his fingers in slow circles, gasping when he applied pressure exactly where I needed it. His free arm wrapped around my waist, securing me to him as he stroked me, his touch skilled, and patient.

"That's it," he whispered against my skin. "Take what you need, baby. Let me make you feel good." His mouth traced slow, wet kisses along my shoulder.

My head fell back against his shoulder, my body trembling.

"Fuck, Malinda," he groaned, his grip tightening. "You're so damn perfect."

I whimpered as the pleasure built, higher and higher trying to hold in the moans clawing at my throat, but when he tapped my clit just right, a sharp gasp escaped me.

He groaned low, his lips grazing my ear "You like that?"

I whimpered in response.

He turned me back around to face him, our eyes locking. The burning intensity in his gaze made my breath catch. Then, slowly, he knelt before me, kissing his way down my stomach, down my hip, down to the aching space between my thighs. I watched as he lifted my leg and draped it over his shoulder.

I barely had time to brace myself before his tongue met me. I gasped, gripping his shoulders as he licked and sucked, his hands gripping my thighs, keeping me in place. My head fell back against the tile as waves of pleasure rolled through me. The world melted away—there was only his mouth, his hands, the devastating skill of his tongue. I shattered against him, my body trembling, my fingers gripping his wet curls.

He stood, his hands sliding up my body, anchoring me to him as he lifted me, pinning me between his body and the cool tile of the shower wall. He kissed me deeply, swallowing my soft whimpers, his erection teasing my entrance.

"Tell me you want this," he demanded, his breath ragged.

"I want this," I gasped.

That was all he needed. With one slow thrust, he filled me. His lips found mine, hungry and desperate.

A strangled moan left my lips as he stretched me, his rhythm measured but deep. His forehead pressed against mine, our breaths mingling, his hands gripping my thighs to keep me in place.

My nails clawed at his back; my moans swallowed by his mouth. He set a rhythm, rolling his hips with precision, each stroke pushing me closer to the edge.

The pleasure was unbearable, overwhelming, an all-consuming fire. And then he hit something deep inside me, something devastatingly perfect, and my world shattered.

"Amir," I cried out, my climax ripping through me, my body spasming around him.

I didn't mean to say it.

Didn't even realize the words had left my lips until I heard myself whispering, "I love you."

His rhythm faltered. His grip tightened. A shaky breath left his lips as he buried himself deeper inside me, his body trembling. Then, with a ragged groan, he lost control, thrusting harder, deeper, faster, chasing his release until he shattered with me, his voice raw in my ear.

"I love you too, baby. Oh, I love you so much."

We stumbled out of the shower, collapsing onto his bed in a tangle of limbs dripping and breathless. My limbs felt like jelly, my chest rising and falling in sync with his. He wrapped his arms around me, his hold protective, like he was afraid to let me go.

He kissed me then, slow and deep, like he was sealing a promise.

My body was spent, but my mind was racing.

I wanted to run. I wanted to take the words back.

As if sensing my inner turmoil, Amir tightened his hold on me, his hand slowly tracing up my body, grounding me. His lips pressed soft, lingering kisses to my shoulder, his breath warm against my skin.

"You're thinking too hard," he murmured.

I swallowed, staring at the ceiling, unsure what to say.

He shifted, rolling onto his side so he could look at me, really look at me. His fingers brushed over my cheek, down my jaw, tracing me like he wanted to memorize every inch.

"You okay, baby?" His voice was soft, thick with sleep but laced with something deeper.

I could only nod, afraid my voice would betray me.

He chuckled, pressing a lingering kiss to my forehead, his hand still resting at my waist, holding me close.

As his breathing slowed, drifting into sleep, I stayed awake, my heart pounding.

I messed up.

There was no undoing it.

I had let myself love him.

And now, I would have to break his heart.

CHAPTER 40

MALINDA

The next morning, I woke up still naked in Amir's bed, but he was nowhere to be found. The room was dimly lit with the early morning sun, and for a brief second, I let myself believe everything was normal. The sheets beside me were cool, the absence of his warmth making my stomach knot. I glanced at the clock on his nightstand—7:32 AM. The familiar scent of breakfast drifted through the air, a mixture of eggs, cinnamon, and fresh-brewed coffee. Before I could move, he walked in, balancing a breakfast tray piled with food with the ease of someone who had done this a hundred times before.

"Good morning, baby." His voice was warm, still thick with sleep, full of something deep and rich.

Memories of last night flooded back, making my stomach twist. My whispered confession. His unhesitating response. His arms were around me like they belonged there.

I swallowed hard. "Morning." I pulled the covers up over my chest, suddenly feeling too exposed.

I should have left while he was asleep. I had stayed too long already.

He set the tray down and leaned in to kiss me, slow and lingering. I let him, but my body tensed against the tenderness. He didn't seem to notice.

"I just put together something real quick for you."

I eyed the spread—pancakes, scrambled eggs, turkey bacon, fresh fruit. Even my coffee was made exactly how I liked it. It was thoughtful. Too thoughtful.

"This is quick?" I quipped, trying to keep the mood light.

He chuckled, "You know I'm extra."

I blushed, looking down, suddenly fixated on my plate.

"Thank you. You didn't have to do all this."

"It's nothing, baby. Enjoy." He ran a hand over my curls before stepping back. "I gotta go into the office early today, so I won't be able to join you for breakfast."

"It's okay."

I watched as his shirtless back, sweats hanging low on his hips, moved to his closet, grabbing a fresh suit from his wardrobe. I'd seen him in suits countless times, but this morning, something was different. Maybe it was the way he selected his tie, the way his movements carried a quiet contentment.

I forced myself to focus on cutting into my pancakes, pretending like I didn't notice the way he moved around the room, the way my body still hummed from his touch.

When he stepped out of the closet in his navy-blue suit, adjusting the cuffs of his shirt, I made the mistake of looking up.

Damn.

I'd seen Amir in a suit more times than I could count, but today, I felt like I was seeing him for the first time. The crisp tailoring, the sharp angles, the effortless confidence he carried—it made my pulse skip in a way I refused to acknowledge.

He caught me watching him in the mirror and smirked. "You like your man in a suit, baby?"

My man. My chest felt tight. He was already talking as if last night had sealed something between us. My heart clenched painfully. Why did he have to say that? Why did he have to ruin this?

I swallowed and quickly turned back to my breakfast; my appetite suddenly nonexistent.

Moments later, I felt the bed dip as he sat next to me. He tilted my chin up and kissed me deeply, his fingers brushing against my cheek, his warmth anchoring me to this moment. I melted into it before I could stop myself.

"I love you so much," he murmured against my lips.

And just like that, the spell was broken. The words hit me like a knife to the gut.

My stomach clenched painfully. Why did he have to say that? Why couldn't he just leave it unspoken, let it hang in the air between us, unacknowledged? Everything was already unraveling, and he had to make it worse by putting words to it.

He kissed me again, softer this time, grinning as he pulled away. Then, as if this was just any other morning, he turned back to the mirror, adjusting his tie. "By the way, what do you want for dinner, baby? I can set some lamb chops out to defrost before I go"

Panic pressed against my ribs. "Umm, don't worry about dinner. I don't think I'll be here."

The air in the room shifted. His hands stilled. "Oh?" His voice was carefully neutral. "Where are you gonna be?"

I kept my expression blank. "Out."

He sighed, His shoulders squared slightly, turning to face me fully. "You do remember that you're in hiding, right, Malinda? You won't tell me anything about the situation, but you wanna run around Maryland like it's no biggie."

I gritted my teeth. He wasn't my man. He didn't get to question me like this.

"Amir, look—" I sighed, forcing myself to stay calm. "I am very grateful that you let me stay here these past few months, but I need to get my things in order. I can't stay here forever."

Something flickered in his expression, but he quickly masked it. He studied me for a long moment before exhaling through his nose.

"Why can't you?"

I blinked, caught completely off guard. "Huh?"

His eyes locked onto mine, unwavering. "You heard me, babe." His voice was softer now, but it carried a weight that made my chest tighten. "Why can't you stay? I can't imagine you leaving me anymore. So just... stay."

I opened my mouth, but no words came out.

"You love me, right?" he pressed, stepping closer. "So, stay."

I sucked in a sharp breath. There it was. The moment I had been dreading. The words hit me like a blow to the chest.

You love me, right?

I had said it. I had let those words slip out in the heat of passion, in a moment where I was weak, where I needed him too much. And now he was holding them in his hands, like proof, like a promise.

I inhaled sharply. "You're not my man, Amir." My voice came out flatter than I intended. "This isn't a fairytale. I'm not some princess in a castle. I had a life before this. I still have a life."

He flinched, just barely, but enough for guilt to claw at my insides.

His jaw tightened. "Okay," he said, his voice hoarse. "But what about us?

The raw vulnerability in his voice nearly shattered me.

"I love you, and I want to be with you. I need you to be safe, babe."

I forced my expression to harden. "I can't do this right now. You should get going. You're gonna be late."

He didn't move at first. His jaw clenched, his fingers twitching at his side like he wanted to reach for me, to shake me, to force me to say something different.

The light in his eyes dimmed. He watched me for a long, heavy moment before nodding once. "Right."

Without another word, he grabbed his briefcase and left.

The moment the front door closed behind him, I felt it—the crushing weight in my chest.

I stared at the untouched breakfast; at the effort he had put into making this morning something special. Something normal. And I had ruined it.

What the hell is wrong with me?

I clenched my fists and forced myself to push it down. All of it. The guilt. The ache. The confusion. I couldn't afford to care. Not now. I had work to do.

I wasn't built for this. Love. Stability. Any of it.

But I was built for survival. And right now, I need to focus on that.

I got up, ignoring the hollow feeling in my stomach, and forced myself into motion, getting ready for the day. I tied up my curls, showered, and changed into something comfortable. Then, I sat down with my laptop. My parts had finally arrived, which meant I could finally fix the damage.

I took my time, carefully replacing what needed to be replaced. When I powered it on and saw the screen light up, a breath of relief left me. Finally.

I plugged into the dark web, sifting through encrypted forums, Discord servers, and old underground contacts. I put word out that I was willing to drop $10K for information on an old fence named Sergei. The underground always knew something, if the price was right.

And then I waited.

One lead. That's all I needed. One step closer to the truth.

I wasn't thinking about Amir anymore.

I wasn't thinking about how he'd looked at me before he left.

I wasn't thinking about how, despite everything, I wished he'd come back through that door.

No.

I had a mission.

And I was going to finish it.

CHAPTER 41

AMIR

I felt tortured on my drive to work. My fingers tightened around the steering wheel as I navigated through the city streets, the morning sunlight doing nothing to ease the heaviness in my chest. The warmth of Malinda's whispered confession from the night before still clung to me, an intoxicating high that had carried me through my restless sleep.

She loves me.

I had woken up feeling lighter than I had in years, convinced that last night had changed everything. That maybe—just maybe—I wasn't in this alone anymore. That she was finally ready to let me in.

And then this morning—the coldness, the shutdown. Just like that, she ripped it away. She had dismissed me like I was nothing.

Her words played on a loop in my head, each one cutting deeper.

You're not my man, Amir. This isn't a fairytale.

Were Aria and Dorian right? Was Malinda really one big walking red flag? Was she using me just for a place to crash?

That can't be true. Not after everything that's happened.

Last night was... I let out a shuddering breath as a flashback flooded my memory. I had no words to describe what happened between us. I prided myself on being a romantic, but last night felt like something out of a damn movie. A perfect moment.

She had laid herself bare in front of me. She had moaned my name and clung to me like I was her lifeline. She had told me she loved me.

And now? Now, it was like none of it had even happened. She had retreated behind her walls and left me standing there, reeling.

She confessed that she feels for me everything I feel for her. So why did she pull away so brutally?

What the fuck am I supposed to do with that?

A loud honk behind me jolted me from my daze. The light was green. My jaw clenched as I pulled into the SparTech parking garage, gripping the gearshift a little too hard before shutting off the engine.

I parked in my designated spot—**Director of Marketing.** I had fought hard for this job. Twelve years of grinding, dedication, proving myself and moving up the ranks. It wasn't just a job; it was my pride, my stability.

I had hesitated when they first offered me this promotion, not sure if I was ready to move up. But after eight years in middle management, I took the risk, and it paid off. Now, at thirty-six, I had everything I thought I wanted.

Everything except a wife, kids, and a family of my own.

My brain had tricked me into believing that Malinda might be it, but now? I wasn't so sure.

I sat there for a beat, running a hand down my face, trying to force myself into work mode. I had a full day ahead—meetings, projects, deadlines. Shit that made sense.

I could lose myself in the work and push Malinda out of my head.

At least, that was the hope.

Walking into the building, I went through the motions, exchanging nods and greetings with colleagues, but my head wasn't in it.

My secretary, Veronica, handed me my schedule, rattling off my morning meetings, but I barely heard her as I made my way to my office.

The view of Baltimore from my corner office was one of the few perks I allowed myself to enjoy. It was breathtaking, a reminder of how far I had come.

So why did it feel like everything was slipping through my fingers?

I buried myself in back-to-back meetings, welcoming the distraction. A call with my Berlin counterpart, Hans, helped refocus me. I liked Hans—smart guy, straight shooter. Working with him has been seamless so far.

As I wrapped up the call, something on my calendar caught my eye. A meeting had appeared.

I frowned and buzzed my secretary.

"Vero, what's this meeting I have in 15 minutes?" I asked, pressing the intercom.

"Not sure, sir. Mr. Sawyer requested to see you in his office."

I stiffened. Mr. Sawyer? The CEO never called me in personally. I had never met with Clay Sawyer. In the twelve years I had been with SparTech, I could count on one hand the number of times I had been inside the CEO's office, and that was back when Clay's father, Brian, was in charge.

I racked my brain, trying to think of what this could be about.

Something wasn't right.

"Alright, thanks," I muttered before ending the call.

I straightened my tie, adjusting my suit jacket before making my way to the executive floor.

After a brief wait, I was called inside.

My gut twisted as I stepped into the sleek, high-rise office, the air thick with power and intimidation. Clay was seated behind his massive mahogany desk, the floor-to-ceiling windows casting a perfect frame around him. He exuded the same confidence and control that made people nervous.

"Mr. Stevens, have a seat," Clay said smoothly, gesturing to the chair across from his desk.

I sat, keeping my posture relaxed even though everything in my gut told me something was off. Clay was watching me with that smug, unreadable expression—the kind that made it impossible to tell if he was about to offer you a promotion or slit your throat.

"I wanted to commend you on the last campaign," Clay said, leaning back in his chair. "Your team really delivered."

I nodded. "Thank you, sir. We've been working closely with Berlin to ensure a smooth transition. Hans and I just wrapped up a meeting."

Clay smirked. "Hans speaks highly of you."

Something about the way he said it put me on edge. There was an undertone—something smug, something knowing.

"How do you think the merger is going?"

"In reference to my department, I think things are progressing smoothly, sir. Relying on more visual media helps us transcend language barriers in both Germany and China. The transition has been nearly seamless.

Clay nodded only half listening. Then his lips curled slightly.

"Speaking of transitions," Clay continued, his tone deceptively casual. "You ever hear from Malinda?"

My stomach clenched. My face remained neutral, but inside, alarm bells rang. I knew, without a doubt, that everything going on with Malinda had something to do with Clay. I forced a casual shrug, my poker face sliding into place.

"Malinda Burns? Nah. She quit, I heard."

Clay held my gaze, tilting his head, studying me like a predator sizing up its prey. Something was unsettling in his expression. A knowing glint in his eye.

"Yeah, she did. I only ask because I know you two are friends. Wondering if she's doing okay."

"Wouldn't know," I replied smoothly. "We're not that close."

"It was all just so sudden. Family emergency, maybe?"

I forced another shrug. "No clue, sir. Maybe HR knows?"

A flicker of amusement crossed Clay's face, but his eyes remained cold.

The air in the room thickened, tension settling between us like a live wire. Clay leaned forward, resting his elbows on the desk, his smirk not quite reaching his eyes.

"Right. Down to business, then?" He cleared his throat and pressed a button on his desk. "Send in Stephanie Ming."

Before I could react, the door opened, and Stephanie Ming, the head of HR, stepped inside. She avoided my eyes as she took a seat near Clay.

"Mr. Stevens," she began, voice clipped, professional. "Due to company restructuring as a result of the merger, we're consolidating departments—"

The rest of her words blurred into static as dread curled in my stomach.

"Wait." My voice cut through the air; my eyes locked on Clay. "You're firing me?"

Stephanie shifted uncomfortably. "Mr. Stevens, please understand—"

I cut her off, my focus solely on Clay now. I nearly got up from my seat but thought better of it.

"Sir... I'm barely eight months into this position. My team managed to increase revenue by six percent in the last two quarters alone."

Clay's smirk didn't waver, looking almost amused. "And we appreciate your contributions. However, a merger of this scale comes with the consolidation of some departments. The Berlin team has a more established department and a long track record of successful marketing campaigns. This makes the most sense. It's not personal."

Bullshit.

My pulse pounded in my ears. I was being discarded. Just like that. My years of work, my sacrifices, my loyalty—none of it meant a damn thing.

I clenched my fists. "But my team is in the middle of some very important projects. You're dissolving us?"

"Your team will be absorbed into Berlin's team and will answer to Hans moving forward," Clay said, his voice cool and detached. "Again, It's not personal. We're just trying to run a leaner operation after such a capital-intensive move with the merger."

I swore I saw the ghost of a smirk on Clay's lips.

"I can't believe this is happening..."

Stephanie spoke up. "You've been a very valuable member of this company, Mr. Stevens. Please see your personal email for the details of your severance package. If you'll just take a look at these documents confirming your personal information, retirement accounts—"

"This is some bullshit," I bit out.

"Your benefits will continue for six months—" Stephanie added, her voice careful, like she was trying not to poke a wounded animal.

Clay exhaled sharply, shaking his head with mock sympathy. "It's just business, Stevens. You understand."

I clenched my fists, my whole body taut with rage. I had to get out of there before I did something stupid—like lunge across the desk and knock that smug fucking grin off Clay's face.

Clay stood, adjusting his suit jacket. "As per company policy, you will have to turn in your badge and any access fobs. Your access to your email and the SparTech server will be terminated at the top of the hour. Mrs. Ming will escort you down to your office to finalize some details, and Security will escort you out once you've packed up."

Escort. Like I was a criminal.

I forced myself to my feet, my dignity hanging by a thread.

Clay gave a curt nod. "Mr. Stevens." Dismissing me.

The asshole didn't even offer a handshake. He turned to Stephanie. "Steph? We'll touch base later."

I turned on my heel and walked out, heart hammering, shame crawling up my spine as Stephanie and Security trailed behind me like I was some fucking intern caught stealing office supplies.

The most shameful part of my day was being escorted off the premises like a criminal.

I gave twelve years to this company, and they discarded me like trash.

Twelve years.

Gone. Just like that.

This was the worst day of my life.

CHAPTER 42

MALINDA

C lay hadn't contacted me in three months.

He said he would check in, and Clay was a man who kept his word. The silence wasn't a good thing—it was a warning. He was waiting. Watching. And I had been banking on the fact that he had no idea where I was.

Staying at Amir's house was never part of the plan, but it had kept me safe, kept me hidden. But today, I had to take a risk.

I needed to go back to my apartment.

The thought alone sent a sharp chill down my spine. The last time I was there, Clay's guys had cornered me outside and stuffed me in a trunk. I knew Clay had eyes on my place—I'd have been stupid to think otherwise. He wanted to know where the money was, but I didn't have the answers he was looking for. And even if I did, I wouldn't have given them to him.

I spent the morning waiting, my patience thinning with every minute that passed. My burner phone stayed silent; my online inquiries sat untouched. Hours ticked by, and I was running out of faith.

Then, at 12:30 sharp, my chat pinged.

A QR code.

My heart pounded as my burner rang.

"Half now, half after the information is verified," a gruff voice said.

"Fair enough," I responded, barely masking my excitement.

I moved fast, transferring half the amount into the crypto wallet.

"Done."

The voice on the other end exhaled. "You're looking for an older man who goes by Sergei. Late 50s, early 60s. 6'3. African American."

"What?" My brain stalled. "He's Black?"

"The name had me expecting some old Eastern European, ex-KGB-type."

"That's the point, sweetheart," the voice chuckled dryly. "People go looking for some white Russian dude and never think to check for a brother."

I closed my eyes for a beat. That son of a bitch—George. Even after all these years, my father still had me jumping through hoops.

"Where can I find him?" I pressed.

"He's been out of the game for years, but he still works. Doorman at the Waldorf Astoria in DC."

I frowned. "You're telling me the man I've been chasing for months is hailing cabs and holding doors?"

"Gotta lay low somehow. Goes by Kwame Johanson now."

Of course, he does.

"Anything else?"

"When you see him, the code phrase is: *Chicago is beautiful this time of year.* He'll give you a time and a location."

I nodded to myself. "Got it."

"Second half of my payment?"

"Sent."

The line went dead. I didn't hesitate, snapping the SIM card in half and tossing it in the trash. Then I leaned back in my chair, exhaling a shaky breath.

Finally. A lead. A real one.

This is the first sliver of progress I've made since I started digging. My chest felt lighter for the first time in months. I wasn't just running in circles anymore—I had a target.

I moved quickly, throwing on a black turtleneck, my leather jacket, and my dark-wash jeans. Functional but stylish. I secured my hair into a loose bun, something simple. I needed to blend in and be just another woman enjoying a brisk DC afternoon. My nerves felt sharp and frayed as I booked a car, and by the time I slid into the backseat, my knee was bouncing.

An hour and a half later, I was walking down Pennsylvania Avenue, my hands deep in my pockets.

I loitered at a nearby park, taking my time, watching. I couldn't just walk up and blow my cover. My eyes darted across the street, scanning the entrance of the Waldorf.

And then I saw him.

A tall, older man, dressed sharply in a pressed black uniform, greeted guests with easy charm. He hailed cabs, tipped his hat, and exchanged pleasantries like he wasn't the key to everything I had been searching for.

This was Sergei?

I took another deep breath, gathering my courage, before making my approach.

His sharp gaze landed on me as I neared, his professional smile unwavering. "Good afternoon, miss. How may I be of service to you?"

I stopped beside him, keeping my posture relaxed, my expression neutral. "Just taking in the sights. I love this weather."

"Ahh, yes," he said, tipping his hat slightly. "Spring is just around the corner. Beautiful time of year, ma'am."

I swallowed, lowering my voice slightly. "Chicago is beautiful this time of year."

His smile barely faltered, but I caught the flicker in his expression—the brief shift in his gaze before he recovered.

"Ah, Chi-town," he mused, his voice carrying a different weight now. "Yes. Gorgeous this time of year."

He studied me for half a second, his stance shifting almost imperceptibly before he continued, "If you're ever craving authentic Chi-town cooking, there's this cozy little spot near the docks, off of Key Highway. Goes by the name of Lucy's. Mmm mmm mmm. They sure can throw it down. I like to get there by 5:30 for the early bird special."

There it was. My time. My location.

I nodded, playing along. "Thanks for the tip. I'll have to check it out."

"You're welcome, madam." He tipped his hat again. "Enjoy your evening."

I turned on my heel and walked away, my heart hammering. Every nerve in my body was on high alert. My hands trembled slightly as I glanced at my watch.

2:25 PM.

I had less than three hours before the meeting. And I needed documents out of my safe.

I booked a car plugging in the address to my apartment.

This was happening. Finally. I was so close.

And nothing—*nothing*—was going to stand in my way.

CHAPTER 43

MALINDA

I was cautious while getting out of the cab and walking into the building. It's 3:0, so I knew Clay was at work, but you can never be too cautious.

I kept my head low, scanning my surroundings. The heavy, suffocating weight of paranoia pressed down on my chest.

It had been three months. Three months since Clay last contacted me. Three months since he had thrown me in a trunk and held me captive in that damn warehouse. Three months of silence, of waiting for the other shoe to drop. And now, here I was, stepping into my apartment building, knowing damn well I was tempting fate.

I told myself it was because I hadn't left Amir's house, that I'd played it safe. But deep down, I knew better. Clay was patient when he needed to be. He was always watching. He had promised to check in. And Clay was a man who kept his word.

The elevator ride to the 23rd floor felt like an eternity, the ding of each passing floor echoing like a countdown in my ears. I tried to tell myself that it was just paranoia, that I'd be in and out quickly, but the pounding in my chest wouldn't let up.

When I reached my door, I hesitated. My fingers trembled slightly as I turned the key. Ready to be greeted by the wreckage that had been left in Clay's wake months ago.

I stepped inside and froze.

Everything... was pristine. The air was thick with the scent of fresh polish. My breath hitched.

My couch was replaced. The broken glass—gone. The broken furniture—restored. It looked exactly like it had before. Untouched, as if nothing had ever happened. My heart pounded as my mind raced to make sense of it.

What? No.

No, no, no.

I spun on my heel, every instinct screaming at me to run.

But I was too late. I barely had a second to process before I felt it. A shift in the air.

"Hey, my love... Long time no see." His voice slithered down my spine, smooth and rich, like he was savoring the moment.

My blood ran ice cold.

I turned, and there he was leaning against the door frame of my server room, his body relaxed, and his lips curved into a smug, knowing grin.

Clay.

I quickly backed away, but Clay moved faster. He grabbed my wrist before I could flee, his grip firm but not yet bruising. His gray eyes, sharp as cut glass, raked over me, drinking me in like he was starved.

"Don't be like that, babe," he murmured, his voice smooth as silk, but there was an edge to it. "Don't be difficult. Have a seat, and let's talk."

My body coiled tight, my pulse hammering in my throat.

"What the fuck are you doing here?" I spat, trying to wrench my arm away.

His jaw ticked, but then his expression smoothed, his smile thinning.

"Don't be vulgar, baby," he tsked. "It's unbecoming. You know I hate that. Stop tryna piss me off."

I glared at him, but my fury only seemed to amuse him further.

Then, just as suddenly, his expression softened. His hands loosened as he pulled me into his chest. He exhaled against my temple, his voice lowering into something almost fragile. The mask cracked.

His hands slid to my waist, his body pressing into mine. My breath caught as my back hit the wall. His touch was warm, his grip possessive. He let go of my arms, but his body kept me pinned.

"I hate that you still make me feel this way," he murmured, his voice raw. His fingers brushed my jaw, tilting my face up to his. "I've missed you so much, Dove. Especially your kiss."

His eyes were dark and unreadable.

"I know you've missed me too."

His lips descended on mine, firm, demanding.

I didn't move, my lips pressed in a tight line, refusing to give him the satisfaction. He pulled back slightly, his breath ragged, warm against my lips.

"Kiss me, baby. Please." The way he said it—like he ached for me, like he had been suffering

I shook my head. "Let me go, Clay."

"I wish I could," he whispered, pressing his forehead against mine. "Truly. But I *can't* because I am so in love with you, Malinda. Obsessively so. You're my soulmate."

My stomach clenched. "Clay—"

He let out a bitter laugh, shaking his head.

"Whether or not this was all a game to you, it was real for me," he rasped, his thumb running over my lips. "Our chemistry is real. The way we make each other feel. That shit is real."

"Stop, Clay."

"Kiss me," He pleaded, his voice cracking slightly. "I've missed you so much that my heart aches. You broke me baby. For the past month, I've been coming here on my lunch breaks. Just to feel close to you. Hoping that maybe you'd show up. Just to...—fuck, Malinda—do you realize how down bad I have to be to do some shit like that?" His grip on my waist tightened. "So just fucking kiss me."

I tried to push against his chest, but he wouldn't budge.

"Let me go, Clay."

"Do you remember that weekend we spent here in your apartment?" His voice dropped lower like he was whispering something forbidden. "Just you and me, laughing, fucking, eating, and talking until the sun came up."

I stilled.

"And those summer Fridays on my yacht," he continued, his fingers brushing against my hip. "You used to lay out on the deck, reading, while I worked." He chuckled fondly. "Then we'd make love in sync with the rocking of the waves."

His hands moved, tracing the curve of my spine.

"And Spain." He let out a ragged breath. "God, Spain. I still dream about you in those white sheets, covered in my cum, your voice hoarse from screaming my name."

A shudder ripped through me.

"You still think about it, don't you?" His lips brushed my ear. "How good I made you feel. How well I know your body."

"Stop it, Clay," I snapped, trying to push him off me.

He exhaled against my ear, sending a chill through me.

"Why does everything have to be a fight, hmm, baby?" His voice turned low, sultry. "Does that turn you on? Or is it something else? Someone else...?"

I tensed. He felt it.

"What are you talking about?" I forced my voice to stay even.

He chuckled darkly, the sound making my stomach twist.

"Aw, baby. You're so cute. You think I haven't known where you've been this whole goddamn time? Playing house with that motherfucker."

My blood ran cold.

I forced my expression to remain blank. "I don't know what—"

"I know everything, baby. I told you... I'm obsessed. Is he the reason why you left me?"

My throat tightened. I forced myself to hold his gaze.

"What are you talking about?"

"You don't want me anymore because of Amir?" he snarled, "You made me feel like I was overreacting about him. You told me not to worry about him.

Even when I knew, I fucking knew that something was going on with you two. The way he was flirting with you. Like I was crazy for seeing what was right in front of me. Then you go running straight into his arms the minute we hit a rough patch. How fucked up is that?"

"Clay—"

"Tell me, Dove—is he a better lover than me?" he sneered. "Did I not satisfy you enough?"

"Clay, stop it."

His breath hitched as his hands dug into my waist. "You think I don't imagine his hands on you? Him kissing you? Taking you to bed?" His lips curled, his voice shaking with rage.

Terror crawled up my spine. Clay was unraveling.

He grabbed my face again, tilting it up. I could see it now—the unraveling. The desperation. The hurt.

"I hate that you've moved on," he whispered, his voice still shaking. "I hate that I have to see his fucking face every damn day. I've had to sit back and watch him breathe easy while I've been fucking drowning without you."

"Clay," I murmured, my voice low, controlled. "Listen to me."

"Sometimes... sometimes I wonder if I'll feel better if I just... kill him."

Fear slammed into me.

"Clay, what the hell?"

"I fucking mean it, Malinda," he growled. "He stole you right out from under me. And I have to listen to his jokes? See him happy while my heart is broken?"

"Clay you sound-..."

"I sound what, babe?" He leaned in, his voice shaking. "Crazy? I feel fucking crazy. I feel so fucking sick not having you in my life anymore."

He was spiraling. I had to stop this.

I grabbed his face, forcing him to look at me.

"Clay, listen to me—"

"You think I'm bluffing?" His expression darkened. "I promise I have the money, resources, and determination to get rid of him. I'll make him disappear. And then maybe we—"

I kissed him. It was the only way to shut him up.

He went still for a split second, then groaned deeply, pulling me tighter against him, his fingers digging into my waist. The kiss was desperate, consuming. His tongue swept against mine, deep, possessive, claiming.

My stomach churned.

He lost himself in it. I felt the shift—his anger melting into something else.

I hated this. I hated that I knew exactly how to kiss him to make him lose himself. And I hated that, despite it all, my body still remembered him.

I kissed him back like I meant it. I can't bear the thought of him hurting Amir. If a stupid kiss will save him, I'd do it 10 times over.

When he finally pulled back, his breath was ragged, his pupils blown wide. He nuzzled my neck, his voice raw.

"Damn, Dove... them lips get me every time."

I forced myself to stay still as he trailed kisses down my jaw, my pulse roaring in my ears.

"I miss you so much, baby." He kissed my ear and then down my neck as his hand caressed my breast. I felt his erection pressing into my stomach. He pinched my nipple hard, and I gasped and grabbed his wrist. I used my other hand to try and push him off.

"Clay, chill".

"Baby..." his voice was husky and aching with desire. " I'll make you feel so good. I always make you come. Every. Single. Time. In Spain you came so intensely you sobbed."

I had a brief flashback to our time in Spain. It was unforgettable. I got chills just remembering it, but I had to pull myself together.

He groaned as he felt my body react.

"I get chills thinking about it too, my love. Remembering how it feels to be inside you drives me crazy. Do you miss how I stretch and fill you?" He kissed my neck. My heart was racing.

"Clay—"

"Just one last time baby. I never got to say goodbye. Being inside you... it intoxicates me. It's my drug and you just cut me off."

"Please stop Clay. I don't want anything to happen here."

He pulled back searching my eyes desperately then sighed deeply and squeezed my hip. He kissed my face over and over like he used to when he missed me. Peppering kisses on my nose, forehead, eyes, temples, and cheeks. It pulled me back to a different time, his tenderness. He rested his forehead against mine and sighed shakily. When he finally spoke, there was an ache in his voice.

"It's not just about sex Malinda...you know that, don't you? I miss you. Your presence. Our talks. You consumed my life for those months, and...I felt a little less—"

He stopped talking. I knew he was going to say that he felt less lonely. I tried to ignore it but the pain in his voice twisted my heart up. I touched his face. We stayed like that in silence for a few minutes. He pulled away and stared at me, his gaze still intense. Finally, he took a deep breath, letting go of me and taking a step back. He cleared his throat, running a hand over his face. Then he exhaled, slipping a mask of indifference back over himself.

"Alright. Sit," he commanded, voice clipped. "Let's talk business."

I took slow, deliberate steps to the chair across from him, my mind racing as I sat down. Clay leaned back on the wall and watched me, sharp and calculating, the yearning from moments ago nowhere to be found. How could he shift so effortlessly? Just minutes ago, he was spiraling—desperate, unhinged, clinging to me like I was the only thing keeping him tethered to reality. And now? Now he was cool, composed, the ruthless CEO once again.

It unnerved me.

His arms were crossed, his eyes, scrutinizing me, analyzing every flicker of my expression.

I forced myself to hold his gaze. "I still don't know anything, Clay."

"It's been three months since our last check-in. Do you mean to tell me that you haven't worked on this at all?" His voice was even, but there was a razor-thin edge to it, sharp enough to slice through my carefully constructed defenses.

I shrugged, feigning indifference. "It's a twenty-year-old cold case, Clay. There's nothing to find."

He tilted his head, his tongue running over his teeth in slow amusement. "Your father was an infamous con man. Do you expect me to believe he's dead and gone, leaving no trace behind? I find that hard to believe."

I exhaled sharply, my fingers digging into my thighs. "He is dead."

Clay arched a brow, waiting.

"My father loved me," I continued, my voice steadier than I felt. "He wouldn't have ever willingly left me. He would have never let me get put into the system. He would have never allowed me to experience all that I did."

Something flickered across Clay's expression—something that almost looked like sympathy—but it was gone before I could be sure.

He leaned his head back, exhaling through his nose. "I'm losing patience here, Malinda." His voice was softer now, but that only made it worse. "I've given you ample time to provide me with information, but you're not delivering."

I swallowed hard, my pulse pounding as his darkened eyes locked back onto my face.

"I'll have to start following through on my threats," he murmured, "I don't wanna have to hurt you, baby...or anyone else...but I will if need be."

A chill shot through me, spreading across my skin like ice.

I knew who he meant.

Amir.

I sat up straighter, keeping my voice light, and dismissive. "I'm trying, Clay. But keeping me here won't help." I softened my expression, injecting just enough exasperation into my tone. "Let me go. I have work to do."

His smirk widened, and he shook his head like I was the most amusing thing he'd seen all day.

"That assertiveness is still so sexy, boo." His voice was thick with something—fondness? Desire? Amusement? Maybe all three. He dragged his tongue over his lips slowly before sighing and turning away from me.

"You're right."

I forced myself not to react too quickly, not to let the relief show.

"You should get going." He stood straight, adjusting the cuffs of his shirt, that same smirk still playing on his lips.

Then he turned back to me, his eyes serious. "But I'll be showing up more often now."

My stomach twisted.

"I'm always watching, babe."

His words lingered in the air long after I got up and walked out. The file I needed would have to wait.

Chapter 44

Malinda

I rushed over to the docks, my pulse hammering with every step. Night was already falling.

The only place I could find with the name Lucy's was an old abandoned warehouse—the kind that looked like a relic from a long-forgotten era. The faded sign above the entrance creaked as the wind rolled in from the bay, and the air was thick with the smell of salt and rotting wood.

I hovered outside, my breath forming small clouds in the crisp evening air. Everything inside me screamed setup.

I scanned my surroundings, pretending to admire the docks as I slowly checked for cameras, hidden watchers, anything that might be off. Nothing. But that didn't mean I wasn't being watched.

The place was eerily silent. No lights. No cars, no movement—just the distant sound of water sloshing against the pier. I hesitated before stepping inside, the heavy metal door creaking as I pushed it open.

I felt like I was walking into a trap, but I had come too far to turn back now.

The interior was dark and mostly empty—dusty crates stacked against the walls, cobwebs hanging from rusted chains, save for a faint glow coming from an office on the upper level, its door slightly ajar.

The vast emptiness of the warehouse made every small sound feel deafening—the echo of my footsteps, the creak of aging beams, the distant water lapping against the pier outside.

I swallowed hard. I hate this.

I forced my legs to move, climbing the rickety staircase with caution. The light in the office flickered slightly, illuminating the dust swirling in the air. I approached the door, my body tense.

I stepped inside.

And then—I froze.

Sergei sat behind a cluttered wooden desk, the faint glow of an old desk lamp illuminating his weathered, dark skin. He was tall, even seated, his broad shoulders filling the space with an unspoken authority. A silver pistol gleamed in his hand; the barrel aimed dead center at my chest.

I went completely still.

His deep-set eyes studied me like I was a problem he needed to solve, his grip on the gun steady as stone. Grizzled, but sharp—the kind of man who had seen and done enough to make a legend out of himself. He exuded a quiet, effortless danger, the kind that didn't need loud threats to be taken seriously.

"Who are you, and what the fuck do you want?" His voice was smooth as silk, but his tone carried an unmistakable edge of danger.

I slowly raised my hands. The scowl on his face didn't budge as he adjusted his grip on the gun.

I've been in a lot of bad situations. I've conned dangerous people, slipped out of traps, lied my way out of tight corners—but I've never been on the wrong end of a gun before.

It made every inch of my skin crawl.

"My name is Malinda Burns."

His expression didn't change.

Then, in a low, almost menacing voice, he said, "Every night before you went to bed, your daddy would sing you a song. What was the name of that song?"

My pulse spiked.

"What?"

The click of the hammer being pulled back sent ice through my veins.

"You heard me. You got five seconds before I put a bullet in you."

Of all the questions he could've asked...

My mind scrambled, tearing through old, buried memories.

The lullabies my dad used to hum. The nights I'd curl up beside him, safe, warm, unaware that one day he'd leave and never come back.

The answer hit me like a punch to the gut.

"My Girl." My voice was hoarse, my throat tight. "By The Temptations."

A tense beat of silence.

Serge's scowl cracked, a slow smirk tugging at the corners of his mouth.

"Well, I'll be damned."

He finally lowered the gun, shaking his head slightly as he let out a rough chuckle.

"Malinda." He said my name like he was tasting it, testing it. "You're more beautiful than I imagined. Have a seat."

I exhaled sharply, forcing my shoulders to relax, though my heart was still hammering. I carefully slid into the chair across from him clenching my knees to steady my trembling hands.

I studied him, taking in the deep lines on his face, the way he carried himself like a man who had seen too much, done too much, and survived it all.

"You damn near got yourself smoked, little miss."

"You told me to meet you here," I said bewildered. "Not like I snuck up."

He chuckled, the rumble was warm, like one you'd hear from a loving grandparent.

"That code phrase you used. I specifically use it when I'm in dealings with the mob. And we're...not on the best terms right now, let's say."

"Oh..."

I cursed that tipster internally. He almost got me killed. But I guess that's the risk when dealing with criminals. There's no honor amongst thieves.

Sergei leaned back, folding his massive arms across his chest, studying me like I was a puzzle missing a few pieces. He let out a gruff sigh.

"I take it you've gotten yourself into some trouble."

I exhaled, rubbing my temple. "You could say that."

Sergei nodded knowingly. "SparTech?"

I stiffened. My poker face slid into place.

"Possibly."

He watched me for a beat too long, then grinned. "Hmph. That right?"

I didn't blink.

"So why did my dad send me to you? How can you help me?" I pressed, eager to get my next lead and get the hell out of there.

Sergei studied me for another long beat before letting out a heavy sigh. "Alright, alright. Down to business. You're feisty. I like that."

He pushed himself up from the chair and made his way to a large steel safe in the corner of the office. The thing looked old as hell but sturdy—like it had kept secrets for decades.

"Your papa approached me about twenty-two years ago," he said, turning the large dial on the combination lock. "Back when I was still in the game. He bought an identity for you, just in case you ever needed one."

My stomach dropped.

"What?"

Sergei pulled out a thick envelope and tossed it onto the desk in front of me.

"Go on. Open it."

I hesitated, then slowly peeled back the flap.

Inside were documents. Official ones.

- A birth certificate

- A passport

- A social security card

- Credit cards

- Even a damn library card

All belonging to a woman named Melodie Blanchard.

I looked up sharply. "Are these forgeries?"

Sergei scoffed, rolling his eyes. "Do I look like a half-ass forger?"

"I already have aliases."

He sat back down and leaned forward. "This ain't an alias, sweetheart. This is an *identity*."

My hands clenched the edges of the envelope, my mind racing.

"I don't understand," I admitted. "Am I stealing someone else's life?"

Sergei shook his head. "No, sweet pea. This life was *made* for you."

I swallowed. "How?"

He rolled his eyes like I was being slow.

"Read the damn report, girl."

I frowned. "Just explain it."

Sergei sighed but relented. "Look. Back in the day, before they changed all the laws and whatnot. In small Caribbean villages, most births happened at home. None of that hospital records bullshit. Fathers would go register their babies at the capital a few days later, and get the paperwork squared away. Me? I found a way to get some of those records *without* the actual babies."

I felt my stomach turn.

"You're saying you... created people?"

Sergei shrugged. "There was a need in the market. The problem with aliases is they just pop up outta nowhere, and the problem with identity theft is they already have a face attached to 'em. Think of this as identity farming. I 'raised' them—on paper. Birth certificates, passports, school records. I built their histories, made 'em real. So when someone needed to disappear? Boom. Step right into a life that's already waiting for you."

I couldn't wrap my mind around it.

"But how did-..."

"The how is none of your damn business!" he barked sharply.

I stilled. Startled.

He sighed realizing he was being grumpy. " Look with a few bribes and the right records clerk, anything is possible.

"So... what? I just leave everything behind and become... Melodie Blanchard?"

Sergei nodded. "Whenever you're ready." His gaze darkened slightly. "Your daddy wanted me to hold on to it for you—just in case something happened to him. Guess he was right."

A lump formed in my throat.

"How much did something like this cost?"

Sergei gave me a slow, satisfied smile. "Back then? No competition, no problem. I could charge whatever I wanted. When Your pops approached me I only had a few left. I was getting out of that business. It was getting way too difficult. He got the friend discount. Seventy-five grand."

I exhaled sharply. "That's a whole lot of cash."

He chuckled. "Well, sweetheart... it's a whole new life. I got them passports, and library cards, I home-schooled them, they all graduated high school and some went to college. Others didn't. And I just waited for people to buy them from me. When you're ready you just seamlessly step into your new life. "

"I don't need an escape," I snapped. "I need answers. Where is my father?"

Sergei exhaled hard, rubbing his temple. "Malinda, I don't fucking know. I haven't seen your father since the day he paid me for this identity."

I narrowed my eyes. "Did he buy one for himself?"

He hesitated, just for a second.

"No. Didn't have any male adults mature enough to match him at the time. He only paid for two—one for your mom, one for you. Said that was enough."

My stomach twisted.

"Bullshit," I hissed. "Someone like you—someone with your reputation—could find him if you wanted to."

Sergei's eyes turned cold as steel. "That ain't my problem. Your pops disappeared after pulling the biggest con of his life. He played his cards. Now you gotta play yours."

My breath came sharp. "What do you mean, biggest con of his life?"

Sergei let out a slow exhale. "You already know. He bled SparTech dry. Hundreds of millions. Some folks say he was spotted in Colombia a month later, but after that? Nothing. No whispers, no sightings. Like he turned to smoke."

Colombia?

My chest tightened.

That's where my mother had been imprisoned. Was still imprisoned? Or at least, she was twenty-five years ago. Had he gotten her out somehow? Was that the plan all along?

My stomach twisted. If he had found a way to bust her out... and left me behind... what did that make me? Just another piece on the board?

I exhaled sharply, the bitterness curling in my throat.

Silence stretched between us, as my thoughts spiraled.

Finally, Sergei cracked his neck and sighed. "Now, enough chit-chat. You got what you need, so go." He leaned back, looking done with me already. "Don't contact me again unless it's life or death. I'm officially retired."

He gave me one last look, his gruff expression softening just slightly.

"Good luck, baby girl."

I shoved the envelope into my bag, stood, and met his gaze. I nodded once and walked out.

CHAPTER 45

AMIR

I sat in my car, gripping the steering wheel so tightly my fingers went numb. My entire body buzzed with anger, humiliation, and heartbreak. It felt like my whole life had just been dismantled in a single day.

I replayed it all in my head—Clay's smug fucking smirk as he took everything I had worked for, Malinda's cold, detached expression as she told me I wasn't her man. The way she had pulled me in so completely, only to push me away the moment I got too close.

I slammed my fist against the dashboard. The dull pain in my knuckles didn't do a damn thing to quiet the roaring in my head.

With a sharp exhale, I grabbed my phone and dialed Dorian.

"Yo," Dorian answered almost immediately, his voice alert. "What's wrong?"

I let out a dry, humorless laugh. "Where do I start?"

"You sound like shit, bro. Talk to me."

I leaned my head against the headrest, staring at the ceiling of my car. "I got fired today."

There was a beat of silence. "Fired?" Dorian's voice was laced with disbelief. "From *SparTech*? What the hell happened?"

I closed my eyes. "Clayton Sawyer happened."

"That motherfucker," Dorian spat. "I knew I didn't like him."

I let out a bitter chuckle. "Well, he don't like me either, apparently. Called me up to his office and told me my department was being 'absorbed' by the Berlin team. Then had security escort me out like I was a fucking criminal."

"Bullshit. They can't do you like that. You've been with that company since we were what? *Twenty-four?*"

"Yeah, well… loyalty don't mean shit, man. Not in this world."

Dorian exhaled sharply. "Damn. So what now?"

"That's the million-dollar question, ain't it?" I said bitterly. I ran a hand over my beard. "I got nothing, D. I'm thirty-six, no job, no wife, no kids. I worked my ass off for over a decade, and now I got *nothing* to show for it."

Dorian's voice turned cautious. "You're not thinking what I think you're thinking, are you?"

I didn't respond right away. It was almost annoying how well Dorian could read my mind.

"You are." Dorian sighed. "Man, don't even go there."

"It's not like I got a lot of options."

"You *do* have options. Re-enlisting ain't one of them."

I clenched my jaw.

"Look, I get it," Dorian continued. "Shit's all fucked up right now. But the military? Bro, it took you *years* to get back to yourself after you got out. The therapy, the nightmares, the fucking *isolation*. You really wanna throw yourself back into that?"

I was silent.

"*Do you?*" Dorian pushed.

I exhaled sharply. "No."

"Good. 'Cause I swear to God, I'd drag your ass outta basic training myself."

I let out a dry chuckle. "I appreciate it, man."

Dorian softened slightly. "Listen, come to DC. Stay with me and Katie for a few days, clear your head. Get out of Baltimore."

"I can't."

"Why?"

I hesitated.

Dorian groaned. "Let me guess. Malinda?"

"D..."

"Bro. *Bro.* What the fuck are you still doing? Why are you so loyal to a girl who keeps breaking your damn heart?"

"She's going through some shit."

"And so are *you*, Amir! When was the last time she checked in on you, huh? You just lost your job, your whole damn *career*, and I bet she ain't even called."

I swallowed hard. "It ain't like that."

Dorian let out a sharp, frustrated breath. "Man. Just... take a few days. Relax. Figure out what the hell you wanna do before you make any reckless decisions."

I ran a hand down my face. "Yeah. Yeah, alright."

"Good. And *don't* go signing up for the military, 'cause I'll be the first one to whoop your ass."

I smirked. "Noted."

We hung up, and I sat there in silence. The ache in my chest hadn't eased. If anything, it had settled in deeper, curling around my ribs like a vice.

I needed something to take the edge off.

I pulled out of the parking lot and headed for the nearest liquor store. When I walked in, I didn't even browse. I grabbed the biggest bottle of whiskey I could find, paid in cash, and walked out without a word.

Tonight, I was gonna drink until I couldn't feel a damn thing.

CHAPTER 46

MALINDA

I got back to Amir's house slipping into the house through the back door, moving quietly through the dimly lit kitchen. The house felt... off. Heavy. By now Amir was usually cooking, the scent of spices permeating the air. When I stepped into the living room, I saw him.

Amir was still in his suit, slouched on the couch with a nearly empty glass of whiskey dangling between his fingers. His tie was loosened, his shirt rumpled, but it was his face that made me pause. His expression was unreadable, his jaw tense, his gaze distant as he poured himself another drink.

Something was wrong.

"Hey..." I greeted softly, setting my messenger bag down near the counter.

He didn't respond. His eyes flicked toward me for the briefest second before he downed the whiskey and refilled his glass.

A pang of guilt shot through me. Was he like this because of this morning? I knew I'd hurt him with my words, but I didn't think it would push him to this.

I hesitated before slowly walking over and sitting next to him on the couch. "Amir," I tried again, this time a little softer. "Are you upset about what I said earlier?"

Nothing.

I sighed. "Look, I— I know I was cold. I know I hurt you. But I have to figure my life out. I can't get caught up in... this. I don't want to hurt you any more than I already have."

Still, he didn't say a word. He just stared ahead, expression unreadable, and poured himself another drink. I watched as he lifted the glass, the amber liquid catching the light, and swallowed it in one go.

Something about the way he was acting put me on edge. I'd never seen him like this before. Amir was warmth, light, and laughter. Even when he was frustrated, he was expressive. This... this was something else. A quiet, brooding storm that I didn't know how to navigate.

A knot of unease twisted in my stomach.

I stood. "Fine," I muttered. "I'll leave you to it."

I grabbed my bag and went upstairs, my skin crawling with a mix of frustration and guilt. As much as I wanted to keep my walls up, seeing him like that made my chest ache.

By the time I made it to my room, I was on autopilot. I hid my bag away, stripped out of my clothes, threw on a shower cap, and got into the shower.

The hot water scalded my skin, but I needed it. I needed to wash the tension off, to rinse Clay's touch from my body, to ground myself in something that didn't feel like my entire world was tilting on its axis. I scrubbed my arms, my neck, my legs—anywhere I could still feel the ghost of his hands. My stomach twisted at the memory of his desperation, his possessiveness, his threats. This side of him is the worst and it honestly disgusts me. His callousness, paranoia, and borderline sociopathic behaviors are terrifying.

I let out a shaky breath and pressed my forehead to the shower tile, keeping my hair tucked safely under the cap while the water beat down around me. I needed to breathe. Focus. Pull it together.

Amir.

I hated how much he affected me. How much I wanted to fix things when I knew I shouldn't. But I couldn't shake the look in his eyes. The weight of sadness pressing down on him.

By the time I got out and changed into sweatpants and a tank top, I had made up my mind. I needed to check on him.

Walking back downstairs, I saw him still in the same position, glass in hand, his face unreadable. His suit jacket was discarded now, but the exhaustion in his posture hadn't lessened.

Something wasn't right.

"Amir," I said again, softer this time. "Why are you home so early?"

No response.

This was getting ridiculous.

I moved closer and carefully took the glass from his hand. "Okay, that's enough," I said, setting it on the table.

His head snapped toward me, his gaze sharp and dark. "Give. That. Back," he said, his voice low, controlled—but laced with something simmering just beneath the surface.

I stiffened.

"Talk to me," I urged. "Tell me what's going on."

His jaw clenched. Instead of answering, he grabbed the bottle and took a long, slow swig from it.

"Amir." I reached for it again. "Stop it."

He ignored me.

That was it.

I yanked the bottle from his grip and stormed into the kitchen, dumping the remaining whiskey down the sink. I could feel his eyes burning into my back, his silent fury weighing heavy in the air, but I didn't care. He needed to eat, to sober up, to snap out of whatever haze he was drowning in.

I opened the fridge, scanning for something quick but comforting. The marinated beef caught my eye.

I pulled out the ingredients and got to work, the sound of chopping and sizzling filling the silence between us. Ten minutes passed, then I felt it—his presence behind me.

The warmth of his body, the subtle scent of whiskey and cedar, the weight of his arms as they wrapped around my waist from behind.

His lips brushed against my neck. "Malinda..." His voice was softer now, almost pleading. "Kiss me."

I froze, caught between surprise and something deeper, something fragile. He turned me gently, his hands firm but careful, and pressed his lips to mine.

The kiss was slow, and tender. Nothing like our usual fire.

I melted into it, just for a second.

Then he pulled back, his forehead resting against mine.

I studied him—really looked at him. His eyes were heavy with exhaustion, his expression raw. Something inside me twisted painfully.

"What's wrong, Amir?" I murmured, brushing my fingers along his jaw. "Talk to me."

He exhaled, closing his eyes for a beat before finally whispering the words that shattered everything.

"I was terminated from SparTech before lunch today."

I sucked in a sharp breath. "What?"

"That asshole Clay did it himself," he said bitterly. "Didn't even have HR handle it. Called me into his office and just—ended it. Twelve fucking years, Malinda."

I felt like the floor had dropped from beneath me. "Are you serious? Why would they do that?"

He let out a humorless laugh, shaking his head. "Baby, I wish I knew."

The way he said baby made my heart clench. I swallowed hard.

"This afternoon?" I whispered. "And you're just getting home now?"

"Nah." He ran a hand over his face. "Been here for hours. Just didn't have the energy to change."

A fresh wave of guilt rolled over me. I had thought his drinking was because of us. Because of me.

But this?

This was so much worse.

"Amir," I breathed. "I'm so sorry."

His hand found my hip, his touch grounding. "Clay knew exactly what he was doing," he said, his voice dark. "He's been waiting for an excuse to do this to me."

My stomach churned. He's doing this because of me.

"What was his reason?" I asked, even though I already knew the answer.

Amir sighed. "Budget cuts. Company restructuring. Some bullshit excuse." He paused, looking me dead in the eyes. "But you know what's wild?"

"What?" I whispered.

"When I walked into his office, he asked about you."

I went completely still.

"What?"

"He asked if I'd heard from you. If you were still in town." Amir's gaze searched mine, his expression unreadable now. "I lied, of course. Told him we weren't close. That I hadn't seen you since the day you quit."

My pulse pounded in my ears.

This was bad.

Really, really bad.

"Do you think he believed you?" I forced myself to ask.

Amir hesitated. "I don't know," he admitted. "I don't think he bought it. He gave me this look—smug as hell—and said, 'okay.' Then fired me."

I exhaled sharply, pressing a hand to my forehead, my heart racing.

Of course he'd asked about me.

Of course he fired Amir.

This was a calculated strike—clean, quiet, and personal.

He wasn't just watching anymore. He was acting.

And Amir was collateral damage.

I needed to act fast.

I turned from him and went back to making dinner. Amir sat at the counter and quietly sipped whatever whiskey was left in his glass. 30 minutes later it was ready. I grabbed two plates and plated the food and the steamed rice.

I set the plates down in front of Amir, pausing for just a moment as the scent of stir-fried beef, garlic, and soy sauce filled the room. The irony wasn't lost on me—Clay was the one who taught me how to make this dish. I remembered the night clearly, standing in my kitchen, watching him move with expert ease as he guided my hands.

Now, I was serving it to Amir.

The thought left a bitter taste in my mouth. Life has a cruel sense of humor.

"Here," I said softly, nudging a plate toward him. "Eat."

At first, Amir didn't move. His head was still heavy with alcohol, his body sluggish from the weight of the day's devastation. But then he looked up at me, his eyes dark and searching, and something in them softened. Slowly, he reached for his fork and took a bite.

I watched as he chewed, waiting for his reaction.

He froze mid-bite, his brow furrowing slightly. Then, a slow smirk curved his lips.

"What's with the look?" I asked, arching an eyebrow.

"This is the first time a woman has cooked for me in over a decade," he admitted. His voice was husky, a little slurred, but genuine. "I've always just done it myself." He shook his head, letting out a low chuckle. "It's sexy as hell, boo."

I rolled my eyes, ignoring the way his words sent a ripple of warmth through me. "I'm not as skilled as you, but I got a little something in the kitchen," I teased, smirking.

"Yeah, okay, baby," he mused, stabbing another piece of beef with his fork. "Let's see how it tastes first."

I scoffed, crossing my arms as he took another bite. But then his expression shifted—his usual playful demeanor faded into something more serious. He chewed slowly, savoring the flavors, and then set his fork down.

"Damn," he muttered. "I didn't know you could throw down like this."

I felt my cheeks warm. "Don't gas me."

Before I could react, he turned and leaned in, pressing a soft kiss against my cheek.

"You are perfect, baby," he murmured.

My heart clenched. *Don't do this, Amir.*

I knew exactly where this was heading—the tenderness in his voice, the look in his eyes. The moment felt too fragile, too intimate. He was hurting, and I was terrified of giving him something I knew I couldn't sustain.

I cleared my throat, desperate to shift the energy between us. "So," I said, reaching for my plate. "What are you gonna do now? Are you gonna sue?"

He sighed deeply, setting his fork down and rubbing a hand over his face. "I honestly don't know," he admitted. "I want to sue. They fired me without merit, Malinda. I know damn well this isn't about budget cuts."

My stomach twisted. I knew exactly why Clay had done this.

My presence in Amir's life had cost him his job.

"You should," I said, trying to keep my voice steady. "You dedicated years to SparTech. You deserve better."

He let out a humorless laugh. "Deserve don't mean shit in business, boo."

I hated the defeated look in his eyes. Hated that Clay had stripped him of something he loved, something he had built for himself.

Amir reached for his glass again, but before he could take another sip, I gently slid it out of his reach.

"Drink some water instead," I said softly.

He didn't argue. Just sighed, leaning back against the stool, staring at the ceiling like the weight of the world had collapsed onto his shoulders.

I exhaled slowly. I couldn't let him get hurt any more than he already had. Clay was escalating. He knew I was here—and now he was punishing Amir for it.

The clinking of his fork against his plate filled the silence as he ate. He was still drunk, his movements sluggish, but at least he was eating. The whiskey had dulled the fire in his eyes, replacing it with something weary and searching.

Even as I focused on my meal, barely touching it, I could feel his gaze on me.

"Thank you for keeping my secret... for protecting me," I said softly. "I appreciate it more than you know."

His chewing slowed, and I already sensed where this was headed before he even opened his mouth.

"Did you have a thing with him?" His voice was calm, but there was an edge beneath it— something dark and heavy. "Is this whole thing because of some breakup? Or something worse? He has an off vibe—stalkerish, control freak, possessive. You're hiding, Malinda. Did he do something to you? Did he hurt you?""

My stomach tightened. I should've seen this coming.

I stayed silent, focusing on pushing my rice around my plate. He exhaled and reached out, rubbing slow, steady circles on my arm. His touch was warm. Grounding

"Baby..." His voice softened, almost pleading. "You're gonna have to tell me sooner or later. You still don't trust me?"

I sighed. My throat burned with the words I wanted to say, but I knew I couldn't.

"Amir..." I shook my head, keeping my voice low, and controlled. "The less you know, the better. Okay?"

His grip on my arm tensed before he pulled away. He ran a hand over his face, exhaling deeply.

"No, Malinda," he muttered, shaking his head. "I'm already involved. I might as well know what I'm dealing with."

He wasn't wrong. Clay had made sure of that today.

I turned to him, meeting his eyes. "I'll tell you, Amir. Just... not now, okay?"

A muscle in his jaw twitched, but after a moment, he sighed and nodded. "Okay, baby." His fingers brushed my cheek in a way that made my heart ache. "For now."

He pushed his plate back, stretching his arms over his head. "I'm gonna go shower and try to sober up." Then, he tilted my chin up with his finger, flashing that lazy, familiar grin. "Join me?"

A jolt of heat rushed through me before my brain caught up with the question. My breath caught, a full-body memory of last night hitting like a wave—his mouth on my neck, his lips tracing every inch of my skin, his hands everywhere, the weight of him pressed against me, the way I came apart under his touch.

I gripped the edge of the counter, steadying myself.

I cleared my throat, willing my voice not to betray me. "Tempting," I said, keeping my tone dry. "But I just showered."

His gaze lingered on me, studying me in a way that made me feel exposed. Then, as if sensing the shift in my mood, he softened. Gently, he tucked a damp curl behind my ear.

"Okay, babe." He stepped back but didn't let go. "Will you sleep with me tonight?"

I tensed.

He caught it immediately and smiled, warm and easy. "Not like that, baby." His voice dropped to a soft murmur. "I mean—sure, that would be amazing—but right now? I just want to hold you. That's all."

Some of the tension drained from my chest. I exhaled slowly, nodding.

"Yeah. Okay." My voice was quiet. "I'd like that."

"Good." He leaned in, pressing a lingering kiss to my forehead. "Thanks for dinner, baby."

I watched him disappear upstairs, the sound of the shower turning on a few minutes later.

Then, the house was silent.

I stood at the kitchen counter, gripping its edge as reality crashed down on me.

I didn't know how I was going to leave now.

For the past few months, I'd convinced myself that this was temporary. That this was just a safe place to regroup, to plan my next move. But it wasn't just that anymore, was it?

I had a life here.

I had Amir.

I swallowed hard, my vision blurring. I never should've stayed this long.

I wished things were different. I wished my father had never conned the Sawyers. That I hadn't inherited his mess. That I didn't have to keep running.

Because now, Clay was escalating.

And Amir—my sweet, patient, big-hearted Amir—was right in the middle of it.

I gripped the counter tighter as a tear slipped down my cheek. I angrily wiped it away, but another followed. Then another.

I hadn't cried in years.

Not since the night social services showed up and dumped me into the system.

But tonight, the weight of it all—the past, the present, the impossible choices ahead—pressed down on me until I broke.

I covered my mouth to muffle the sound, my shoulders shaking.

I didn't want to leave him.

But if I didn't...

I might just get him killed.

I inhaled sharply, forcing the sobs back.

I wiped my face, straightened my spine, and started clearing the table.

I'm Malinda Burns.

I can do this.

The act of clearing the kitchen grounded me, helping me push aside the emotions clawing at my chest. One by one, I wrapped up the leftovers, placing them neatly in the fridge. I loaded the dishwasher, the rhythmic clatter of plates against each other filling the silence. My hands worked on autopilot as I wiped down the counter, the damp cloth sweeping away the last traces of our dinner.

Finally, I turned to the sink, filling it with warm, soapy water. The wok from earlier sat at the bottom, the remnants of seared beef and sauce clinging to the surface. I scrubbed it methodically, letting the motion soothe me, letting my mind go blank.

I was good at compartmentalizing. I had to be.

I was Malinda Burns. I could do this.

I straightened up, inhaling deeply, and turned off the sink. Drying my hands, I took one last look around the kitchen, making sure everything was in its place.

Then, without another thought, I headed upstairs.

As I approached Amir's bedroom, I slowed, pausing in the dimly lit hall-way.

The door was slightly ajar, and from where I stood, I had the perfect view of him.

He was sitting on the bed, still in his towel, his skin glistening slightly from the shower. His broad shoulders were hunched forward as he furiously scrib-bled notes onto a legal pad, his brow furrowed in deep concentration. That little wrinkle between his eyebrows appeared—the one that always surfaced when he was thinking too hard about something.

The sight of him made my breath hitch.

The rich chocolate of his skin stood in stark contrast against the white towel around his waist. His muscles flexed with each movement, the tension in his arms visible even from where I stood.

God, he was beautiful.

And I loved him.

The realization slammed into me like a freight train, but I didn't fight it this time. I just let myself feel it.

For a moment, I let myself believe this was normal—that I was just walking into the bedroom of the man I loved, coming to lay beside him, to be held in the safety of his arms.

I pushed the door open fully and stepped inside.

"Amir..." My voice was soft as I approached.

He looked up at me, blinking as if pulling himself from deep thought.

"I figured it out," he murmured, his voice thick with determination. "I know what I'm gonna do. I just gotta get my ideas down real quick."

I frowned slightly, sitting beside him on the bed. "What are you talking about?"

I ran my fingers through his damp hair, my touch lingering at his nape. The moment I made contact, I felt him relax under my fingers.

His hand shot out, catching mine. He lifted it to his lips, pressing a slow, lingering kiss to my knuckles.

"Malinda..." His voice was softer now. "Did you mean it when you said I should start my own catering business?"

"Yes." I nodded without hesitation. "Definitely. I meant every word of it."

He exhaled, some of the weight on his shoulders lifting. "Well, that's what I'm gonna do," he said, a small, hopeful smile playing on his lips. "I need to get some figures down, but...I think this is it."

"That's amazing, Amir." I squeezed his hand. "I'm so glad you're pursuing this."

"I feel good about this, boo," he admitted. "With my severance pay added, I have enough to dip into my savings for start-up costs, and then I'll get a loan to back that up—just in case I don't do too well the first year."

I scoffed. "Loan? Remember that I'm investing too. I can cover the start-up fees. You don't need to apply for a loan."

His eyes softened, something deep and unreadable flickering behind them.

"You are the most magnificent woman on this planet, Malinda."

He tossed the notepad aside and kissed me, slow and deep.

I melted into him, my fingers tracing the hard planes of his chest, his damp skin warm beneath my touch. Before I knew it, he was pressing me back against the mattress, his body hovering over mine. His towel barely clung to his waist, and there was no mistaking the heat between us.

His arousal was hard against my thigh, and I knew he wanted me.

Hell, I wanted him.

His lips brushed against my neck, his breath hot, his hands gripping my hips like he was grounding himself in me.

But then—he stopped.

With a sharp inhale, Amir pulled away, running a hand down his face. He exhaled, sitting up and gripping the edge of the bed.

"I'm sorry," he muttered, shaking his head. "I got carried away."

I leaned forward, cupping his jaw, forcing him to look at me.

"Don't apologize, baby," I murmured, pressing a soft kiss to his lips.

He smirked, his hands running up my sides before settling on my waist.

"I'm your baby now?" His voice was teasing, but there was something else there, something vulnerable.

I smirked and changed the subject before he could pull me in too deep. "So, what are your plans?"

He exhaled, standing up and sliding on a pair of boxers under his towel.

"Honestly? I'm all over the place right now," he admitted, running a hand through his curls. "It's been a long day. I just wanna get a business plan together, figure out the funding, register an LLC...all of that."

"That sounds like a solid plan," I said, nodding in encouragement.

He sat at the edge of the bed, his shoulders heavy with tension. I grabbed the lotion from the nightstand and moved behind him, squeezing some onto my palms before rubbing it into his back.

He groaned lowly, the sound making my stomach clench.

"Baby, you don't understand how amazing this feels right now," he mumbled, leaning into my touch.

I took my time, kneading the tension from his muscles, my fingers working slowly over his broad shoulders and down the ridges of his spine. He exhaled deeply, letting himself relax completely.

When I was done, he turned, cupped my face, and kissed me.

"Thank you, honey," he whispered against my lips. "I needed that."

"You're welcome," I murmured.

We got under the blankets, and he immediately pulled me close, tucking me against his chest. His warmth surrounded me, his heartbeat steady beneath my palm.

I never thought I'd like this—cuddling, being held, feeling safe in someone's arms.

But with Amir...

It felt right.

Chapter 47

AMIR

I woke up to warmth—soft, delicate, and completely wrapped around me. Malinda.

Her body was curled into mine, her breathing slow and even. The soft glow of the nightlight cast a golden hue across her face, highlighting the curve of her lips, the gentle slope of her nose, and the deep brown of her skin against my sheets. She looked angelic. Perfect.

My heart swelled. Yesterday had been hell, but falling asleep with her in my arms made everything feel manageable. She believed in me. She saw me. Invested in me, not just with money, but with trust. And that meant everything.

I trailed my fingers down her bare arm, then lower, across the curve of her hip, feeling the way her body instinctively leaned into my touch. A deep warmth spread in my chest. My love for this woman was undeniable, all-consuming.

I pressed my lips to the back of her shoulder, then moved up to her neck, kissing her slow, deep, savoring the way her breath hitched even in sleep.

"Mmm..." she stirred, her body shifting in my arms.

"Good morning, baby," I murmured against her skin, voice low and thick with sleep.

She sighed softly, barely awake. "Mm... it's too early."

I smirked against her shoulder, my hand slipping under the blanket, sliding over her waist and higher until my fingers grazed the soft swell of her breast. I rolled her nipple between my fingertips, feeling it stiffen under my touch.

"It's never too early for me to have breakfast."

She let out a breathy laugh. "At 3 a.m.?"

I nipped at her neck, chuckling as I moved down her body. "Especially at 3 a.m."

I kissed my way lower, pulling the blankets off her body as I worked my way down. I wanted her completely exposed to me. Her scent, the feel of her, the way she squirmed under my touch—it was intoxicating.

Malinda's legs parted instinctively as I settled between them, my lips grazing the sensitive skin of her inner thighs. I slid two fingers inside her, groaning at how ready she was for me.

"Damn, baby," I whispered, watching her gasp.

Her body trembled as I slowly withdrew my fingers and brought them to my lips, licking them clean. My eyes flickered up to hers, half-lidded and hazy with pleasure.

"You taste so fucking good," I murmured, before diving back in.

She arched against me, hands tangling in my hair, a gasp slipping from her lips as I sucked her clit into my mouth, teasing and playing with her until she was shaking. She tried to suppress her moans, but I wasn't having it.

"Let me hear you, baby," I commanded, fingers curling inside her just right.

That was it. Her body tensed, her thighs clamping around my head as her orgasm crashed over her. She let out a soft cry, trembling, her hips bucking against my mouth. I licked her through it, drinking her in, until her body sagged against the mattress, spent.

I climbed back up, kissing her deeply so she could taste herself on my tongue. "Did you enjoy that, baby?"

She nodded, still breathless.

"Good." I ran a hand down her side, feeling the shiver that followed. "My dick is so hard right now, Malinda. I need to feel you."

I guided myself inside her, both of us groaning at the sensation. Her warmth, her tightness, the way she held me—it sent a deep shudder through my body. I moved slowly, and deliberately, setting a rhythm that had us both unraveling. She rocked against me, matching my movements, our bodies perfectly in sync.

I kissed her deeply, fingers tangling in her hair, whispering between each kiss, "I love you... fuck, I love you."

She moaned, nails dragging down my back. My strokes became rougher, deeper, each thrust pushing us closer to the edge.

Then—

A loud crash echoed through the house.

Malinda stiffened beneath me. "Amir—"

"Shh, baby." I kept moving, my rhythm never faltering. "Let me finish."

"But—"

"I heard it," I murmured, my voice tight, my strokes deeper, more intense. "I got you."

She gasped, her body tightening around me, her nails digging into my back as her orgasm hit, pulling me with her. I groaned, gripping the sheets as I spilled into her, our moans lost in the tension-filled air.

The second we caught our breath, I was moving.

I rolled off her and sat up pulling my shorts on. I reached into my nightstand. A beep. A click. The lockbox opened, and I pulled out my gun.

Malinda's eyes went wide. "Amir... what the hell?"

I stood, cocking the gun, my SEAL training kicking in, instincts taking over.

"I know what I'm doing," I said firmly. I kissed her forehead, my tone leaving no room for argument. "Stay here."

Then I was out the door.

Gun steady in my grip, I moved swiftly, my heart pounding in my chest but my mind eerily calm. It had been years since I'd needed to operate like this—since my training had kicked in so naturally. But muscle memory was a powerful thing.

My senses sharpened. Every creak in the wood, every gust of wind outside, every inhale from Malinda behind me—it all registered in my brain, but I filtered out the noise, focusing on the task at hand.

Clear the upstairs first.

I kept my footsteps light, barely making a sound as I checked the hallway. My eyes swept left, then right, every instinct in me on high alert. I nudged open the guest room door with the barrel of my gun, peering inside.

Clear.

Office—clear.

Bathroom—clear.

The house was dark, only the dim glow from streetlights filtering through the windows. I crept toward the staircase, staying close to the wall. If someone was downstairs, I wasn't about to give them a clean shot.

With every step down, my heartbeat drummed steadily, as it used to when I was on deployment, waiting, watching.

I remembered the nights in the desert, the ones where the air felt too still, where danger lurked just beyond the edge of sight. The feeling was the same now. A tension, a tightness in my gut telling me that whoever had been here was sending a message.

When I reached the bottom of the stairs, I paused, listening.

Nothing.

Too quiet.

I moved to the living room, sweeping my gun in an arc, checking corners, checking shadows.

Clear.

Then, the kitchen.

I turned the corner and stopped.

The sight sent a fresh surge of adrenaline through me.

One of the large glass panels in the back door was shattered, and pieces of wood and glass splintered across the floor. A heavy brick sat in the middle of the wreckage, dust, and debris clinging to its surface.

I clenched my jaw, stepping closer, my eyes scanning for anything else out of place.

The back door was still locked. No forced entry. No footprints in the dusting of dirt by the threshold.

They didn't break in.

They just wanted me to know they could.

I exhaled slowly, rolling my shoulders as I processed what this meant.

I had a damn good guess who did this.

I flipped the lock, easing the door open with my foot, keeping my gun low but ready. A gust of cold air hit me as I stepped outside, scanning the alley. The streetlights cast long, eerie shadows, but the space was empty.

Silent.

As if nothing had happened.

But something had.

I took a slow, steady breath, adrenaline still pumping as I listened. Nothing but the distant hum of traffic.

After a long moment, I stepped back inside and locked the door.

I put my gun down and ran a hand down my face, exhaling hard.

This was a warning.

And I had a damn good idea who the message was for.

CHAPTER 48

MALINDA

My heart was racing, hammering against my ribcage as I threw on my clothes. My hands trembled slightly as I grabbed Amir's cell phone, just in case we needed to call the police. The weight of it felt cold in my palm. I stood at the door of his bedroom, straining to hear any sound, anything that would tell me he was okay. The silence stretched too long. My stomach twisted.

Then, finally, I heard his voice.

"Baby, come here."

I exhaled in relief but remained cautious as I made my way downstairs. Amir flicked on the light, and my breath caught when I saw the broken glass panels in the back door. Jagged shards still clung to the frame, the night air filtering in through the opening. The sight chilled me to my core.

"What is it, Amir? What happened?" I asked, my voice tight.

He ran a hand over his head, looking grim. "It's nothing, Malinda."

Nothing? My skin prickled. "It has to be something."

As he responded, his phone buzzed in my hand. Instinctively, I glanced down at the screen. My stomach clenched.

Lorraine: You up? I miss that mouth.

A tight, foreign feeling twisted inside me. Lorraine. That name. I'd heard it before, but Amir never explained, and I never asked. Now, staring at the text, something bitter and unspoken lodged itself in my throat. I forced myself to breathe.

It doesn't matter. He's not my boyfriend. I have no claim to him.

I steadied my voice. "You have a text from Lorraine."

I handed him the phone without meeting his gaze and turned my focus to the shattered glass. I needed something—anything—to distract from the pang in my chest.

Amir sighed heavily. "Babe... nothing is going on with—"

"Do you think it was an intruder?" I cut him off, my tone clipped. Willing myself not to care.

His jaw tightened before he exhaled, letting it go. "Maybe. I'm about to call the police."

I nodded. "Okay. Don't tell them I'm here. I don't want my name in any reports."

Amir hesitated, then nodded. He stepped toward me, reaching for me, his lips brushing my temple like he always did, but I turned my head away.

He stilled. "Baby..."

"I'll be upstairs," I murmured, already pulling away.

He caught my hand, kissing my knuckles, but I barely felt it. I slipped from his grasp and climbed the stairs, each step heavier than the last. I didn't know why this hurt, why the text bothered me when I knew I was leaving. When I knew we were never meant to be anything more than temporary.

But I couldn't let myself dwell on it.

Amir and I will never be together in this lifetime.

I needed this reality check. I had been too distracted, too caught up in the warmth and security of his arms. Clay's warning was clear now. The broken window was a message. 'I see you. I can get to him whenever I want.' Firing Amir was just the beginning. This was an escalation.

I curled up on the guest bed, my fingers gripping the blanket as I stared blankly at the ceiling. My mind churned, mapping out every move I had left. I needed to speed things up.

Three weeks. That's how much longer I'm giving myself. Tomorrow, I had to start making my final moves.

Go through the identity packet. Transfer my money into new, untraceable accounts. Secure housing. Plan my escape. Figure out how to keep Clay pacified long enough to get out without him dragging Amir down with me.

Because this wouldn't stop at a pink slip and a broken window. Clay wanted revenge. And I couldn't—*wouldn't*—let Amir pay the price for something that started long before he ever met me.

After about ten minutes, I heard Amir speaking with the police. His voice was measured, and steady, but there was an undercurrent of frustration beneath it. They didn't stay long. Typical. Nothing was stolen, and no one was injured, so the cops wouldn't do much beyond making a report and telling him to call if anything else happened.

I listened to the sound of the door closing, followed by his footsteps ascending the stairs. He hesitated, then went into his room. I exhaled, my fingers gripping the blanket as I stared at the dim glow from the hallway light beneath the guest room door. Maybe he'd leave me alone.

A soft knock.

I should've ignored it, but I couldn't.

The door creaked open, and Amir's silhouette filled the space. He stepped inside, closing the door halfway behind him. His broad shoulders looked tense; his face etched with something unreadable.

"Malinda..." His voice was quieter now. More careful. "Are you okay?"

"I'm fine." The words were clipped, distant. I refused to look at him.

Amir sighed. "Cops said they'll file a report, but since nothing was taken, there's not much they can do."

I scoffed under my breath. "Figures."

Silence stretched between us. I could feel him watching me, waiting.

"Are you sure you're okay?" he asked again, his voice softer this time.

"I said I'm fine."

He exhaled sharply. "Okay... are you coming back to bed?"

I stiffened. "Um... I don't think that's—"

"Malinda, come on." His voice was firmer now, cutting through my resistance. "Don't do this. Things were going so well between us. Just come back to bed so I can hold you, and we can get a few more hours of sleep."

"There is no us, Amir."

I regretted saying it the moment the words left my mouth.

His jaw clenched, and his eyes darkened. "Is this about Lorraine?"

I scoffed. "It's not about anything."

"Bullshit." He stepped closer, his voice edged with frustration. "Nothing is going on with her. We hooked up last summer, yeah, but it's done. She knows that. I haven't touched her since."

I looked away. It wasn't my business. I told myself I didn't care.

"You don't have to explain," I muttered. "I'm not your girl."

His nostrils flared. "But I want you to be."

The words landed like a punch to my gut.

"You know that, Malinda," he pressed, his voice heavy with emotion. "Stop with the games. We're grown. You're not ready for this, fine—I've been dealing with that. But don't act like there's nothing between us. I just want to be near you. Now cut this shit out and come back to bed."

I swallowed hard, my chest tight. I should've resisted. I should've stayed in this room, built more distance, and reminded myself why I needed to leave.

But I didn't.

I sighed, defeated, and stood up.

Amir didn't smirk. He didn't gloat. He just nodded once and turned, leading the way back to his room.

And I followed. Because I didn't have much time left with him.

And I wasn't ready to let go just yet.

Chapter 49

Clay

I sat back in the plush leather chair of the private room at Tassels, whiskey glass dangling between my fingers. The bass of the music throbbed through the walls, a low, steady vibration that barely touched the chaos inside my head.

The dancer—new to the club, eager to please—straddled my lap, rolling her hips against me, her oiled skin glistening under the dim, sultry lighting.

I didn't even know her name. Didn't care.

She had Malinda's build. The same curves, the same deep brown skin, the same way her waist dipped just enough to drive me mad. If I closed my eyes, if I got just drunk enough, I could pretend.

Pretend that my Dove was back where she belonged—on top of me, whispering my name, dragging those nails down my chest before sinking her teeth into my bottom lip the way she always did.

My head rested back against the chair.

Malinda.

She'd fucked me up today.

I thought firing Amir would be enough. Watching that motherfucker's world crumble before me, seeing the frustration in his face, the way he tried to hold it together like a professional—it filled me with sick satisfaction.

I wanted Amir to suffer. Wanted him humiliated. Wanted him to understand, in no uncertain terms, that he was a fly buzzing too close to something he would never, ever have.

But then Malinda had to show up at her apartment.

Looking like sin in that tight little jacket. Her scent was still the same—warm vanilla and something else, something uniquely her.

Her hands were on my face when I spiraled.

Her lips on mine.

For those brief moments, I felt like myself again. Like we were back in Spain, back on my yacht, back in my bed where she belonged. Where she'd always belonged.

It wasn't just sex. It was the way she talked to me. The way she could settle me when no one else could.

She saw me. The real me.

And she still left.

My grip on the whiskey glass tightened.

The dancer ground down against me, smiling when she felt my reaction. But I wasn't reacting to her.

It was the memories—the ghosts of Malinda's hands, Malinda's moans, Malinda's soft breath against my ear. I let my eyes slip closed, let myself imagine, and let myself get lost in the fantasy.

And then I broke.

I shoved the girl off my lap so abruptly she yelped. Digging into my pocket, I threw down a wad of cash without a word and stormed out.

"Rick. Keys. Now." My voice was gravel, rough, and uneven.

I didn't give a fuck about the stares I got as I pushed past the patrons, barreling through the exit into the cold night air.

Rick hesitated. "Boss, maybe we—"

"Keys. Now."

Rick cursed under his breath but handed them over. I barely got the Escalade started before I peeled out of the parking lot, whiskey burning hot in my veins, fury bubbling just beneath my skin. I didn't even think. My hands moved on their own, turning the wheel, guiding me through the streets of Baltimore, past the landmarks, past the memories.

My mind was a loop of Malinda—her laugh, her voice, the way she'd looked at me like she still felt something.

And then the other memories crept in.

Malinda curled up in Amir's arms.

Malinda, in his goddamn house, playing house with that motherfucker.

My grip tightened on the wheel until my knuckles turned white.

She was mine. *Mine.*

I'd die before I let Amir fucking Stevens take her from me.

By the time I reached Amir's house, my breathing was ragged. My pulse was erratic, and the world had narrowed to one singular thought: getting Malinda back.

I yanked the truck onto the curb, barely throwing it in park before I was out, my boots hitting the pavement hard. My eyes swept the darkened yard, my breath coming fast, my chest heaving. The house stood quiet, the windows dark except for the faintest glow of light upstairs.

She was in there. *With him.*

A tremor ran through me, violent and electric, setting my whole body on edge. I stumbled toward the back door, fists clenched, my mind screaming for something—*anything*—to tear through, to shatter the barrier keeping me from what was mine.

My gaze landed on a brick near the edge of the patio.

Perfect.

With all the strength I had, I hurled it. The sound of shattering glass filled the air, the jagged shards catching the moonlight as they rained down inside the house. The impact sent a jolt of sick satisfaction through me. But I needed more. I needed to get inside. The brick had already done its job, splintering the glass and sending a clear message—but it wasn't enough. My blood roared in my ears, my whole body vibrating with the need to act, to take, to *fix* what had gone wrong.

I needed to grab Malinda, shake some goddamn sense into her, make her remember what we had, and make her believe that we could work.

I moved to the door, reaching for the handle—

A hand clamped around my collar, *yanking* me back with brutal force. I stumbled, twisting to break free, but another hand—iron tight—latched onto my arm, jerking me off balance.

"Clay, that's enough," Rick whispered harshly.

"Get the fuck off me," I snarled, but Rick didn't budge. He twisted my arm, yanking me back so hard I stumbled again. Before I could shout, Rick clamped a hand over my mouth and dragged me back toward the SUV.

"I'm saving your ass right now, Clay," Rick muttered low and sharp. "Shut the fuck up."

I thrashed, my whole body vibrating with rage, but Rick was solid. A wall—unmovable, steady, deadly calm. I *hated* it. Rick wasn't supposed to stop me. *Rick was supposed to understand.*

My muscles strained as I fought, but Rick was stronger, his hold unrelenting. He shoved me into the backseat and slammed the door shut.

The second Rick slid into the driver's seat and took off, I exploded.

"You don't tell me what to do!" I shouted; my voice raw, unsteady. "I *call* the fucking shots!"

Rick didn't flinch. "The hell you do."

"Turn the car around, Rick," I growled, my voice shaking with barely restrained fury. "I need to see her."

Rick exhaled slowly, gripping the wheel tighter. "You really wanna do this?" His voice was calm—*too* calm, like he was talking to a wild animal he didn't want to spook. "You think storming in there, dragging her out, is gonna make her love you again?"

I stiffened. A sharp breath ripped through my nose. "She *does* love me."

Rick's jaw ticked, his eyes fixed on the road. "You sure about that?" He let the question sit heavy between us. "'Cause from where I'm standing, she's in there with another man, and you're out here throwing bricks through windows."

My head snapped toward him, my glare searing. "You don't know what the fuck you're talking about."

Rick let out a slow, measured breath, shaking his head. "You're out of control, man. You wanna throw your whole life away? Over *her*?"

My chest rose and fell, my whole body wound tight, fists clenched so hard my knuckles ached. My voice came low, raw.

"She's *mine*," I growled.

Rick let out a humorless chuckle, shaking his head. "I've been watching you lose your mind over this woman for months, man. I've seen you go through bad deals, seen your old man try to break you, seen you at rock bottom—but *this*?" His gaze cut through me, hard but not unkind. "This is different. You don't even look like yourself anymore."

I slumped back against the seat, the tension in my body refusing to settle. My head hit the cool leather, but it didn't cool the fire raging in my chest. My breath still came ragged, my pulse still hammered. Rick had dragged me away before I could make an even bigger mistake, but the fury hadn't left. If anything, it had *deepened*.

My Dove was in there. With *him*. With fucking *Amir*.

The words sliced through me like a blade, sharp and unforgiving. I swallowed hard. "She's confused."

Rick's jaw ticked; his voice steady but firm. "She's *moved on*," he corrected. "And you need to accept that before you do something you can't take back."

I turned away, my chest rising and falling in uneven breaths. "You don't get it," I grumbled, voice rough. "I *had* her. She was *mine*. I made her *happy*."

Rick sighed, his tone dipping into something softer. "Maybe that was true *then*. But now?" He gestured toward the street we had left behind. "You think *this* is what love looks like?"

My hands curled into fists, nails biting into my palms. "I just—I *can't* let him have her."

Rick gave me a long, measured look. His voice came quieter now, but no less sharp. "So, this ain't even about her anymore, huh? This is about *him*."

Something twisted in my gut. The answer sat thick in my throat, but I couldn't say it.

Rick exhaled heavily like he was carrying the weight of my destruction right alongside me. "Look, I know what it's like," he admitted. "I *know* how bad it burns. Loving someone so much it fucking *wrecks* you. But Clay—" He shook his head, gripping the wheel tight. "You *can't* force her to love you back."

My jaw clenched, my throat tight, words caught somewhere between my pride and my grief.

Rick's fingers flexed around the wheel before he glanced at me through the rearview mirror. His voice was quieter now, more exhausted than anything else.

"You're losing it, man."

I didn't respond. I just stared out the window, jaw locked, watching the blurred city lights streak past like ghosts in the night.

Rick turned onto a quieter street, the tension thick in the car. "You don't even see what you're doing, do you?" His voice was calm but edged with frustration. "You're spiraling. This isn't like you. Because she—what? Moved on?"

My head snapped up, my glare burning through the mirror. "She hasn't moved on."

Rick scoffed, shaking his head. "She's living with another man."

"She's *hiding*."

"She's hiding from *you*, Clay."

My breath came heavy, nostrils flaring. "I don't need a fucking lecture right now."

Rick's grip on the wheel tightened. "This ain't love. This is desperation."

I let out a sharp scoff. "You don't understand."

Rick held my gaze in the rearview mirror, unwavering. "No? Seven years, Clay. Seven damn years, I've cleaned up more of your messes than I can count. I've seen you ruin men for looking at you wrong. But this?" He paused, his voice dropping, steady, and pointed. "This is the first time I've seen you ruin *yourself*."

Silence stretched between us, thick and suffocating. My hands balled into fists. I wanted to tell Rick he was wrong. That Malinda *wanted* me just as much as I wanted her. That if I could just get her alone, get her back in my arms, she'd remember. She'd *feel* it, just like she did in Spain, just like she did every time we were together. She'd stop fighting me.

We pulled into the car elevator leading up to my penthouse. As we reached my door, Rick let out a heavy sigh. He didn't turn to look at me, and for that, I was grateful. My embarrassment was creeping up, twisting into something hot and ugly in my chest.

Rick exhaled, voice firm but not unkind. "Boss... go inside. Go to bed. Sober up. And tomorrow? Move the fuck on. No more going to her place during your break. No more obsessing over her. You're Clayton *fucking* Sawyer. You run a multibillion-dollar empire. *One girl* won't break you." He paused, letting the words sink in. "You *can't* let her."

I swallowed hard, staring at the door to my penthouse. But for the first time in a long time, I wasn't sure if Rick was right. Because deep down, I already felt broken.

CHAPTER 50

MALINDA

We sat in his office after breakfast, the sunlight filtering through the blinds as we went over figures and projections, finalizing his business plan. By the early afternoon, we had mapped out demand in the area, marketing strategy, and a timeline. If he stuck to the plan, Amir's catering company would be up and running in three months. He was beaming, his excitement palpable, while I sat there with the weight of an impending goodbye pressing on my chest. It had been just under a week since the brick in the window incident but I kept it at the forefront of my mind. I can't get comfortable. I can't forget because the longer I stay, the more danger he's in.

Amir pulled me close, his body warm against mine. "Thanks so much for helping me, baby." His voice was soft, full of affection. He wanted to kiss me—I could see it in the way his eyes lingered on my lips. But after I had rejected him twice this morning, he was cautious and hesitant in a way that made my stomach twist with guilt. I had to create some distance. Detachment. Anything to make this easier.

I forced a small smile. "You have great ideas, Amir. You know what you're doing. I was just your soundboard."

He studied my face as if trying to read between the lines. "What are your plans for today?"

I swallowed. "After the repair guy comes, I have some banking to take care of." A half-truth. A necessary one.

"Sounds productive," he said with a grin. "I gotta go visit my mom and sister—let 'em know I'm not still falling apart over getting fired. They've been blowing up my phone. Then I'm heading to Costco to pick up some ingredients. Gonna make some sampler plates for you to try so I can narrow down my menu."

"Oh...okay." I kept my tone light, but my pulse quickened. He was moving forward, making plans. Planning for *us* —for a future I wouldn't be in.

He hesitated, his hand still resting on my hip. "You should come with me."

The words made my stomach drop. *Meet his family?* I felt panic creep up my spine. He was pulling me deeper into his world, into something I could never be a part of. That was a line I couldn't cross.

I forced a small chuckle, shaking my head. "I have too much to do today. Another time."

He reached out, tilting my chin up with his fingers. The warmth of his skin sent a rush of conflicting emotions through me. We still haven't talked about how harsh I was to him the other morning and I'm in no rush to. He searched my eyes, looking for something— reassurance, maybe. A sign that I wasn't slipping away from him.

"Okay," he murmured. "Next time then."

His trust in me, his certainty that there would be a 'next time,' sent a sharp pang through my chest.

He kissed my forehead, lingering for just a moment longer than usual, before pulling away. The tenderness of it nearly shattered me.

He grabbed his keys and headed for the door. "I'll be back later, baby."

I didn't answer. I couldn't. I just stood there as the door shut behind him, pressing a hand to my stomach to steady myself. When I was sure he was gone, I exhaled shakily and went straight up to my room. I pulled my messenger bag from the closet and opened my laptop, logging into my email. The leasing agent I had contacted in London had responded. The apartment was still available.

Ms. Blanchard, it began, using the name Sergei had handed me. *Your application is attached. Please complete and return at your earliest convenience. Please confirm your tentative move-in date.*

I stared at the screen, my vision blurring slightly. This was real. I was actually doing this. I was leaving.

This would destroy Amir. We'd been living together for almost 6 months. We've shared our feelings, our bodies, our laughter, our pain. And I was going to rip the rug out from under him.

How do you tell someone you love that you're about to disappear from their life forever?

I rubbed my temples, willing the ache behind my eyes to go away. I know the kind of life he wants—a house, a couple of kids, a dog, and a wife who can be his anchor. And he deserved all of that. A woman who could give him stability, and commitment. Love without an expiration date.

But that wasn't me. It could never be me.

I sighed and ran my hands down my face, trying to shake the thoughts away. I had too much to do to let emotions cloud my judgment. I opened a separate tab, checking my offshore accounts. I needed to start transferring money into new ones, breaking the trail as much as I could. I had to liquidate my remaining assets, close accounts that could be traced, and finalize my exit strategy. If I was going to disappear, I needed to do it flawlessly.

I was deep in my work when I heard the front door open downstairs. My heart lurched. He wasn't supposed to be back yet. How much time had passed? I glanced at the clock, registering that it was already 4 pm.

I quickly shut my laptop and closed my bag, getting up just as Amir walked into the room.

"Babe, the repair guy rescheduled for—"

He stopped mid-sentence, his eyes immediately locking onto my face, scanning me with quiet intensity.

"You okay?" His voice was softer now, careful.

"Yeah. Just getting some stuff done." I forced a casual shrug, even as my heart raced.

He didn't look convinced. Leaning against the doorframe, arms crossed, he watched me carefully.

"You sure? You've been kinda... distant this morning."

I swallowed. "I'm fine. Just still rattled about the window, I guess."

It wasn't entirely a lie. The broken glass had been a wake-up call, confirmation of what I already knew—I was putting Amir in danger just by being here.

But that wasn't what had me on edge.

It was him. His unwavering trust in me. The quiet certainty in his eyes that I wasn't going anywhere.

And the crushing truth that, soon, I'd prove him wrong.

He exhaled and nodded. "Yeah... I get it. I hated leaving you alone today, but I had to check in on my mom."

"It's fine, Amir. I promise."

Another pause. Then, with a small nod, he pushed off the doorframe. "Alright. I'm going to start dinner. You hungry?"

I forced a smile. "Yeah."

I sank back onto the bed, gripping my knees. Three weeks. I kept pushing the date back, convincing myself I had more time. But this time, I meant it. Three weeks. That was all I had left here.

Then I'd be gone. And Amir would be safe.

So why did that thought make my stomach feel like it was caving in on itself?

I exhaled shakily, closing my eyes. *Three weeks.* That's how much longer I had to figure out how to break his heart in the least painful way possible.

Or maybe... maybe there was no way to make this hurt less. Maybe I just had to go.

CHAPTER 51

MALINDA

Three weeks went by too quickly.

I had forced myself to compartmentalize, slowly pulling away in subtle ways. I was careful—making sure I was always busy, out for most of the day, getting my affairs in order while Amir was laser-focused on launching his business. It was perfect timing. He barely noticed my distance. He was pulling late nights, deep in numbers, recipe testing, and supplier calls. Our moments of intimacy, of sleeping in the same bed, had dwindled. And it *had* to be that way. It made this easier.

At least, that's what I kept telling myself.

But the night before I left came too fast.

In private, I cried more than I ever had in my life. But in front of Amir, I was steady, composed, and *perfectly* normal. It scared me how well I could mask it. It terrified me how convincingly I played the role of simply celebrating his achievements.

I made him dinner. His favorite. Baked Mac and cheese, Cajun Butter Salmon, Roasted Maple Brussels Sprouts, and for dessert Peach Cobbler. I played it off as a *celebration*—for getting his licenses approved, finalizing his menu, and taking another step toward his dream. And it was. But I also needed him to remember this. Because this was my goodbye.

I had planned this for days.

I felt so proud of him. He had rebuilt himself from the ground up, refusing to let getting fired break him. He had reframed, reinvented, and leaned fully into his dream. So tonight, I made sure it would be a night he would never forget.

The faint scent of cinnamon and nutmeg filled the house as I pulled the peach cobbler from the oven, the golden crust bubbling at the edges. The mac and cheese sat cooling on the counter, layers of perfectly melted cheese and crispy edges just like I'd seen in his grandmother's cookbook. I had found it tucked away in his cabinets weeks ago, the pages worn, the spine cracked, and decades of love poured into its recipes.

I had studied it, and followed it to the letter, wanting to get it just right. Because this wasn't just dinner.

This was for him.

The man who had given me safety when I had none. The man who had loved me despite my rejections, my distance, the walls I refused to lower.

I adjusted the dim lighting, making sure the candles on the table flickered just enough to cast a warm glow over the space. The rich notes of a '90s slow jam playlist hummed through the speakers—his favorite.

I wanted him to have this memory—something untouched by pain, by uncertainty, by all the things I would leave behind tomorrow.

I stepped back, glancing at the scene I had set. The soft candlelight, the music, the food made with my own hands, the bottle of his favorite wine breathing on the table.

It was deeply romantic. It was everything Amir deserved.

And it broke me.

The moment Amir walked through the door, he stopped cold.

His gaze dragged over the room slowly, like he wasn't sure if he had walked into the right house. The candlelight, the table, the scent of baked cheese and peaches in the air—it all settled into his eyes before finally landing on me.

I had taken my time getting ready. I knew what I was doing. The dress—elegant, sexy, deep red, hugging every curve—was meant to stagger him. My curls were defined to perfection, tumbling over my shoulders. My makeup was flawless, sultry, just enough to make him want to ruin it.

Judging by the way his throat worked, by the way heat flashed across his face, down to the way his hands clenched at his sides, I had succeeded.

He took a slow step forward, his hazel eyes burning through me.

"Damn, baby." His voice was rough, uneven. "You trying to kill me tonight? What's all this?"

I lifted a bottle of wine, keeping my expression smooth, and unreadable. "You've worked hard, Amir. You deserve to be celebrated."

He didn't answer right away. Just kept staring at me, like he was trying to commit me to memory. Then, a slow, almost disbelieving smile spread across his lips.

"Damn." His voice dipped, hunger thick in his tone. "I love it when you do things for me."

I swallowed, feeling my throat tighten at how soft his voice had gone.

Don't do this, Amir. Don't make this harder. I prayed internally.

I forced myself to smile, tilting my head toward the table. "Sit down before your food gets cold."

Amir took a seat, but his eyes never left me.

I poured his wine, watching his hands brush over the linen napkin, his fingers trailing along the rim of his glass like he was savoring the moment.

And then I sat across from him, taking a slow breath.

"Amir," I started, my voice softer than I meant it to be. "I need you to hear me right now."

His brow furrowed, his focus locking onto me with an intensity that made my chest ache.

"I've watched you work for this," I said, gesturing toward him, toward the world he had built. "I've watched you push through when most people would have broken. I saw you take something that should have been your downfall and turn it into something incredible. I saw you trust yourself when no one else would."

His throat worked, but he didn't interrupt.

"And beyond all of that—beyond the talent, beyond the ambition—you are one of the most thoughtful, selfless people I have ever known. You see people, Amir. You make them feel safe. You've made a mark on my life, and I know you'll make a mark on everyone you cook for."

I stopped, swallowing back the knot in my throat.

Because I wouldn't be here to see it.

I wouldn't be here to watch his business soar, to see him become everything he was meant to be.

But I needed him to know how much I believed in him.

His jaw flexed, fingers tapping against the table as he exhaled slowly. "Damn, baby," he murmured, shaking his head. "You trying to make me emotional?"

I huffed a small laugh. "Just telling you the truth."

He didn't tease, didn't deflect. Just watched me. His eyes were softer now, warmer like he was seeing me in a way he hadn't before. Then, he took my hand, lifting it to his lips, pressing a slow, lingering kiss to the back of it. I caught the glimmer in his eyes—he was holding himself together.

After a measured breath, his voice came out rough, "Thank you, Malinda."

I couldn't handle the sincerity. I was barely holding my tears back. I gave his hand a gentle squeeze before lightening the mood. "Try it first before you thank me."

He chuckled, and I smiled softly at him. Then, finally, he picked up his fork.

Amir's first bite of mac and cheese was slow and deliberate. He chewed, swallowed, and set the fork down before looking at me.

"You used my grandma's recipe."

I froze.

How the hell did he know that?

"You did, didn't you?" He smirked, shaking his head. "I can tell."

"How?"

"She's the only one in the family who uses pepper-jack cheese for a spicy kick and a bit of nutmeg to deepen the flavors."

I lifted my chin. "Well?"

He exhaled, the smile on his lips bordering on something deeper.

"My grandma taught me how to cook when I spent summers with her as a kid," he said, his voice quieter now. "Aria hated that shit," he smirked. "So it was just me and Nana. Every morning, she'd have me in the kitchen, teaching me how to make everything from scratch. She used to say food wasn't just about taste—it was about love. That if you made something with care, people would feel it when they ate it." He shook his head slightly, a distant look in his eyes. "She's the reason I love cooking the way I do."

The words hit me harder than I expected.

I had wanted to make him feel special, to celebrate him. But I hadn't realized I had reached this deep.

This wasn't just a meal to him—it was a piece of his childhood, a connection to someone who shaped the man he had become.

I swallowed, suddenly feeling like I had stepped into something sacred.

His gaze found mine again, warm, unreadable.

"I love you for this—for all of it. The effort, the thought... bringing this memory back for me."

I stilled, my fingers curling into my lap.

He had no idea how much that one sentence meant to me—how deeply it touched me, how much I wanted to tell him everything, but feared I'd fall apart if I tried.

I took a sip of wine instead. "Eat before it gets cold, Amir."

He chuckled, but his eyes never left me as he took another bite of mac and cheese, chewing slowly, his face unreadable. Then a bite of salmon. Lastly, a brussel sprout.

I held my breath, watching him like a hawk, my pulse pounding in my ears.

He made a soft sound of approval, but I needed more.

He paused. Looked at me appraisingly. Then smirked.

"So, you mean to tell me you had me cooking all the meals when you had these skills hidden up your sleeve?"

I exhaled, rolling my eyes to mask the warmth flooding my chest at his approval. "Damn right, I did."

We ate together, laughing, teasing—just existing in a moment untouched by everything outside this house.

Then he took a bite of the peach cobbler. His eyes fluttered shut, his head tilting back slightly as a moan rumbled through his chest.

"Oh my God," he groaned. "This is delicious. I love cobbler. You browned the butter perfectly."

A grin stretched across my lips before I could stop it, pride swelling inside me.

"You doubted me?"

He opened his eyes and flashed that devastating smile, the one that always did something to my chest.

"Never." His voice was soft, deep, full of something I didn't want to name.

I held his gaze, and for a moment, time stopped.

Then he said it.

"You're incredible."

The sincerity in his voice knocked the air out of me.

I looked away first, my fingers curling against my lap, my throat tightening.

I felt the tears before they even surfaced.

No. Not now. Not yet.

I swallowed hard, blinking quickly, forcing them back.

Because in a few hours, I'd be gone.

And when he woke up to an empty house, a hollow bed... I wouldn't be incredible anymore.

I'd be the woman who broke his heart.

The night stretched between us, intimate, heavy, exactly how I wanted him to remember it.

Dinner was perfect. Too perfect.

I sat back in my chair, fingers wrapped around the stem of my wine glass, watching Amir as he polished off the last bite of peach cobbler. He ate like a man who didn't know this was a farewell meal. Like someone who believed in tomorrow.

I wanted to believe in it too.

I was memorizing him.

The way his eyes lit up when he talked about his plans. The sound of his laugh, deep and genuine. The way he instinctively reached for my hand across the table, brushing his thumb over my skin.

The warmth of the room—the flickering candlelight, the smooth hum of music playing low from the speakers, the way Amir kept stealing glances at me like he was trying to memorize the night—it was almost enough to make me second-guess everything.

Almost.

That's why I bought my ticket days ago—to make sure I stuck to the plan. To ensure I remembered why I was leaving. To keep Amir safe.

To protect him from—

No.

I caught myself before my mind could go there. I refused to say his name tonight. Tonight was for Amir.

"That was the best meal I've had in ages, boo." Amir leaned back, rubbing a hand over his stomach. "I might have to let you take over kitchen duty."

I scoffed. "You'd have a mental breakdown if you couldn't cook for twenty-four hours."

He grinned, dimples deep, eyes warm and golden under the candlelight. "Nah. I could get used to this."

My heart twisted violently.

He was picturing a future that didn't exist. One where we did this again. One where I didn't disappear in the morning.

I pushed back from the table before the guilt could swallow me whole.

"I'll clean up."

Amir shook his head. "Leave it. I got it, babe." He stood, grabbing our empty plates, and stacking them neatly. "You cooked. I clean. That's the rule of the kitchen."

I wanted to argue. Wanted to keep my hands busy, keep myself moving so I wouldn't have to feel.

Instead, I nodded. "Okay."

I took another sip of wine, slow and deliberate, as he moved around the kitchen.

It was ridiculous how at home he looked there, like he belonged in that space, like he belonged with me. Like I belonged with him.

Stop it. I scolded myself.

I couldn't let myself believe that.

Couldn't let myself want that.

Because the truth was, Amir was a good man. And I was about to hurt him in the worst way possible.

He didn't deserve this.

But neither did I.

After he finished cleaning up, Amir strolled over to me, exuding a kind of raw, masculine sensuality that made my breath catch. As "Tell Me It's Real" by K-Ci & JoJo started to play, his gaze locked onto mine, heavy with intent. He held out his hand, and I took it without hesitation.

He pulled me into his arms, his grip strong, warm, safe.

"You look so fucking sexy, Malinda." His voice was low, and raw, sending a shiver down my spine. "You take my breath away."

I let myself sink into the moment. Into the weight of his body against mine, the warmth of his skin, the way he smelled. Clean, masculine, with that deep, familiar mix of cedar, amber, and the faintest trace of spice that always lingered on him.

I let myself pretend.

He swayed me slowly in rhythm with the song, his arms holding me like he never wanted to let go.

I tried not to listen to the lyrics. Tried not to let the meaning of the song sink in. Because if I did, the tears I had been holding back all night would spill over.

Then the track transitioned smoothly to "All My Life."

Amir held me just a little tighter.

His face buried in my hair; his breath warm against my scalp. His deep voice hummed along, the sound vibrating through me.

I held it together.

I let him hold me, love me in the simplest way.

And when the song ended, and Brian McKnight's "Back At One" started playing, I pulled back, my fingers trailing down his chest.

I kissed him—soft, slow, and full of something too heavy to name.

Then, wordlessly, I took his hand and led him upstairs.

I let him undress me slowly, his hands worshiping, his touch cherishing every inch of my skin.

But when I was bare before him, I took control. And when we made love, I gave him everything.

I held nothing back—no walls, no guarded distance. I let him consume me.

I kissed him with every ounce of love I felt, let him touch me, take me, imprint himself into my soul.

Because this was the last time.

We came together, my body trembling, spent, raw. I collapsed onto his chest, his heartbeat still racing beneath my cheek.

He wrapped his arms around me so tight, like he knew something was off.

"Damn, baby." His voice was hoarse, sated. He pressed a kiss to my forehead, his fingers absently playing with my curls. "That was... amazing."

I lifted my head, and the moment our eyes met, mine welled up. I tried to blink it away. But the tears betrayed me. "I love you so much, Amir," I whispered, my voice breaking.

His frown deepened. His fingers tilted my chin up, searching my face.

"Hey, why the tears?" He gently wiped them away with his thumb, concern darkening his features.

I forced a shrug, my throat tight. "I've never felt like this before." The truth.

His frown softened into a grin, his lips grazing mine. "Well, I'm honored to be your first... and your only love."

His words cut straight through me.

I swallowed the lump in my throat and kissed him before he could see the devastation in my eyes.

Then he rolled on top of me, smiling down at me like a man who believed he had forever.

"Round two?"

I forced a chuckle, playfully rolling my eyes. "You talk a big game."

We made love again, slow and unrushed, until he was spent, his body exhausted, his breathing deep and steady in sleep.

I couldn't sleep. I refused to.

I lay there, beside him, memorizing him, curled up against him, his warmth surrounding me. He instinctively pulled me closer, even in his sleep, like his body *knew*.

I buried my face in his chest, inhaling his scent, memorizing the feel of his skin, the rhythm of his breathing, and the weight of his arm around me.

The way his arm draped over me protectively, the slow rise and fall of his chest, the way his face softened when he slept.

I let myself exist in this moment just a little longer. Then I slowly, carefully, untangled myself.

I tiptoed to my room, my heartbeat thrumming wildly in my ears. I was already packed. Everything was done. I washed up quickly, dressed in all black, and went over my checklist. Triple-checked.

Nothing left behind. No loose ends.

Except *him*.

I pulled out the letter I had written earlier, my final words to the man I loved, and placed it on the bed. It wasn't enough. It would *never* be enough to explain this.

My heart clenched as I looked around one last time.

Then my phone buzzed.

Uber's outside.

I exhaled sharply, fighting the panic that clawed at my throat. I crept down the hall, pausing at Amir's bedroom door. He was still there, peaceful, unaware of what was coming.

I took one last look.

Then I rushed downstairs, out the front door, and into the waiting car.

CHAPTER 52

MALINDA

The ride to the airport was quiet, but my thoughts were deafening.

Every streetlight felt like a spotlight. Every car trailing too long behind us made my chest tighten. I kept glancing at the side mirrors, half-expecting to see an SUV speeding toward us, a shadowy figure in the backseat—*Clay.*

The Uber driver made casual small talk, but I barely responded. My mind was elsewhere, running through every possibility, every worst-case scenario.

Had Clay figured it out already? Had he *known* all along I was planning to leave?

Would he be waiting for me at the gate?

By the time we pulled up to the terminal, my palms were damp. My heart was thudding against my ribs like it knew something I didn't.

I tipped the driver in cash, my voice barely above a whisper as I thanked him. I reached for my bag, but before I could step out, my body froze.

What if this was it? What if the second my foot hit the pavement, someone would grab me? Drag me back?

I forced myself to move.

I walked fast, head down, gripping my passport and boarding pass so tight my fingers ached. The airport was half-empty, the early morning hush making every sound more ominous.

A sudden *clack* of shoes behind me had my breath stalling in my throat. My mind flashed to Clay's voice, to his last words to me:

"I'm always watching, baby."

I turned my head slightly, just enough to see a man in a dark coat walking a little too close behind me.

My pulse skyrocketed.

I sped up, weaving between a group of travelers, my stomach twisting when the man seemingly adjusted his pace to match mine.

Fuck.

I ducked into the nearest bathroom, my breathing ragged. I locked myself in a stall and stood there, gripping the cold metal walls, counting my breaths.

He's not following you. He's just some guy. He's not following you.

I waited a full three minutes before peeking out.

No one was there.

I stepped out, my legs shaky, my hands trembling as I ran them under cold water. The mirror reflected a woman who looked nothing like her-self—shoulders tense, jaw clenched, fear in her eyes.

I had to pull it together.

I made my way through security, trying to act normally, but every second felt stretched, unbearably long. The TSA agent barely looked at my passport before waving me through, but I still felt *watched*.

I kept my head on a swivel as I approached my gate. A man in a gray suit caught my eye, his expression unreadable. Was he staring at me? Or was I losing my mind?

A group of businessmen laughed near the windows, their conversation overlapping in a blur of noise. A woman cradled her baby, rocking it gently as she murmured a lullaby. An older couple sipped coffee from a thermos, their hands intertwined.

Normal. It was all *normal*.

So why did I feel like my whole world was seconds from shattering?

They called my flight.

I hesitated.

One last glance over my shoulder.

No one was there.

I forced one foot in front of the other. Walked toward the gate. Stepped onto the jet bridge.

The second I sank into my seat, I let out a shaky breath, my body still too wired to relax.

The plane doors were sealed shut.

The engines rumbled to life.

It wasn't until we lifted off—until I saw the city shrinking below me—that my body finally *collapsed* against the seat.

I was in the air, flying away from *Clay* and his obsession. Away from *Amir* and his love.

I had no solid plan beyond this. No real next step.

But I will figure it out. And with all the money I had, I could stay off the grid for years.

A driver was waiting at the gate when I landed at 7 p.m. London time.

My original flight had been to Chicago. A diversion.

I had another ticket booked under my new name, new documents, and new life.

It had all gone smoother than expected—no suspicion, no questions. Even the passport photo I'd rushed from a forger I knew had passed without issue.

The driver stepped forward, offering a polite nod.

"Ms. Blanchard? Welcome to London."

I nodded, adjusting the strap of my bag. "Thank you."

The ride to the Novotel was short. The city lights blurred past, the foreign streets unfamiliar and oddly isolating. I had chosen this location strategically—hiding in plain sight, surrounded by the chaos of London's financial district. If anyone was looking for me, they'd never find me in the crowd.

Check-in went smoothly.

The silence was deafening as I stepped into my suite.

It was beautiful. Spacious. Floor-to-ceiling windows with breathtaking city views, a private balcony, and a sleek, modern design.

This should have felt like a fresh start. Like freedom.

Instead, it felt like grief.

I fought the urge to think of Amir, but my mind betrayed me. By now, he knew. He must. It was after noon in Baltimore—he'd woken up, reached for me, and found nothing but an empty bed and a letter that could never explain enough.

I imagined it all. The way his brows would knit together as he read my words. The way his face would fall when the realization hit. Would he curse my name? Tear the letter apart? Drown himself in whiskey, trying to make sense of why I left?

The thoughts suffocated me. I squeezed my eyes shut, willing the images away, forcing back the tears that burned at the edges.

This was for the best. I had always known this day would come.

I had to forget.

Forget the way he held me. The way he looked at me like I was something to be treasured. Forget the home I found in him.

Because I wasn't done. Not even close.

I still had work to do. Still had a ghost to chase.

Clay's control, his relentless scrutiny, his suffocating grip—his obsession, his hunt for me—none of it could reach me now.

And Amir? He'd be heartbroken, but he would heal. What mattered was that with me gone, he was finally safe.

At least, that's what I had to keep telling myself. What I had to believe.

I moved on autopilot—ordering room service, bolting the door, and layering on every security measure I had left. Then, finally—finally—I collapsed onto the bed.

For the first time in a long time, I felt completely alone.

The tears came fast and hard, shaking my body until exhaustion took over.

I let them fall.

But only for tonight.

Because tomorrow, the mission continued.

Sleep pulled me under.

CHAPTER 53

AMIR

My 6 AM alarm rang, pulling me from the deepest sleep I'd had in weeks. I blindly reached over, silencing it in one practiced motion. My body was sore in the best way. The last few weeks had been an absolute whirlwind—meetings with vendors, licensing applications, and menu refinement. Long days, longer nights. I had barely been able to keep up.

Thank God for my mom and Aria—they had been my rock. And Malinda...

My breath hitched as I thought about her. *Malinda.*

The woman who had taken my half-formed dream and put real weight behind it. She believed in me in a way I hadn't even believed in myself. The day she transferred sixty thousand dollars into my account, I almost dropped my phone. I had expected maybe ten, fifteen at most. But *sixty*?

I had tried to refuse, tried to give it back, but she just smiled, kissed me, and told me she believed in me. That she wanted to see me win.

My snooze alarm blared again. I groaned and silenced it quickly, mumbling, "Sorry, baby. Forgot to turn it off."

I rolled over, reaching for her—only to find an empty bed.

My eyes blinked open groggily.

Where'd she go?

Probably in the bathroom.

Sleep dragged at me again, my limbs too heavy to fight it. I let myself sink back into the pillows, inhaling her faint scent on the sheets. The tension I had carried all week was gone, replaced with a lingering warmth from last night.

Last night...

The memory washed over me in waves, like something out of a 90's Black rom-com. The kind of love story my young, hopeless romantic heart used to dream of.

She made me dinner. From my grandmother's cookbook.

She had looked me in the eye and told me she was proud of me—that she believed in me, that I would leave a mark on this world.

She danced with me, pressed against my chest, swaying slowly to the music I grew up on.

K-Ci & JoJo crooned in the background; I got lost in the lyrics.

Praying all your life to find that special person.

Two souls made for each other.

Feeling so grateful and so blessed to have found them.

I held her tighter because I knew.

I knew what it meant to love someone so deeply that words would never be enough.

To look at them and feel the weight of every prayer, every wish, every quiet hope you ever had for love.

To finally find the person meant for you.

And as the song played, I thanked God for her. Because I had never been more sure of anything in my life.

And then she had taken me upstairs, stripped me bare, and given me all of her—the way she touched me, the way she cried in my arms, whispering that she loved me. I'd never felt so connected to someone before. It wasn't just sex. It was something deeper, something real.

When I finally stirred awake again, it was 8 AM. I yawned and stretched, reaching for her again.

Still empty.

My brows furrowed slightly as I sat up.

"Babe, you okay?" I called out, my voice raspy from sleep.

Silence.

I swung my legs over the side of the bed, rubbing the back of my neck. Maybe she had an early errand. She'd been busy these last few weeks, but we had been so wrapped up in our own things that I hadn't asked too many questions. Still, she always woke me up if she left before me.

I checked my phone for a message. Nothing.

A small prickle of unease ran down my spine. I shot her a quick text, expecting the usual dots to appear.

Message not delivered.

My stomach twisted.

Her phone must be dead.

I tried to shake it off. I checked the bathroom—empty. Walked down the hall, calling for her—nothing. I even peered down the basement stairs, flicking on the light.

The house was still.

She wasn't here.

I forced myself to calm down. She probably just went out to grab breakfast for us. She'll be back soon.

I tried to believe it. Tried to go through my morning routine like everything was normal. I put on coffee and kept myself busy. But as the minutes dragged on, the silence felt heavier.

By 10, I gave up.

My pulse picked up as I jogged back upstairs, grabbing my phone and calling her. The line rang once before a robotic voice cut through.

The number you have dialed is no longer in service.

My body went ice cold.

What the fuck?

I dialed again, then again. *Disconnected?* That didn't make sense. Maybe she changed her number?

No.

No, Malinda wouldn't just disappear like that. Not now.

A new, sickening thought slithered in.

Clay.

What if he had her? What if he had somehow come in the night, and dragged her away while I was sleeping? What if she was trapped somewhere, terrified and alone?

Panic squeezed my chest, my breathing quick and unsteady. My hands were shaking as I grabbed my car keys and rushed outside.

I called her again—carrier message. I drove straight to her apartment, hands clammy, gripping the wheel so tight my fingers went numb. My pulse pounded in my ears, my mind racing as my foot pressed harder on the gas with every passing second. Traffic blurred around me, horns blaring as I weaved between cars, but I didn't give a damn.

I just needed to see her, to know she was safe.

By the time I screeched into a parking spot outside her building, my heart was in my throat. I barely threw the car into park before I was out, moving fast, toward the entrance.

I rushed through the lobby, past the concierge who barely had time to glance up before I was already at the elevators, jabbing the button impatiently. The doors slid open, and I stepped in—only to stop cold.

Shit.

I didn't have a fob.

I turned back toward the front desk, walking up to the receptionist, a fresh-faced woman who smiled politely at me.

"Morning, I'm here to see Malinda Burns. Apartment 2320."

She typed something into her system, then frowned. "I'm sorry, sir. That apartment has been vacant since last month. Maybe you have the wrong number?"

My stomach dropped.

"What?"

She repeated herself, still giving me that polite, apologetic look.

"No, no, that's not possible," I muttered, shaking my head. "Malinda *Burns.* Spelled B-U-R-N-S."

She typed again. A pause. A tilt of her head.

"I'm sorry, sir. We don't have a resident by that name."

I just stood there, staring at her like she had spoken a foreign language.

Vacant?

No resident by that name?

My lips parted, but no words came out.

The front doors opened, and a woman carrying a gym bag strolled inside, heading straight for the elevator. She lives here. She has access. I moved without thinking, falling into step beside her.

The concierge was wrong. I had to check for myself because it had to be a mistake. A glitch in their system, nothing more.

The moment she swiped her fob and the elevator doors slid open, I stepped in right behind her, my breath tight in my chest. Every second that passed felt like another wave of dread crawling up my spine.

I got off on 23 and made my way down the hall to the end.

Then I smelled it.

Fresh paint.

My steps slowed, my stomach twisting as I took in the sight ahead. I didn't need to reach her door to know what the concierge said was true.

I stopped.

The apartment was empty. A worker was rolling a fresh coat of paint over the walls, covering any trace that she had ever been here.

I stood there, frozen. My body felt numb like I had left my skin.

I turned and walked out of the building in a daze, my legs moving without permission. I got into my car and sat there, staring at nothing, my mind scrambling for something that made sense.

She moved? When? How?

Why didn't she tell me?

I called her again. Then again. Each time, the carrier message taunted me, its repetition gnawing at my sanity. I tried texting her again, then a fucking email—anything, everything—desperately trying to reach her.

An hour passed.

Two.

I stayed parked in front of her building, praying that maybe—just *maybe*—this was some huge misunderstanding. Maybe she would just appear, walking out of the doors like nothing had happened, smiling at me like she always did.

But she never came.

By the time I got back home, I felt like a shell of myself. My movements were robotic as I stepped inside, looking around the house again like she might somehow be there, like this whole day had been some sick dream.

And then I saw it.

An envelope.

It sat on the bed in the guest room, my name written in her careful handwriting.

My breath caught in my throat.

I grabbed it quickly, tearing it open, my hands trembling so violently I almost ripped the letter inside. My eyes scanned the words, the explanations, the apologies.

And my heart broke. I grabbed my phone and texted Dorian.

Amir: *I'm spiraling, bro…*

Dorian: *What happened?*

Amir: *She's gone…*

Dorian: *You two broke up?*

Amir: *We weren't together officially…*

Amir: *But we were committed… and when I woke up this morning, she was gone.*

Dorian: *Gone how? Like left for work?*

Amir: *No, man.*

Amir: *GONE gone.*

Amir: *Like packed-up-in-the-mid-dle-of-the-night-and-disappeared gone.*

Amir: *Like fucking vanished.*

Dorian: *Wait, what? Did you call her?*

Amir: *Her fucking number is disconnected. Not voicemail. Not a dead battery.*

Amir: *DISCONNECTED, D.*

Amir: *She cut the line.*

Dorian: *What the fuck?!*

Amir: *I drove to her place thinking maybe I could catch her, maybe she was there and just needed space or some dumb shit like that.*

Dorian: *And?*

Amir: *She moved out. Security at the front desk said the unit's been vacant for a MONTH.*

Dorian: *Are you fucking kidding me?*

Amir: *Wish I was.*

Dorian: *Nah, bro.*

Dorian: *That's crazy.*

Dorian: *That's beyond crazy. That's straight-up cold.*

Amir: *I don't fucking get it, man. She told me she loved me.*

Amir: *I was building a life with her. We shared a goddamn bed, a home—she was my future.*

Amir: *And now she's just… gone like it never meant anything.*

Dorian: *That's what I'm saying, A.*

Dorian: *She always had one foot out the damn door. I told you from the start—Malinda is a walking red flag.*

Amir: *Don't start that shit right now, D.*

Dorian: *Nah, man, I am gonna start because I watched you bend over backward for her, give her your heart on a silver fucking platter, and for what? For her to run like a coward in the middle of the night? That ain't love, bro. That's some selfish-ass bullshit.*

Amir: *She's not selfish. She's just…*

Dorian: *Just what?*

Dorian: *Complicated?*

Dorian: *Misunderstood?*

Dorian: *Spare me, bro. I get that you love her, but wake the fuck up. She left you. And you deserve better than that.*

Amir: *I can't just turn that shit off, Dorian. I don't work like that.*

Dorian: *I know you don't, man. I know how deeply you love. That's why I'm telling you this.*

Dorian: *You can't stay there right now. It's gonna eat you alive.*

Dorian: *Come up here, stay for a few days. We'll celebrate your birthday early.*

Amir: *I don't care about my fucking birthday, man.*

Dorian: *Yeah, well, Dora does. She's been asking about you every damn day.*

Dorian: *Told her Uncle Amir was too busy building his empire, but guess what? That empire ain't got shit to do now.*

Amir: *That's low.*

Dorian: *Is it working?*

Amir: *...Fuck.*

Dorian: *Pack your shit and get up here. I'll have a drink waiting.*

Amir: *I don't know, man. I don't think I can face people right now.*

Dorian: *Then don't.*

Dorian: *Just come sit on my couch and drink my liquor. Katie will make dinner, and let my kid climb all over you.*

Dorian: *Do it for her if you won't do it for yourself.*

Amir: *...Fine.*

Dorian: *Good.*

I put my phone down, my fingers still curled around it like it might ring, like she might change her mind and call me. But the silence stretched, thick and suffocating, filling the space where she used to be. My head fell back against the couch, my gaze locked onto the ceiling as I forced myself to breathe.

Malinda was gone.

Not just gone for the day. Not just pulling back like she did when things got too real. Gone.

My chest tightened, the weight of it pressing in, making it hard to inhale. I should be angry. I wanted to be angry. But all I felt was this gaping, hollow ache where she used to be. I clenched my jaw, blinking hard, willing myself not to cry.

She said she loved me. She said she *fucking loved me.*

Then why the hell did she leave? Why couldn't she just let me love her? Last night was special. *Why couldn't she stay?*

My hands curled into fists against my thighs. I wanted to move, to break something, to do *something*. But I couldn't.

I was stuck here, drowning in the absence of her.

The house was too quiet. Too empty. The faint scent of her still lingered in the air—vanilla, cocoa butter, and honey, the warmth of her skin, the ghost of her laughter.

God, I wanted her to walk back through the door.

Just one more time.

Just long enough for me to tell her she didn't have to run. That I would have fought for her. That I still would.

But deep down, I knew the truth.

She wasn't coming back.

CHAPTER 54

CLAY

The skyline of Beijing stretched endlessly beyond my office windows, glowing with the soft haze of evening. My mind should have been focused on the merger—on strategy meetings, projected revenue, and re-structuring logistics—but I was on autopilot, signing papers without reading them, nodding through conversations I didn't care to register.

This was the first time I'd been away from Baltimore in months, the first time I'd put real distance between myself, and the chaos Malinda left in her wake.

Rick's words had rung in my head every damn day. *You're spiraling, Clay. Move on.*

So, I had. Or at least, I was trying.

Until my phone pinged.

Rick.

> **Rick:** Hey Clay. Check your email. I forwarded you something from the P.I.

I froze, my heartbeat picking up before I even knew why. I stared at the message for a moment before exhaling slowly.

The investigator. Fuck. I forgot he still sent monthly updates. I'd pushed those reports to the back of my mind, deprioritizing them in the chaos of everything happening with the merger.

When I first found out Malinda quit, I had been out of my fucking mind—unhinged, desperate, making calls, sending people to get answers, putting pressure on everyone I could. I had exhausted every resource, grasping for anything that could tell me what the hell had happened.

When no one could give me a good answer, I took matters into my own hands. I put the guy we already had on the books onto her case. He's the one who flagged the fake documents in HR, the tax ID number where a social security number should've been, and the offshore accounts.

Then the kidnapping happened. And when that went left, Rick took over communications with the PI. It had been consuming me, so I let him. I let myself breathe.

I hadn't even thought about it since.

Until now…

I opened my laptop and found the email. The subject line was simple:

Malinda Burns – Flight Records

I clicked the attachment, scanning the details.

She had boarded a plane.

To Chicago.

My pulse roared in my ears as I scrolled further.

One-way ticket.

A one-way ticket?

My grip tightened on the edge of my desk, the words blurring for a second.

I sat back, tension creeping into my shoulders. I stared at the information, trying to understand, trying to piece together what the fuck she was doing.

I exhaled through my nose, willing my jealousy down before it consumed me. My mind raced to a thousand different conclusions. Was that *bitch boyfriend* of hers taking her on a getaway? No—Amir didn't have that kind of money, not anymore.

And besides, the pictures attached to the report showed her alone.

I picked up my phone, typing fast.

Clay: *When was this?*

Rick: *Last Friday.*

Clay: *Was she alone?*

Rick: *Yeah, from what the pictures show.*

Clay: *Find out where she's going.*

Rick: *You want our guy to go out of state?*

Clay: Yes. I don't care if it's international. I'll cover his expenses.

Clay: Find her.

Rick: *And what do you want him to do when he does?*

Clay: *Nothing. Just document and report back.*

Clay: *Also, go over to her apartment and Amir's house.*

Clay: *Let me know if anything seems off.*

Rick: *Got it, boss.*

I clenched my jaw, staring at the email again, the information glaring back at me.

She's running.

The question was—*from what?*

Or who?

My mind raced through possibilities. Did she find something? Had she uncovered something about her father? Something that made her disappear in the dead of night? Or was she guilty? Had she been part of it all along? Had she played me just like he played my grandfather?

The thought made my blood burn.

I ran a hand down my face, breathing hard, before rubbing the tension at the base of my skull. I tried to shake it off, tried to center myself, but I knew better.

I *needed* to know.

Another text buzzed in.

> **Rick:** *Clay.*

> **Clay:** *What?*

> **Rick:** *I need to say something. And I need you to listen.*

I frowned, tapping the screen.

> **Clay:** *If you're about to preach, spare me.*

> **Rick:** *I'm not preaching. I'm warning you.*

> **Rick:** *You went off the deep end last time. I had to drag your ass out of Amir's backyard.*

> **Rick:** *And now you're talking about potentially sending a guy overseas to track her?*

My teeth ground together.

> **Clay:** *It's not like that.*

Rick: *It's exactly like that.*

Rick: *She left, Clay. On purpose. She doesn't want to be found. That should tell you something.*

Clay: *I don't care.*

Rick: *Yeah, that's what fucking worries me.*

I leaned back in my chair, staring at the ceiling.

Rick had known me long enough to see through my bullshit.

But this wasn't obsession.

Her running meant she was guilty. Meant she played me.

So this was justice... right?

Yeah. Had to be.

This was about making things right.

I loved a liar. This would be my closure.

And I'd keep saying that until it felt true.

I texted back.

Clay: *Just do what I asked.*

Rick didn't respond right away. When he finally did, it was short.

Rick: *I hope you know what you're doing, boss.*

I threw down my phone, exhaling sharply, then looked back at the laptop screen.

The airport security footage showed Malinda at the gate, sitting alone, her face unreadable. A backpack rested at her feet. She had her earbuds in, her head tilted slightly like she was deep in thought.

I stared at the screen for a long time.

Then I clicked on the next image.

She was walking down the jet bridge.

Stepping onto the plane.

Leaving.

My jaw ticked as I closed my laptop.

Whatever the answer was, I would find out.

I would *find* her.

And when I did—

She wouldn't run again.

Letter from the Author

To my readers,

From the moment I started writing *Identity*, I knew it would be a story unlike any I had written before. This book is a tangled web of love, deception, obsession, and survival. At its heart, it's about a woman who has always relied on herself, navigating a world where trust is a luxury she cannot afford. Malinda's journey is one of resilience and reckoning, shaped by a past that refuses to stay buried. She is flawed, sharp, and complicated—never the damsel, always the strategist. And yet, even the strongest walls crack under the weight of love, desire, and betrayal. Clay and Amir are forces in their own right—both powerful, both unyielding, yet complete opposites in how they love. One is a storm, consuming and reckless. The other is an anchor, steady and patient. Neither is willing to let her go without a fight. This book is for readers who crave high stakes, intense emotions, and characters who refuse to fit into neat little boxes. It's for those who love the thrill of romance entwined with danger, where love isn't always pure, but it's always undeniable.

Identity was born 11 years ago during an overnight shift at the psych hospital where I worked. I was fighting to stay awake when I found myself reflecting on a story my mom told me. She explained how my grandmother's birth certificate had the wrong year because, back in the day in the Caribbean, families would send a representative to the capital to register a child's birth.

The person sent to register my grandmother went a year late but never mentioned she was already one year old. The same thing happened with our family name—when my grandfather's birth was registered, the representative mistakenly gave my great-grandfather's first name as the surname instead of the actual family name. Rather than correcting it, they just went with the new name moving forward. That story stuck with me, and as I sat there in the quiet hours of the night, I thought—what if someone turned that into a business? Not registering births late, but manipulating identities altogether. Selling identities without the babies. And then a deeper question struck me: *What makes an identity? Is it your name? Your memories? Your experiences?* From that moment, the idea began to grow.

To my readers—thank you for stepping into this world with me. *Identity* is only the beginning, and I can't wait for you to experience every twist, every heartbreak, and every unforgettable moment. Turn the page for an exclusive sneak peek into Book 2, where Malinda's journey takes an even darker, more dangerous turn—with higher stakes, deeper betrayals, and dangers lurking in the shadows. As she fights to uncover the truth, she'll have to decide who she can trust—if anyone. The game isn't over yet... and neither is she. With love and obsession,

N.S. Igwe

FIRST LOOK

Identity: Book 2

Malinda

I wiped the sweat from my brow as Joann and I climbed the winding roads back from the marché, the scent of ripe mangoes and fresh spices thick in the warm evening air. The hills of Pétion-Ville rose around us, the city lights flickering below like fireflies, pulsing in time with the heartbeat of the streets.

A moto roared past down the hill, the driver weaving recklessly between pedestrians and street vendors. Joann sucked her teeth, shaking her head. "Moun sa yo ap chèche lanmò," she muttered. (Those people are searching for death.)

I swatted at a mosquito biting into my arm and cursed under my breath. "Gade mizè!" (Look at this misery!)

Joann laughed, waving her hand dismissively. "Ou pa abitye ak yo depi dat sa?" (You're still not used to them?)

I shot her a glare, but the corner of my mouth twitched despite myself. The streets buzzed with life, voices rising in a rhythmic hum—vendors calling out their last sales, the scent of fritay—griyo, pikliz, and plantains—drifting through the humid air, the distant echo of kompa music spilling from a nearby yard. The night was alive, pulsing, thriving.

I met Joann months ago, during a guided tour of the Musée du Panthéon National in Port-au-Prince. I had been desperate to learn more about my father's heritage, and his upbringing, and hopefully uncover clues that could bring me closer to the truth. Along the way, I had hoped to learn more about myself. But my horrible Kreyòl and only passable French had made it difficult.

Joann had taken pity on me. She had some English, enough for us to communicate, and over time, we had become close. Joann was more than a house helper—she was my lifeline, the closest thing to a friend I had ever had.

Over the months, Joann had become my roommate and confidante. I paid her well, of course, but our bond went beyond that. She had taught me how to haggle in the marché, cook traditional meals, navigate the language and culture, and even, on two occasions, dragged me to a soccer match and a night out with friends. We ate, danced, played music, and talked until dawn.

Back at the house, we spent the next hour tidying the porch, peeling plantains, soaking rice and beans, and starting dinner, moving in an easy rhythm that had become routine. For once, I allowed myself to exhale. It had been months since I last felt the stirrings of danger, and I had almost convinced myself I was safe.

That night, I drifted off, lulled by the distant sounds of laughter from the neighbors down the hill and the steady chirping of crickets.

Until a noise shattered the silence.

A panicked whisper tore through the darkness.

"Madame Mélodie! Réveillez-vous!" (Wake up!)

Joann's urgent voice, thick with fear, snapped me awake.

"Un voleur est à la porte!" (A thief is at the door!)

I sat up so fast my head spun. A thief? No. It wasn't a thief. Couldn't be. It was something worse.

I heard it—the unmistakable rattle of the front gate, the scrape of metal against metal as someone tested the lock. My blood ran cold.

What are the odds?

I had covered my tracks. I had been careful.

Then I remembered the postcard.

A few months into my stay, Joann and I had stopped by the post office near Chanmas on our way back from the nail salon to pick up a package. It had been waiting for me, tucked in between advertisements and junk mail. A simple white postcard, postmarked Switzerland. No name. No message. Just a random, nameless warning from nowhere.

I had ignored it. Brushed off the uneasy tingle it sent down my spine. And now I was paying for it.

Joann grabbed my arm, her voice trembling. "Madame! Fòk nou kache." (We have to hide!)

I swallowed hard, forcing myself to think. Hiding was not an option.

"Non. Ann ale." (No. Let's go.)

I reached under the bed, grabbing my go-bag, my heartbeat pounding against my ribs. Joann and I crawled silently along the cool tile floor, muscles tight with tension.

We reached the back door, every noise outside amplified by our fear. The night was alive with the sound of frogs croaking, iguanas rustling in the brush, distant cows lowing, and pigs snuffling in their pens. Somewhere down the hill, a group of men played dominoes, the sharp clack of tiles striking wood punctuated by bursts of laughter. The smell of charcoal smoke and sizzling meat drifted from a nearby home, mingling with the damp earthiness of the late-night breeze.

I should have prepped for this. Should have known.

That postcard had been a clear warning. I had brushed it off, convincing myself it was just my paranoia creeping in. I had been happy here, at peace for the first time in years. Leaving meant running again. And I wasn't ready to run.

But now—now I knew better. Safety is an illusion. Peace belongs to the dead.

The sounds of the men outside masked our careful footsteps as we slipped into the backyard. The cool night breeze cut through the lingering heat, making me shiver despite myself. We had to move fast.

I led Joann through a gap in the fencing, ducking behind a row of banana trees before slipping down the rocky incline. My feet moved from grass to gravel to uneven dirt, the familiar terrain of the hills. We vaulted over a barye, landing hard on the other side before pressing ourselves against a wall.

A dog barked in the distance. Another answered. Too loud. Too close. Shit.

I turned, scanning the shadowy rooftops ahead. We had to move lower and blend into the maze of corrugated tin roofs and narrow alleyways. I pulled Joann along, weaving through yards, past a makeshift pen where a donkey shifted restlessly. Somewhere, a baby cried. Someone called out in rapid Kreyòl, asking for a missing sandal. Normal sounds masked the fact that somewhere behind us, armed men were still searching.

It hit me then. I had put Joann in danger. Joann, who had been nothing but kind, who had taken me in, showed me how to live, how to survive here. And now, because of me, Joann was running for her life too.

We fled to her brother's house in Delmas, arriving breathless, the weight of unseen eyes pressing down on us. Her brother didn't ask questions. He knew better.

We spent the night at his house, but I lay awake, my mind racing. Her brother kept his ears open the next day, listening for word of a break-in in Pétion-Ville. The thing about Haiti was that someone always knew something. Word of mouth traveled fast, carried on the back of the wind.

But by the time he returned that evening, he had heard nothing. No break-in. No commotion. Nothing at all.

My stomach twisted. It had to be mercenaries. Professional. Quiet. Precise. This wasn't just someone trying to rob me. This was someone hunting me.

But who? Not Clay. That wasn't his MO. He was obsessive and possessive, but he wasn't this crazy. Right?

He had kidnapped me once before. But mercenaries? That was different. That was too much. Even for him.

That night, I couldn't sleep. I lay awake until 3 a.m., when I finally embraced Joann, whispering a soft goodbye. Joann clung to me, eyes wet, whispering urgently.

"Protégez-vous, chérie. S'il vous plaît. M'ap priye pou ou." (Protect yourself, my dear. Please. I'm praying for you.)

I nodded; my throat too tight to speak. Then I slipped into the back of a camionette, one owned by their family friend, heading toward Jacmel. It wasn't ideal, but it was the safest option. The truck rumbled through the hills, heading south.

Four hours later, just as the sun began to rise over the coast, I arrived at Jacmel's airport. Sitting stiffly in a corner of the waiting area, I watched, my nerves humming, my skin prickling with unease.

I was kicking myself.

How could I be so careless? So reckless? I knew better than this. I had spent the last year on the run, bouncing between countries in Europe and the Caribbean, always watching my back, always making sure I lost whoever might be following me.

But in Haiti, I had been happy...

I felt a deep ancestral pull to the country, something I had never experienced before. Like I belonged. I laughed more than I had in years.

For the first time since—

My heart twisted. Amir.

I had thought of him often in the beginning. Too often. But eventually, I forced myself to store those thoughts away.

Now, sitting in the airport, the weight of loss settled into my bones.

This couldn't be Clay.

Then who?

The realization settled deep in my gut.

It was bigger than Clay.

And that terrified me.

Clay

I sat in my private study, the dim lighting casting long shadows across the room. A glass of perfectly aged whiskey rested in my hand, the ice barely melting as I stared at the six-foot painting hanging over my mantle.

A woman—bare, weightless, divine. A halo of curls framed her face, her back arched in an almost ethereal surrender, as if the sheets beneath her were the only thing tethering her to this world. Her full breasts rose with the hint of a breath, dusky nipples peaking against the cream-drenched silk. Her deep, honeyed skin, rich as aged mahogany and smooth as velvet, stood in bold contrast against the softness of the canvas, its warmth radiating even in the dim light.

Malinda.

It had been over a year since she disappeared.

My heart randomly cries for her. My chest aches—a random pang of grief that hits without warning. This was one of those times.

I had this painting commissioned while we were still together. Was that what we were? *Together?* Or was it just an illusion I let myself believe in?

It was supposed to be a surprise for an anniversary I assumed we would have. I had forgotten all about it—until the call from the artist three months ago.

Now, it taunted me every day. Made me more agitated than ever. An unbearable reminder of what I lost. Of what I couldn't let go of. But I couldn't stop staring at it. Couldn't stop reminiscing.

I wanted my Dove.

But my Dove didn't want me.

Rick's words still rang in my ears, reminding me that I needed to move on. To help that along, I kept reminding myself that she was not even who I thought she was.

We followed her trail to London Heathrow, tracking her from Chicago O'Hare through security footage. But that was where it ended. The PI assumed she used an alias to board the flight, but without knowing what it was, she could have been anyone. There were 263 passengers on that plane.

It would take months, maybe years to track her down.

Back here, her apartment was cleared out. No sign of her at Amir's place, though I made it a point to fuck with that asshole whenever I could.

Where the hell could she possibly be?

I hated not getting what I wanted.

The PI eventually gave up and said it wasn't worth the time or effort.

But the not knowing was unbearable. Knowing where she was and not being able to have her was painful enough. But this? This was worse.

I exhaled sharply, exhaustion creeping into my bones. The weight of it all pressed down on me. Brooke's laughter drifted down the hall, light, and grating, as she chatted on the phone—no doubt about the wedding. Or the house. The house she picked. The massive fifteen-room monstrosity I only agreed to with the prayer that she would stay in her wing, and I would stay in mine. I made a mental note to get this room soundproofed.

Knock.

I tensed. My jaw clenched.

She knew not to interrupt me when I was in this room.

I inhaled deeply, forcing myself to take a slow breath, forcing myself to stay calm.

"What?"

"Clay?" Brooke's voice was too bright, too expectant. "Architectural Digest is coming tomorrow for the feature on our perfect new home!"

She was excited. She expected me to care.

I didn't respond.

My gaze lingered on Malinda's likeness.

A whisper slipped from my lips— "Why'd you leave me, Dove?"

I shut my eyes, gripping my drink, drowning in thoughts of her.

I just had to remind myself to focus on SparTech. On my family. On anything but her.

She was gone.

She wasn't coming back.

Amir

I was in the kitchen, cleaning up after catering to 200 guests—my guests. The birthday party for Aria and me had wrapped up, but the remnants of the celebration still lingered in the air. The distant hum of music, the faint sound of laughter from stragglers saying their goodbyes, the scent of grilled meats and sweet cake still clinging to the air. These last few months had been a whirlwind of events and exponential growth for my company, but right now, I just wanted silence.

After getting back from a week with Dorian and his family, I had fallen into a bit of a funk. My sister, her husband, the kids, and my mother had been around me as much as possible. They secretly took shifts—thinking I didn't realize—to be in my home for various reasons. My mom suddenly needed to cook in my kitchen, my sister needed to drop things off, and my brother-in-law found excuses to stop by. They thought they were being slick.

I was grateful for them. I knew why they were nervous. They had seen me at my lowest after deployment, and I could see the same fear creeping in again. Back then, they were afraid they'd lose me. And now? I think they were afraid I was breaking again. So, I worked hard to keep myself busy.

It only took one silly cooking video to change everything. I had been sad that day, missing Malinda badly. Instead of drowning my sorrows in whiskey, I set up my camera and filmed myself making dinner. I made a joke—something dumb, something that wasn't even that funny—but the algorithm loved it. Eight months later, my bookings were full, my social media was popping, and I barely had time to breathe.

And yet, Malinda still crossed my mind more often than I wanted to admit.

But she was gone.

And she wasn't coming back.

"There you are!"

Aria's voice broke through my thoughts. "Manny, why the hell are you working? It's our party."

"The party is over, Ri. Only person still out there is Uncle Leroy, drunk and slow dancing by himself. Matter of fact, go tell the DJ to cut it out and stop enabling him."

Dorian chuckled as he walked in. "Aria, he's hiding."

"Hiding?" She glanced back at him. I shot him a deadly glare, but he ignored it, a mischievous smile spreading across his face.

"Yeah," he answered. "Hiding from Tasha."

"Shut the fuck up, D," I barked. He ignored me again. I clenched the rag in my hand, resting my fisted knuckles on the stainless steel counter in a weak attempt at intimidation.

"Tasha?" Aria looked between us, obviously confused.

Tasha was sweet. A lawyer I had met a couple of weeks ago while catering a luncheon for the Black Women Lawyers of America. She was attractive, interested—forward. She had gotten my number from the host, under the guise of wanting to book me for an event.

It only took about a minute of conversation over the phone for her to let me know she was interested in more than just my cooking.

"She's sweet," I admitted. "Smart. Funny. Easy to talk to."

"So what's the problem?" Aria asked, raising an eyebrow.

I hesitated, my grip tightening on the rag.

Over the months since Malinda left, I had grown callous. I told myself it didn't matter. *She* didn't matter. A lie. I forced myself to stop being overcritical, to stop overthinking about what I did wrong or why she didn't love me enough to stay. I forced myself to accept that I had moved on, rebuilt myself, and left it all behind.

And for the most part, it was true.

But some nights, when the world was quiet, I still found myself looking at the door. Waiting. Wondering. Knowing, deep down, that if Malinda ever walked back into my life, nothing I had built would be strong enough to keep me from falling for her all over again.

Aria stomped over in her gown and sparkly heels and thumped me upside the head.

"I'm talking to you, dummy. Why aren't you out there talking to her?"

"That's what I'm saying," Dorian added. "That girl is fine as hell and applying crazy pressure."

"I'm not looking to get into anything right now."

"Why the hell not?" Aria gasped, perplexed. "We're thirty-eight now! My kids need cousins."

I rolled my eyes, acting annoyed, and went back to loading the dishwasher. "Ri, you know I want a family."

"So, what's stopping you?" she challenged.

I hesitated again. They knew. They both knew.

Aria sighed. "She's not coming back, Manny."

I swallowed. "I know that."

Dorian watched me carefully. "Do you?"

Silence stretched between us. Did I?

Aria huffed and walked out when she heard her daughter calling for her. As she left, she shot Dorian a pointed look. "Talk some sense into him, please."

Dorian cautiously walked over, fully aware that I wanted to throttle him for blabbing.

"Look, A, I know you're still healing over Malinda, but you haven't entertained anyone in over a year. You deserve to hold a little *sutin'* soft. It's your birthday. If you don't want anything serious, then aight, that's on you. But you got a baddie out there desperate for you. At least consider a casual hookup."

He paused, letting the words settle.

"This might be just what you need to scrub Malinda from your mind."

I stared at the counter, fully aware that no matter what I did tonight, my heart still belonged to her.

Coming Fall 2025. Stay tuned for Book 2, where the action intensifies, the stakes are higher, and the enemies have multiplied. The past refuses to stay buried, and a shadow lurks in the distance. Is it Clay—or someone far worse?"